The Solar Murder
By Stan Daneman

Published by and available from
theendlessbookcase.com

Printed Edition
Reprint
Also available in multiple e-book formats.

The Endless Bookcase Ltd
71 Castle Road, St Albans, Hertfordshire
England, UK, AL1 5DQ

Copyright © 2015 Stan Daneman
All rights reserved
ISBN: 978-1-908941-39-8

9 781908 941398

i

Dedicated to my wife and daughters,
Anita, Taryn and Lauren
with all my love

About the Author

Stan Daneman was born in South Africa. He is a graduate of the University of South Africa obtaining a B.Com (Accounting) and a postgraduate Hon. B.Com (Business Economics). He also holds a diploma in Organization and Methods and is a certified management consultant.

He is a past president of the institute of management consultants of South Africa and was awarded fellowship of the institute.

During his business career he held senior management positions as a management consultant with professional firms and Director of Education positions in the IT Industry.

Mr Daneman has published five books. His three books of poetry were published in 1987, 2002 and in 2013. In 2009 he published a book on the positioning and measuring of learning in an organization. His two previous books through The Endless bookcase were; 'From my hilltop – a living history of South Africa' (a unique look at the changes in the country as narrated by a tree) and 'Reflections of heaven' (2013).

Mr. Daneman immigrated to Canada in 1995 and resides in Richmond Hill Ontario. He is married with two adult daughters. This book is dedicated to his wife and daughters.

This is Stan's first novel.

"The Solar Murder"

CHAPTER 1

The post-verdict statement to reporters and TV stations were always a blur. The lights, focus of attention and basically inept or plain stupid questions were certainly not where Greg Winters got his most favorite moments. In truth he loathed the experience.

But it was a necessary evil that he unfortunately had to deal with. And one that he had dealt with so many times before. Like all of the other high profile cases that he had won for his clients, he knew that statements of satisfaction with the verdict, relief for his client and the families and confirmation in the justice system, were all processes that he had to go through. He would have preferred to have slipped out of the court and gone home to rest. When you are Greg Winters, the most successful defense lawyer of high profile clients in the state, if not the country, then it is not possible to just slip away from the limelight.

Over the years he had realized that his best advertisement for his next high profile murder case is the post-verdict interviews. He usually took a long break between cases but he understood that the limelight of a recent successful verdict was like melting gold. One had to take advantage of it before it just evaporated away. Standing in front of the TV cameras outside of a courthouse was not in his natural character comfort zone but he knew that it had to be done.

This case had been different. All cases were different.

This one was different because he knew that it was his last.

He had applied himself and made demands on his team like he had never done before. He was a driven man once he took on a case and he drove his associates to the point of self-destruction. Just as he drove himself - to the full extent of his abilities. He had not

1

always been successful. In the early years he was involved with the law – a highly acclaimed student but more interested in his life style than in his career. Somehow his mind set was that the profession owed him something. His ego had got him into trouble with clients, with the partners of the law firm that had recruited him and with the staff that worked with him. It was only after he was encouraged to seek alternative career opportunities outside of the firm that had spent so much on recruiting him that he finally began to settle into his own boots. The oversized boots that he thought were a perfect fit began to feel uncomfortable and were eventually discarded. He now became committed to the law instead of just being involved with it. Mind you his assignments were to have his clients found not guilty so in a way he used the law as opposed to only being committed to it.

He had started his own practice and began to function as a lawyer worthy of his outstanding academic achievements. It took a long time – and maybe he never really outgrew his ego or sarcasm – but he became a highly sought after defense lawyer. He was not only gifted with a genius IQ but with a mind that could almost see into the complex and sometimes disturbing thoughts and actions of his clients. He could almost "feel" if they were guilty or innocent of the murder charges brought against them right from the time that he first interviewed them. What he felt was beside the point because his sole job was to have his client found not guilty. His reputation came to the fore after he successfully defended a famous host of a TV Morning Show charged with murdering his wife. That case gained national and international attention – and vastly increased his fees for taking on a case. There had been over a dozen equally as high profile cases since that milestone one some twenty five years ago now.

As he had heard the most recent set of NOT GUILTY verdicts been delivered in the courthouse he had become distracted by just how he was now becoming also disengaged with the actual process of the reading of the verdicts. He was so convinced that his case was sound and that he had all but destroyed the arguments and evidence provided by the prosecution, he just expected what would be the outcome. He had picked up these danger signals some time back and each of the last few cases forced him to keep total focus right to the very end of the case, including the reading out of the verdicts. His distraction this time was more of a self-farewell than one of disinterest.

Greg counted himself to be the luckiest guy in the world when he met Mary.

He had never really had any serious relationships with anyone prior to meeting the bouncy five foot four brunette who simply stole his heart at their first meeting. To his utter amazement she said that she fell in love with him from that very first time too.
Being romantic was not in his nature but just being with Mary made him feel free and excited about life. They married about a year after meeting – a meeting that friends swore was just a co-incidence and had never been planned. Neither Greg nor Mary believed them. Greg was almost thirty when they got married and was in the process of branching out alone at the time. There was not much work around in the first year or two and financially things were pretty tough. But Mary never complained. She was the light of his life and never stopped being positive about the future. To a large degree she helped him find that pair of shoes that fitted him. How he developed as a lawyer and how he began to use his skills was all because of one Mary Winters. She would never have agreed with his assessment that she was the change in his life.

They put off having children for several years until they felt that they were becoming financially stable. Unfortunately by that time it was too late as Mary had been diagnosed with cancer.

Mary had always wanted a cabin in the country overlooking a small lake and with a village nearby so that she could walk around and enjoy the local wares. While Mary was well enough they started searching for a weekend cabin that would match her dream location. Finally they found it. Well, they found the land and had a cabin built. It was just off of the I80 near Alpine Meadows, not far from Reno and just inside the Nevada border with

California. They designed the cabin themselves and had it built in record time – but only after the endless delays due to local town red tape. It was during this time that Greg had met the local sheriff, Norm Wilson who became his dear and personal friend. Whenever Greg was in town he would take Norm for a coffee and they would chat about fishing or the local mountains that Greg and Mary had fallen in love with. They never spoke about Greg's cases. Norm somehow knew that Greg was in Alpine Meadows to "detox" from the extreme stresses of his profession.

They moved into their cabin early one spring and experienced the full bloom of mountain wild flowers and the early morning hazy sunrises over their small lake. The cabin was only a mile from the main road directly through the bush. It was a difficult terrain and one that could take an hour or more to navigate through. To drive was an extra five miles as the road had to cut around dense brush and other small lakes. The village was seven miles away and that gave Greg and Mary their personal space but also to be close to town if they wanted to pop in for groceries or just to walk around. They spent two months there that year and it was sheer bliss.

By late summer Greg had taken on another case and his time was very limited over the next eighteen months. They did drive up to the cabin several times but Greg needed to be in the city and these visits were not that relaxing. Finally the case came to an end and Greg obtained a NOT GUILTY verdict. He was exhausted from the ordeal and could think of nothing better than moving into his cabin for several months. He had become so absorbed in the case that he had not noticed that Mary's health was deteriorating. Even with such a small frame, he should have seen that she was losing weight. She had never complained and even stayed out of his way for several weeks as the trial was underway and gaining national headlines. She had volunteered to go up to the cabin and make it ready for their stay – Greg had mumbled his approval and a few days later he recalled that she was leaving that morning. He was fighting hard on the case and he felt distracted when they said goodbye.

They spoke briefly each of the first few days but he'd forget to call until it was too late at night and he knew that she would be asleep. She was only several hours away but it seemed like the other side of the world to him right now.

He could not wait for the post-verdict interviews to be over so that he could wrap things up and pack and drive to the cabin.

When he arrived late the next day he was horrified to see what Mary looked like.

She had refused treatment and had sworn her doctor to silence.

Greg had won his case but lost his wife just two weeks later.

She was his soulmate and his one-and-only love. She had asked to be buried near their beloved cabin and it took some negotiation with the towns authorities for this to be allowed. Sheriff Norm Wilson was like a brother to Greg for the next few months. He could not have asked for a better friend in life.

It took a full year before Greg returned to his office in the city and began the process of looking for a new client. With his reputation it did not take long.

That was over twenty years ago and now he stood outside of the courthouse thinking that the road was now over and that he could retire.

He was wrong.

"The Solar Murder"

CHAPTER 2

Paxton Starr came from an upper middle class background. His father owned a small construction company and made an honest living building and renovating homes within his community. Every day was an honest day's work and the family home was a reflection of a simple yet prospering life style. Nothing was ever over the top but as the family wealth had increased new kitchen appliances were purchased and even an in-ground swimming pool for the kids was installed.

Paxton's love for swimming started right there in the backyard pool. He was a high school swimming champion and was on the shopping list of several of the top colleges around the country. His six foot three and broad-shouldered frame were almost lost to most people who met him – rather it was his crop of untidy blonde hair, his smile and most of all his boyish charm and his gentle personality. Many high school girls would easily have given their all to be in the embrace of the gangly young Paxton Starr – and many indeed had.

To the utter surprise of his parents and his swimming coaches he had decided not to take up a swimming scholarship but to attend a well-rated university where he could obtain a respectable degree in Business Management. He had been tempted to join the college swimming club but declined all offers and only played some social sports.

His potential in the swimming pool was never realized and after a year or two the name of Paxton Starr was taken off of the short-list of future potential Olympic competitors.
Four years later Paxton graduated *cum laude* and joined his father's building business.

Over the next few years he reshaped the business and became President of Starr Property Development Inc. the company that his father had started. The business was now ten times bigger than

7

ever before and was a sought after development and construction corporation in California. His personal reputation was outstanding and many prospective property developers sought him out as partner in joint ventures.

Paxton had one major weakness. Not really a weakness at all but rather an obsession. He had met and fallen in love with Maxi Long at university and after some sowing of the seeds he and Maxi had linked up. And totally linked up they were.

As much as she adored him and everything about him (and his family) he was simply head-over-heels in love with her. She was his soulmate, his best friend, his lover and the center of his universe. No one was surprised when they had married. She called him "Gentle Giant" as she thought that he could never hurt anyone not even a fly.

Maxi was a success in her own right. She had qualified as an Interior Designer and had established herself as a sought after consultant to the upper class of the city. From successful home décor she had branched out into the interior design of both new and existing office blocks. To remain neutral she only became involved in the interior design of Paxton's buildings and apartments if she was approached to do so by incoming tenants or owners. Maxi Starr did not come cheap and she had compiled a sizable fortune of her own over the years.

The Starr's bought a house on an exclusive coastal road just ten miles from the city. The community was comprised of several small streets but the ocean facing homes were the most expensive. The homes sat on large lots and each house was about a hundred and fifty yards from each other. Over time Paxton and Maxi had become firm friends with their neighbors on Ocean Drive. All of the families were certainly well off and there was no real need to show off or brag about their wealth. Those that became friends were bonded by true friendship and not by their social standing.

Over the years the families took turns in hosting Saturday night get-togethers. The gatherings would take place once a month and rotated between the homes on Ocean Drive. Sometimes the parties were a little wilder than others but generally the evenings were casual, great fun and a time to relax and enjoy good food, wine and wonderful company. Sunday mornings were a time to clear the head from the activities of the previous evening. The guests generally walked to and from their homes and more than once the walk home with the fresh breeze coming off of the ocean was a cure from that one-too-many glasses of wine.

When the families met, some already had small children while others expanded the size of theirs as the years passed. Ocean Drive was a little world of its own with a group of friends raising their children together. The children of one family became the children of all as the well-knit community prospered over time. Unfortunately the only family that did not grow in numbers was that of Paxton and Maxi Starr. After years of trying they finally accepted the fact that Maxi was unable to become pregnant. Without the love and support of their friends on Ocean Drive they would not have managed their situation well. It was almost as if the other families gave up some of the "ownership" of their own children to Paxton and Maxi. This was none more evident than with the only son of Wil and Jenni Wright. Ryan Wright was as much a part of Paxton and Maxi as he was of his own parents. They were the first visitors when Ryan was brought back from the hospital and the bond between Ryan and Paxton and Maxi only developed from then on. Wil and Jenni often said that Ryan loved the Starr's more than what he loved his own parents. This comment was not taken too seriously as Ryan loved his parents a great deal – but he loved "Mom and Dad" Starr a great deal too.

Like most teenage boys however Ryan became more and more rebellious as he grew older. He was a big broad shouldered teen. Wil and Jenni were becoming more and more concerned about Ryan's drinking. At the age of sixteen Ryan Wright was becoming a problem in the Wright household.

CHAPTER 3

Greg Winters maintained a small office staff. He prided himself by selecting the very best that he could find. His legal associates were the cream of the crop and he trusted them completely. It was of course a moot point if he had selected them or in fact if they had selected him. Any aspiring defense lawyer wanted to work for Greg Winters. By being recruited by him was a sure sign that you had what it took – the legal qualifications were paramount but of even greater importance to Greg was whether they had the desire, the hunger, the intellect and the ability to think through the finest set of evidence and to ask questions.

Over the years he had turned away applicants that had achieved almost perfect academic records but that lacked the ability to think through the evidence and to put themselves almost inside the heads of their clients and indeed inside the heads of the prosecutors. They had to almost feel where a string of evidence was going and how they could pick apart the most solid set of arguments. Most of all they could have a feel for what the members of the jury were hearing, seeing and believing. Casting doubt in the minds of members of the jury was so significant in winning a case. Over the years Greg's team had always seemed to have come up with something that would discredit or discount evidence. Was it luck? Maybe sometimes but more likely it was because they were the best talent that could be found – and that they were taught by Greg. More than anything it was Greg Winters. He would work himself and his team into the ground but they stayed with him – year after year and case after case.

Not all of Greg's support came from his legal team. There was Elizabeth McKenzie.

Elizabeth McKenzie was Greg's personal assistant. She ran the office like a Sergeant Major but with the smooth loving care that made everyone respect and admire her. Some feared her – for good reason. Elizabeth made everything happen. She was the

Project Manager, the resource allocator, the mother hen, the motivator-in-chief, the sounding board and one of Greg's most trusted employees. Greg could never replace Mary and could never replace Elizabeth. Their relationship was strictly professional and yet they knew that an immense bond existed between them. Often Elizabeth would pour two glasses of whiskey and walk into Greg's office late at night. They would talk about everything but the case at hand for ten maybe fifteen minutes, drink their whiskey and then get back to work.

Greg had often thought of retiring. This time he thought that he had made up his mind to do so. He wanted more than ever to move into his cabin and do all of the things that he had been planning to do for so many years now. Greg's staff was fully aware of his desire to retire and they dreaded the end of each case as they never knew if Greg would leave them.

But one did not simply close down a thriving legal practice – not only a thriving practice but a highly successful one. In all likelihood Greg would sell his practice to one or more prominent defense lawyers and they would seek to attract the type of high profile clients that had selected Greg to defend them. Greg had often wondered if his staff would remain part of a practice if he was not there – this thought had bounced around his mind far more than what he would have anticipated that it would. In a way his team was what had kept him going all of these years – he believed in his own skills sets and knew that he was good at what he did but his team was the ultimate pool of talent that made Greg Winters the success that he was. In reality his team had also wondered what they would do if Greg finally decided to retire. To a person they all believed in him just as much as he believed in them.

This most recent case had taken its toll on Greg and he seemed more irritated than normal if he could not get the information that he wanted when he wanted it. Greg put it down to the extreme stress of the case and not getting enough sound sleep. Sleep was his greatest ally while he was on a case. Just a few hours at a time and he would be ready to be re-immersed in the most minor details of the case. He often said that it was one little thing at time that ended up destroying the argument of the prosecutor and finally convincing a jury that his client was innocent. Maybe innocent was not the correct word to use as Greg was not that much concerned if his client was innocent or not but rather that he was found not guilty.

Since the end of the last case Greg had taken a few days off and had enjoyed the solitude of his cabin. He even found time to meet with Sheriff Norm Wilson. After all, his coffee with Sheriff Norm was part of his recovery process. He admired Norm Wilson as he was always the same – even tempered and mild mannered.

Elizabeth McKenzie never telephoned Greg at the cabin. He would telephone her when he needed to chat or to catch up with things in the office. It was about a week after Greg had left for the cabin that Elizabeth received a call saying that he would be coming back into the city on the following Monday. She was surprised that he had decided to return so early – just a week was not like him. She kept her opinion to herself and informed the staff that Greg would be back in the office the following week. The office chatter was immediate and there was much speculation that Greg would be coming in to announce his retirement. The next few days in the office was not a happy place to be.

On the following Monday morning Greg parked his Landrover in his parking space at his office. He smiled every time that he pulled the Landrover into his reserved parking bay. Several years ago the staff had given him a special birthday present, a sign which read "Reserved Parking for the Boss". Walking into the lobby of the office park he wondered how his life would be different one day.

Greg spent the first hour or more in the office in greeting his staff and walking around with his Giants coffee mug firmly attached to his right hand. He seemed very relaxed and although there was still an atmosphere of expectancy from the staff no one minded

Greg just mingling. That was his way – and it was also a way of binding together his "family".

It was midmorning when Greg was finally alone with Elizabeth and he gave her 100% of his attention as she updated him on everything in the office, from client payments to office maintenance. No wasted time with Elizabeth. She was short and to the point. When she had completed her update to Greg and he was satisfied with the answers that she had given to some of his questions then and only then did she ask if he had enjoyed his time at his cabin. Even this almost personal slant from Elizabeth was kept brief. Greg knew that Elizabeth cared deeply about him and his health and peace of mind. Greg replied that he had a wonderful week. He even told Elizabeth a few things that he had done to keep himself busy during his week away. She almost beamed from ear to ear when Greg confirmed that he had also made up on his lost sleep.

Monday and Tuesday soon passed. Just after lunch on the Wednesday, Greg asked Elizabeth if she could organize a full staff meeting in the boardroom for 4 o'clock. Elizabeth's face turned a dark grey as if she had lost all life in her body. She knew that Greg had made up his mind to retire. She could hardly breathe as she left his office. Elizabeth walked slowly to the ladies washroom – slowly so not to raise the attention of anyone that might see her look like death walking down the hall way. In the washroom she found some privacy behind a cubicle door. She just sat there trying to breathe and bring herself under control. She knew that she could not hide away for long and not raise suspicion from anyone who might have seen her walk into the washroom. Partially recovered she walked back to her office and was about to send out an office-wide email notification of the staff meeting when the telephone rang.

Elizabeth screened all of Greg's telephone calls – and even his mail for that matter. She took down all of the details from the caller and promised that she would return the telephone call.

14

Elizabeth knocked and entered Greg's office. He looked up and saw Elizabeth. She stood in front of his desk and then sat down before she fell down. Greg asked her if she was unwell and she replied that she was fine although stunned by the telephone call that she had just received. Greg put his pen and glasses down and looked at her. Elizabeth was a professional and he knew that she would gather herself and soon tell him about the telephone call that she had just received.

Although she tried to remain calm she finally said, "The telephone call was from police headquarters. They have arrested Paxton Starr for the murder of his wife. Mr. Starr has asked for you to represent him".

Greg replied, "THE Paxton Starr?"

Just a simple "Yes" was all that Elizabeth could utter. "Mr. Starr has asked for you to represent him. The Chief of Police asked if you would come downtown as soon as you can."

Greg sat in silence. He knew that this could be another case. He inwardly shook his head and said to himself, "No, no, no, I do not want another case". He looked out of the window and almost forgot that Elizabeth was still sitting in his office. He thought of spending more time at the cabin and being near to Mary. His mind drifted back to times gone-by. He so desperately wanted some peace in his life. He also thought that above all he was a defense lawyer and that he had a job to do. He sat for another minute and then he became aware that Elizabeth was still sitting there. Somehow she had read every thought that had gone through Greg's mind.

Greg turned and faced Elizabeth, "Have you sent out the notification about the staff meeting?" he asked her.

"No, not as yet."

Greg was already gathering up his note pads, jacket and briefcase as he said to her, "Hold back on the meeting until we know what this is all about". He disappeared out of the office and Elizabeth was left sitting by herself. With a slight smile on her face she returned to her office and returned the telephone to police headquarters. Greg's instinct as a defense lawyer had taken over his emotional desire to think of retirement – at least for the moment. Once a lawyer always a lawyer!

CHAPTER 4

Greg was well known at police headquarters – sometimes for the wrong reasons. He had successfully represented the rich and famous and there was a general feeling that in many situations justice had not been served when NOT GUILTY verdicts were delivered. The Homicide Squad also knew that they had to be particularly careful with evidence and other information when Greg Winters was on a case. He could destroy the most tightly and convincing piece of evidence that they could assemble. This case would be no different.

Chief Detective Martinez had a love-hate relationship with Greg. They had been involved in too many cases together and Bill Martinez knew that Greg's arrival would turn up the heat in his department – as would the heat from the Press and TV media.
Greg's involvement was sometimes like a full blown media circus. Bill had often had to tell his officers that Greg had made them a better police department. In reality this was very true.

Greg was ushered into a briefing room – a room that he had been in far too many times in his life. The room was very bland and although it had been refurbished and smartened up with a good paint job it still seemed to be a rather dull and depressing room to be in. As per his usual practice Greg would take up a seated position in the middle of the one side of the long table. He never wanted to be too near to the presiding officer as this might give the impression of being "close" to the police department. Being a defense lawyer 101 was all about optics!

Within a minute of Greg coming into the briefing room Chief Detective Martinez arrived with some of his officers. Martinez had also studied the Detective Manual 101 which states never keep a respected defense lawyer waiting!

"Good morning Mr. Winters, how are you?" sounded all rather civil as the Chief held out his hand to greet Greg.

"Great, thank you, Chief, how are you?" enquired Greg and not really caring in what state the Chief's health was in.

"Gentlemen", Greg greeted the other officers as they entered the room and nodded at Greg.

"What do we have today?" asked Greg.

The Chief felt more comfortable delivering a briefing to Greg than actually holding a conversation with him. These briefings were themselves very short as they were intended to bring a potential defense lawyer up to speed on developments. They would, in quick order, have the attorney in front of the arrested person to establish some facts before deciding if he was going to represent the said arrested person.

The Chief started his brief. Greg took notes in his self-developed style.

"On Sunday morning we received a 911 call from Paxton Starr stating that his wife, Maxi, was unresponsive and under water in their bath tub at home. The call came in at 9:35 and we had Emergency Vehicles and officers on the property at 9:44. Mrs. Starr was slightly submerged in her bath tub and was pronounced dead by the coroner.

We have a portfolio of photographs of the body available for you."

Greg nodded his appreciation without answering the Chief directly.

"Mr. Starr provided us with a statement that the couple had attended a party at a neighbor's home on Saturday evening. The neighbors, a Wil and Jenni Wright – and the Wrights confirmed that Paxton and Maxi Starr were at their home. Mr. Starr stated that his wife had consumed a high volume of alcohol at the party. They were driven home – a distance of about 150 yards by Wil Wright. Apparently it is their custom to walk to-and-from the

18

neighborhood parties but Mrs. Starr was not well enough to make the walk back home".

"And was there a reason for her intoxication?" enquired Greg.

"According to Mr. Starr and confirmed by the guests at the party, Mrs. Starr appeared to be very drunk. The blood tests taken from Mrs. Starr showed a high alcohol content – and most likely she was well over the limit the night before."

"Did she normally drink that much at these parties?" asked Greg, again hardly looking up from his notes.

"Both Mr. Starr and the other house guests confirmed that these neighborhood parties that they held once a month varied in intensity – some dinner parties were sedate while others not so much – all friends from Ocean Drive – would let their hair down more – but at all of them some drinking took place – sounds as if Mrs. Starr normally had a good few drinks and had previously been drunk once or twice". The Chief hesitated then continued, "But not like on Saturday night, by all accounts she was pretty much out of it – and an argument broke out between the Paxton's and Maxi slapped her husband".

"Do we know what about?" asked Greg in a monotone.

"No, not as yet, we know that Maxi Starr was very drunk and that her husband took her outside by the arm and appeared to be talking with her. Some of the other guests were watching the argument – and apparently their first ever argument in public in over 20 years that the neighbors have been getting together – and then all of a sudden Maxi slapped her husband".

The Chief hesitated for a second and glanced up at Greg. If he expected to see a reaction he was mistaken. He should have known better by now.

He continued.

"From the statements by the guests that witnessed the argument from inside the house, it appears that there was a stunned silence and then Maxi buried herself in her husband's chest and he put his arms around her. The house guests dispersed from the windows when the Starr's walked back towards the house – Mr. Paxton holding his wife around the waist and with her resting her head up against him."

Greg chipped in, "Did anyone hear what they were arguing about?"

"No" replied the Chief. "All of the guests were inside the house – but those that witnessed the argument said that Maxi Starr seemed to be very drunk – for someone apparently in her state she sure clocked her husband a shot. He had a welt across his face when he guided his wife back into the house. In fact he still had a welt on Sunday morning when we arrived at his home after the 911 call".

"So we have no clue why she was drinking heavily or why she clocked him", asked Greg. "None at all at this stage", replied the Chief.

The Chief took a breath and then went on.

"Once inside the house the guests gathered around and asked Mr. Starr what had happened outside – and some of the female guests were talking to Mrs. Starr and checking out if she was okay. The group of friends reported in their statements that Mr. Starr seemed genuinely embarrassed and kept apologizing. He said that he had noticed that his wife was drinking a great deal that night and he asked her if she would walk outside with him. They walked out onto the patio and some of the guests looked up and witnessed what occurred. At first they were talking and then Mr. Starr seemed as if he wanted to bring his wife back indoors – then bang she slapped him.

In Mr. Starr's statement he said that he had noticed that his wife was getting out of it and he approached her to ease up – she

20

rebuked him and said that it was none of his business – he then stated that he convinced her to walk outside as he wanted to know if anything was wrong or why she was drinking so much. He said that he then suggested that they should leave the party and go home. He said that his wife started to yell at him that she was fine and he should go and keep company with the men. He stated that he suggested to her again that they should leave and it was at this point that she slapped him."

The Chief paused again and then continued.

"By all accounts it appears as if finally Mrs. Starr gathered herself together enough and accepted that they should leave the party. They had walked to the Wright's home – which is one house away from the Starr's property. Wil Wright drove them home. There was no discussion in the car – Mr. and Mrs. Starr were in the back seat. Mrs. Wright had offered to go with them but Paxton refused.

Upon reaching the Starr's home Wil Wright assisted Mr. Starr in getting his wife out of the car. Mr. Wright did say that Maxi seemed more lucid than she had been before the incident took place. He said that he thought to himself that maybe the shock of realizing what she had done had sobered her up a little but he admitted that this was an unscientific observation. Wil Wright offered to assist them into the house but that Mr. Starr said that he could manage. Paxton apologized again for the incident and Maxi kissed him on the cheek and said how sorry she was and that he should give his wife a kiss from her. Wil drove back to his home. Pretty soon thereafter, the guests left. They were all rather shocked by what had happened and had never seen the Starrs argue before. They all seemed stunned."

"And to confirm again that no one knew why the Starrs argued or what was said outside", asked Greg. "No", replied the Chief.

"What happened at the Starrs home after they were dropped off?" Greg probed.

21

"From Mr. Starr's statement he said that he asked his wife if she was okay and that she hugged him and said how sorry she was for her outburst. From the hallway they walked through to the kitchen and Paxton Starr made his wife coffee – and we did find coffee in her stomach when the coroner conducted his examination".

"Did Mr. Starr have any coffee or just his wife?" enquired Greg.

"Just his wife. Mr. Starr said that he poured himself a whiskey – and we found the whiskey glass in the kitchen when we went through the house."

"Was there any unknown substance in Mrs. Starr's coffee?"

"None at all, there were no substances found – except for a high alcohol level and the equivalent of a cup of coffee in her system. The alcohol content was about double the legal limit and for a small framed person that is a great deal of liquor in her system."

Greg interjected again, "When was the last of the alcohol taken in – or put another way did she drink any more after she got home?"

"The coroner believes that she consumed her last alcohol about 60-90 minutes before she died, so it looks as if all she had when she returned home was the coffee."

"Let me get back to Mr. Starr's statement". The Chief wanted to get through this initial briefing as soon as possible.

"Mr. Starr said that he asked his wife why she had drunk so much and her reply was that she had no reason – she was just having a good time. Mrs. Starr had her coffee and said that she was going upstairs to have a bath. Mr. Starr offered to assist her up the stairs but she refused. She kissed him and then walked upstairs. Mr. Starr said that he had another drink and then felt extremely sleepy. He poured himself a mug of coffee and took it upstairs with him. He walked into the bedroom and sat on the bed and took his shoes off. He said that he must have fallen asleep. He awoke and was still fully dressed. He stated that he remembered that he had brought a mug of coffee upstairs with him – the untouched mug was beside the bed. He said that he realized that his wife was not next to him and that her side of the bed had not been slept in. He stated that he called out but she did not answer. He said that he then remembered that his wife had said that she was going to take a bath. He found his wife naked in the bath tub slightly submerged in the cold water. He tried to revive her but her body was cold. He ran through to the bedroom and called 911."

The briefing room was silent for a minute. The police officers were almost waiting for Greg to say something. Indeed Greg's mind was working overtime – there were already aspects of the story that he had just heard that required much more investigation – and he still had not decided if he was going to take the case.

Greg looked up and asked Chief Martinez,

"What transpired after the police arrived?"

"Mrs. Starr was pronounced dead at the scene. We took a statement from Mr. Starr and then visited the neighbors who were at the party and informed them of the death of Mrs. Starr."

"And what was their reaction to the news?"

"Utter shock is an understatement! Just utter shock. We asked about the party and received independent confirmation that Mrs. Starr had consumed more than her usual and we recorded the witness statements of the argument and Wil Wright taking them home. All of the statements are very similar. There was genuine grief at the news".

The Chief continued before Greg asked the obvious question.

"We moved quickly to ascertain if Mrs. Starr's drowning was an accident or not.

Certainly Mr. Starr was the only person in their home so he had the opportunity, and he had cause based on the argument of the night before – although we have not investigated in detail what the argument was all about. The coroner's initial assessment was that Mrs. Starr drowned slowly and he found it strange that she did not wake up or start sputtering as she started to take in water. Granted her alcohol level was high but he felt that a slow drowning seemed uncommon in such circumstances. If she had fallen asleep and slipped under water she would have drowned quicker than what she did.

Although Mr. Starr has no record of any kind – in fact he is almost squeaky clean – we did establish from Mrs. Starr's lawyer that Mr. Starr was the sole beneficiary of her Will. Give or take about $16 million in cash and stocks but a Life Policy worth $25 million. Giving a total of around $41 million that would go his way. We have concerns regarding the events of the night of her death and that Mr. Starr was the only one at home and that he states that he did not even venture into the bathroom before he apparently fell asleep in his clothes on the bed. We decided on the facts that Mr. Starr had the opportunity, cause and motivation to murder his wife."

Again the room fell silent and everyone appeared to be waiting for Greg Winters to ask further questions. Whatever was bouncing around in Greg's mind was solely for his personal consumption at this point in time. He merely started to gather up his papers and then asked if he could now see Mr. Starr. Chief Martinez of course agreed and Greg followed some of the police officers to the holding room where Paxton Starr was seated.

CHAPTER 5

Paxton Starr had been held in the room for several hours since he had asked for Greg Winters. He had sat almost motionless in his chair and had only occasionally walked around the room. Twice a police officer had entered the room and asked him if he would like a cup of coffee. On both occasions Paxton had accepted the offer. He had sat sipping at the strong black coffee – not the quality that he was accustomed to drinking at home, after all this was a police station – and both times he had left almost half of the coffee standing cold in the plastic cup. The plastic had just made the coffee taste even worse. The time on Paxton's watch hardly seemed to move and yet at other times he must have been deep in thought and when he checked the time again over half an hour had gone by. He was sure that he had not fallen asleep but he could not be sure. His mind seemed too full to want to sleep.

He had gone over and over the events of the last few days in his mind. Had he forgotten something, had he missed something no matter how small – something just something that would make him relax a little.

He had gone over every minute from the time that he and Maxi had dressed to go to the party, their walk to the home of the Wrights, the exchange of greetings when they had arrived and the events of the evening. The mingling as they always did before dinner – the guy and gal groups in two parts of the house. Nothing strange there – this was always the case when they got together as a group. He thought of the other events of the evening – the barbeque and the normal banter that took place between the strong group of friends (more like his extended family). Some of those evenings together were the most enjoyable of his life. He had learnt to laugh with them, to open up and be more relaxed than what he was with anyone else. They had witnessed the families grow and saw the children turn into young adults. Some had now moved out and were in college. It was as if they were his and Maxi's own children. His mind turned back to the Saturday evening. He tried to recall when he had noticed that Maxi's mood might have changed. Was it brought to his attention by a comment from some of his friends?

He remembered taking Maxi's arm and walking outside with her. He remembered asking her some questions and he remembered her response.

The slap to his face still seemed like a blur. He had not seen it coming – and had not even expected it. The sting to his ego and his embarrassment with his friends was worse than the blow itself. Maxi had reacted like he would never have expected.

The next moment they were inside the house and their friends were all around them. He just wanted to get his Maxi home. The quick drive home with Wil came and went. He remembered Maxi kissing him inside the hallway. What else had she said? In the kitchen he made her coffee while she sat on a stool next to the serving island. He remembered pouring a drink and sipping at it while Maxi drank her coffee. They might have said some meaningless things – nothing really of substance. Then she walked up to and pressed herself to his chest and held him. She kissed him and then said that she was going up stairs to take a bath – as she always did after a party. He had stayed down stairs, had another drink and then decided to pour himself a coffee. Then he was in the bedroom.

He woke up when it was light. He found her body in the bath. She was cold. Then he had called 911. Had he missed anything? Paxton had replayed the "tape" in his mind over and over again. Had he covered everything?

The door of the holding room opened and a police officer ushered Greg Winters into the room.

It did not take Greg more than a second to realize that Paxton Starr was a tall and strong man – strong enough to drown a slightly built and apparently drunk wife. But he was not here to find Mr. Starr

26

potentially guilty but rather to assess if he would take the case and then have Paxton Starr found not guilty.

Having dispensed with the formalities Greg Winters sat down opposite Paxton Starr. Before he could pose his first question Paxton said,

"Thank you for representing me".

Greg Winters was very cool and direct in his reply.

"I have not as yet decided if I will represent you. That would depend on how you answer my questions. I expect you to tell me every single detail of what happened the night of your wife's death, plus to answer a range of other questions that I might ask you now or later. Nothing less will be acceptable. Do I make myself clear, Mr. Starr?"

Paxton Starr was somewhat stunned by the response from Greg Winters. He thought for a second and then replied,

"Yes Sir!" That was the only words that he could get out of his mouth, Greg Winters was not to be taken lightly. Besides which his life was in the hands of the famous lawyer and he had better remember that.

Greg nodded and continued.

"Mr. Starr I have been briefed of the death of your wife by the police department and I have read the statements that you and others have made. You no doubt realize the seriousness of the charges brought against you. A potential charge of Second Degree Murder is never one to be taken lightly. I expect full and complete co-operation from you".

For the next two hours Greg asked Paxton Starr a range of questions. Sometimes the questions flowed in sequence and other times they jumped around. Greg would then return to a topic and ask the same or a similar question again. He took notes while Paxton Starr spoke and sometimes seemed to be adding ticks and crosses against his notes. Sometimes a question mark was quickly drawn next to a comment that Greg had recorded.

At approximately 8 P.M. Greg stopped the interview. He rose from the table and merely said, "Mr. Starr, I will consider representing you. I will decide by the morning. Until then please talk to no one about the case. My standard fees will apply and I will require a deposit to be made to my law firm within 24 hours of you signing an agreement that you have appointed me. Good evening, Mr. Starr" and Greg Winters left the room.

Paxton Starr was relieved, exhausted and elated that he had hopefully secured the services of the best defense lawyer in California.

Although it was now after 8 P.M. Greg telephoned Elizabeth at the office. She could have been available on her cell phone for Greg but she felt that it was more professional to take his call at her desk. He always called after he had gone out for an initial interview. It was therefore not uncommon for her to sit and wait. When the telephone rang she greeted Greg and then sat silent waiting for his instructions.

"Elizabeth, please contact the team and all associates and ask them to be in the boardroom at 11 A.M. tomorrow morning – we are considering representing Paxton Starr."

Elizabeth put down the telephone and allowed herself a personal little smile. Then she started making telephone calls and making arrangements for the morning. It was well after 10 P.M. when she left the office. She would be home by 11 o'clock, be up by 5:30 A.M. and be in the office by 6:30 A.M. The Sergeant Major would be at her best again.

CHAPTER 6

A long time ago Greg Winters had represented a well-known personality in a high profile case. He had put a tremendous amount of time into the case – as he always did of course – and indeed as his team at the time had also done – that was the nature of the beast, once a case started almost all other life events came to a halt.

Greg's legal office was on the ground floor of an office park. It was well situated near an interchange and getting to and from home, the office and the city was within the norm of being a respectable drive in the traffic. No ground transportation in San Francisco was ever easy or quick but this commute proved to be a good selection for everyone in the office.

The preparation for the case had gone well and an air of self-confidence had slipped into their attitude towards the outcome that they expected – an outcome that some on the team believed that they had deserved. No one really noticed they were becoming sloppy. No one really noticed that they were being set up to lose the case.

The popular belief was that the client was guilty – no matter what the evidence of legal verdict might be. The client was highly unpopular and remained arrogant throughout the trial. Not a good attitude to have when the next twenty five years of your life could be spent behind bars. But based purely on the evidence and the skill of the defense team it was anticipated that the accused would be found not guilty. Not a verdict that the man-in-the-street in California wanted to hear.

Not a great deal of attention was paid to the fact when one of Greg's associates had the back window of her car smashed and an attempt was made to grab her belongings on the back seat. Auto crime is certainly not uncommon through the Greater San Francisco area. The associate was not near her car when the attempted smash-and-grab was committed so the incident was merely thought of as another act of wanton crime. Several days later another associate on the case was mugged near the courthouse but before the assailant could make off with her attaché case he was apprehended. Although the incident was viewed as a lucky escape as the associate was carrying case files back to her car, no connection was made between the first and this incident.

About a week after the second incident the case came close to being lost. Greg's team – like in any case had gathered a vast amount of information. Based on how the case was proceeding the information was presented, interpreted or even not presented at the trial. After all it was their whole and soul objective to have their client found not guilty.

Greg's office security had become slack and it was not uncommon for white boards to be left uncovered (they were the folding types that locked away), or for some files to be left on top of desks instead of being locked away. In the so-called heat of battle of being immersed in a high profile case and the fatigue of the staff the security of information on the case tended to suffer. In the post mortem investigation after the third incident had occurred it became evident that Greg's practice had let their guard down.

The office park had its own security service and routine checks were carried out during the night. It was fairly common for the lights to be on in Greg's suite of offices until late at night. The security company was aware of this. On the night the incident occurred Security Guard Owen had just completed his walk around the business unit of the office park that housed Greg's law practice, when he saw associate Ken Parker leaving and locking up. The Guard greeted Ken, passed some comment about having to work late to earn a buck – the two men exchanged a few words and the Guard moved on. It was while he was walking around the next office unit that Guard Owen noticed a light beam coming from the direction of Greg's law offices. He then heard a distinct crack and the breaking of glass. Owen pressed his Radio and requested

30

assistance as he began running back towards Greg's offices. As he turned the corner to the front entrance of the office unit he saw the reflection of broken glass in the beam of his flash light. The glass doors to Greg's law offices had been broken.

Guard Owen knew that the standard procedure was to wait for back up – and that it should reach him within two minutes from the time that he alerted his team mates of a break-in. He hid the beam from his flash light but tried to peer inside the law offices. He could not see any movement. As he slowly moved his head he heard the low mumble of voices from inside. He carefully lowered himself through the hole in the broken door way but stood directly onto the broken glass lying just inside the entrance. He froze. The mumble of voices went silent. Owen tried to remain completely still but his large boots were sliding on the glass under foot. He looked down to try to see where he could move his feet without making any further noise. The intruders must have been watching him and as he looked down they rushed him. He heard the running steps but it was too late. Two bodies piled into him and he went crashing back into the front doors which were directly behind him. As he fell he felt the sharp pain as his side hit the area where the one door had been broken. A pointed piece of the glass cut into his body suit. He remembered looking up and seeing someone swinging his arms at him. And then he felt the dull pain on the front of his head. Then nothing more – it was all black.

Security Guard Owen woke up several hours later. Instinctively he tried to move but his body felt like it was trussed up like a bird caught on the hunt. He struggled to breathe but there was no pain. He opened his eyes and it took a while before he realized that he was in a hospital ward. He had no idea why he was in hospital. He tried to speak but what came out sounded more like a mumble than anything else.

Then a voice said, "Oh, you are awake!"

Owen looked to his side and saw a nurse standing next to him.

"You took a whack on the head and you have a nasty cut on your side. Do you remember what happened?"

Nothing seemed to register. He just lay there almost in a state of being in a dream.

"I'll go and call the Doctor. You just rest until I get back", said the voice.
He closed his eyes and everything went blank again.

It took another three days for Guard Owen to fully wake up from his massive concussion and to remember what had happened that night. The pain in his side hurt every time that he tried to breathe in and out. It was not a deep cut but it was almost eight inches long. His security vest had almost certainly saved his life. The blow to the head had left him with a headache to top all headaches. His entire forehead and side of his face was swollen. Whoever had struck him had rained down several blows.

Greg Winter through his detail to attention and prying mind had set associate Ken Parker onto a track of investigation into their existing case. Their somewhat unorthodox methods of fishing for information had led them to believe that their client – no matter how disliked by the masses – could not have committed the crime. Ken was putting some final touches to the package of information for Greg to review. It was late and he was exhausted. He put off the office lights and locked the front doors. He had however, forgotten to lock away the dossier of critical information on the case. The dossier lay on his desk. Not that the intruders that night knew that the dossier had been left out but if they had found it the case might well have been lost.

When Greg was alerted to the break-in he was on site within 45 minutes. To say that he lost his temper that night would be an understatement. Such displays of emotion were a very rare occurrence and one not to be witnessed. If the intruders had reached the back offices where Ken had his office they might well have taken possession of the dossier. As luck would have it by

Security Guard Owen entering the broken doors the intruders never reached Ken's office.

The next morning had seen a change in Greg's demeanor and he was once more even minded although still very edgy – to say the least.

Ken Parker asked to see Greg and he tendered his resignation from the firm.

Ken was amazed at the reaction that he received.

Greg read the letter.

"Ken, you are one of the smartest young associates that I have ever hired and you have a great future in front of you. There are three reasons why I will not accept your resignation. One, we all slip up sometimes! We should have linked the other two incidents together and realized that some forces are trying to steal information and evidence from us. We all failed on this one. Our guard should have been up so I cannot blame one person. Two, if you resign because of this your reputation in the market will be ruined. That would not be justice and I simply cannot allow you to ruin your life over this. And thirdly, on top of your legal duties I am giving you the position of leading our review of office security."

Ken Parker had expected the worst and falling on his sword seemed like the only thing that he could do. He knew that Greg Winters was a special man but he had not expected this outcome. He just sat there and looked at Greg with utter respect – and portrayed with a very dumb look on his face.

"Ken, are you with me on this one? Do you understand what I have said"?" asked Greg.

"Yes, yes, thank you. Thank you. I do not know what to say" was the only answer that Ken could manage.

"Right then, let's get this security thing under control shall we!"

Several weeks later Greg recruited Elizabeth as his personal assistant/office manager (aka Sergeant Major McKenzie) and with Ken Parker they came up with a number of key security improvements. In the next few months a new member joined their team. Security Guard Owen had been "pink slipped" by his company because he had not followed procedures when reporting or investigating a break-in. When Greg heard of this he went to visit now Mr. Luke Owen. Greg assisted Luke in forming his own security consulting company. Greg Winters and Associates was his first client.

A number of months after the incident the security team of Elizabeth, Ken and Consultant Luke recommended to Greg that they should take the opportunity of moving from the ground floor of the office park unit to the second (and top floor) of the same building. Being on the ground floor was not a good idea for a law firm.

It was standard procedure after every major new case was opened that Elizabeth would give Luke Owen a telephone call. All locks and security cards were replaced as a matter of course. A lengthy check list of security measures would be addressed before the new case even got off of its feet – and regular audits would be conducted throughout the duration of the case. As technology changed, the firm became leading edge in information management and communications. New challenges seemed to face the firm each year as the changes moved from paper dossiers to computer files and then to personal computers, laptops and now tablets. Security over information was an on-going issue.
The impact on the business was such that even when Greg interviewed potential employees, he had their skills on technology management tested – this included a private review on their use of social media and other networks. Those potential candidates that were assessed to be too active in these activities were eliminated from the selection process. Security over information had become a living bible in the Greg Winter's law firm.

By the time Greg Winters and the associates gathered for their 11 A.M. meeting to be briefed on the Paxton Starr case Elizabeth, Ken and Luke had already met. Steps were already in progress to change all office locks, passwords and even cell phones. Greg insisted that nothing should be left to chance when his firm was entrusted with the future life of his client.

CHAPTER 7

Before the planned 11 A.M. meeting in his office Greg drove to police headquarters and asked to see Paxton Starr. After greeting Paxton Starr Greg sat down opposite his soon to be client and pulled some papers out of his Brief Case. To Paxton Starr it seemed an age before Greg addressed him again.

"Mr. Starr do you still wish me to represent you?"

Paxton replied, "Yes, Mr. Winters, I do".

There was no visible sign of excitement in Paxton Starr's voice or his action but he was absolutely elated with the news. Even by now he knew not to overly engage Greg Winters in conversation.

By the same token Greg also felt a surge of excitement run through his body. He had never kidded himself that he felt most alive when he was working on a case. The lights inside his brain seemed to come on when he was working. These "lights" had certainly kept him going since Mary had passed away. Every time he switched himself over into the "ON" mode he knew that she was there to support him, to guide him and to love him. The strange thing was that while she was alive he had almost ignored her and sometimes even forgotten where she was or what she was doing. Yet she was always there, never failing and madly in love with him – as he was with her. He would never forget how shocked he was when he drove up to the cabin and saw just how ill she was. He told her that he had neglected her. He sat next to her and sobbed. She held him close and said that she knew that he loved her – and reminded him that he had just saved a life. His legal career seemed pointless then as he was losing the last days of being with Mary. He had won another case but had lost his wife forever. That is what made this feeling all the more strange that by starting a new case she was with him.

He knew that this time it would definitely be his last case.

"Mr. Starr the DA has been convinced by the police department that there is sufficient evidence to lay charges against you in the death of your wife. This is a serious state of affairs. Do you comprehend the seriousness of the situation?"

"I do", replied Paxton, without any hesitation.

"Mr. Starr, the charges against you still need to be defined by the DA's Office, but irrespective my firm will represent you".

"Mr. Starr," Greg continued, "These papers lay out the agreement between us that my firm will represent you – please read the agreement and sign them. A representative from my office will be by to collect them from you. My firm requires an advance on our anticipated fees. I have filled out the amount in the document. Please initial the amount quoted. Once the paper work is in order then I will require that you have the sum mentioned deposited into my law firms account".

There was no offer of negotiation on the deposit amount required. Paxton Starr picked up the papers that Greg Winters had pushed across the desk. Greg was looking for any sign from Paxton that he would be shocked when he saw the size of the deposit required

While Paxton Starr read the document, Greg continued, "The deposit amount is $1 million. Should the final fee come to less than this amount then my firm will reimburse you within 30 days of the final outcome of the case – taking into account any Appeals etc that might come about at the end of the case. Should the fee be greater than the deposit then we reserve the right to request a further deposit to my firm or the difference will be billed to you within 30 days. Payment would be expected by Direct Bank Transfer within seven days of date of statement".

There was silence in the room and then Paxton Starr spoke.

"I will have the transfer take place before close of business today if that suits you."

38

"Thank you" replied Greg without even showing any surprise, "That will be fine".

Greg then continued.

"I will be meeting with the DA within the next day or two to establish the exact charges to be brought against you. Once we have that in place then we will proceed down the road of having you released on bond – and to determine what the amount of the bond will be – these things can take some time as we of course need to meet with the prosecutor and the appointed judge. You might have to sit tight for a while – but we'll be working away for you. Do you have any questions?"

In truth Paxton Starr didn't know what to say. He was not the type to jump up and down or show much emotion. For a big man he was very placid and had hardly ever lost his temper his entire life. Those that did not know him might think that he was a very timid man – and indeed he was. At this moment in time however, he felt like leaping up and down and shouting with joy. He had been afraid that Greg Winters would turn him down but now he knew that he had the best that money could buy. He had to be found not guilty of the murder of his wife – his dear Maxi.

He tried not to show too much emotion and he struggled not to shake. Unbeknown to Paxton, while Greg almost looked on in boredom he was watching ever emotion that showed on his body. His hands were shaking, he sucked on his lips and he blinked his eyes repeatedly. Greg did not miss any of these reactions. He was too well trained in his observation skills to have missed them. Over time he would replay every frame of movement in his mind and analyze every emotion that Paxton had displayed – as he would observe and analyze everything that Paxton Starr would say or do throughout their relationship as lawyer and client – and possible beyond.

Sometimes it took Greg a long time to move on after a case and he had often wondered if he had served the community by having his clients found not guilty of the charges that had been laid before them. Most times Greg had moved on but sometimes the thoughts had stayed with him. He wondered if this case would be a "quick forgotten" or a "long reminder". Maybe as his last planned case he would remember it longer.

Finally Paxton asked.

"Mr. Winters, I asked for your services and I know that you will do everything to make me a free man. I will wait here until you have arranged my bond and then we'll move forward as you determine".

Greg Winters would record that comment long and hard into his mind.

So would Paxton Starr.

"Right then, let me get moving on things. My Financial Controller will be back this afternoon to collect the signed paperwork. Until later, Mr. Paxton – and let me know if you require anything", said Greg as he handed Paxton his business card. "The number on the card will get you through to my personal assistant. Elizabeth will do everything to assist you if you require some things. Just sit tight"

Greg Winters left police headquarters and drove to his office. He had an important case to defend.

Driving to his office he was already replaying his conversation with Paxton Starr.

He never gave one thought to the size of the deposit that he had requested from his new client. The money was never important – it was the challenge, the ability of unearthing evidence, or discrediting evidence presented and to place enough doubt in the mind of the jury to have his client found not guilty that was important. The money had made Greg Winters a wealth man but he could never place fees in front of his task at hand.

The "ON" button in Greg's mind had been engaged for several hours already

After Greg Winters had left police headquarters Paxton Starr was already replaying the meeting in his mind.

"The Solar Murder"

42

CHAPTER 8

There was a distinct buzz of excitement in Greg's law firm – not only that morning but from the previous evening already. Greg's quick departure for police headquarters had started things rolling. Elizabeth was her normal stone-wall self but the associates could read her better than what she thought. They admired her, feared her, trusted her and like everyone else over time loved her. No one would ever say it as Elizabeth was not the type of personality that would openly accept or tolerate affection – but they knew that she knew and she knew that they knew it too!

No one wanted to be the last person into the office that morning. They could not stand to miss anything. The cat was out of the bag that something big was afoot when they saw Luke Owen arrive and go into a meeting with Elizabeth and Ken Parker.
All of the associates had been contacted by Elizabeth late the previous evening and given the usual message when an oncoming case was imminent. Some of the associates were working on other more minor cases but their attendance at the meeting was mandatory. Once a major client was brought on board the case loads of all professional staff were assessed. Greg did not like to make changes to client representation but sometimes this was unavoidable.

The meeting would not only brief the staff on the new case but also assess all existing workloads and determine when specialist resources might be required. A murder case usually takes a very long time to conclude and the allocation of resources is vital. No professional legal associate likes to sit on the bench without work – not that is has ever happened in Greg's firm – but the opposite was also true. One person cannot be running with too many cases. A distraction or by not thinking through vital pieces of evidence or argument could cost someone a life-time behind bars. In Greg's world of defense law this could never be allowed to happen. His 100% record on major murder cases was proof enough. He would much rather contact law firms with which he had very sound business relationships with and discuss the possibility of transferring client cases to them rather than have a vital internal resource not available to his case at hand. The transferring of cases to another firm had to receive the permission of his clients and this was always a tricky situation. Greg had to balance the reputation of his firm with current situations at hand and he immensely disliked having to consider such actions.

Greg parked his SUV in the parking lot at his office. He sat for a moment to consider what lay before him and his team. Another long slog – incredible stress, missed family functions and missing months off of the calendar of life. He asked so much of his team – and they gave so much. It was actually easier once the case had commenced and a bunch of activities were taking place. It seemed odd to think that but in many respects it was the getting going that was the most difficult. It was like looking at an unopened jigsaw puzzle – just were on earth to begin – and would any sense be made of all of the different pieces – would things fit together – what would the outcome be. Once an "Order" was established then discipline, experience, common sense and a touch of luck always came into play. He had often told his associates that their ability to think and ask questions was of greater importance to the law itself. The law would be applied to situations and outcomes but it was how they thought through evidence, counter-evidence, arguments and even the apparent little point that made the case for their clients. Years before, IBM had used the slogan "THINK" and he still believed that this was the cornerstone of their success as a firm.

Greg had to gear himself up to walk into his suite of offices and take charge of the case launch meeting. He was ready.

Greg walked straight through to his office, greeting his staff as he passed by. The greetings were warm but brief. A simple, "Good Morning!" or "Hi Sue" was all he said as he walked by. He knew that everyone was looking at him intently but that no one would break the protocol by asking him about the upcoming case. In truth by now they all knew as the grape vine and Press speculation had already started. Elizabeth had not said a word out of place but she did not have to. There were also too many eyes at police headquarters for things to remain confidential for too long. In the legal profession walls have ears and eyes – and people cannot help themselves from talking out of turn.

Rumors might come into the law offices of Greg Winters but rumors never came out – unless of course it was so intended! Misinformation – no matter its original source – can be of greater importance than information itself – although all information is subject to interpretation!

Greg and Elizabeth exchanged good morning greetings and she followed him into his office. They did not close the door as that was not Greg's custom unless he was deep in thought on a case. More often than not he met his clients in a meeting room as to avoid any eye-wondering around the room while they were talking. Greg also felt no need for his clients to see his framed certificates on his wall. He knew what qualifications he had and to be frank his clients no longer cared. A certificate does not attract new clients or generate fee income – results do.

Greg handed over some papers to Elizabeth and some audio notes that he had made while driving. He was not a great fan of cell phone discussions while driving and who could be listening in on his conversations. Elizabeth zipped off to type up the notes and to make copies for everyone before the meeting started. She would be holding binders for the professional staff at the meeting and only distribute them once Greg had gone through his introduction. He hated people paging through their binders ahead of what he had to say. Also present at the meeting of professional staff would be Hector Franks, Greg's law firm financial controller. Hector would need to set up a new Client code for the case and keep a very watchful eye on fees booked against the case and expenses incurred.

Every last penny would be booked to the client case number – no exceptions. At the end of the case Greg and Hector would decide if any expense write-offs would occur. At the beginning of a case everything would be recorded.

At 10.45 A.M. Elizabeth was in the boardroom alone making sure that all was in order for the meeting. Luke Owen was on stand-by to have all office security codes and locks changed upon Elizabeth's command.

CHAPTER 9

Just before 11.00 A.M. Elizabeth opened the door to the boardroom (sometimes known as the WAR ROOM!) and within a minute or two the professional staff and Hector began to take their seats. There was no pecking order as who sat where but over time tradition or maybe sheer habit had determined who sat in which seat. In the Greg Winters law firm there was no pecking order – every person had a significant role to play – sometimes individually because of their experience or skill set, or as a group in debating, probing and dissecting evidence or statements made by witnesses. There was no doubt that egos existed – it would not be normal in any professional firm, legal or otherwise, if egos did not exist. With a Sergeant Major that everyone respected – feared and loved in one breath – egos were reasonably well managed. A motherly or cutting comment or two by Elizabeth tended to bring down boiling points or potential conflicts of personality. Besides which Greg was a stabilizing force. He encouraged individual thought, questions and probing. He developed lawyers who were sought after in the market place. To work for, and with Greg Winters was in itself an ego boost in the market. Mr. Winters managed and led his staff well. They would walk over hot coals for him – undoubtedly they had worked at high levels of intensity many times throughout their careers with him.

Greg employed some unusual practices when a major case was undertaken. He always contracted a retired lawyer to be the "Independent Safe Guard". The lawyer would not be involved in the case at all but would be called in to review procedures, ask questions, to ensure that legal protocols were being followed and that nothing material was being missed. The "obvious question" was so often missed when one becomes immersed in a case that a distinct risk exists of the team losing sight of the rather plain facts at hand. The Independent Safe Guard could also review case files and ask to see that compliances were being met where required either by the firm or by statute or law. He or she had proved to be

47

worth their weight in gold on more than one occasion by reviewing evidence information or asking basic questions.

Greg entered the boardroom just on 11 o'clock. No need to keep anyone waiting - there was certainly no time for theatrics. His staff again said "Hi" or words to that effect and Greg acknowledged their greeting. As he seated himself and arranged the papers that Elizabeth handed to him a silence enveloped the room. Some might say that it was a deathly silence but in a murder case that would not be appropriate.

Greg broke the silence.

"So, why did you call this meeting?"

A mild ripple of laughter spread throughout the room. It was the same line that he had used to commence many a meeting.

Greg continued.

"You have no doubt gathered that we have been approached to represent Paxton Starr. He stands accused of drowning his wife last Saturday night. The incident took place in their home after they returned from a house party with their neighbors. From what we understand Mrs. Maxi Starr was intoxicated. Mr. Starr, concerned about her drinking, confronted her in an outside garden of their neighbor's home. They argued and she reportedly slapped him. They were taken home by their neighbor, Wil Wright. Mr. Starr states that he made his wife coffee when they returned home. Mrs. Starr then said that she was going to take a bath. The following morning Mr. Starr found his wife dead in the bath".

Greg nodded at Elizabeth and she began to distribute binders to each of the associates.

"The police department, based on the coroner's report and other evidence believe that Mr. Starr had the opportunity (being alone with his wife at home at the time of her death), the means (he is a

48

well-built man and Mrs. Starr could be described as slight of build) and he had motive (Mrs. Starr left her entire estate to her husband). It is estimated that he stands to receive about $41 million in cash and stocks and from the proceeds of her insurance policy and various investment holdings.

It is not only the opportunity, means and motive that triggered the arrest of Mr. Starr but also the belief of the coroner that Mrs. Starr's drowning appears to be suspicious – first reports queried the position of her body in the bath tub and the amount of liquid in her lungs. He believes that someone drowning, even if intoxicated, would sputter and wake up if they began to take in water. He believes that Mrs. Starr would have coughed loud enough to wake her husband – ah, let me add that Paxton Starr maintains as per his statement to the police, that when he made his wife coffee when they returned home, that he poured himself a number of drinks. His blood tests indicates that he had alcohol in his system and that it was taken only several hours before – indicating that he consumed alcohol just before he went to bed. Further, Starr maintains that just before he went to bed he poured himself a coffee, took it upstairs with him. He states that he sat the coffee down on his bedside table and as he was very tired he took off his shoes and lay on the bed. He fell asleep fully dressed. The next morning he awoke and noticed that his wife had not slept in the bed. He found her dead in the bath tub. The police were called – and by the way they found Mr. Starr's empty whiskey glass in the kitchen and the coffee that Mr. Starr had poured for himself was found on his bedside table – cold and untouched. There were no traces of coffee in his blood".

Greg's team were taking notes and scanning the binders that Elizabeth had given – all while actually not missing a word that Greg was saying. There would be plenty of time for questions – first Greg had to pour out his information gathered thus far.

"Hector, let me digress for a moment so that you can get going with your paper work. I have instructed Mr. Starr that his deposit to the firm will be $1 million".

49

Before Greg could continue there was a ripple of noise in the room. Greg's staff actually looked shocked at the size of the deposit that had been imposed. Although Greg was planning to spend time on questions later in his brief he was interrupted by one question that seemed to represent everyone present.

"Gee, boss, why such a high deposit? Do you expect a long trial?"

Greg was a little taken aback by the question so he paused for a second to gather his thoughts – then he answered.

"I wanted to assess just how much our new client wanted to be represented by our firm. I wanted to give him a clear signal that we are expensive but we get the required results. Maybe I was testing him at the interview. If he had shown shock or be reluctant to pay then it might have made me feel that he was really innocent but could be found guilty of whatever charges are laid – or maybe he is guilty and realized that he would have to pay almost anything to have him found innocent. Not sure yet what I interpreted from his reaction – still mulling that in my mind – but he hardly blinked an eye and accepted the amount. And, hey let's not forget that he will be facing a pretty hefty bond to have him released from jail. Certainly the man is very wealthy".

Greg would have preferred not to open up the briefing for questions at this point but another one came from one of his associates.

"If he is wealthy then would it not discount his having the motive for apparently murdering his wife for the $41 million?"

"That is what you will have to investigate" was the reply from Greg Winters. He wanted to press on with his briefing session.

"Hector, I gave copies of the documents to Mr. Starr; he is expecting you later on to collect the signed copies –let's see if Mr. Starr can keep his first promise of arranging the funds transfer within a few hours". Greg need not have worried. Hector collected

50

the documents from their Client by 2 P.M. that afternoon. The confirmation of the deposit into the law firms' account was made by 6 P.M. that evening.

Greg spent the next hour or so going through events of the evening of the apparent murder. He referenced his notes and copies of the statements taken by the police. It was now time to open the floor for questions and then to allocate resources to the case. Greg employed a dictum that he used on his cases, "DAIIPAS" – his staff pronounced it DAEPASS – but it actually stood for the various stages that he used in working through a case.

He would again remind his staff of his approach – as he had done many times before. They knew that he would go through it again. They also knew that it worked.

"DAIIPAS" stood for "Discovery, Assessment, Investigation, Interpretation, Positioning, Argument, Summary". It was how the firm gathered information, assessed its accuracy and validity, and investigated any apparent anomalies, how to interpret the evidence and other facts at hand, how to position the information (even not to use some information if it would not benefit the outcome of the case), how to present their argument and prepare their summary.

At about 12 30 P.M. Greg called a "bio" break but not before he was asked a few more questions. During the ten minutes of the break the coffee was refreshed and a light lunch brought into the boardroom. Elizabeth could certainly multi-task – listening to Greg's briefing and ordering food on her Tablet.

The meeting reconvened and lasted another two hours. Questions were asked from the floor and Greg either provided answers or indicated that the point required investigation – as surely all of the questions would be investigated – over and over and over again!

Greg believed in allowing the information to seep into the minds of his staff. Sure, many things would pop into their minds right away but he wanted that private time for thoughts to take hold. He closed the meeting by midafternoon. Shortly thereafter Elizabeth had forwarded a transcript of the meeting to all associates – including scanned copies of the statements taken by the police. Greg insisted that he did not want them to have electronic files in front of them during the briefing – he was old-fashioned in that regard and wanted his staff to listen and to make notes while he spoke.

With the information at hand the associates scurried off to their offices and began to review the information and gathered evidence thus far. They would spend the next few hours in drafting questions, raising concerns or issues. They were free to draft their questions in any format as Greg did not want uniformity at this stage – the more diverse the questions – even the same type of question but in many different angles – the better right now.

By early evening the first cut of information was sent to Elizabeth. She would then, in her mind group the questions into categories. Again, Greg did not want fixed legal-minded opinion as yet as where the questions would belong in the upcoming investigation – and in any event the same question would most likely appear in several different categories – that was the nature of a complex set of investigation in a murder case.

Elizabeth completed her analysis by approximately 8 P.M. Before leaving the office she forwarded her analysis back to each of the associates and a copy to Greg. This was the first of many a long night for her and for the legal team of Greg Winters and Associates. Ken Parker would lead the group while Greg met with Paxton Starr and the DA in the morning.

CHAPTER 10

Before Greg had drained his third cup of coffee the next morning he had read the files that Elizabeth had sent him. In fact he had read them twice. The first read was before breakfast, and the second after his meal of cereal and eggs on toast. During breakfast was never a good idea as he became so involved in reading his notes that his meal went cold, or he spilled on everything in sight while trying to co-ordinate eye, hand and mouth functions. This was never an easy task. He used the time while enjoying his breakfast to think about the notes that he had just read. That he could manage while negotiating his meal. He had formulated his notes and sent them to Elizabeth.

He knew the questions that his team would come up with. This was not surprising as in essence the type of questions would be the same for any murder case. What he was more interested in was what his team was thinking about this particular case – the why, the how, the when, - what was behind the face of their client, the victim, what needed to be explored behind the evidence and the statements taken.

DAIIPAS – Discovery, Analysis, Investigation, Interpretation, Positioning, Argument, Summary,

Greg had drilled his dictum into his staff over and over again. Missing something at the Discovery stage means countless time and effort (and a potential lost case) at a later stage. He knew that discovery was like peeling an onion and the consequences of some things did not become apparent right up front, so a particular set of evidence might not be explored to the fullest extent as a case commenced. Nevertheless rework and analysis was very costly and potentially disastrous for a case. He knew that when he arrived in the office later in the day that Ken would have DAIIPAS written up on one of the many white boards in the boardroom and that much debate would be taking place on structuring how to commence this first phase of the case.

53

He had a tremendous team.

Soon he would be faced with the situation of considering his retirement. He was by no means an old man but he was tired and he wanted to spend his time near Mary. What to do with his law practice was forever in his mind. He had not really made any attempt to search for a potential merger or even an acquisition by other leading law firms. He was however, not that naïve to know that should he ever decide to pursue some options that he would have an avalanche of enquiries. Some he might not even consider but others would certainly be worth reviewing.

But for now he had to keep focus on the case at hand – and the objective of finding Paxton Starr not guilty.

The telephone rang. It was Elizabeth confirming that she had received his notes.

He would be in the office after he had met with his client and the DA.

CHAPTER 11

As it turned out Greg met first with the DA. He could only get an appointment in the morning so he stopped off there first. He had telephoned the police department and left a message for Paxton Starr that he would be visiting him later in the morning.

The district attorney and Greg Winters went back a long time. Charles Hawkins was as tough as they came as a lawyer. He was as charming as one could wish for when exchanging initial greetings and briefly enquiring how you were – not that he really cared. But once it came down to matters of the law and the application of the law then he could be a brute. One had to dance around him and show tremendous respect for the law to get anywhere with him. Not that he never gave an inch but it had to be based on legal merit and deserving of the circumstances presented.

Greg and Charles had first crossed paths about twenty five years before. Both were making their mark in the legal profession. Both had vast potential in their chosen field.

Charles Hawkins wanted to prosecute and apply the law while Greg wanted to defend clients. Neither man had a great outgoing personality but where Greg could befriend people and want to nurture his staff, Charles was far more distant and difficult to fathom sometimes. The assistant DA's admired their boss but they never really liked him – or he them for that matter – he was too distant to be reached as a loving human being. He had found a partner who loved him and they had a family that seemed well bonded – a difficult thought to comprehend sometimes when one was dealing with Charles Hawkins on a bad day. Which was on most days of the week?

One could not say that Charles Hawkins had a love-hate relationship with Greg Winters as Charles could not be accused of loving anyone too dearly, let alone in a business setting. Charles did however realize that Greg Winters was equally as tough as they come, a highly skilled defense lawyer, someone would could draw doubt onto the most clearly defined piece of evidence, confuse a witnesses for the prosecution and have them reconsider their previously water-tight evidence. Greg Winters was not a man – or a law firm for that matter – to toy with. With Greg in the other corner of a high profile legal case was no easy task. A 100% track record on murder cases tends to make the best of DA's and prosecuting lawyers redouble their efforts. The comments made by the Police Chief Martinez that having Greg around made them a better police department was also held true in the DA's Office.

Charles had often wondered if Greg Winters had any morals in defending those that had been accused of taking the life of another person. Life was simply too important, too precious to be taken away under any circumstances. That is maybe why he had also struggled over the years with the death penalty. His views had changed over the years – just as society's views of the death penalty had changed – he simply could not reconcile himself to the taking of a life be it through murder, conviction or through armed conflict.

Many years before, he was a staunch supporter of United States armed intervention around the world. He believed that it was bringing stability and civilized rule across the globe – assuming that the United States model be imposed on all types of peoples in all regions. He had long since given up that belief – although he was an absolute believer in the United States of America and its judicial system. He saw his mission as bringing criminals to justice and he deplored the thought of men and women having committed murder and then going free. Somehow, his feelings of imprisoning the innocent for crimes that they had not committed seemed less repugnant.

But for all of his personal opinions and character peculiarities Charles Hawkins was a good DA – he supported the police department and tried to run a well-respected law abiding (or at least law enforcing) district. There had never been a push to have him replaced or retired. In highly political times this was rare. Maybe those in power knew what they had and did not want someone that could be unpredictable. Charles Hawkins was the same every day of the week and maybe that is what a solid DA has to be.

Greg was ushered into Charles' office and as per the usual they exchanged greetings.

Greg got things going.

"You might have heard that I have decided to represent Paxton Starr?"

"Yes indeed." Charles replied.

"I thought that you were thinking of retiring after the last case. I thought that I'd seen the last of you". The attempt at humor failed. Both men knew it.

"No, not just as yet", replied Greg. "Still some hills to climb I am afraid".

"Pity – we need some new faces around here" Again the attempt at humor failed.

A silence seemed to fill the room for a moment then Greg spoke.

"Mr. DA – what charges are being brought against my client?"

Charles Hawkins' reply was completely without emotion.

"Mr. Paxton Starr will be charged with Second Degree Murder in the death of his wife Maxi Starr, a second charge of Criminal Negligence will also be filed".

"Second degree murder – on what grounds?" asked Greg Winters.

"Mr. Winters, your client had opportunity – he was the only person with his wife when she drowned – and the police department feel that evidence exists that Mrs. Starr was drowned – he had cause – we know that they had an argument just before they left the home of Wil and Jenni Wright – and he had motive – she left him an estimated $41 million – a tidy sum".

Greg thought for a few seconds and decided not to debate the issue now. Instead he asked, "Criminal Negligence?"

Charles Hawkins was just as matter of fact in his comments as before.

"Mrs. Starr had by all accounts – and confirmed by her blood tests – consumed a great deal of alcohol at the residence of Mr. and Mrs. Wright – once the Starr's returned to their home Mrs. Starr indicated – as per her husband's statement to us – that she said that she was going to take a hot bath. We believe that by not preventing his wife from taking a bath while in her state that he is criminally negligent in the death of his wife. He had opportunity to prevent her from taking actions and he failed to take actions himself."

Again Greg sat in thought for a few moments. His mind was working at a hundred miles an hours. And again he decided not to have any debate now with the DA. No need to upset him this early in the proceedings.

After his pause Greg asked.

"When will your office be in a position to consider bond for my client and what will it be set at?"

Charles knew the drill and was waiting for the question.

"We have considered the fact that Mr. Starr has no previous convictions and we do not believe that he is a threat to society. In view of this we have set the bond at $1 million dollars. He will however, have to surrender his Passport and not travel outside of the State of California without the written consent of my office. Is that understood, Mr. Winters?"

Greg Winters was left in no doubt that the DA was serious. His tone alone was indication itself – but it was the look in his eyes that struck Greg even more.

"A million dollars is a high bond considering that my client has no previous convictions. Why so high?"

Charles Hawkins had baited Greg Winters to challenge him.

"That, Mr. Winters is the decision of my office – would you prefer that your client remain at police headquarters for the next few months until we decide to take him to trial?"

"No, Mr. DA that will not be in the best interests of my client. May I ask however, when is a grand jury to sit and hear the charges brought against my client?"

"At this point in time I do not have a date for a grand jury to be called but I suspect that it will be within the next two months or so. You will of course be advised well in advance".

"By when could we expect the paper work to be completed for the bond?"

"That will be ready by Friday of this week. Once issued and the bond paid – and we have your clients Passport – then he will be released".

There did not seem to be much more to say at this point in time. Greg thought that Round 1 had gone to the DA. Without showing any emotion at all he thought to himself ALWAYS LET THE DA WIN ROUND 1!

Greg rose from his seat and thanked the DA for his time. He said that he would wait word on the availability of the paper work for the bond and then arrange payment.

He left the DA's Offices and walked slowly to his car.

He called Ken Parker and updated him on his meeting with the DA.

CHAPTER 12

On the way to police headquarters Greg decided to stop and have a coffee at a small street-side diner that he frequented from time to time. He knew that his client was expecting him but somehow his desire for a coffee and a slice of homemade cheesecake overpowered his duty to Paxton Starr. Besides if he arrived 15 minutes later than what he had expected Mr. Starr would not know that he was late at all.

Joe's Diner had been around for longer than Greg could remember. The diner had been recommended to Greg by a client many years before but although he drove within a block of it almost every day it had taken him some time before he decided to take the one block detour one day. From his taste buds point of view this was one of the best days of Greg's life. The small diner was certainly nothing to write home about but the food certainly was – and the cheesecake in particular. On any given day the menu board listed not only the original Joe's cheesecake but at least two other cheesecake specials. None were friends with ones waistline but treating oneself every so often was completely within acceptable dietary practices.

Joe knew every ones by name as they came into the diner. That was not a wonder of his memory – it was rather because he only used a slight variation of two main words when greeting his loyal patrons. It was either "Hi boss", or "Hi lady". Nothing fancy – just his way of saying hello. This was followed by "What you like today?" Sometimes Joe's wife would serve you if he was at the back of the diner but when he came through he would still say "Hi boss" or "Hi lady" and then say "What you having today?"

Greg honestly believed that neither Joe nor his wife knew the proper names of any of their patrons – nor did they care what their names were or in fact who they were, or what they did in life. Their livelihood was to operate a small and successful diner and to take their cash from the register every evening and to deposit the money in the overnight banking facility at the nearby bank. Who knew if they ever made a good living or not? The diner was open six days a week and from 8 in the morning to 8 at night. Not unlike tens of thousands of family operated business around the country. They did not care which political party won the election, who was Mayor of San Francisco or who won the World Series. What was important is that they had the choice of making a living and be in a country where they were free. In all the years that they had operated their diner not once had they been hit by a gang or even had a car stolen from their street side parking lot.

Greg ordered his coffee and cheesecake and sat looking blankly outside the window of the diner. Thinking of nothing in particular –just mindlessly enjoying some brain-empty time! His order arrived and his focus of attention switched to the anticipation of consuming his piece of cake.

Greg had hardly started his mouth-watering adventure when two men entered the diner and were greeted by "Hi boss". The men sat at the table behind Greg. They started talking and Greg could not but over hear their conversation.

"So what you think about this Starr murder? - it is just another freaking rich guy killing his wife."

"It stinks if you ask me. These guys think that they own the freaking world. Do what they like – get pissed with their woman and just kill them off. Pile of shit if you ask me."

"Yeah! What bull shit! Then they get some smart lawyer type to defend them and he gets off. Walks free! How can the lawyers live with themselves? Freaking murders walk free – but if you and I do "sumfing" wrong then we'll go away for a few years. No freaking justice. If you ask me the lawyers are just as guilty of a murder if the scum bag gets to walk free".

Greg Winters almost gagged on his cheesecake. He froze as her heard what the two men said. He replayed it over in his mind "No freaking justice. If you ask me the lawyers are just as guilty of a murder if the scum bag gets to walk free".

At first he could not believe what he had just over heard. Then his instinct was to turn around and correct the perceptions of the two men behind him. But that would have been a very bad idea. He sat almost breathless for another minute. He realized that his hands were trembling. "No freaking justice. If you ask me the lawyers are just as guilty of a murder if the scum bag gets to walk free".

He was brought back to life by "Hi boss, you not like cake today?"

He looked up and smiled, "Oh, no, the cake is good, just day dreaming!"

Greg left money on the table and a minute later he walked out of the diner without finishing his coffee or his cheesecake.

"The Solar Murder"

CHAPTER 13

Greg was ushered into see Paxton Starr.

Mr. Starr had received clean clothes and although he looked tired and rather stressed he seemed genuinely pleased to see Greg. The two men shook hands and Greg enquired if from Paxton if he was comfortable.

"As good as can be expected Mr. Winters, thank you for asking".

Greg sensed that his client seemed less distant than their previous meetings.

"Mr. Starr I have just come from the DA's Office. Two indictments will be brought against you when the grand jury is called. The indictments will be for Second Degree Murder and Criminal Negligence – I get the feeling that the DA will be pushing hard on the case".

"Criminal Negligence? What is that?" asked Paxton.

"Well, as I said, the DA will be pushing hard on the Second Degree Murder charge – that will be their prime target when the grand jury is called – but they need a second and fallback charge. They seem to believe that by you not stopping your wife from taking a hot bath when you knew that she had consumed a vast amount of alcohol was neglect on your part – and therefore you had a role to play in her death".

"I see. That seems unfair. I had no inkling that Maxi was in danger – it never occurred to me – otherwise I would have stopped her. I would have stopped her".

Greg watched his client very carefully as he spoke.

"The law has got nothing to being "fair" – so let's forget about what might or might not appear to be fair" retorted Greg.

"We'll address all of these issues in due course, but now we need to work on getting your bond approved. The DA has set your bond at $1 million – that is our first priority right now."

"$1 million!" sputtered Paxton, "They want one million dollars bond – why? I have no previous convictions? I do not understand. Why on earth such a high bond?"

"Good question. I am not sure why they have pitched it so high. Maybe because other high profile murder cases recently have set seven-figure bonds. To be honest I do not know. But what I do know is that it has been set and we're not going to be able to negotiate – too early to piss off the DA. On top of that he has required that you surrender your Passport – is that an issue with your business?"

Paxton's mood seemed to have become more sullen again. It was not often that he became overly emotive – a life-long character trait.

"I have a building project commencing in the United Arabia Emirates in the next month or so – that could be a problem as we move forward – but if we have to make the DA happy then I'll arrange for my Passport to be brought in". Paxton paused for a second then went on, "By when will the DA require the bond to be paid – I could have it arranged within a few hours?"

"It will not be that quick. When I get back to my office I'd need to talk with the DA's Office and move things forward it could take a little time". "Also, and this might appear to be harsh on you by keeping you here a little longer but we should not just pop up with the bond too quickly. The optics might not seem important to you but by coming up with the funds so quickly might make the DA think that he is dealing with just another rich guy who can buy his way out of police custody. We'll get this done soon but just not that quick."

It was now Greg's turn to pause for a moment, then he continued.

"Mr. Paxton I must advise you of a few things. A murder trial is not a pretty thing. We will have to delve deep, sometimes very deep into the evidence presented, what has not been presented, what might appear to be personal or trivial to you. Rest assured that the DA's Office will be doing exactly the same. Their intention is to prosecute you on the indictment brought against you – while our assignment is to have you found not guilty of these charges. We will have to probe and probe and keep probing – sometimes cases are won or lost on a series of small inconsistencies rather than one big piece of evidence – in fact this is mostly the case. I will be introducing you to lawyers from my office – they are all highly skilled defense lawyers – every one of them – I expect total co-operation on your part – even if we keep asking the same questions over and over again. We must never get the feeling that you are hiding anything from us – remember that we are presenting you – representing you with the sole purpose of having you found not guilty at the end of the process.

"In presenting the indictment and calling for a grand jury the DA believes that he has a cause against you. He believes that you had the opportunity, the cause and motive to take the life of your wife. We need to explore every avenue to take away their evidence against you.

"The media will be all over the case – as indeed they are already - and sometimes they will seem out of control – and sometimes indeed they are – but in a strange way they are doing their job – whether we like it or not. You will have to work with us in containing the media – for instance no talking to the media – no statements, nothing at all. The next few months must be well orchestrated – this might sound a little phony but it is absolutely vital that we keep a clean slate with the DA and with the media.

Either me, or one of my lawyers will make statements to the Press – no one else, not your PR Company, no one. Do you understand?"

"Yes, Mr. Winters, I completely understand".

"There are a few other things that I would like to discuss with you if you do not mind" he continued.

"Of course, Mr. Starr, of course – I have not really given you much opportunity to ask me anything – I apologize". Greg replied. He sometimes did get too caught up in his side of preparing for a grand jury and Trial. "Please, go ahead".

"There is not much really. I know that you and your team will have to probe into my life and into that of other people and the circumstances surrounding the death of my wife – I do understand that". He paused as if not too sure how to continue, then he asked. "I had a great relationship with our friends on Ocean Drive – great, great friends – family really – but I know now that their feelings towards me might have changed because of what has happened. That would be completely natural – you see they all loved my Maxi very dearly – and, well now I am sitting here accused of murdering my wife". He paused again and looked down at the floor – a sign of emotion that Greg had not seen before.

"Mr. Winters, I cannot face my friends now – if they still call me a friend – I cannot go back and live in my home again – I cannot walk into the rooms and see Maxi sitting there, I cannot sleep in the bed without her next to me, and I cannot face my friends on Ocean Drive – I am sorry, I just cannot do that".

Greg did not answer immediately – that would have been insensitive and inappropriate. This was the first time that he had seen any real emotion from his client and he had to digest what had just taken place. It was too early to judge the authenticity of the scene or not – too early to judge if it was a well thought out play-act for his benefit. He had seen similar scenes before. He waited for a minute and then replied.

68

"Mr. Starr, I understand. It is a very sensitive time right now. I cannot make the call how your friends will react to you – that we will have to discover as we move forward – but maybe do not under estimate them. Once we get you out of here then we can think about moving you home for a while – that should not be a problem – just by way of interest do you have anywhere in mind?"

"No, not as yet – but there are furnished apartments near to my home and that could be an option but maybe that is too close to Ocean Drive".

"Well, let's not worry about that now. We'll sort out something as we move forward."

Greg said goodbye to Paxton Starr and walked slowly back to his SUV.

"The Solar Murder"

CHAPTER 14

Ken Parker and the team of lawyers had certainly been very busy. They knew the drill of developing questions, queries and identifying oddities in statements, facts, opinions, observations and suggestions. Of course, not all evidence and oddities were on the table as yet but they were expert in slicing up information (or lack of information) into bite size pieces of logic. If an item was divided up into its smallest logical entity and then tested for validity, common sense or rationale then some result would be forthcoming. If these small units of information added up and were agreed upon then they were so documented onto their systems – if the units of information did not seem to add up then either the units had to be smaller or they were highlighted as Attention Points.

Greg had put it another way to his staff "Keep shaking the tree and eventually all of the leaves will come down – if you are still not satisfied then start digging up the roots."

Logic was a most powerful tool in the array of tools and skills found in any top class lawyer. Keep following the "logic trial and see where it takes you" had been a catch saying of one of the Law Professors that Ken Palmer had at law school. Another famous saying brought to the table by Michelle Grant – one of Greg's upcoming lawyers was,
"Logic test: is it logical that if A took place that B, C, or D would have happened as a result – if YES, "WHY" if NO try to establish what E, F, or G could be. Keep following the logic tree!"

Ken had been with Greg the longest and had grown accustomed to Greg's methodology, his sense of instinct, his attention to detail but most of all his power of thought and logic. He had not perfected these – and other talents that Greg possessed – that would be too much to assume – but there was no doubt that he possessed many fine talents. Ken had not however, as yet picked up Greg's ability to read body language – to watch for slight

71

twitches of the mouth or nose, the shaking of a hand or foot, the deep look of the eyes when lying, the fake portrayals of remorse or the lack of display of joy or happiness. Sometimes Greg shared his observations other times not. He would never jeopardize his role as a defense lawyer by mentioning things that could damage their case. Ken was sure that Greg had a truck load of observations stored away in his brain over the years – and no one would ever find out about them.

This case would no doubt be the same.

Greg arrived at his offices about two hours later than he had expected. He had kept Elizabeth posted re his activities during the morning so she was not surprised when he walked into the office – he had called to say that he was 15 minutes away – and then on time he walked in.

The boardroom (war room) was at the very back of the suite of offices but Greg could see his team seated around the table as he walked to his office. His office was closer to the front of the suite as he did not like the thought of clients entering too far into their "confidential spaces". Even the boardroom only had a narrow glass panel next to the door – otherwise it was closed off from view. Through the narrow glass panel down at the end of the hallway Greg could see Ken standing at the front of the room.

Elizabeth followed Greg into his office and allowed him time to remove his jacket and hang it up behind his door before she began to brief him on some of the developments in the office. Whether he listened or not the notes would be on his PC when he required them. Greg was actually more interested in getting into the war room and catching up on the progress being made by his team – just as they were now eagerly awaiting his arrival and for him to update them on the activities of the morning.

Greg's seat in the boardroom was always left vacant when he was not attending a meeting. He enjoyed sitting in the middle of the one side of the boardroom table – he could not tolerate the thought of sitting at the head of the table and pretend that he was some type of God overseeing his subjects. In fact there was no chair at the head of the table at all. Not only did this symbolize the fact that Greg did not want the focus on himself all of the time but also that is was easier for someone to lead a discussion from the whiteboard at that end of the room if no one was sitting there.

Greg knew that one day his seat in the middle of the boardroom table would not be his spot anymore. He would no longer have a vacant chair left waiting for him. He would miss his favorite place at the table. Deep down his staff also knew that Greg was just about ready to move on to other adventures in his life. Maybe in their minds Greg's chair would simple remain "Greg's Chair" and that no one would ever sit there. If they had given more thought to the idea – which they really did not want to do – they might have thought of retiring Greg's spot like the Pro Sports teams do when famous players finally retire from the game. Even if they should ever do something like this Greg's chair would never have the number "1" stuck on the back. Greg would not like that.

"The Solar Murder"

CHAPTER 15

After the round of greetings and some jibes at always being late for meetings, Greg settled himself into his favorite seat. The mild banter lasted only long enough for the coffee table to be refreshed and the muffins to be brought in. No muffins were brought into the room before Greg arrived for a meeting – an "Elizabeth Rule" – so no wonder Greg took a little rap from his team for being late!

It took just a minute or two for the hungry staff members to fill their plates and to pour a coffee before the room settled down to discuss the Paxton Starr case.

Greg briefed the team on his meeting with the DA and confirmed that the two indictments to be brought against Paxton Starr were Second Degree Murder and that of Criminal Negligence. As Greg spoke Ken Parker wrote the indictment charges up on a corner whiteboard – and of course, the information was being captured onto the online case files of the team members.

Greg was very open to questions coming from the various members of the team. Each question would be recorded in order that they did not lose sight of something that might be vital later on in the case, or even the way in which Greg answered the questions.

The questions came.....

"What makes the DA think that he has a Second Degree Murder indictment against our client?'

"What is the logic behind the Criminal Negligence charge?'

"When do we expect a grand jury to be called?"

"What are the chances of the grand jury recommending that the case goes to trial?"

"Why was the bond set so high?"

"What was Paxton Starr's reaction to the size of the bond? How did he react?"

Greg answered all of the questions as they popped up. He referenced his own notes and indicated when he thought that the necessary paper work would be completed by the DA's Office in order that a bond Hearing could take place and bail be granted.

Greg did not mention his visit to Joe's Diner or the conversation that he had overheard. He wondered if he was just as guilty of murder as the clients that he had so successfully defended. He was not going to share this thought with his team.

After some discussion around what the team described as the "mechanics" of the case – the indictment, bond, grand jury date etc. Greg turned the conversation to what the team had discussed while they were eagerly awaiting their muffins. They had indeed been very busy – as was to be expected.

Ken arose from his chair and opened up the fold-away whiteboards that the team had been working on. The whiteboards were in fact more like "smart boards" with the functionality to copy written notes, hide information or even have some information under security only access. All information gathered on the boards would be grouped, analyzed and divided up for investigation. This was the starting point of using Greg's DAIIPAS methodology (Discover, Analyze, Investigate, Interpretation, Position, Arguement and Summary).

Ken now had the floor.

"As our first cut of the statements on hand our view that no apparent incident occurred between Mr. and Mrs. Starr before they arrived at the home of Wil and Jenni Wright. We might of course be mistaken here but from accounts there did not appear to be any strain between them when they arrived. None of the witness statements indicate any abnormal behavior or edginess between Mr. and Mrs. Starr. Based on this initial cut of the evidence we feel that something must have either happened at the home of Mr. and Mrs. Wright – as demonstrated by their argument on the patio and Mrs. Starr slapping her husband – or that he had preplanned the incident, provoked his wife and that he had the intention all along of murdering her after their return home."

Ken paused and waited for any comment from Greg. Greg merely indicated with his hand for Ken to continue

"We have a difference of opinion as to this latter possibility as by creating an incident would have drawn attention to himself and then their friends might have become suspicious when Mrs. Starr was then found dead the next morning. Generally we cannot see the logic of Mr. Starr in doing this. If he had planned to murder his wife then why raise suspicion – if she was found drowned the morning after the party then none of the group of friends would have suspected foul play. After all the Starr's apparently had a solid marriage so the sudden death of Mrs. Starr would be tragically viewed but there would have been no suspicion of foul play".

This time as Ken paused Greg spoke.

"I thought through that one as well. To me it makes little sense for Paxton Starr to create an incident and then raise suspicion. I agree that it does not seem logical but let's not dispel that thought. We will have to robustly analyze the scenario".

Ken continued.

"So, for the time being let us accept the fact that a non-planned incident occurred at the home of Wil and Jenni Wright. From the statements it appears as if Mr. and Mrs. Starr did not spend much time together at the party after they arrived. This seemed to be the pattern of these monthly get together events with the families on Ocean Drive. Just as an add-on here, these monthly gathering have been going on for over twenty one years. The events rotate between the households with each family hosting twice a year – give or take. Over the years the adults and those with growing kids attended the gathering. We'll need to probe deeper here but on the surface there does not appear to be any visible or clear issue that arose at the party in question.. As I said, it seems as if the families and their children attend – or the kids attend some of the functions – and although it was recorded in the statements taken by the police that every so-often one or two of the adults had a few too many drinks – there does not appear to be any misuse by anyone – including the kids."

Greg interjected.

"I would not say that the assessment included Mrs. Starr – from my discussion with her husband and my opinion of the statement evidence gathered so far, it appears as if Maxi Starr – although not all of the time – but that she had the highest consumption rate – not saying that she was always intoxicated but that she did enjoy a few drinks at these functions. We must be careful in gathering evidence here because if she indeed did have a few drinks – as a general habit – and, and let me stress AND she always took a hot bath when she got home after the party then we have a crack in the DA's argument that Paxton Starr was criminally negligent in allowing his wife to have bath when they returned home that night – we need to focus hard on this point".

"Yes, we picked up on this issue – and our investigation will focus on this. Just seems strange at this point that never before was there an issue between her and her husband in public about her drinking – and such a visible display by slapping him – that is the confusing point right now – why at this party? What set it off?"

"That, my dear "Watson" could be the kernel of the entire case!" stated Greg without even appearing to be humorous or being pointed.

Ken continued.

"So we know that the Starr's went outside – most likely Paxton Starr wanted to be discreet in talking with his wife about her drinking that evening...." Before Ken could continue, Greg interjected again.

"Let's not make that assumption. What if she wanted to talk with him?" commented Greg.

"But the witnesses at the party saw Mr. Starr take his wife by the arm and walk with her towards the sliding doors to the patio. He wanted to talk with her about her drinking that night." The comment came from one of the other lawyers in the room,

"Indeed. That appears to be what happened. But we cannot merely assume that Mr. Starr instigated the move outside.....what if Mrs. Starr had asked to talk with her husband alone and he then took her by the arm to walk outside. We cannot link together him taking her by the arm to leave the house and his statement that he asked to speak with her – those are two separate issues. Sure, we might never know who instigated the proposed private discussion but we cannot assume that it was Paxton Starr just because he said so in his statement. Statements are not pure fact in any case."

The young lawyer made some frantic notes and looked down at his finger tips for a short while. When he looked up Greg had a fatherly slight smile on his face. Nothing too demonstrative to make the team member embarrassed. Other lawyers in the room had experienced similar moments with Greg. Although slight they picked up the hint of a smile from Greg.

Ken cleared his throat to bring back the attention to himself. He continued.

"We know – again via the statements only at this point in time that Paxton Starr and his wife appeared to be talking, then became more animated – and then that she slapped him. We have two perspectives of the incident – those that watched from inside the house and Mr. Starr's statement. Again, let's not make any assumptions here – this is what we have but it proves nothing really.

Next we know that Maxi Starr appeared to bury her head in her husband's chest.

At the moment we can only interpret this as a sign of remorse. If so, then she might have realized that she had overreacted by slapping him – but the fundamental questions is rather why she hit out at him – was it something that she did, something he said – or most likely both. It is just another avenue for us to try to find a logical answer for. With the incident having taken place outside and with no one actually having heard the exchange between them we only have Mr. Starr's account of what happened.

We know that they came inside after the incident and that Maxi Starr was crying and apparently very upset – as was Mr. Starr. He still carried the slap mark on his face when the police arrived after his 911 telephone call on the Sunday morning. For a small woman she certainly unloaded on him. Brings us back to the point that something fundamental must have taken place between them while they were with the neighbors that night. Greg, is there any other indication from Paxton Starr what they argued about?"

"No. None at all! In my second interview he told the same story as the first time around, and this information is rock solid with that in his statement to the police. He maintains that he calmly confronted his wife as to why she was drinking so much that evening. He asked her to walk outside and he asked her on the patio – he said that he wanted to keep it private – which I suppose is understandable." Greg replied.

A question from one of the lawyers caught their attention.

"Is there any chance that Mrs. Starr staged the event outside?"

"Why would she do that?" asked Greg. "What's on your mind?"

"Maybe Paxton Starr was being unfaithful to his wife and she then staged the incident and later in the evening drowned herself and wanted her death to be pinned on him?"

This time Ken answered.

"Um, it takes a very brave person to plan to drown themselves. Can't see it – no guarantee that the staged event would work or that you'd be successful in killing yourself – I've never heard of something like that - no, can't see it happening."

"I have not heard of it either – she would most likely start choking and gasping for breath and the noise would have attracted the attention of her husband – no, I think that is not what happened. But we can be sure that something set off the string of events," said Greg.

Ken took up the lead again.

"Ok, we know from the statements taken that the couple came inside – were surrounded by their friends and that Paxton Starr suggested that they leave the party and go home. Several of the guests confirmed that Mr. Starr looked very shaken – embarrassed, shocked, confused even – not mad at his wife but appeared to be very comforting. Another reason why I do not think that the scene was staged – this looks as if it was a real event that occurred – unplanned if you would.

"Wil Wright then drove the Paxton and Maxi Starr back to their home and saw them to the door. Paxton Starr said that he was fine and that he would get his wife to bed. Mr. Wright then returned to the party. From the statements taken from the guests the incident took place at around 11:30 P.M. – give or take a few minutes. After Mr. Wright arrived home there was some discussion among the group of friends as to what had led to the incident. It sure seems as if the guests were all pretty stunned. Not seen anything like this since they had met the Starr's – never an argument – nothing – if anything just the opposite – they were very much in love with one another and it was pretty visible to see. The guests were really stunned.

"By about midnight all of the guests had left the home of Wil and Jenni Wright.

"We've all read the statement made by Paxton Starr to the Police about what transpired when he and his wife returned home. We know that they were dropped off at home at approximately 11:40 P.M. as stated by Wil Wright. When they entered the hallway he said that his wife broke down and cried again and that he embraced her in the hallway. She apparently said how sorry she was for what had happened – but of course we cannot independently confirm that this is what Mrs. Starr said – if she said anything. Paxton Starr states that he offered to make his wife coffee and that they walked through to the kitchen. He said that while the coffee was brewing he poured himself a drink. We have no indication if the drink was a single or double shot but he stated that it was about a half an inch of liquor – say close to a double. He said that they hardly spoke while the coffee was brewing. He poured his wife her coffee and she sat and drank it without saying a word. He maintains that he poured himself another drink – again about half an inch.

"According to Mr. Starr when his wife had finished drinking her coffee she said that she was going upstairs to take a bath. He maintains that he asked her if she was alright and that she replied that she was. She kissed him and told him that she loved him. Mrs. Starr then went upstairs. Mr. Starr maintains that he had another drink and then poured himself a mug of coffee. He maintained that he felt very tired and walked up the staircase to go to bed. Per his statement he sat on the side of the bed put his coffee down, took of his shoes and must have lay down and went straight off to sleep. When he awoke when it was light outside he noticed that his wife had not come to bed. He called out for her, received no answer and then walked into the bathroom and saw her in the bathtub.

82

"He telephoned 911 and the Emergency Vehicles arrived about nine minutes later at 9:44 A.M. - as per the Police records.

"Not many of the neighbors on Ocean Drive were up and about when they heard the sirens coming down their Drive on the Sunday morning. The Drive is about three quarters of a mile long with the Starr residence being the end home before the dead-end. The emergency vehicles would have had to pass-by all of the other five homes on the way to the end of the road. That was about 9.44-45 A.M. The estate lots are fairly well spread out with about 150-180 yards between each of the homes.

"Mrs. Starr was found naked in the bath and was pronounced dead at the scene. The coroner's initial estimate of the time of death is approximately midnight to 1 A.M. The full report from the coroner will only be available in several weeks. The blood alcohol content in her indicated that she had consumed a good amount of liquor the night before – the initial report indicates that the consumption had stopped around 11 P.M. Mr. Starr provided a blood sample on the Sunday morning and his residual alcohol content was high – indicating that he had consumed liquor up to about 1 A.M."

Greg interjected.

"So, it appears as if that part of Mr. Starr's statement holds true"

Ken replied almost instantaneously.

"You say, "that part of Mr. Starr's statement" what makes you say it as if other parts are not true?" "No, real reason as yet, just to say that we should not assume that every statement made to the police is totally true or valid. Maybe more than that, maybe he just comes across a little plastic to me sometimes – not sure yet – we've heard that he is a very reserved man so that may be it – we'll have to see as we get to know him over the next few months."

Somehow Ken knew that Greg had picked up more than what he was saying right now – rather be on guard as a well-respected lawyer that he was.

"Ken, please continue", said Greg – it sounded as if the more pertinent information was still to come.

"Mrs. Starr was found naked in the bath. We've taken a look at the photographs of her body. As we know Mr. Starr has been charged with Second Degree murder and Criminal Negligence - and his bond has been set at $1 million.
I open the floor for questions".

Now the questions and queries came more rapidly from the other lawyers in the room.

What could have caused the scene at the home of Wil and Jenni Wright?
What could have happened when Paxton and Maxi Starr returned home?
Why did Paxton Starr not enter the bathroom when he went upstairs?
If he had Cause, Means and Motive then what were they?
Was he having an affair and was caught out?
Was she having an affair and was caught out?
Were either of them having financial difficulty?
Why raise the suspicion of the group of friends by murdering your wife after just having had a public incident? What would have caused him to react in this way?
Why was the coroner convinced that something was amiss at the scene of the crime?

The questions and debate around the events of the evening of the death of Mrs. Starr lasted for some time. Proposing a question then listening to speculation or points of view. Venturing theories and exploring possibilities. Finally Greg stood up and took the floor.

"All of these questions no doubt require answers – and we will probe as deep as we can when we interview the witnesses and other parties of interest. But ladies and gentlemen there are three questions that I pose to you....

Precedence, Precedence, Precedence."

Greg staff looked at him confusion written all over their faces. What had they missed or not discussed as yet?

"My young friends," Greg answered the question that they had on their faces.

"Have we considered Mr. Starr's behavior or demeanor at previous gatherings with his friends? Was he a heavy drinker or only a social sipper? If he drank heavily then how did this potentially impact the incident with his wife or even his actions or inactions when they returned home? Was he abusive to her outside on the patio of the home of the Wrights and that lead to the visible incident that took place? What if he was UI when they got home and did not comprehend the potential risk of his wife taking a bath? What if he was UI and then went to bed without entering the bath room before he apparently fell asleep on his bed.

The next precedent to consider.....

What if Mrs. Starr had a reputation of being UI at these gatherings? What indeed if she did not? How does either scenario affect the events that took place that particular evening? If she had a record of drinking then maybe she routinely just passed out when she got home? - maybe this time in the bath? If she did habitually drink then why was this time different and she became violent – what set her off? Her drinking habit might have a substantial bearing on what transpired that night.

And the third precedent to consider is this....

Did Mrs. Starr routinely have a bath when she returned from these social events? Is there a precedent here? If she never took a bath when she and her husband returned home from these or any other function for that matter – then why this particular night? In fact did she ever even commit to a bath or is that an item of information provided solely by Mr. Starr? If she always took a bath when they returned home then maybe Mr. Starr – irrespective if he had consumed liquor or not that evening – might not have thought anything of it when his wife said that she was going to take a bath.

These are three key precedents that we need to investigate. We need to keep shaking the tree until all of the leaves fall from it.

Let me remind you that we are defense lawyers. We will explore every avenue of the case – think like the prosecution team – think like the coroner – think like the police department. It is our job to have our client found not guilty of the indictments against him – and in doing so we need to turn over every conceivable piece of evidence and then decide if we are going to use it or not".

Silence had fallen over the war room. The staff had not heard Greg Winters be so animated in a very long time – and for some it was their first time. It had certainly been an experience. And even to suggest that some evidence might not be used if it would potentially damage their case. Maybe this had always been implied but never so vividly expressed before. Greg Winters seemed so determined that Paxton Starr be found not guilty.

Ken arose again and stood at the front of the war room.

"OK, let's take a look at our methodology. DAIIPAS.

D is for Discovery – so let's plan to populate our approach...
D1, Would be Paxton Starr – gathering everything about him and reviewing the evidence that he provided.
D2, Would be Maxi Starr – same, gathering everything about her

86

D3, This will be Wil and Jenni Wright and their account of what transpired
D4, The other group of friends
D5, The police report
D6, The coroner's report
D7, Other evidence."

The last part of the meeting was dedicated to the allocation of resources and action plans and timescales to begin their preparation for the grand jury.

Greg returned to his office and felt completed exhausted by the activities of the long day. This would be the first of many long days and nights still to come. He swallowed down some headache capsules – he thought to himself that the pills seemed to have less and less impact over the years.

He sat in his chair and thought about what he had overheard in Joe's Diner. Was he just as guilty of murder as his clients that he had presented over the last thirty years?

Over the next few days the bond was finalized and Paxton Starr was released. The media were in full attendance when Mr. Starr was taken out of the police department and driven away by Ken and Greg. Not however before Greg had to make some statement to the Press about the innocence of his client and that he was sure that the grand jury would find no cause to pursue the case. Greg did not believe what he said – and in fact some time later he was proven correct when the grand jury decided to recommend Paxton Starr to stand trial for the indictments brought against him. Greg knew that DA Charles Hawkins was going full out to have Paxton Starr found guilty.

"The Solar Murder"

88

CHAPTER 16

Ken Parker would become more and more prominent as the defense case for their client developed. He would lead interviews, oversee other interviews, gather information, ask questions and keeping chipping away at the evidence that the DA might be stockpiling against Paxton Starr. Ken was a fine lawyer and learnt more and more about instinct on each case that he worked on with Greg Winters. There was no doubt that Greg was in charge of the entire case – as he should be but without Ken he would have been severely handicapped.

On the day that Paxton Starr was released on bond Ken and Greg had offered to pick him from police headquarters and drive him home. They were not only playing at being Good Samaritans – they were both very eager to see their client's reaction when he entered his home – how would he react to being in the home where his wife had died.
Greg had explained that they also needed to visit the scene of the death of Maxi Starr and by taking Paxton home it would kill two birds with one stone

On the journey to Ocean Drive the three men spoke more about the beautiful scenery on the way to the Starr home than about the case. Once they were in Ken's car and asked Paxton if he was "ok" after the ordeal of working through the crowded media circus that had gathered outside of the police headquarters, the conversation was kept away from the case. Greg and Ken had rehearsed their roles for that day – and somehow Paxton might have guessed that they were attempting to steer the conversation away from the immensity of the case. Greg had previously asked his client if they could conduct a "walking-interview" around the house and Paxton had readily agreed.

Once they turned off the main road the scenery became breathe-taking. The low forest line gave way to the beach and the brilliant blue ocean. Greg enjoyed the view while Ken could only glance at the magnificent sight in front of them as he drove. The road then turned through a small neighborhood and almost at once they turned into Ocean Drive. Paxton kept providing Ken with the driving directions.

Ocean Drive consisted of six homes – or rather estate homes. Not small in anyone's book. Greg thought to himself that there was a great deal of capital invested in these few properties. Some wealthy people inhabited these homes. As they slowly drove by each home, Paxton told Ken and Greg which family from their group lived in which house. Both Ken and Greg made mental notes about the information provided – although they had already received these details from the police department. From the lawyers' point of view every morsel of information was being soaked up and stored away for reference later on. As per Paxton's description, the homes were well spaced apart. There were no fences between the properties – some small trees or some stone features but nothing that looked permanent or divisive. Each home had a featured electric front gate and a short drive way to the front door and garages. On the side of each electric gate were bushes that ran across the front of the property and a small ditch that would keep any unwanted vehicles from by-passing the gates. The architect of the homes had totally brought a sense of tranquility into the overall development. From front gate to front gate between the homes, the distance seemed to vary between about one hundred and fifty to maybe one hundred and eighty yards. Greg recalled in his meeting with the Chief of Police that the homes were well spaced out.

The second last house was that of Wil and Jenni Wright - the scene of the argument between Paxton and Maxi Starr. Greg and Ken would still be visiting the Wright's for an interview.

As they approached the Starr residence it was easy to see that it was the more rustic looking. It was an estate home at the end of the Drive and with rocks and beach on the right-hand side and the beginnings of the forest on the left-hand side. The yellow police tape and car parked outside the front gate seemed totally out of place as they slowly approached the home.

The police officer walked up to the car as they pulled up in front of the gates. Ken and Greg lowered their windows and greeted the officer. They identified themselves and waited while the officer checked his list of persons that could enter the property. The unsmiling officer returned to Ken's car and asked him to sign-in on an electronic pad – even police forces are now using new technologies! The authorization form that Ken had signed would be logged into the case file at police headquarters and also be available to both the DA and to the defense team should they request information on visitors to the crime scene.

Ken drove through the large entrance gates and parked his car in the drive way near the front door of the house. The partner of the police officer stationed at the front gate was standing at the front door of the house as they approached the home of Paxton and Maxi Starr. Again Ken was asked to sign-in on an electronic keyboard.

Greg and Ken were on full internal alert as they prepared to enter the home with their client. They intended to watch every reaction of their client. They would be totally mentally drained when they would leave the home several hours later.

They entered the home and stood in the hallway. Even from this limited vantage point they could see that it was a beautiful home – the colors of the walls were of a sandy shade and the floor tiles a shade darker. The staircase was of a grainy wood that seemed to flow upwards and almost appeared to be not like a staircase at all but like a magic carpet gliding upwards. As the hours passed and Greg and Ken went from room to room with their client they experienced the full force that was the interior decorating skill of the late Maxi Starr. The lasting impression was one of simple class – of tremendous thought and care that had gone into planning the entire interior of the home.

Not one room felt overstated or of being a reflection of the wealth that the Starr's had at their disposal. There was no doubt that the furnishings were expensive but there was not the feeling of the home owners showing off. The home was simply stunning. Later when they ventured into what the Starr's called their common room – where most of their entertaining took place – and from there onto the outside deck and barbeque area – and the view over the beach and onto the ocean was breath-taking. The kitchen was situated next to the common room and sliding doors opened onto the deck and in-deck small swimming pool. At the end of the deck steps led down directly onto the beach. Most of the beach area was to the right hand side of the property – on the left was a shorter expanse of beach before the rocky outcrop led up to the forest line. From the deck each of the other homes on Ocean Drive could be seen – although they were spread apart with the curving of the small bay. Whoever had discovered this little bay and turned it into a developers vision of private estate homes was a genius.

Paxton Starr walked through to the kitchen and offered to put on coffee for Greg and Ken. He appeared to be completely relaxed but he knew that soon the business at hand would need to be addressed. He could not avoid it – and he did not know how his emotions would hold up.

Finally it was time and Greg suggested that they should talk about the case. Paxton had been the most talkative since Greg had first met him but now there was a more somber man sitting in the kitchen of his own home. Greg tried to comfort him by saying that they were there to listen and to gain evidence in order to represent him successfully at the trial. Greg had noticed that there appeared to be a very sincere and kind man inside Paxton Starr. A gentle giant – but was he a wife killer?

Greg suggested that before they undertake the walking-interview that Paxton recap from the events leading up to the party.

Were there any matrimonial issues between the couple?
No

Had there ever been matrimonial issues in the past?
No

Where there any financial worries?
No

Some questions were a repeat of those asked before but Greg wanted to listen again and Ken watched and made notes.

Did your wife usually drink at these parties?
Yes

How much did she normally drink?
Maybe 2-3 drinks, not really sure.

Did she ever become loud or rowdy at other party's?
No – more full of fun than rowdy.

Did your wife usually drink more when with the group on Ocean Drive?
Yes

Why was this?
She seemed more relaxed in their company.

How many drinks would she have at these events?
Not sure, maybe 4-5 – maybe more on the odd occasion.

Did she ever become loud, rowdy at these group functions?
Yes, but mostly in a playful manner. Maxi was very playful. She loved life. She never caused a scene before the incident of that evening.

What caused the incident?
I asked her why she had been drinking more than normal.

What caused her to drink more than her normal?

I do not know. I really do not know.

Did you observe her drinking or was it brought to your attention?
Before dinner she was fine. After dinner the guys hung out together so I did not see Maxi drinking. Later in the evening Jenni Wright mentioned to me that Maxi had been drinking heavily. I then saw that she was pretty much out of it.

That is when you asked her to join you outside on the deck?
Yes, that is correct.

What would have caused her to start drinking more heavily after dinner?
I do not know. I wanted to talk with her out of ear shot to see what was going on.

Did she tell you when you asked her?
No. She told me that she was fine and just having a good time.

Did you press her on the topic?
Yes. I kept trying to ask her what was going on. She became frustrated with me asking her questions.

Did you assault your wife on the deck?
No, absolutely not. I believe that that folk inside the house could attest to that. I gently held her by the arms and then on her shoulders but I did not use force.

Then what happened?
I pressed her again and she used foul language at me. I was totally shocked. I told her not to talk to me that way and to get a grip on things. The next thing I knew she slapped me. I was stunned – not only by what she did but by the force that she used.

And then what happened?
She burst into tears and fell into my arms and said how sorry she was. We held each other. I looked up and saw my friends looking at us. I asked her if she was ok to go inside and she just said "yes"

94

I then held her and took her inside the house.

And then?
Everyone gathered around us and asked if we were ok. Maxi sat and sobbed for a few minutes while the ladies comforted her. One of the guys brought me a cold towel as my face stung like hell. I then suggested that we go home. We had walked over so Wil gave us a ride home.

Greg then suggested that they walk to the front door of the home and pick up the events from the time that Wil Wright dropped them off. Ken had been writing away and making cryptic notes for himself – while at the same time trying to look carefully at his client. He was now thankful for the opportunity to stand up and walk to the front door.

"Mr. Starr, why don't you take it from here – go through everything that you can remember - take things slowly and just relax." Then almost as an afterthought he added,
"I know that this must be very difficult for you".

Paxton Starr led them through the events that transpired after they had entered their home.

"After I closed the front door and turned around my wife embraced me and said how very sorry she was for slapping me. She sobbed her eyes out with her head in my chest – she said that she had behaved so badly and embarrassed herself in front of our friends. She said that she could not face them again after what had transpired. I remember that I held her with my arms around her – her forehead on my chest – I told her that things would be fine and that I forgave her – I said that we'll call Wil and Jenni and the others in the morning and make plans to go for lunch or something.

I asked her if she'd like some coffee and she said that she would. I walked with my arm around her to the kitchen".

Greg interrupted.

"Did you have any coats or jackets on that evening? Did you put them away when you arrived home?"

"I was wearing a long sleeve shirt and Maxi was wearing a wrap-type of thing – do not know what you call them – a shawl - she had it around her shoulders when we came home. It was a favorite of hers – she'd purchased it at a home-industry event in the village."

"And where is it now?" asked Greg.

Paxton Starr though for a moment – he seemed unsure of the answer. Then he replied, "If I recall she kept it around her shoulders while we were in the kitchen and I think – yes, I am sure that she still had it on when she went upstairs."

"So we might either find it in the kitchen or possibly upstairs – if you are correct", stated Greg.

"Yes, I suppose so" answered Paxton.

"Okay then, why don't you walk us through to the kitchen and pick up the events from there again", Greg suggested.

Paxton walked them through to the kitchen and indicated where Maxi had sat that evening. It took a great deal of concentration for both Greg and Ken not to stare outside onto the view of the beach and the ocean.

Paxton Starr continued his recollection from the night that his wife had died.

"As I made the coffee Maxi just sat there – we did not say much – she did ask if Jenni would forgive her and I said that she would – Wil and Jenni are very close friends and we love them – so I told Maxi that things would be fine. Besides that we did not say anything. I poured her a mug of coffee and gave it to her. She

96

thanked me for it. I decided not to have a coffee and instead poured myself a drink."

"Is this a normal practice for you to have drink so late at night?" asked Greg.

"No, not at all – I think that I just felt very upset at what had happened that night – I really do not know – I can only think that it was because I was upset."

Paxton Starr was visibly becoming more upset right now – he was struggling to keep himself under control.

After a brief silence he continued.

"Maxi finished her coffee and I asked her if she wanted another. She said that she did not" Paxton then paused before he said in an apparent state of shock, "This is her mug", pointing to the side of the bar counter, "This is where she sat and this is her empty coffee mug".

Greg commented, "Strange that the police did not remove it for testing – Ken make a note of that would you – and maybe just inform the police officer on duty outside."
Ken walked outside for a moment.

It took Ken all of maybe two minutes to walk to the front door, speak with the police officer and return to the kitchen. The brief time that he was outside of the house brought fresh air into his lungs. He had not realized just how much he had been concentrating on the task at hand of his client recounting what had happened the night that his wife had died – if indeed the story that they were being told was true or not. So far there had not been anything really unexpected that had been said – except maybe Greg's interest in the shawl that Maxi Starr had worn the night that she had died. He was sure that Greg would share his thinking on that one when they left the home of Paxton Starr. Ken took in a very brief sweeping view of the landscape outside of the home –

how the scene changed from the homes on the left hand side and the ocean view to the more rugged forest area to the right of where he stood. He briefly smiled to himself and thought that one day if he became a successful lawyer that he could afford a place half the size of those on Ocean Drive. He then turned and walked back to the kitchen knowing that the more emotional part of their "walking interview" still lay ahead.

As he entered the kitchen Greg smiled and said, "I thought that you got lost!"

Ken replied rather sheepishly, "No, just admiring the view."

Greg smiled in agreement and then restarted the proceedings by asking Paxton a question.

"You said that you made your wife coffee that night, Right? We've just found her coffee mug – but a thought just came to mind - we've just had coffee – before you used it did you not wash it out? If you did wash it out would there had not been some coffee over from what you made for your wife? I had not noticed any when you cleaned out the pot."

Paxton paused and seemed to be thinking through the events of that fateful evening. Then he replied, "The pot was empty when I made coffee now but I had made myself coffee after – after my wife had died." He seemed to struggle to get the words out.

"I also made several pots of coffee for myself in the few days before I was detained by the police. So, I suppose that I must have washed it out every time that I'd used it."

It was now Greg's turn to pause for a minute. His mind was racing – he knew what he wanted to say – finally he just decided to ask the question as it came out.

"You used the coffee pot several times after the passing of your wife – you've just confirmed that – and I've noticed that there are no other dirty dishes in the kitchen – any reason why you might have missed the coffee mug?"

"No, I most probably just did not see it – although looking at it now it is rather obvious I must admit – no, I have no reason why I might have missed it."

Greg thought it rather odd that his client would live alone for several days after the death of his wife and not see the dirty coffee mug on the kitchen serving counter. Ken, likewise, had made some notes for follow up. He had briefly thought that maybe Paxton Starr had put something in with the coffee to make his wife sleepy – would he then have drowned her? The lab test on the coffee mug could be revealing. It had also passed through Ken's mind that how come the police department had not seen the mug or considered it for testing – surely the prosecutor would be most interested in the results from the lab.

Just then the police officer walked into the kitchen and carefully placed the coffee mug into a plastic bag and tagged it as evidence and removed it from the kitchen.

Once the officer had left the house Greg suggested that his client continue his recall of the events of that evening.

"Please continue." Greg prompted.

"Maxi finished her coffee and we seemed to sit for an eternity – but most likely only a minute or two – we had nothing to say I suppose. My wife then said that she wanted to take a bath and go to bed. I asked her if I could help her and she said that she could manage. We walked out of the kitchen and at the bottom of the staircase she turned and again said to me that she was sorry for what had happened. She came up to kiss me and I held her briefly before she slid away and turned and walked up the steps."

"You did not follow her?"

"No, I got the feeling that she wanted to be alone. Even her kiss was more like a small peck and I noticed that the hug was – was, well, it was almost weak."

"And this did not make you feel that maybe your wife was either still too much under the influence of alcohol or just too tired and that a bath could be dangerous?"

"No, most likely I just felt – I really do not know how to describe it – I felt hurt – and not just my face which still stung – but I felt rejected – maybe that is not the right word either, confused , I do not know, most probably I just wanted to be alone."

"Go on." prompted Greg.

"I walked back into the kitchen and poured myself another drink and sat on the bar stool where I had sat earlier."

Greg interrupted again…

"Mr. Starr do you believe that you were drunk?"

Paxton Starr seemed to react rather abruptly, "NO, Mr. Winters, I was not drunk.
I had a few drinks at the party but I am not a heavy drinker – most likely two drinks all night – from sometime after 8 P.M. until about 11 P.M. – my friends can vouch for that."

Greg was a little surprised but also somewhat pleased at Paxton's reaction – the man had feelings!

"Mr. Starr, the reason why I asked the question is not to doubt your morals or drinking habits but from a legal perspective it is important to try to establish if you were in control of your senses when your wife decided to go upstairs. Not that being UI is an excuse in the eyes of the law if you were criminally negligent but being reasonably sober means that you had the power of reason and that you should have known better than to have allowed your wife to take a bath in her condition. Mr. Starr, it is my job as your defense lawyer to ask you difficult and probing questions – and I expect nothing but the truth – you must realize that you have very serious indictments against you. We are not playing games here."

There was no doubt that Greg's tone although sharp was still under control. He wanted to rattle his client and see what the reaction was. He has succeeded.

After a short silence Paxton replied, "I am sorry if I appeared rude, Mr. Winters but it is difficult to be objective at the moment – to answer your question more precisely, I was not drunk and I have very seldom been drunk in my entire life."

"Mr. Starr, I need to take the view of being both your defense council and that of the prosecutor – I am on your side, but to have you found not guilty I need to explore all avenues".

"I understand." Paxton said and then he just seemed to wait for Greg to take the lead again.

"Right then, moving on.......you said that you had three drinks, right? Over what period of time was this, and ah, how big were the drinks?"

"Mr. Winters, I am not actually sure over what period of time – I think that it was about 20 minutes max – I had the first drink in sips while my wife drank her coffee, then I poured the second almost by instinct – the second one I seemed to drink faster – maybe I was getting tired or even that the alcohol had just hit me sitting on top of the emotional events that had taken place. I then had a third drink. If I recall I poured myself a mug of coffee before I finished off the last drink – drained the glass and then just wanted to take the coffee up to the bedroom with me. You asked me how big the drinks were – again I am not sure but each shot must have been about half an inch or so – not much more."

"Is this a normal sized drink that you pour yourself?" asked Greg.

"No, not at all, - if anything I normally have a small shot – but mostly I enjoy a beer or two." Paxton paused and then continued, "I really do not drink very much my friends can confirm that – I am rather boring most of the time"

Ken was busy taking notes for follow-up. He had placed little stars next to the notes about his client's view of himself being rather boring a character and also not being a big drinker. These would be easy to check out with the neighbors on Ocean Drive or even with other potential witnesses. Against some other points were bigger stars for those points that would most likely require further digging or confirmation. As with these type of interviews the pace sometimes moves forward too quickly and Ken had been drawn back into taking notes while listening intensely and also watching Paxton Starr all of the time. Looking, listening and writing in short-hand script is no easy task. Ken marveled at Greg as although his boss also took notes, watched and listened he was also guiding the pace of the interview and probing for weaknesses in his client's story. This was an exhausting activity and Greg had the experience, skill, knowledge and competency to keep going for hours if necessary. Ken had never seen him falter or show signs of fatigue. Greg Winters was certainly a man-amongst-men in the legal profession.

Ken's moment of self-thought was snapped back into the present as he heard Greg push forward with the interview.

"Mr. Starr, your character traits might be a positive or a negative in this case – but it is too early to decide how we will spin it with the prosecution – but rest assured we'll work out the right strategy as to how we will play it"

"OK. Moving on then," said Greg, "You had finished your last drink, had a coffee ready and you were preparing to go up the stairs, right?"

Paxton Starr nodded.

"Please continue, what did you do next, go straight up stairs?"

"Yes, I walked out of the kitchen with my mug of coffee in hand, and headed for the staircase and...."

Greg interrupted, "Sorry, to interrupt but did you switch off the kitchen light – or the hall way light, or lock the front door before you went upstairs?"

Ken's pen and note taking became more nervous as he knew where Greg was going with this sudden question. If Paxton Starr had felt that sleepy and exhausted after his last drink but he was still alert enough to put off the lights and check the locks then he might not have been as drained as what he had made out. If he was more alert then maybe he had thought through a plan to murder his wife and was fully in control of the upcoming events of the evening in question. Clear thoughts could incriminate Paxton Starr.

Both Greg and Ken held their breath waiting for the answer. They were both surprised with the answer that their client provided.

"I locked the door as we walked inside the house after Wil dropped us off. That is a routine that I never miss. Ocean Drive is a little remote and on occasions we have had some trouble with attempted burglaries or break-ins. The security system is armed once we lock the door – the system is integrated throughout the house. And just by-the-way all of our homes on Ocean Drive are linked so that should something strange go off during the night then not only is the security company pinged immediately but an alarm also sounds in the next house on the Drive". Paxton paused and when he had no response from Greg he went on.

"There is no doubt in my mind that I locked the door as we got home. About the kitchen or hallway lights, I most likely never even thought about them – because we never do. The rooms have motion detectors and if after 15 minutes there is no movement

103

then the system switches off the lights – so, no we never worried about the lights, I suppose that they looked after themselves".

This was not the answer that Greg or Ken had expected. They both had different thoughts about how the wealthy lived or the sophistication of house gadgetry.

"So, you feel pretty sure about the whole light and lock up thing?"

"Yes, Mr. Winters, in a way our home is stupid proof!" This was the first time that either Greg or Ken had seen Paxton Starr smile and appear to be less stiff. What struck Greg was that his client appeared to be a very gentle man, withdrawn, even shy, and a fine looking man, tall and very handsome – in particular when that smile lit up his face. Was this the smile of a man who is charged with murdering his wife? Greg needed to keep that thought with him as the building of their case continued.

"Just on the subject of security, do you own a firearm, Mr. Starr? You did mention that you've had some trouble from time-to-time." asked Greg almost casually.

Again Greg and Ken were a little taken aback by the answer to the question.

Paxton Starr began to chuckle – almost a strange type of laughter mixed with snorting. Greg and Ken looked at each with raised eye brows.

"Please forgive my laughter," answered Paxton, "THAT is good question! My wife suggested that I buy a handgun because of some of the problems in the area. I hated the thought of getting one but Maxi insisted. We both went for shooting lessons to a place just over the hill – about 20 minutes from our home – Maxi seemed a natural and although not too accurate, she hit the targets. I, on the other hand, well, um, this is embarrassing – I missed the targets completely. I could not hold the gun properly and was absolutely hopeless. Maxi got her license the same day that Wil and Jenni got

104

theirs but it took me an extra two months before I got mine - it was a huge joke in our group and they teased me that I could not hit a target at 15 feet let alone stop an intruder."

Both Greg and Ken smiled openly at the statement made by Paxton. Almost not to gain attention Ken made a slight flick on his note pad – a reminder to himself to check out Paxton Starr's story with his friends and with local shooting stores.

"You might have been safer if your wife stopped an intruder!" commented Greg smiling. Then he allowed the smile to quickly melt off of his face as he realized that he was referring to his client's late wife and the centerpiece of the case at hand – the indictment against Paxton Starr in the murder of his wife.

"Right, let's move along then" suggested Greg. "Please lead the way up stairs if you would".

The three men walked out of the kitchen through the so-called common room and came out at the bottom of the staircase near the front door of the home. Just as Paxton was about to take his first step going up Greg asked another question.

"Just by way of interest what other rooms are downstairs in the house – I can't get over just how beautiful your home is?"

"Thanks again, yeah, we really loved the home – downstairs we have a washroom, right here." as Paxton pointed to a door fairly near to where they were standing.

"Then down that way" as he pointed to the opposite side of the house from the kitchen, "is the entrance from the garages, storage room, two bedrooms and bathrooms – in the front of the house we've just come through what we call the common room – where most of our entertaining takes place, there is a larger dining room than the one near the kitchen – and another washroom there. The laundry room is off of the kitchen under the main bedroom. All of the front rooms lead off onto the deck, the barbeque area and the swimming pool, wet bar and changing room. The home is very functional really." Paxton paused and then added. "There is one or two novel features upstairs that I'll show you – those were Maxi's touches". He stopped again as if he were in mid-sentence. It was obvious that he was still talking about her in the present tense and then realized that she was gone – and he then almost stopped himself from speaking.

"If I may should we go upstairs?" he asked Greg.

"Yes, or course – please lead the way." Greg replied. He felt a small twinge inside as he suddenly thought of his Mary and how he missed her. On top of that his headache was coming back again – way too much concentration! He was so involved in gathering information, keeping mental notes of potentially key facts and also managing the walking-interview – and not to mention carefully watching his client's reactions to his questions, that he felt rather fatigued. He also seemed to understand what Paxton Starr was going through. But he could not afford to become involved with the person – just the case. He was taught that at law school and could hear it in his mind over and over again, "do not get involved with the person but the person in the case".

The two lawyers walked up the staircase behind their client. They exchanged very brief wide-eyed looks. Maybe it was just an admiration of the beautiful house – maybe it was more than that. In front of them on the steps Paxton Starr knew that they were exchanging some type of nonverbal opinion.

More surprises awaited the two lawyers up stairs.

Paxton Starr stopped on the landing and waited for the two men to join him.
He stepped aside as they reached the top of the curving staircase.

"If I may, I would like to point out some features upstairs before we go through to the main bedroom". The two men nodded in agreement. Maybe Mr. Starr was just putting off having to go into

106

the main bedroom and into the bathroom where his wife had died. Maybe he was gathering himself to have to go through that hell again. Or could it be that he was just a show-off and was more interested in highlighting his wealth – only time would tell when the lawyers would examine their thoughts on their time with their client.

Paxton pointed down the left hand hallway from the top of the steps and started his static tour of the upstairs of the house.

"The house is actually odd shaped upstairs with both sides being longer than the downstairs. One cannot really tell from the front of the house because it is slightly curved. Both sides overlap the downstairs by about ten feet. Down on the left side right at the end we have another bedroom and washroom – that room overlooks the ocean on two sides. It has a stunning view looking back right over the bay – and one can see the other homes on Ocean Drive as they are spread out facing the beach. Sometimes we'd move into that room as the season changed Next to that bedroom we have two offices – one each for my wife and I, then a washroom and then..." Paxton smiled as he pointed towards the two doors that were just to the right from where they were standing and looking down the hallway going left.

"These next two rooms are – rather were – our special hide-a-ways – come I'll show you quickly if you'd like" Again the two men just nodded and followed their client.

The two rooms were side-by-side. On each there was a sign. The one had the word SUMMER and the other WINTER on small gold trimmed plaques.

"I had better explain." said Paxton with a slight grin.

"Although we loved having company and to entertain our friends the upstairs of our house was our private space. Before Maxi's parents were killed in a car crash several years ago they sometimes stayed over in the room down the hall – but mostly

107

they slept downstairs. Upstairs was our space. The two rooms became a bit of a passion with us as we spent so much time there.....let me show you." He opened the door to the SUMMER room. They stepped inside behind Paxton Starr.

The room was bright and sunny with sliding doors leading off onto the upstairs balcony – the balcony which ran along the entire outside of the sea facing side of the house. Inside the room there were comfy looking lounge chairs – certainly not cheap – there were bright colored paintings on the walls – giving the room almost a Greek island setting. The room was simplistic – even the small bar on the right hand side wall looked perfect. One might think that fresh juices could be served from behind the small bar – more like a mini-bar – but very smartly fitted into the room.

Paxton smiled and said, "Yes, this is the summer room. We would spend hours here in the summer – either inside or outside, reading, talking and even snoozing. This was our little summer relaxation room".

Ken could not contain himself.

"It is absolutely magnificent – just fantastic. My! It is beautiful!"

"Steady on Ken, next thing you'll be asking me for a raise!" Greg chipped in. He was also totally taken in by this private little island of their own. He thought that Mr. and Mrs. Starr must have deeply loved each other to spend so much time together. That confused Greg's thinking even more. He never stopped thinking about the case.

The three men stood outside on the balcony for a few minutes talking about the scenery before Greg suggested that they move on. Paxton seemed in no hurry to visit the main bedroom. Although it was windy out the view was breath-taking. On a clear day it would be beyond description.

108

Back in the hallway they moved towards the door with the sign WINTER on the door. Paxton opened the door and they walked in behind him. The room was completely different from the first. The rooms in fact could not have been more different. WINTER was darker inside with heavier drapes on the walls and covering the sliding doors. The furnisher was plush leather sofas and beautiful coffee and casual tables. There were hundreds of books up on the well-organized book shelves - shelves made out of dark wood. The shelves rose from the floor to the ceiling. A thick pile carpet covered the floor. The room was like a small library found tucked away in a mountain retreat lodge – including a gas fire place and a TV screen placed above it. Instead of a bar like in the SUMMER room this one had a small wooden push cart that held a number of half-filled bottles of most likely fine brandy or whiskey. Greg could almost see Paxton and Maxi Starr reading a book in the light of one of the small lamps or even cuddling up together on the large sofa and watching a movie on the TV. With the heavy drapes drawn across the sliding doors the Starr's would have been so very snug in their WINTER room.

"This is where we spent the cooler winter nights – we would read a book or watch TV together." said Paxton, as if they needed the explanation. For no particular reason Greg tried to estimate the size of the SUMMER and WINTER rooms. His best estimate was that each room was over 500 square feet. What an enormous area for two people to relax in their special world.

Greg edged towards the door to leave the room as the visions in his mind were becoming very confused again. Was this the household of a man accused of murdering his wife?

The two men stood on the landing while Paxton Starr closed the door to WINTER.

They all knew that the guided tour was now over and that they had to visit the scene of the crime.

The entrance to the main bedroom was just to the right of the top of the staircase.

Paxton opened the door and the two men followed him in. The immediate impression – besides the fact that it was very large and with its own electric fireplace was that it had been very carefully planned out. It was simple without a clutter of furniture and the color scheme was gentle and almost sleepy. Standing inside the bedroom Paxton pointed out the entrance to the two large walk-in closets and dressing rooms. One could only imagine the size of these two rooms – most likely bigger than a bedroom in a standard home.

There were sliding doors onto the balcony – the view from this angle of the house would be more naturally away from the other homes on Ocean Drive – but of course outside on then one would be able to have the full vista from left to right.

There were two long sofas near the fireplace and a table that would have held their tray of morning coffee or evening cocoa. It was not difficult to let one's mind run away with the imagery of the routine that took place in this beautiful but simple looking room.

Across the room was the entrance to the bathroom.

Greg finally asked, "Is that the bathroom?" He had waited for his client to say something but there were no words now from Mr. Starr. He just nodded in acknowledgement. However, Greg did require him to speak.

"I know that this will be very tough for you to do but we do require you to tell us everything that happened on the night that your wife died – just take your time – but please try to remember everything that you can.....whenever you are ready, Mr. Starr."

Greg and Ken moved to a side wall as if to be out of the way of Paxton Starr – giving him space to think and to feel what happened the night that Maxi Starr died.

Still there was no response from Paxton Starr; he seemed to have half-frozen when he had entered the bedroom. Greg waited another short while and then said, "Why don't you first think through what your wife might have done when she came into the room – and then you can go through what you did?"

It took another maybe twenty seconds before Paxton spoke.

"As I said, my wife gave me a kiss at the bottom of the staircase – a half kiss really – I think that I called it more like a peck. She then turned and walked up the steps."

Greg asked, "Did you watch your wife walk up the steps?"

If Paxton Starr had watched his wife walk up the steps he was interested to find out if she used the handrail for support – confirming that she was still intoxicated – and if not then she might have been more alert than might have been described. Her condition in walking up the steps was therefore very important in Greg's mind – as it would be in the mind of the prosecutor.

Paxton put his hand over his face as if he was trying to remember. He thought for a second and then replied – but maybe he was onto what Greg was driving at and needed time to think about his answer.

"Yes, I watched her walk up the first few steps and then I turned and walked back into the kitchen".

"You did not watch your wife walk all of the way up the staircase – or maybe hold the handrail for support?"

"I watched her turn – she took the handrail – which on the left hand side of the staircase and she started to go up the steps – I

111

then turned and did not see her going up the remainder of the steps".

"And that was the last time you saw your wife alive?" asked Greg.

"Yes, Mr. Winters that is the last time I saw my wife alive."

"Please go on", asked Greg, almost disappointed with the answers that he had just received. But who knew with Greg Winters. Paxton had answered the first question both ways – not to incriminate himself at all. "Yes" he had seen her take the handrail but basically "no" I had not seen if she struggled to get up the steps. Greg knew that Paxton Starr was a much smarter man than what his character might portray.

"Well, I would think that my wife would have opened the door to the bedroom – the doors are always closed - "

Greg interrupted again.

"Sorry to interrupt you again but when you came upstairs was the bedroom door open or shut?"

"It was open but by maybe only an inch or two - may I go on?" It was not so much of a question as a statement.

"I do not know what she did that night but normally she would have walked into her dressing room – taken off her clothes, most likely have put on a bathrobe and then sat down and taken off her make-up. She would then go to the bathroom".

Paxton could see Greg's hand coming up as if to speak so he stopped again. He was not enjoying the interview now.

"Just a thought, did your wife take a bath as a habit after you came home from a function – or meeting with friends?"

"Yes, she normally cleaned up her make-up and then took a bath – was it every time, no, but I would say that it was 95% of the time - Maxi hated going to bed without having a bath ....the odd occasion might have been if we had come home very late from the theatre and then dinner. Then she would take-off her make-up and pop straight into bed...otherwise it was her routine to take a bath".

"And she always took her make-up off – even if you'd been with your friends on Ocean Drive and she had had a good time?"

"Mr. Winters, I do not appreciate your tone or line of questioning! My wife was not a drunk."

There was no doubt that the line of questioning was beginning to bother Paxton Starr. His pale-skinned face was a flushed red and he actually looked as if he was going to explode with anger. Greg read the signals and said, "Mr. Starr, I again apologize for pressing you on these apparently small or sensitive issues but we had better get them out now and consider any weaknesses in our story if we are to present our case successfully at the trial. If I do not ask these questions now then we might be surprised if the prosecutor lets them jump out at you. If you lose your temper or become irritated with him then we would have lost valuable influence over the jury. As I have said to you before – this is a very serious situation – and I and my lawyers take our jobs very seriously – I thought that I had made myself clear on this point!"

As had happened earlier when Greg had let off some steam at his client a silence occurred. No one really wanted to say the next word. Greg Winters just waited until his client recovered some stability - he could have stood there all afternoon if that is what it would take. It took maybe another twenty seconds for Paxton Starr to recover his composure – even if the color in his cheeks were still a mild red!

"Mr. Winters, I am sorry...I am just finding this very difficult. Question after question, small detail after small detail.....I feel as if I am being examined and x-rayed all at once – with a rough brush!

113

I am really very sorry, it is not easy……I loved my wife very dearly - -- let's try again". He paused again almost to control his breathing and then he continued (he had noticed Ken making a larger tick on his note pad).

"In all the years that we were married I cannot remember Maxi coming to bed without taking her make-up off. She was a very beautiful woman but the make-up and the way she wore it made her look like a million bucks – but she always said that she "had to take her face-off" before she came to bed – she used that expression thousands of times over the years – so to answer your question, NO, even if she'd had a great time at a party or we'd been out late she would always take her make-up off before going to bed - does that answer your question?"

Greg carried an attaché case. In it was a collection of his papers on the case and a number of photographs taken by the coroner's team when they examined the bathroom of the Starr's home the day that Mrs. Starr was found dead. Also in the attaché case was the coroner's report. Greg was tempted to open the case and show Mr. Starr the report but he decided against it. The report stated that Mrs. Maxi Starr was found dead in her bath tub. Traces of make-up were found on her face. She had not done a good job of removing all of her make-up. Not the actions of someone who was always particular about removing her make-up. Was Mrs. Starr still under the influence of the alcohol that she had consumed? If so, could she have fallen asleep in her bath and drowned? Did that mean that Paxton Starr was criminally negligent in allowing his wife to go upstairs by herself and take a bath? Did it make him not guilty of murdering his wife? Only time and the manipulation and interpretation of evidence would tell.

"Thank you, Mr. Starr I appreciate your comprehensive answer, please continue" said Greg.

Ken had also made a particular mark on his note pad – a cryptic reminder to check out the evidence about Mrs. Starr's body on the day that she was found dead.

114

"Sorry, where were we?" asked Paxton.

"Your wife would normally have walked into her Dressing Room, taken her clothes off, put on a bathrobe and then taken off her make-up....that is the point that we were at...."

"Yes, she would then go run a bath" Paxton waited to be interrupted but he was not so he continued. "She would bathe and then put on her night clothes and come to bed."

There was no interruption this time but there were more questions.

"And what would you be doing while your wife took off her clothes and her make-up?"

"I would be in my dressing room taking my clothes off. I would then go through to the bathroom and wash-up. The bathroom has two sections, three actually, a front room if you like that had the washbasins, closets etc, then the toilets further on – and then the bathroom proper which also has a shower. Most times I would already be changed and washed up when my wife would come through – she'd walk through to the bath room section and begin to run her bath. I would finish up and then lie in bed and wait for her."

"How long would she usually take in the bath?"

"Oh, not that long maybe 5-10 minutes no more than that."

And then Greg asked a very difficult question.

And maybe Paxton Starr was waiting for it.

"Had your wife ever fallen asleep in the bath tub before?"

The answer was quick and very decisive.

115

"No, there had never been an incident like that before – she would bathe and then come to bed."

Greg self-assessed where they were on the recollection of what would normally happen when Mr. and Mrs. Starr made ready for bed. There was one more point that he wanted to check up on but he decided to wait until his client began to recount his actions of that fateful evening.

"Right then, shall we then begin your account of what happened that evening when you came up stairs, Mr. Starr if you please", as Greg motioned for his client to begin his recollection of the facts – or at least what he was going to share with them. Greg started him off by saying, "You had your mug of coffee in hand, you left the lights on downstairs as they shut off automatically, you felt fatigued and you were preparing to go upstairs."

"Yes, that sums it up" Paxton had a mild smile on his face as Greg had basically remembered every point that he had said earlier, in fact Greg had remembered everything without taking notes.

"I walked up the staircase and walked towards the bedroom – the door was standing open by a few inches as I mentioned earlier; I walked into the bedroom." True to form Greg interrupted his client. "You walked straight to your bedroom, not any other room first, and when you entered the bedroom was the bathroom light on?"

"Yes, I came to the bedroom directly after I reached the top of the landing. When I came into the bedroom the bathroom door was closed – that is the door that leads into the basin area – with the bathroom beyond that – the door was closed but I could see the light on under the doorway."

"Did you call out to your wife try to greet her or hear her make any sound at all?'

116

"I did say something to the effect like, "Hi Hon – will you be long?" but I did not receive a reply. I had put my mug of coffee down next to the bedside table. I then said, "I am going to bed", I had no reply. I then felt totally drained sitting there on the bed. I took my shoes off and lay down on the bed. I must have fallen asleep immediately - next thing I woke up and it was morning."

"Do you recall if you woke up during the night and maybe went to the bathroom?"

"No, I was out all night – still flat on my back in fact – as I had lain down after taking my shoes off". He waited for a comment from Greg but when none was forthcoming he went on, "It took me a good minute or two to fully wake up...I think that I said something like, "Morning Hon, what time is it?" I had no answer so I rolled onto my side and saw that my wife's side of the bed had not been slept in"

"What did you think then?"

"My initial reaction was that she was still maybe upset about the night before and that she had decided to sleep in another room". Before Greg could ask the question Paxton Starr continued, "But she had never done that before so I dismissed the idea. I lay on the bed for, I don't know maybe a few seconds before I looked up and although it was light outside I saw that the bathroom light was still on. I was confused, I looked at my watch and it was just after 9.30 – I was still confused and then I remembered that my wife had gone for a bath the night before – I jumped off of the bed and yelled her name as I ran towards the bathroom door – I pushed it in and ran through to the bathroom area."

Then Paxton Starr stopped suddenly. His voice dried up and he seemed in absolutely pain to try to speak. Neither Greg nor Ken said a word. As painful as this was to witness they had to allow the scene to unfold.

Greg slowly walked towards the doorway to the bathroom. Paxton and Ken followed him. At the doorway he said, "Please, Mr. Starr, this is important, what happened next?"

Paxton Starr was shaking. Not the shake of a fake act of remorse but a true knee-knocking, hand-trembling shake. This was no fake but was it because he had found his wife dead in the bathtub or because he was reliving what had actually taken place that night.

"I, I ah, ran through into the main bathroom area – and there she was – she was lying underwater - I screamed "oh God, no, no, no! I pulled her out of the water and screamed at her to wake up, please, please wake up. I held her in my arms and cried, yelled, everything,   just everything   ....".

This was heartbreaking for Greg and Ken to watch. They both felt sick to their stomachs.

Paxton Starr was crying and they let him be for a minute.

Greg walked up the entrance of the bathroom area and looked in. A police cordon was still across the door so that he could not enter the room. In a way he did not want to.

He had studied the photographs taken of the room in great detail and he was now mentally comparing his life-images to those that the coroner's team had taken. He was asking himself why the coroner still had the bathroom taped off. Was he still looking for further information? What was concerning the coroner and the police department?

Greg walked over to where Paxton Starr was sitting. He almost felt as if he did not want to disturb him but he had to. He also knew that Ken had been watching his client very closely while he had walked to the entrance to the bathroom area.

"I am sorry Mr. Starr but we need to cover a few more things. If you're ready we should continue."

118

Paxton stood up and walked with Greg back towards the entrance to the bathroom.

"Please tell us what happened after you found your wife in the bath tub".

Paxton took a deep breath and then spoke in a very soft voice. The tone surprised both Greg and Ken.

"I held my wife – maybe for a minute or more – I do not know – she looked so tiny, so meek, so helpless – she was my love, my true love and soulmate. I eventually placed her back into the tub and walked back into the bedroom and telephoned 911. I knew that she was dead I could feel her cold body clinging to mine – it was a strange sensation."

"When you placed your wife back into the tub did you submerge her – put her back as you found her?"

"No, I do not think so. If I recall I left her face out of the water."

"What did you do while you waited for the police to arrive?"

"I sat on the bed – I just sat on the bed. A few minutes later I heard the sirens coming down the road. I then got up and walked down stairs and opened the front door and let the police in through the security gates. I went upstairs with them and took them into the bathroom."

Greg heard his client speaking but his mind was on one last question that he had to ask. He did not know if the answer would be significant or not – in cases such as these one never knew the value of information until later – now he had to ask everything – that is why he called it the Discovery Phase in his methodology.

"Mr. Starr, do you remember what your wife wore that night that she died?"

119

"Yes, as I mentioned earlier my wife had on a dress and her shawl."

"Can you describe the clothes in more detail for me."

"The dress was strapless, a light brown color with a lighter shade on the sleeves. The sleeves were just above the elbows. I remember it well because it was one of her newer dresses and she had said that she wanted to wear it that evening."

"Do you perhaps know where she bought the dress and when?" asked Greg.

"I am not sure of the date but it must have been within the last few weeks before she wore it. I remember her talking on the telephone with Jenni Wright that she had found this wonderful dress and that she was planning on wearing it for the first time to the function at their home. I can check the credit card statements for the exact date of purchase. I think that she bought the dress at "Beverly's" which is just a few miles away in the village. They stocked smaller sized dresses that my wife enjoyed wearing – she had such a small body and the clothes from Beverly's made her look so young and beautiful."

"Any idea what your wife would have paid for the dress?"

"That I cannot remember off hand but I would think that it would be around $400 – but I am guessing, I do not know off hand – that was about the average that she paid for dresses from that store. It will only take me a minute or two to check the information for you."

"Thank you, we can do that in due course." Ken made another note on his pad.

"Do you know where the dress is now?" asked Greg. He was building towards his main question.

"If I recall the dress was found in her dressing room and was removed by the police for evidence – I believe that the dress is with the police department."

"Do you perhaps recall where the dress was found in the dressing room?"

"Yes, it was found on the floor with my wife's underwear that she had removed when she got undressed – why is this important?"

"I am trying to tie together the picture in my mind of all of the events and nitty gritty of what happened where, when and how." Greg had still not come to his main question. He had reviewed all of the photographs taken by the police team and he was filling in the blanks in his overly active legal mind.

"Let's just try to recap one or two things if I may....we expect – but do not know for sure of course – except for the evidence trial – that your wife entered the bedroom, she left the door slightly open as you have confirmed – then as is her habit she would have gone to her dressing room to undress, put on her bathrobe and removed her make-up – right? " Greg did not wait for an answer but went on. "We know that she still had some make-up on when she took her bath – and in fact the cotton buds and other waste found in her dressing room garbage can proved that she had removed some of her make-up."

Greg's referral to the waste in the garbage can indicated that he had more information about the evidence in the bedroom than what he had earlier eluded to. This was not lost on Paxton Starr. He had to be more careful when he provided information to Greg Winters.

"So, we do know that your wife had spent time in her dressing room. Her underwear was found in a pile on the floor and not in a wash basket – maybe indicating that she removed them and in her apparent state of weariness just threw them onto the carpet. Not an uncommon gesture if one is very tired." Greg had used the word

121

"tired" on purpose so not to offend his client that Maxi Starr might still have been intoxicated. Mind you, if she was then drowning by accident could be more tenable.

"Your wife's dress was also found on the carpet. Providing further proof that she might have just wanted to get undressed, bathed quickly and get to bed that night." Greg paused as he readied himself for his main question.

"She removed her clothing and dropped them on the floor – indicating to us that she was maybe tidiness was not a priority in her mind. She dropped a dress costing about $400 – that she had purchased for the function that night – and was proud to wear – she dropped on the carpet. Mr. Starr, do you have any idea where the shawl is that your wife wore the evening that she died?" Greg had sprung his question.

There was a brief silence before Paxton Starr answered the question.

"I do not know where this question is leading to Mr. Winters but as I told you down stairs that I thought that my wife was wearing the shawl around her shoulder when she left me at the bottom of the staircase – is there a point here?"

"Indeed there is Mr. Starr – the point is that we have photos of all of the evidence from your bedroom taken the day that your wife was found dead. We have photos of her clothes on the floor, expensive clothes lying on the floor – signs maybe of a very tired person wanting to bathe and go to bed – and yet not on one of the photos do we see her shawl. I asked you if you had seen her walk upstairs with the shawl and you confirmed this. My question is then "Where is the shawl?"

Paxton Starr looked stunned. Yes, indeed, where was Maxi's shawl?

"I do not know – I was pretty sure that she had it over her shoulders when she had her coffee down stairs – and I was sure that she was wearing it when she turned to go up the steps – I do not know, I can't think where it might be. Why is it important?"

"It is important if the prosecutor latches onto it – he, or she, might spin something around it that your wife was more alert than what we could portray – indicating that accidental drowning is therefore questionable – the story line could go anywhere so we had better be ahead of it. We cannot afford to be placed behind the Eight Ball with the grand jury or later if we go to trial – we need answers to questions that they might not even think of – that is why it is important.

"Where could the shawl be? Did your wife have a special place where she kept her wraps, scarves, shawls – maybe in her dressing room?"

"I suppose – I am not familiar with how she organized her things – but I do know that she was pretty well organized."

"Should we go and check?" suggested Greg.

Paxton led the two lawyers to his wife's dressing room. The room was enormous. It was fitted out with closets, shoe racks; open hanging space, a sitting area with numerous mirrors and drawers for who knows what. Walking into the dressing room was an experience for both Greg and Ken. Although both Paxton Starr and his wife each had a separate dressing room the two rooms did connect at the very end where the laundry hatch was situated. There was no doubt that planning of the house had been very cleverly thought through – as if Greg or Ken had not realized that already?

Greg asked, "Any idea where your wife kept her shawls?"

"Not really", Paxton replied. He started to open closet doors going down the right hand side of the room. One closet after the next

123

was filled with clothes. How could one person have so much clothing – it was just too much to comprehend – and not to think about the cost of each item on the various racks? The three worked their way down the right hand side of the dressing room – each closet revealed more clothing "treasures" but no scarves or shawls. At the end of the room was the storage place for shoes and the opening to the laundry hatch. It was in this area of the dressing room that Maxi Starr's dress and underwear were found after her death. Paxton Starr opened the first three closets coming back down the left hand side of the dressing room – the right and left hand sides of the room were split by a single chair and then a long sofa – then next on the left was an open closet – nothing there to be seen – and then another closet before the seating area with the various mirrors and hand creams and countless other lotions and female beauty products – an array of finery that could most likely keep a bevy of beauties content for years. The men stopped at the final closet. Greg was wondering if he would have to ask his client if he would mind going through all of his closets to try to locate the shawl. There was no doubt that this would cause a scene with Paxton Starr – one that Greg did not want to entertain at this point in time.

Paxton opened the last closet on the left hand side and as he did so he inhaled sharply and then let out a groan – there neatly folded on middle shelf were the collection of Maxi Starr's scarves and shawls. There was no doubt that Paxton Starr recognized the shawl in question from those on the shelf. Even if had wanted to hide his recognition of the shawl it was too late – the groan had given him away. Paxton pointed a finger at the shawl wrap and said, "My God, this is it – this is the shawl that my wife had on the night that she died."

"Are you sure?" asked Greg. He was not in any doubt that Paxton's reaction was because it was indeed the wrap.

"Yes, I am sure – no doubt". He paused and then asked, "I still do not understand the significance of finding the shawl – would this just not mean that my wife put it away as she entered her dressing room?"

"It might well just be that Mr. Starr but as I tried to explain a few minutes ago it does raise the question – was your wife alert enough to carefully fold an inexpensive shawl and place it carefully on a shelf but then almost uncharacteristically just leave her expensive clothes lying on the carpet? Was she alert or not?" Greg put his hand out to touch the shawl. He turned it over to look for a label but there was none. He remembered Paxton Starr saying that his wife had bought the shawl at a local market in the village – so most likely it was home made.

"I must admit that it does sound odd – I can only guess that as she walked into her dressing room that she stopped and took off the shawl and folded and put it away but maybe then just felt lazy or fatigued and just dropped her clothes were she took them off."

Greg provided a reply as quickly as he could in order not to appear to drag out the matter.

"Yes, that could well be it." He was struggling with the concept that Mrs. Starr could have been so precise in folding the shawl and placing it perfectly onto the shelf in her closet but failed to then take care of her expensive clothing.

Greg contemplated removing the shawl for evidence but decided against it. If he did it would become the domain of the case and who knew where that line of questioning might go. As a defense lawyer it was his job to have his client found not guilty and definitely not to provide evidence to his opponents on the case.

"Mr. Starr, could I please ask you to leave the shawl where it is just in case we might need to examine it at a later stage?"

"Sure, Mr. Winters – it will be right here if you need it".

Greg Winters was potentially leaving a piece of evidence at the scene of the crime and he hoped that he had made the correct decision.

The interview with Paxton Starr was suddenly interrupted by a police officer knocking on the door of the bedroom.

"Hello, are you in there?"

"Yes", replied Greg – "Come in officer".

"Sorry to disturb you but we have a bit of a scene at the front gate. A lady says that she works at the house and she wants to gain entrance. We thought that we'd check first."

Paxton Starr's reaction was a surprise to say the least.

"Oh my God, Oh my God, it's Abby, Oh my God, what I am going to tell Abby?"

CHAPTER 17

Abigail Rose Carmichael was born to a lower middle class African American family. She was the eldest of five children – spaced eight years apart to Herbie and Rose her beloved parents. Her parents had married young with the hope of raising a family and of giving their children an education and opportunity in life. While Herbie worked two jobs to provide for the family Rose was kept busy by being pregnant and raising the ever increasing size of the family. There was never enough money to go around and they always had to borrow from members of their family to pay another. Throughout all of their woes and hardship Rose Carmichael never complained. She never spent any money on herself and in most cases there was never any money to spend on young Abigail. All of the family income went to the boys – and some monies to Herbie's liking for the bottle.

Abigail was an extremely bright child and she picked up on most things very quickly. Rose had always wanted Abigail to have a university education but that was not to be. When the economic downturn came Abigail was taken out of school at the age of 13 and she started cleaning homes for the middle class families in the nearby communities. She learned quickly and with her keen wit and engaging smile she took on more and more homes as a cleaner. She missed not going to school but she actually enjoyed what she was doing – and learning from the families that she cleaned for. She learned how to speak politely and to do the extra things that the families liked.

She was an avid reader and she would often borrow books from her clients and read about distant countries – or about politics and history. What Abigail Carmichael missed by not being in the formal school system she learned through the books that she read.

Her dream in life was to go to China. We all need dreams to keep us motivated and alive.

Herbie Carmichael was killed in a car accident when Abigail was just 15 years of age. She was devastated. Her Dad was her hero. She knew that he had his faults but she also knew that he loved his wife and children. With his passing there was no fixed income coming into the family. The small insurance pay-out was soon gone.

Abigail settled into the business of cleaning homes, cooking for some clients or even baby-sitting whenever the opportunity arose. She was always available to work – in truth she had no choice.

On her 16th birthday she was invited to a house party in her neighborhood. Rose thought about not allowing young Abby to attend the party but she finally agreed. This was the highlight of young Abby's life. It was her first real party. It was also the first time that she tasted alcohol. She did not remember being raped and no one at the party said anything – they saw nothing and did not know the name of the boy that she was last seen with. This story – although unlikely - could have been true because uninvited young men from the neighborhood often gate-crashed party's. In any event young Abby was pregnant – it was her last neighborhood party.

At the age of 17 she was a mother and also chief provider for her mother and all of her brothers. Life was hell most of the time but like her mother she never complained.

She was a tough-minded working mother and she had few joys in life. Her one joy was still borrowing books and trying to get some reading in if she had some time to herself –which was not very often. China seemed to her a long dream away!

At 19 Abby met William (Billy) Ross. He was 21 and studying to become an electrician. She was very wary about dating anyone after what happened to her but Billy seemed different. In her heart she also knew that her brothers were taking advantage of her and that she would spend the rest of her life working to keep them in

128

money – Rose often said that none of the boys were like their late Dad. Abby had to get married to break out from the prison that she was trapped in. Abby and Billy married when he passed his electricians examination and received his Ticket to become a junior electrician at a local construction company. She was 20 years old and he was 22.

Even when their monthly income began to increase and they had two of their own children did Abby continue to clean homes and she contributed towards their joint monthly expenses. China was still a distant dream – but now a dream shared with a good man and a happy small family.

Over the years Billy was promoted several times and became a Foreman for his company and he oversaw the electrical installation for the property sites being developed across southern California. The nineteen years of marriage passed by generally without incident – except for the normal pranks of three young boys.

On Friday nights Billy would volunteer at the local Boys Club. The neighborhood that he went to was tough and kids as wild as the wind sometimes. But Billy never missed a Friday night – he was always there to play basketball, hang-out or sometimes even rescue them from police arrest for petty theft. One Friday night that all changed when two local gangs started a running street fight outside of the Boys Club. Billy went outside to try to break it up – there was pushing and yelling and then a shot rang out. Billy Ross died several hours later in the nearby hospital. Billy was just 41 years old when he died.

At his funeral the newly elected President of the construction and development company that Billy worked for attended the church service. After the service Paxton and Maxi Starr introduced themselves to Abby Carmichael Ross. Paxton and Maxi Starr fell in love with Abby the moment that they met her. There was just something about the woman – now in her late 30's that struck both of them. She had class and character. Without Abby knowing

129

Paxton arranged that the funeral expenses be paid by the company. All funds due to Abby by the company were expedited.

Over the next few years Maxi would keep in touch with Abby and telephone her from time to time. Abby felt a little uncomfortable with the president's wife calling her every so often. Abby did feel a very strong bond for Mrs. Maxi Starr – she seemed a lovely person – so small, so gentle, so fun-loving and so beautiful. At the time of the company Christmas Party Maxi would telephone and invite Abby and her children to attend. Mrs. Starr explained that it was common practice for the spouses of deceased employees to attend the Christmas get-together.

Abby's work routine was living on the bus system. One day a ninety minute ride each way with two changes en route to this neighborhood to clean and then another day a one hour ride to another part of the town. Abby hated the bus service but it was her lifeline to get to and from work.

One day just as Abby walked in the door from work the telephone rang. It was Maxi Starr. The strangest thing happened Mrs. Starr asked if Abby was free on the coming Saturday afternoon as she would like to take her for coffee. This had never happened before and although hesitant she accepted. After Abby put the telephone down she thought that it was a prank by one of her friends – this could not be true.

The next Saturday at 2 o'clock a car arrived outside of her small home. Out stepped not only Maxi Starr but Mr. Starr too. Abby felt that the eyes of her entire neighborhood was on her as she met her guests at her door and then drove off in the blue BMW 5 Series. Even while getting settled into the back seat of the car Abby thought that it was some kind of dream.

Mr. Starr mentioned that they had selected a place just outside of town for coffee and that the drive should be about 45 minutes. What on earth were they going to talk about for the next 45 minutes? But that did not prove to be a problem – Maxi held a wonderful conversation all of the way to their destination. As Paxton Starr turned off the Interstate and then cut across towards the ocean did Abby begin to take in the scenery.

A few minutes later Paxton turned the car into Ocean Drive and they drove past the few homes that were on this estate road almost right on the beach. Abby just sat in silence not knowing what in heaven's name was going on.

The car passed through the entrance gates and Paxton parked the car near the front door of the most beautiful home that Abby had ever seen in her entire life. Paxton helped her out of the car and then he unlocked the front door of the house and ushered Abby in.

"Abby please allow me to show you the new home that my husband and I have just had built. We moved in about three weeks ago." Maxi led the quick guided tour through the downstairs rooms of the house.

Finally Abby said, "Your home is beautiful – the most beautiful that I have ever seen – But I do not understand why you brought me out here to see it".

Paxton ushered Abby back to the kitchen and invited her to take a seat.

"The coffee that we promised you is homemade I am afraid – I make a poor cup of coffee" He was smiling at Abby's total state of confusion.

"You brought me to your new home to make me a coffee!?"

"No, well, yes, I suppose that we did - the truth is Abby that we would like to offer you a job – part-time cook and loving care giver to our new home – we'd like you to come and work for us." said Maxi beaming from ear-to-ear.

This was the closest thing to fainting that Abby had ever come to. THEY want ME to work for THEM. She repeated that sequence in her mind again, THEY want ME to work for THEM – in THIS HOUSE she said to herself.

Paxton and Maxi just sat and smiled at her. Abby just sat and smiled back – dumbfounded would be a better term to use.

Finally, Abby could muster a few words. "Oh, I could not work here – there is no transport out this way – I could never get any transport."

"Well, what we had in mind was that if it suited you you'd work three or four days a week and maybe cook one or two – we can decide that as we go forward – and as for transport, well, we've being doing some investigation with one or two of your friends and they told us that you've always liked American cars – so we thought that if it was acceptable to you we'd help you find a used American vehicle – call it a signing on fee from us – and we'd pay for the gas and insurance".

Now Abby was even closer to fainting.

"What? Why? Why me? I do not understand".

"We've run some informal reference checks on you and everyone says that you are tops, just the best – you are honest, hard-working and trustworthy – and we thought that you'd like a new challenge – looking after us!"

Abby finally accepted the offer the following week. She insisted on giving all of her existing clients' one month's notice. She was like a small child when Maxi took her out and purchased a Dodge Intrepid – red with black seats. The car only had about 5000 miles on her – Paxton had made a few telephone calls to nearby car dealerships and located a red one that had been used as a demonstration model.

Abby started working for the Starr's four days a week and then some time later it was reduced to Monday's and including making dinner, then Thursdays and Fridays.

She was paid a more than fair wage and Maxi spoiled her from time-to-time. Over the years Abby referred to Maxi Starr as her "little princess" and Paxton was "Mr. P".

The trust and love between the three of them was very evident. Abby's children were assisted with funds for education and the term "extended family" was very apt.

Abby had no title – she never wanted one. She cleaned and cooked and managed the gardener who came in twice a week. Sometimes she would buy groceries with the credit card that they had provided her.

Abby had developed a routine for cleaning the house. The task could not be done in one day – the home was too large for that to be possible. She worked through her cleaning routine on Mondays until late afternoon and then she made dinner. On Tuesdays she continued her cleaning and would finish up by late in the day. On Fridays she would clean the kitchen and bedrooms and do a spot check on all other rooms in the house. If the Starr's were having friends over on a Saturday evening then Abby would check the stock of liquor, beers, pop, snacks, buy meat for the barbeque and generally make the home ready for the party. The Mondays following these party's was not as bad as one might expect – The Starr's were never very good at cleaning up after a party but in fairness the home was never really in too bad a state when Abby commenced her cleaning routine on the Monday morning.

Several times over the years Maxi had suggested that Abby sleep in their home on a Monday evening to prevent the commute but she had never taken up the offer.

Abby had been through tough times with the Starr's in particular when Maxi Starr lost her parents in the auto accident. She shared Maxi's grief as if it were her own.

Now her grief would be even greater.

CHAPTER 18

The police officer at the main gate of the Starr's residence backed-up his vehicle in order that Abby could drive her now over 20 year-old Dodge up the drive way. Dodge no longer made the Intrepid but Abby refused to sell it. The car was in immaculate condition and had a very low mileage. She saw no reason to sell it although Maxi Starr had often tempted her to upgrade to a newer model. Maxi had teased Abby about having a new car delivered for her upcoming birthday but the suggestion had fallen on deaf ears.

"You get no smart ideas about changing my car you hear! I like want I got and I am going to drive it until the wheels fall off or until they bury me whichever comes first!"

Maxi's reply was, "We'll see – we'll see!"

The two women would glare at each other while smiling at the same time.

Now Abby drove her car up to the side of the house. As she parked the car she saw Paxton Starr walking out of the doorway of the house and her heart sank. He screamed as she leapt out of the car, "Is it Ms. Maxi? What has happened to my princess? Oh God, what has happened?"

Paxton Starr met Abby half way between the parked car and the front door. He threw his arms out and embraced Abby as it she was his own mother. He buried her small frame in his and whispered in her ear that Maxi had died. Abby fell limp in his body as she fainted. Paxton caught her as she buckled and her legs gave way. At first he seemed to struggle to hold onto her but then he straightened up and lifted her in his arms and walked towards the door of the house. Greg and Ken stepped aside as Paxton carried Abby into the front living room. He laid her out on a large sofa – without even being asked to assist Ken ran into the kitchen found the glass rack and filled it with cold water. When he returned to the room Abby was still lying very still. Paxton Starr was on his knees next to the sofa and trying to revive her. Paxton took the glass of water from Ken and lifted Abby's head to try to make her take a sip of water. At first there was no response from her but then after several tries Paxton succeeded in getting her to splutter and gasp for breath. One does tend to sputter when taking in water when not completely conscious.

It took another minute or two before Abby began to recover. Ken had held Abby's head for a minute while his client went into the kitchen to start making some tea and to come back some cold towels to place on Abby's neck. It was as obvious as plain day light that Paxton was deeply attached to Abby – just as his late wife had been. Ken did not have to make a note on that topic.

Eventually Abby sat up. The police officer who had been on duty at the front door of the house helped sit Abby up and held her steady while Paxton ran back to the kitchen to bring in the tea.

Abby sat silent on the sofa as if not sure where she was or what she was doing there. Then reality flowed back into her veins and she tried to stand up as if it were not her place to be seated. Very gently she was helped back into a seated position again.
When she spoke it was like a weak voice from a dying old person, "My princess, what happened to my princess?"

This was not an easy question for Mr. Starr to answer. He took the cup of tea from Abby and sat it down on the table. He sat next to her on the sofa and instinctively took her hand in his – but as he attempted to speak he began to shake and sob at the same time. For Greg and Ken and the police officer this was a very personal moment to see such a tall, well-built adult become a quivering incomprehensible mumbling man. Was this the reaction of a man who was being indicted for the murder of his wife?

Greg stepped forward and asked his client if he could tell Abby what had happened. Paxton Starr just nodded his approval.

"Abby, my name is Greg Winters and this is my colleague Ken Parker – we are Mr. Starr's lawyers – I am deeply sorry to tell you that Mrs. Maxi Starr was found drowned in her bath tub just over two weeks ago – on a Sunday morning – Mr. Starr found his wife unresponsive – he telephoned 911 and Mrs. Starr was pronounced dead at the scene."

Greg paused as if to give Abby – or his client the opportunity to speak. He waited and as he was about to continue Abby spoke – but her voice was hardly audible.

"Why are you here? Why does Mr. Starr need legal men? I do not understand".

Greg's answer to her question would come like a thunder bolt to Abby – he knew it but there was no way to avoid it.

"Abby, Mr. Starr has been charged by the district attorney for the murder of his wife."

The look on Abby's face turned from the slight flushness still from her fainting to an ashen grey – her eyes widen and her jaw slowly dropped. The last thing that she said before she collapsed onto the floor was, "No!"

The police officer called an ambulance for Abby.

Greg and Ken walked to the kitchen under the pretext of pouring some of the tea recently made for Abby for Mr. Starr. He was just sitting in a single sofa not saying a word. In the kitchen Ken asked Greg, "I do not recall Abby's name being mentioned by Mr. Starr in any of his discussions with you – and yet she has been employed by him for over 21 years – and she certainly appears to be more than a housekeeper – there is genuine affection out there – and she was never mentioned – I do not get it."

"Me neither." answered Greg. "Where has she been the last few weeks that she had no knowledge of the passing of someone that she called "my princess"?

Ken poured tea not only for their client but took the liberty of pouring cups for both himself and for Greg. He then felt guilty that he had not offered the police officers on duty at the front gate and the entrance to the home anything to drink – but they both declined when the offer was made.

A few minutes later when the ambulance arrived for Abby Paxton Starr rose from his chair and walked next to the gurney as Abby was taken outside then driven away.

He then turned and walked back into the house and started climbing the staircase.

"Mr. Starr, where may I ask are you going?" asked Greg as if fearing that his client might want to do himself some kind of injury.

"I am going to wash my face – I'll be right back" was the answer that Greg got – his client had not even turned to address Greg as he continued walking up the steps. Greg was in two minds if they should follow Paxton up the steps. Ken was just about to start walking up the staircase when Greg stopped him.

"Let's give him a minute shall we – then we'll go up – but listen carefully if you hear anything".

They stood at the bottom of the staircase but heard no noise at all. Greg was beginning to regret his decision when all of a sudden Paxton appeared on the landing and started to walk down the steps. He had clearly just washed his face as it was still a little wet as he reached the two men. As he walked passed them he gave a weak smile and said, "Were you waiting for me?" He walked on and sat in the large common room.

Greg and Ken followed their client into the common room and he motioned for them to take a seat. They took up seats opposite from each other – an old tactic so that one could watch their client while the other one held the conversation going. The tactic was however not lost to Paxton Starr.

"Mr. Starr I do not understand why we had not heard you mention Abby's name – she seems such an important part of your lives – more than an employee and yet you failed to mention her to us – and why has she not been to your home since the – since your wife was found dead?"

"Abby is indeed part of our lives – she has been with us for over 21 years and had shared much joy and some sadness with us". Paxton Starr proceeded to recount the story of how he and his wife had met Abby at the funeral of her husband – who had been employed by Paxton's group of companies. He spoke for about fifteen minutes without a pause – and with no interruption from Greg. In fact both Greg and Ken sat almost enjoying the tale that their client told them of the relationship between him and his late wife and their housekeeper – the housekeeper who never wanted a title.

He told them how supportive Abby was when Maxi's parents were killed in a car crash several years before. He failed however to even mention that he and Maxi had funded the education of Abby's children – now all adults and somewhat employed. That information they would later hear from Abby.

Finally Paxton stopped and almost seemed embarrassed the way that he had spoken so freely of the relationship between the Starr's and Abby.

"I still need to know why you did not mention her to us".

"That, Mr. Winters, is a million dollar question. I think that in the anguish of the last few weeks Abby simply did not enter my mind – it might sound like a fake but I cannot seem to even have thought

139

about her". Paxton then hesitated and slapped himself on his thigh..."Of course, I know why Abby was not in my mind or why she had not heard about the death of my wife – she was in China – it was a life-long dream of hers to go to China and finally we worked out some dates for her to go away for a few weeks – ah, let me think, yes, she left on the weekend before – before the passing of my wife and she flew into San Francisco this morning. We had said that she would be terribly jetlagged and that she should only come back to work next week but she had insisted that she return to work from the airport. Her car was in long-term parking and she likely got changed at the airport and came right over here after she landed. My goodness, yes, Abby has been out of the country for the last few weeks."

Greg was not too sure how to take this news. If the facts checked out – and he was sure that they would then maybe – just maybe in the heat of the last few weeks his client had not thought about Abby. It did however seem unlikely.

Greg decided to wrap up the walking interview as indeed it had been intense and eventful. He was exhausted and he was sure that Ken felt the same way. He was also sure that Paxton Starr had had enough for one day. There would be more and longer days ahead for all of them

On their way out of the house the three men walked over to Abby's car. They popped the trunk and there was her suitcase and some other items from her trip to China.

CHAPTER 19

As Ken turned his car out of Ocean Drive Greg was already on his cell phone to Elizabeth. He had not been in contact with her for most of the day and that was not like him when he was out of the office. She knew however not to telephone Greg unless it was for a situation of a dire nature. So Elizabeth had planted herself in her office for most of the day and waited for Greg to call her. She was of the belief that if he telephoned her that she should answer the call on the second ring – no more than that. She had arranged for lunch to be brought into her office and personal breaks were brief and only when she could arrange a stand-by in her office while she was away powdering her nose.

Greg briefly filled Elizabeth in on the activities of the day – but obviously not on the details of the day. That would come soon enough when Elizabeth took down his notes, recorded his thoughts and tried to unscramble some of his ideas into words.
While on the call to Elizabeth Greg suddenly realized that it had been hours since he had last eaten anything – he asked Elizabeth to hold for a moment while he proposed to Ken that they stop at the first fast food place that they could find and have a greasy burger and a coffee – Ken smiled widely and nodded – Greg advised Elizabeth that they were stopping on the way back to the office. It was already late afternoon but the day was hardly done for them.

Elizabeth was very pleased that Greg had telephoned in (reported in to the Sergeant Major!) but she was not too happy about them stopping for fast food somewhere. She looked at her watch and then worked out at roughly what time they would work until that night. She then checked with some of the other lawyers who were working in the office and how late they would be staying. Based on her "scientific" analysis she then telephoned the small steak restaurant near the office and placed an order for a set of meals to be delivered later in the evening. She had used this service many times before and their steak rolls and salads were good value.

141

Over the next few months the owner of the restaurant would thank Greg Winters defense lawyers many times for their evening business – as he had for years already!

Elizabeth knew that a happy and well-functioning law firm – one working on a major case – functioned on its stomach – without the right food and drink the team could not think properly. An unthinking lawyer could miss something – Elizabeth would never let that happen. No Junk food mind you – she would never permit cookies or the like into the war room – that would never be allowed under her watch.

Elizabeth would swing into action soon as the case really got underway.

CHAPTER 20

Paxton Starr felt very exhausted after the long day with Greg and Ken. He felt as if he was under the spot light the entire day. He could almost hear their minds working overtime as he walked them through the proceedings of what happened the night that his wife died. He still could not believe that his Maxi was gone – it seemed like an ugly demented dream – or a joke that was in very bad taste. The last few weeks had truly been a nightmare – and this was only the beginning. The media coverage had been extensive and he knew that it would only get worse – was his name tainted for life even before the grand jury met – and then the trial. Greg had hinted that he thought that the grand jury would recommend that the charges brought against him would have the sympathy of the jury and that a trial would be called.

Paxton sat in the common room thinking about the things that he had to do that day – one of which was to make himself some lunch as he also realized that he was very hungry. Then there were other matters to take care of.

Finally he stood up and walked through to the kitchen.

He threw the milk out, the bread was stale and other items in the fridge did not interest him. There was almost an entire apple pie that Maxi had made on the day before she died – it still looked fresh but he threw that out too. He could not bring himself to sit and eat it. He went through to the pantry – not a room that he was too familiar with and looked around. Nothing looked interesting. Maybe it was just him. He finally decided that a can of soup would have to do. Mixed vegetable – so "unyum" he thought to himself.

While the soup simmered on the stove he wrote some notes of things that he had to take care of that day. The list was longer than what he had hoped.

After washing up after his "unyum" soup he poured himself a glass of water and walked up to his office. As he walked passed the upper stair window he looked out and saw the police officer near his door and the other officer still sitting in his vehicle blocking the front gate. Half way to the office he stopped and turned around and walked to his bedroom. From a window in his bedroom he could see the home of Wil and Jenni Wright. He was interested to see if they were home – maybe he should give Wil a call. Both Wil and Jenni's cars were in their drive way – what should he do? If he saw their cars then they could obviously see his car – and Abby's car too for that matter. Had they been home when the ambulance came to fetch Abby? Why had they not telephoned to see if everything was alright at his home? Maybe they were not home at the time and therefore did not know that something had happened. But if they were home – did that mean that they did not care – did not want to talk to him. After all he was charged with the murder of their best friend. Where did this stand him in the eyes of his good long-time friends on Ocean drive? He did not know. He stood for another minute and then walked back towards his office.

His first call was to his office. He spoke in turn with his personal assistant, his two vice presidents, the company legal council and his general manager of construction.

He was free to resume duties at work but he decided that he needed a few days off to realign his new life. He was not sure if he detected a change in tone towards him from his colleagues – after all he stood accused of murdering his wife – and also someone that they all liked and loved very dearly. Everyone that met Maxi Starr loved her.

He had arranged for a company car and two drivers to come by his home later in the day and collect Abby's car. They would then drive it to her home.

He telephoned the hospital and reached the receptionist who told him that the doctors had decided to keep Abby overnight for

144

observation. The long flights back from China – her jet lag and then the events of the afternoon had taken their toll on her.

Next he called his PA again and arranged for flowers to be sent to Abby's home the next day.

He had previously made arrangements to move into a furnished apartment fairly near to his home. He called the Agent and asked if he could move in that evening. He had signed a one month lease but he was sure that it would be extended – it was several times.

Then he called Greg Winters. Greg was still travelling in Ken's car – having stopped for a late lunch at a MacDonald's – they ate so fast that they did not see the kids at the next table watching them devour their food. He had meant to ask Greg when Maxi's body would be released for burial. Greg did not now but said that he would look into it again with the DA.

Finally Paxton telephoned a security guard company. He knew the President personally as the company had provided security for Paxton's onsite buildings for years. He arranged for a 24-hour watch on his home as he would be moving out. He did not know how long the police would keep a presence at his home but he wanted professional security once the SFPD moved off.

After his telephone calls he went into one of the spare bedrooms upstairs and took a long and much overdue shower. His large frame slowly came back to life as soap and hot water covered his entire body. It must have been one of the longest showers that he had ever taken in his life and he washed himself over and over again. He could only think of one other shower that he had taken that had lasted as long.

He went to his bedroom dressed and packed a suitcase – in fact he packed three suitcases full of clothes and personal effects. He took them down and placed them in the trunk of his car. While he was packing the car the two cars from his office arrived and the drivers greeted him and then were gone in a flash as they drove away with

145

Abby's car. He locked the door of his home and drove down Ocean Drive without looking to see if any of his friends were even outside. Were they still his friends?

CHAPTER 21

After Greg had completed his call to Elizabeth he sat still for a minute or two before he spoke, "So what do you think?" he asked Ken. It was such a short question and yet it covered so much content.

Ken had known that they would discuss the session with Paxton Starr as soon as Greg was off of his call with Elizabeth; that had given him a few minutes to try to arrange his thoughts and come up with something that sounded logical and coherent. He was not sure if his answers or comments would make sense at this stage – most likely they would not – but there was plenty of time to put the information together and to build the case for their client. Still, first impressions or opinions were always important. .

"It is possible that the entire set of circumstances as he described to us – and made in his statement to the police – is true and accurate. Everything could have gone as he explained – right from the beginning of the events from when they arrived home through to the 911 call might have occurred as explained. On the other hand we have no proof that things happened that way – maybe it is a grand plan to throw us off of what really occurred – one thing for sure though it is pretty darn obvious that he loved and cherished his wife." Ken hesitated then continued, "So why would he take her life – I cannot figure that one out – yeah, maybe his story holds up at first glance but there are holes and inconsistencies that we'd have to work through with him before the grand jury sits".

Greg thought for a moment before he provided an answer to Ken's observations. Certainly there were holes that they would have to fill in and coach their client on – this is always the situation on a case – but was there something else deeper down – he did not know.

"I blew hot and cold with him. On occasions I felt that we were right on top of what actually happened and that he was sure of himself – then pop – I was not sure any more.

He seemed much more nervous on some points and darn right testy on others – like inferring that his wife drank a great deal – he was very touchy there. I do not think that he is used to being probed at so hard – he is a fairly timid guy on the outside and does not seem to enjoy confrontation at all – not a good sign if the DA gets hold of him."

"For sure – that could be a disaster for him. But from the outside they looked like a very loving couple – I mean it is clear as day that he adored his wife – a tough thing to convince me that he murdered her – but one can never tell."

Greg stared out of the window of the car as they climbed the small hill that separated the village and shopping area from the beach front homes. From up here the ocean was like a gigantic blanket to their one side. What a wonderful place to make a home. His thoughts jumped to his cabin and he longed to go back and just be by himself again. He made a mental note to look at his calendar when he got back to the office.

He heard Ken talking but in truth he had missed the first few words of what had been said.

"There is nothing to prove for instance that he had not followed his wife up stairs waited for her to get into the bath and relax and then go in and drown her – it is all possible."

"Yes, it is but we know from the coroner's report that there was no sign of a struggle – was she asleep or did he attack her – an attack seems unlikely" Greg inhaled and breathed out very slowly, "I do not think that the actions were premeditated – although it is kind of strange that Abby was away right at this time – but I am not sure that if murder is the case that it was planned." Greg stopped himself and then continued "But who says that he did not

148

stage the incident with his wife – but, we know that she seems to have become tipsy – more than tipsy – did she plan the incident with the view of taking her own life?"

He continued, "No, I am sure that something happened the night of her death – something at the house party - we'll have to delve deep there to try to find something before the prosecutor does."

"I agree." said Ken. "Whatever we do find from the witnesses at the party we'll have to close the gaps so that nothing gets given free to the prosecutor."

"There are a number of things that puzzled me during our interview – one of which was how do some people make so much money and can build a home like that – I have never seen anything like it before – not only the home but the decorating and the scenery. My, it was breathe-taking!" Ken had to brake hard to avoid hitting a car that had stopped in front of him.

"If you keep driving like that you will not live long enough to earn your fortune to build your dream home!" Greg grinned broadly at his young colleague.

As Ken slowly pulled away from the STOP sign he asked Greg, "I was puzzled about your interest in Maxi Starr's shawl – what was bothering you – and it certainly got Mr. Starr's attention."

Just as Greg was about to answer Ken's question he noticed a MacDonald's just up the road and he gestured with his hands if it was he would be happy to stop there to grab something to eat. Ken nodded and changed lanes and turned the car into the parking lot next to the golden arches. Once inside the restaurant they did not discuss the case. That would be unprofessional and walls have ears. Ken would have to wait until later to hear Greg's answer to his question.

CHAPTER 22

Greg and Ken arrived back in the office in the late afternoon. Greg presented Elizabeth with an Action Figure toy that he had bought for her at the restaurant where they had stopped for their late lunch. She was not amused which gave the two men great joy. Sometimes a very stressful day requires a little silliness to relieve the tension.

After a brief discussion the two men retired to their respective offices to begin the process of composing their notes from the interview with their client. Ken sat and transcribed his notes onto his laptop while Greg toyed with a pencil, pulled at his ear while he was thinking and then made another hand scribed note. From these notes he would then record everything for Elizabeth to type-up and send the file back to him. He knew that he was completely technically very outdated but he felt comfortable with his methods – and why change now at the end of his career. He still felt the odd man out when the lawyers gathered in the war room for meetings and he was the only one without a laptop or some other technical device. He had Elizabeth and she was as up to date as anyone in the room.

Elizabeth did not disturb Greg while he was deep in thought – it would be like breaking a trance and that would not be a good thing to do. Greg's mind would go down a number of different tracks and he would let his thoughts flow freely until he came to some sort of conclusion. Then he would start another track – and so he would go on. A few notes made here and there on his note pad and then he'd be back into his own world again.

He thought through various scenarios that might have occurred once Paxton and Maxi Starr returned home the night that she died.

Did Paxton go upstairs at the time that his wife did? Then what could have happened? Did he let her take a hot bath and then enter the bathroom and drown his wife?

151

Did Paxton go upstairs as he had said? Then what could have happened? Greg checked his notes and returned to his inner world of thoughts. Did Paxton then decide to murder his wife? What would have made him do that?

Did Paxton make himself coffee and go up the stairs later as he had said? Did he indeed fall asleep on the bed and discover his dead wife in the morning? Was this merely a terrible tragedy? From all accounts his client loved his wife with all of his heart – surely this must have been a simple case of drowning while under the influence of alcohol?

What – if anything – had been the cause of Maxi's sudden increased intake of alcohol at the party that they had attended? So, far nothing had come out from the police statements – his team still had to interview the group of friends. Why had Maxi slapped her husband?

And what was it about Maxi's shawl that bothered him? He could not put his finger on it – if indeed there was anything at all. He simply did not know.

Greg looked at his watch. It was after 7 o'clock.

He walked out of his office to go to the washroom. Elizabeth was still there waiting for his notes. He decided not to suggest that she should go home – from previous experiences he knew that it was not a good idea. He washed his face and dried it off with one of the small white towels. He looked at himself in the mirror but before he brought himself to comment on his own looks he walked out of the washroom.

Greg looked at Ken's office and saw that he had already left to go home. The lucky guy has a family to go back to thought the world famous lawyer. Being famous is very lonely.

When Greg returned to his office there was a large mug of fresh coffee on his round table and a plate with his steak roll that Elizabeth had ordered for him. There was no point in arguing with her - he sat down at the table and took a sip of his hot coffee. Elizabeth would never allow him to eat at his desk – that was simply not acceptable. Again he had learnt his lesson with her. He asked her if she had had dinner. "Yes, thank you. In fact I had Ken's steak as he decided to go home for dinner."

Greg invited Elizabeth in to share a coffee and some small talk while he ate his dinner. Neither of them spoke about the case. The coffee and dinner break lasted about twenty minutes and then Elizabeth left Greg with the instruction not to go past 9 o'clock because otherwise he was a real pain in the rear end the next morning. She was right of course.

At about 8 30 P.M. Greg had completed his notes and walked through to Elizabeth's office. To her surprise he said, "Do not get these ready tonight – tomorrow morning will be fine. I think that I'll come in later in the morning so do the work then." She thought that she had misheard what Greg had said but before she could ask him to repeat himself he had turned and walked back into his office. A minute later he emerged with his jacket and briefcase. She starred at him in disbelief. "Come on then, lock up your files young lady you're going home – or would you like me to lock you in the office overnight?"

About five minutes later Greg walked Elizabeth to her car and they drove to their respective homes.

That night in bed all Greg could think about was his Mary and how much he loved her. He thought about the love that Paxton Starr must have had for his wife.

All Elizabeth could think about was getting her work organized before Greg came into the office.

.

CHAPTER 23

Greg only made it into the office after 11 o'clock the next morning. He had tried to sleep but there was too much bumping around in his mind. Finally, he had gotten up and made a sandwich and hot milk. It was after 3 o'clock before he had crawled back into bed. Not before he had telephoned Elizabeth's number at the office to tell her that he would only be in after 11 in the morning. After he had hung up the telephone he thought what if she had her calls redirected to her cell number after hours. What would she think if he was calling her at 3 o'clock in the morning?

It was a bright Wednesday morning and Greg had come to the office prepared.

Once he had settled in with his second cup of coffee (in his Giants mug) he walked through to Ken's office. There was no doubt that Ken had not slept much either the night before.

Together they looked at the upcoming interview schedule that his firm had put together for the various witnesses and other key persons of interest for the upcoming grand jury. Not much had changed since the list was first drawn up a few weeks back when they had developed their DAIIPAS list. One addition to the list would be Abby Carmichael who they had met the day before.

It was not the easiest of tasks to set up the interviews. People were busy or out of town and one had to try to accommodate their schedules. It was always a good idea to try to hold the interview in an appropriate setting – for example, Paxton Starr's interview in his home – or to try to arrange for the interview with Wil and Jenni Wright in their home where the incident between Paxton and Maxi had taken place. Visualization played a significant part in trying to piece together what had taken place. In the ideal world an interview would be held at the same time of day as what the incident had occurred – but of course this was hardly ever possible. Most interviews took place in an Interview Room and

155

Greg felt that it made the proceedings feel clinical and bland. He wanted the action to be part of what had happened on a case.

The two men then met with some of the other lawyers on the case and spent an hour or so going through their interview with Paxton Starr. Ken noted that Greg did not mention Maxi Starr's shawl. Maybe there was something that was still bothering him and he did not want to mention it at this point in time.

Greg then ate a small lunch from the deli in their office park before he sat down with the notes that Elizabeth had prepared. To her utter surprise he glanced over them for about ten minutes and then placed them in his attaché case. He announced to her that there was not much happening until the interviews planned for later in the week and early the next week were complete.

"So I am therefore off to my cabin with notes and cell phone in hand – I will see you next Monday!"

Elizabeth was dumbfounded. Speechless – and Greg enjoyed every second of watching the stunned look on her face.

"Ken is aware that I am going away – I need a few days – and he has everything under control so I will only be in the way".

"You're serious aren't you!" exclaimed Elizabeth. "You are going away until next week!"

"Yes, indeed – don't look so glum I'll be back next week – and I know that you'll telephone if you need me".

"Are you going home first – what are you taking with you?"

"I am all packed – everything is in the Land Rover and she is ready to roll" answered Greg with an even bigger smile on his face.

All Elizabeth could muster was, "Well, ok, ah, well, enjoy your few days away!"
156

Two minutes later Greg was in his beloved SUV and starting out on a four day visit to be with his Mary. He knew in his soul that he needed to be with his late wife for a few days.

Somehow Elizabeth realized that too. Greg found peace being near Mary.

Greg went through the drive-through of the nearby Coffee Shop outlet – ordered an extra large coffee and a doughnut and off he went to visit his late wife. He enjoyed the four hour drive to Alpine Meadows.

Just before he arrived in Alpine Meadows Greg stopped at a local grocery store and bought what he needed for his few days at the cabin. It is always difficult to buy for one person – let alone cook for one person – or for that matter to eat alone – but he picked up a few steaks, bread, milk, a bottle of whiskey and some other items. He had shopped there often and it was refreshing to greet folk who lived outside of the city. They did not care a whisker who Greg was – or if they did know who he was they did not care. On his way out of the store he stopped at the magazine rack and picked up a bunch of things to read. He returned to the Cashier and paid for the magazines. When the cashier scanned the prices he said to Greg, "I see that you're interested in renewable energy. It will never work. These new things never do!" Greg had picked up a copy of HOME TECHNOLOGY. It was just something to read.

Greg turned off of the main road and onto the side road that led up to the cabin. About half a mile from the cabin the road turned from the trees and there he stopped the SUV. He climbed out of the vehicle and looked out over the small lake to his cabin tucked in near the trees. His heart almost leapt right out of his chest with the sight of the lake and the cabin. This is where he belonged. This is where his heart was. At this time of his life he just wanted to be here near the trees, the lake and near Mary. He cast his eyes slightly to the right of the house and there he saw the white cross on Mary's grave. The tears ran down his cheek and he made no effort to wipe them away.

He climbed back into his SUV and slowly drove towards the cabin. He wanted to savor the view. It really was picture perfect. Yesterday he had stood on the balcony of a beautiful home and overlooked the ocean and today he was taking in a cabin in the woods with a small lake in front of it. He could not make up his mind which was the more appealing – actually he knew.

Greg stopped his vehicle on the side of the cabin and hauled out the things that he had purchased at the grocery store. He came back for his suitcase after he had opened up the cabin. Greg turned off the alarm system and opened the front door of the cabin. The air was stuffy but that would soon pass when he opened up some windows. He carried the groceries to the kitchen and put them away. He took the bottle of whiskey through to the main living room and opened up the liquor cabinet. There standing in the cabinet were several unopened bottles of whiskey plus another about three quarters full. "Darn" he thought to himself "you keep forgetting that you have this stuff but you never drink much of it". The whiskey would keep for when you retire he thought.

He fetched the rest of the stuff from his vehicle and locked it. He had taken off his suit jacket and his tie as he had left the office and they were lying on the backseat of the SUV. He was tempted to leave them in the vehicle but though better of it.

Inside the cabin he opened up some windows and then went through to the bedroom and soon had unpacked and stripped down to casual clothes. He hung up his suit, business shirt and tie in the closet.

Next was to make himself some coffee and to begin to settle into his cabin.

While the kettle boiled he gave Sheriff Norm a call.

158

"Sheriff Wilson". Norman Wilson's voice was as big as what the man was.

"Good afternoon sheriff I would like to report a break-in at Greg Winters cabin".

Greg used the same routine every time that he called his good friend.

"Greg my old friend, how are you? Are you in town?"

The two men chatted for a minute or two and made arrangements to meet for coffee and their regular place the next afternoon. Greg felt at home.

After Greg had his coffee he went to the shed and took out a broom. He walked over to Mary's gravestone and after he had said hello to her he started to clean up the area where she rested. It does not take long for the dust and dirt to gather up around a cross or for it to take on an off-white color. He did the best he could on that first visit to Mary but over the next few days he spent many hours with her and making her more comfortable. It was not a morbid experience to clean up the site where his wife lay – it was far more like a duty, an expression of love after death – a very meaningful ritual to go through. Greg found the experience to be refreshing and a healing experience.

That evening he cooked one of the steaks that he bought earlier in the day. He washed it down with a glass of red wine. He had found a bottle of Californian Merlot in his liquor cabinet. Eating and drinking alone had been a part of his life for a long time now. It did however seem easier to have a meal so close to Mary. He enjoyed her company as he ate. He had every intention of washing up the dishes and reading one of the magazines that he had bought but he felt totally fatigued and although it was still early he retired to the bedroom. He undressed by remote control and left his clothes on the floor. Within minutes he was sound asleep. Maybe this is what Maxi Starr had done the night that she had died – she had left

159

her clothes on the floor of her dressing room but instead of falling asleep in her bed she had fallen asleep in her bath tub and drowned.

CHAPTER 24

The next morning Greg awoke at first light. He had slept for almost ten hours - for him a record. He washed and dressed and was as hungry as an unfed lion when he walked through into the kitchen. He feasted on a large breakfast and several cups of coffee and finally sat back totally overfed. He decided that a walk was in order and he headed off into the trees to the right hand side of the house. There was no real trail but he knew that the walk would bring him out just beyond from where he had parked the SUV the day before. Years before he had discovered an old stump. The tree was cut down to the height of about three feet. The stump was fairly level so it provided a wonderful seating position to sit and look back towards his cabin. He sat there in absolute bliss just admiring the view and listening to nature. His lungs filled with clean fresh county air. His heart seemed to come alive again. After about a twenty minute rest he arose and walked back down the road to his cabin.

In the early afternoon he drove into town and found a parking spot fairly near to where he was to meet Sheriff Norm. Some of the locals greeted him as he walked around in the small downtown area. No one cared who he was or that he was representing an accused wife killer. He was just Greg Winters part-time local resident. He stopped at the grocery store as he needed to pick up a few things that he had forgotten to pick up the day before - he was out of dish soap and bottled water. He carried his brown paper bag back to the SUV and had just closed the back door when he felt a very large hand on his shoulder. The distinct burly voice of the local sheriff said, "Hello stranger, are you new to these parts?"

Greg turn around and replied, "Yes, but I am just passing through – you'll have no trouble from me sheriff!"

The two men laughed and shook hands warmly. It had been a while since they had seen each other. They found their usual table

161

at the nearby coffee shop and settled in for a good chat. They did not even have to place an order as they had the same thing every time that they visited the coffee shop. It really was like being in a home town – where everyone knew one another and most likely their business too. But it was not a gossip town just more of a good place to be part of.

As per usual there was no discussion of Greg's case – although Sheriff Norman Wilson had seen the coverage on TV and had read all of the news print on the recent developments. He knew that the last few weeks for Greg had been tough. Greg was not an upfront media-loving person so having the spotlight of another murder case could not have been easy.

After their coffee mugs had been refilled Norm Wilson told Greg that there had been some break-ins lately at some of the homes just outside of town. He was sure that it was a gang of idle youth that were breaking into the homes. Nothing much of value was ever taken but every few weeks there would be another break-in. Sheriff Norman advised Greg to recheck his alarm system and not to leave anything of value in his shed.

Their chat was cut short by the sheriff's cell phone ringing and his Deputy informing him that there had been a head-on collision just outside of town and that he should be on the scene as quickly as possible. The two men rose from their table and shook hands and the gentle giant that Sheriff Norman Wilson was turned and he walked as quickly as he could manage to his police car that was parked just a short distance away. Greg sat and finished his coffee and then decided to order lunch. There was no Elizabeth to watch what he ate so he consumed a bacon burger with fries.

He drove back to his cabin by late afternoon. It took a while but eventually he opened one of the magazines that he had bought and he started to read some of the articles. A leading article on Renewable Energy was very interesting. He read it a second time later in the evening as somewhere during the first read he had fallen asleep on the sofa.

162

By late that night he had read the magazines cover to cover. For the most part there was no much that was of interest to Greg but he had waded through them. He decided to do some research on the topic of renewable energy and booted up his computer. A PC and he were not great friends but he knew how to search for various topics. Actually he was not that bad for an "old-timer" – he just chose not to use it too much. Maybe when he retired!

He again had a very good night's sleep and awoke with vigor the next morning. He again wolfed down a large breakfast and enjoyed the light classical music that he played in the background. He spent most of the morning working outside of the house cleaning up the small garden that he mostly left unkempt anyway – he was not at the cabin enough to keep it looking smart. Besides which Mary had wanted a wild little garden on the side of the pathway leading up to the front door. The wild flowers, pebble stones and broken twigs looked almost out of place when taken into the context of the shimmering lake and the forest nearby but it did seem to add a certain luster to the cabin.

It was Friday afternoon now and Greg was wondering when he would be tempted to open his attaché case and bury himself into his notes and the case again. He was sitting contemplating his decision with a mug of coffee when the telephone rang. The sound of a telephone ringing in the cabin is so rare that he spilled coffee down the front of his shirt.
He was still in some pain from the scolding liquid when he picked up the telephone – he had seen that it was Elizabeth and he answered, "Alpine Meadows brothel and massage parlor – where service is our number one priority – how may I help you?"

Elizabeth did not answer. For a few seconds she thought that she had dialed the wrong telephone number. Then she realized that it was Greg on the line. She mentioned what for her was an unspeakable and Greg just burst out laughing. He had never heard her say "Bloody fool" before.

163

After they had both gathered themselves Elizabeth asked him how he was – she was trying to make small talk in order to recover her composure.

"Sorry to disturb you but Ken asked me to give you a call – I'll put you through". There was no goodbye or other farewell greeting – Elizabeth had not forgiven him yet. Greg took great joy at knowing that she was a tad mad at him.

Ken came on the line.

"Hi Greg sorry to bug you but I needed to check something out with you."

"Sure, no problem – what is it?" he asked.

"We'll have all of the interviews with Paxton Starr's neighbors done by this evening – all except for the Wrights. Wil Wright has been away all week and he is away for most of the next two weeks – he is however home on Monday and has said that we could come over for the interview. Would Monday work for you?"

"Of course, what time is the interview?"

"They will be home by 3 o'clock but I thought that you and I could interview Abby in the morning – I called her and we can arrange to meet at a local police station near where she lives. She usually works at the house on Mondays but Mr. Starr has given her some time off until after the police department withdraws their officers from the premises. We could meet her at 10 and then grab a burger before we drive over to the Wrights –will that work?"

"Sure – I'll be in the office early and then we can catch up on things in the car as we drive to meet Abby – and oh, just other thing, please remember to tell Elizabeth that we'll be eating greasy burgers for lunch – that should spoil her weekend! See you on Monday morning".

164

He did not want to be near Elizabeth when she received his message. The glare that she would give Ken would have spoiled his weekend.

Greg changed his shirt and poured himself another mug of coffee. He picked up his attaché case and walked through to his small office. Besides a break for dinner Greg spent the next six hours emerged into the case again and writing more notes. He again let his mind flow freely down the various scenarios of what might have led up to and then the death of Maxi Starr.

On the Saturday he felt restless and took another walk into the forest. It took him two hours to walk in a big circle around the lake and back to his tree stump. He sat and looked at his cabin again and thought about some changes that he might like to make.

After lunch he packed up his garbage and other things that he could not leave behind – including the milk as he knew that he did not have any at home. He checked that the cabin was secure and he set the alarm.

He drove back to the city a day early but he had work to do. He said goodbye to Mary before he left.

He was however totally refreshed from his three days and nights in his cabin.

CHAPTER 25

On the Monday morning he was actually in the office before Elizabeth arrived. He placed a small box of chocolates on her desk. There was no note – she could think of something that she wanted him to say!

When Elizabeth came into the office Greg was sitting in Ken's office going over some notes of the case and preparing themselves for the two interviews that lay ahead that day. At about 8:30 Greg came out of Ken's office and greeted Elizabeth. She just smiled but did not thank him for the chocolates. She knew that it was a peace offering and a smile was all that was needed. Her outer toughness and sometimes personality was only a cover for a very caring person. Greg knew her better than what she thought and she knew him better than what he thought. A very solid professional relationship existed between Greg Winters and Elizabeth McKenzie.

By 8:45 Greg was seated in Ken's car and they were heading off to interview Abby Carmichael.

Ken pulled his car into the police department parking lot at about 9 40 – Abby's car was already parked in a Visitors Bay. It is not difficult to miss a red Dodge Intrepid – and in particular one that still looked brand new after 21 years on the road.

The two lawyers were ushered into the meeting room where Abby was waiting for them. They reintroduced themselves and asked her if she was comfortable. She replied that she was perfectly comfortable. In truth she was extremely nervous and still very upset by the news that had been broken to her the previous week upon her return from China. When she was released from hospital the day after she had fainted twice in the Starr residence she had unloaded a canon at her family for not contacting her while she was away. If that was not enough they had not come to the airport to meet her upon her return to the States – where they could have

167

broken the news to her gently. Her family had no real reason for their oversight which had made Abby even more furious with them. Then she had received flowers from Mr. P. and she was not too sure if she was pleased to receive them or not. He was accused of murdering her "little princess". How could he have done that? She did not believe it but what if it was true?

Abby had made ready to go to work at the Starr's home on the previous Friday when she received a telephone call from Mr. P's office saying that she should take some time off. Mr. P would contact her shortly as to when she could return to work.

Over the weekend she spent time in the local library reading newspaper articles of the discovery of the dead body of Maxi Starr and the subsequent arrest of Mr. Starr. She read the news reports as if she was in a trance – it simply could not be true. Mr. P could not have done it. Several times she started to cry and had to compose herself before she read the next article. And she still could not believe that her family had not tried to contact her – they had a detailed itinerary of her trip. Their answer to her question had been that they thought that she would have heard about it on the TV news in China. That was not likely.

Greg asked Abby some general questions to start with. How long she had worked for Paxton and Maxi Starr. How she had come to work for them in the first place and had been happy with being employed by them over the years.

"Sir, I have spent about twenty one years with them. They treated me with love and respect and I loved them both back too. I started with them just after they moved into their new home – and although it was mostly decorated inside there were things that I saw being done over the years – everything that they did they did together."

Abby went through some general things and Greg allowed her to talk freely. He wanted her to feel completely relaxed in their company.

168

"What hours did you keep with them?" asked Greg after he had allowed Abby to ramble on for a few more minutes.

"I have worked on Mondays, Tuesdays and Fridays for the last few years. On Mondays I cook dinner before I leave. Most times I missed seeing Mr. P as he would have left for work before I arrive on a Monday and he gets home after I have left. Not always – sometimes he gets back by late in the afternoon. I used to see more of Ms. Maxi – she worked from home more. If I missed her on a Monday morning then I would see her in the afternoons. Sometimes we would have coffee or lunch together if she worked at home that day."

"Did you spend much time with Mrs. Starr then?" asked Greg.

"It was a big house to keep clean so I was real busy for most of the time – don't get me wrong now I had no vacation there – I worked really hard on the days there – but sometimes Mrs. Starr would find me in the house and we'd talk for a while, or as I said have a coffee break or make some lunch together."

"You liked Mrs. Starr?" enquired Greg.

"Yes sir, I did l like Mrs. Starr – but I loved her more – she was my little princess – so small and beautiful – it was a real blessing to know her."

"You said that you felt the same way about Mr. Starr?"

"Yes, I loved them both – as I said before – we were very close."

"Tell me more about Mrs. Starr?"

"She was full of life – she loved everyone and everyone seemed to love her back. She did like her clothes and looking real pretty – buying herself things all of the time – my, my, she would shop sometimes as if she had nothing to wear. She could dress the

169

neighborhood with what she bought. Then she would give things away because she said that she did not have space for her clothes. Never heard such a foolish thing – but she had the money I suppose. One thing is for sure she could not survive without her nice things – she was so sweet but a real princess – always so neat and tidy and precise with her things."

Both Greg and Ken made sharp mental notes about Maxi Starr being so neat and tidy – and yet she had just thrown down her clothes on the carpet the night that she died. Maybe she was still under the influence of the alcohol that she had consumed earlier that evening. Another comment that Abby had made was missed by both Greg and Ken but they would recall it later in the investigation into the death of Maxi Starr.

Greg changed the subject. "Tell me about your trip to China. Was it something that you had planned for a long time?"

"I have been planning a trip to China since I was a young girl." replied Abby with a broad smile. "It has been a dream of mine to go one day".

"And what made you go now – anything in particular that was happening in China" asked Greg.

"No there was nothing special – there was a flower show that I wanted to see but otherwise I just wanted to visit the places that I have read about all of my life. I had kept talking about it for years and finally Mr. P and Ms. Maxi suggested that I go and fulfill my dream. When they get badgering it can wear one down – so I eventually said that I would go."

"Did Maxi Starr push you to go?"

"Yes, but it was really Mr. P that kept at me. He even found a great package for me and arranged everything."

"Even the particular dates that you'd be away?"

170

"Yes, even the dates. He helped me get everything done."

Why would Paxton Starr insist on Abby being away over that particular time period? Abby had left for China just a few days before the death of Maxi Starr. Was that merely a coincidence or had it been planned?

The interview went on for another few minutes and then Greg thanked Abby for coming to meet with them. He informed her that they would most likely meet again in the near future.

The two men left the police station and headed off for their greasy lunch and then their appointment with Wil and Jenni Wright.

Abby was left wondering when she could go back to work.

"The Solar Murder"

CHAPTER 26

Greg had telephoned the DA's Office before he had left for his cabin and asked when Maxi Starr's body would be released for burial. He had not heard back from the DA and this had troubled him. What could be holding up the release of Maxi Starr's body to her husband?

While Greg and Ken were interviewing Abby Carmichael Elizabeth had received a call from the coroner's office saying that Paxton Starr could arrange for the collection of his wife's body the next morning. Elizabeth had sent a text message to Ken saying that they should call her after the interview. When Greg called in Elizabeth informed him of the news. Paxton Starr had received the notification and he now set in motion the arrangements for the interment.

The police officers would also be withdrawn from the Paxton home and Mr. Starr would have free access to the en suite bathroom of the main bedroom. He however, had no plans as to when he would return to live in his home. It would take a super human effort to live in the house without his wife. It was always too large for just two people but now with one person it would be unbearable. He could not imagine himself sitting in the common room, or relaxing in the "SUMMER" or "WINTER" rooms without his wife. And he could not imagine himself using the main bath room. The image of his dead wife in the bath tub would forever haunt him.

CHAPTER 27

The Wrights greeted Greg and Ken at their home and ushered them into the front living room. Both men were most likely more comfortable in a well decorated room to conduct the interview than in a room that overlooked the ocean. The ocean view would be distracting.

Jenni Wright had premade coffee and she brought out a tray with some cookies. She was actually very nervous about having the two lawyers in her home – she did not know what to expect. It was Greg's job to make both Wil and Jenni Wright feel relaxed. He had many years of experience making people feel relaxed and then extracting information from them!

As with the other interviews Greg made some general inquiries about the relationships between the families that lived on Ocean Drive. The story was the same as what had been gleaned from earlier accounts – the families got on really very well – a genuine bond existed between the husbands and wives. Jenni Wright related a few accounts of acting as Mom's Taxi to take kids on the street to after school sports activities or to the dentist if one of the other Mom's could not make it. The Dad's and the boys on the street had been to baseball together and hung out often doing guy-stuff – like watching a big football game together.

Jenni mentioned that their son Ryan and the Starr's had been very close. They did not have children of their own and although they loved the Wrights daughter, Stacey, they had a special bond with Ryan.

Greg asked, "I believe that Ryan went missing several years ago, is that correct?"

"Yes" replied Jenni. "He ran away over four years ago – and we have never heard from him." She began to sob and Wil Wright picked up the conversation. "Ryan disappeared but we believe

175

that he is safe somewhere and will come home one day". Even he was getting pretty choked up as he spoke.

"Do you have any idea why he might have run away?"

"No, not really – he was a really good young man – getting on for turning 17 – smart, good looking and kind. He was big and tall for his age."

There was a pause and the Wil Wright continued, "He had gotten involved with some undesirable kids from school – we knew that he was drinking with them – and who knows what else – in the last two months or so before he ran away he was different – more aggressive – more remote – but we thought that he'd work his way through it – we'd spoken with him and he knew that we were here for him. We had an argument with him one Saturday night and on the Sunday morning we noticed that his bed had not been slept in – we called the police later that day – but Ryan was gone – we've never heard from him since."

Greg decided to move on with the discussion – he could always come back to the discussion of Ryan if there was a need.

"Tell me about Paxton and Maxi Starr - what were they like as people and together?"

Jenni Wright answered first, "Maxi was an incredible woman – as small as what she was in stature she made up in heart. She was sweet and kind – to everyone – and not just for show she generally loved people and cared for them – we all loved her. She was like a breath of fresh air – full of fun and her face would light up and she'd glow when she smiled." While Jenni was talking Wil Wright sat and nodded his head in agreement. It was obvious that the admiration for Maxi Starr was mutual and genuine.

"How was she at your neighborhood parties?" asked Greg - knowing that he could get an angry response from Wil and Jenni.

Wil replied to the question. "If you mean did Maxi enjoy a few drinks and have fun then the answer is "yes" she did – but the emphasis was on fun – we had our kids grow up in front of us at the parties – it was the gathering of families that liked and loved one another – there was never anything done in poor taste. Some of the adults would have a few drinks but there was never an incident to be embarrassed about. I suppose that of all the adults Maxi most likely used to drink the most and got tipsy every so often but she was not a heavy drinker Mr. Winters".

"I know that she was not Mr. Wright but I do need to gather information. I am sure that you understand" replied Greg.

"Yes, I understand – but it does make it sound as if Maxi was out of it at these parties – and no she was not ....." he paused and Greg interrupted.

"Except for the night that she died!"...

There was a silence for a few moments then Wil replied, "Yes, except the night that she died. But the evening started out just fine – we socialized and then had dinner and everything was pretty normal – a run-of-the-mill fun get together."

"Then what changed?"

Jenni Wright replied, "We do not know – we've thought about it over and over and over but cannot think of what might have made Maxi drink so much after dinner – and not even right after dinner – it was much later in the evening. But we just cannot think of anything that might have upset her – or if anything had upset her – we simply cannot think of what it might have been."

"Tell me more about Mrs. Starr – anything would help".

Jenni thought for a moment and then said, "Maxi loved her clothes and the way she looked. She was a beautiful woman but she was stunning when all made-up. She loved shopping and spending

177

money – I know as I went out with her on many occasions – she would spend as if there was no tomorrow – not always on expensive items but sometimes on things that just looked good on her – ah, like the shawl that she had over her shoulders the night that – the night that she died."

Both Greg and Ken felt an electric shock run through their bodies. Maxi's shawl – they had still not discussed it and the mention of it almost made Greg fall off of the sofa. What was it that worried Greg about Maxi Starr's shawl?

Jenni had continued talking and the two lawyers had to catch up with her.

"Would you say that Mrs. Starr was under the influence of alcohol when you drove her home that night?" Greg directed his question at Wil Wright.

"Maxi seemed to have recovered from the incident that took place outside on our patio – the coffee seemed to revive her somewhat – but I must say that I thought that she was still pretty woozy when I took them home. She held onto Paxton's arm as they walked towards their front door and he was supporting her by holding her around her waist with his arm".

"Mr. Wright would you make that statement under oath if necessary?" asked Greg

"Yes, I would" Wil Wight answered the question without any hesitation.

Greg thought for a minute and then asked, "Anything else that you'd like to tell us about Mrs. Starr?"

There was another short silence before Jenni Wight offered up a comment that caused Ken to make a large exclamation point on his note pad.

"Maxi loved life – she was full of energy as I said earlier – she could not live another life she would be lost without her car, her clothes and her add-ons – it was who she was – a person who loved the good life."

"What do you mean by your statement?" probed Greg – why had Jenni Wright brought this up about Maxi Starr.

"Just what I say – Maxi loved to be well off and should anything ever happen that would mean that the Starrs should lose their wealth then I think that Max would have struggled being say middle class."

"Mr. Wright, do you agree with this statement?"

"Yes, I suppose that I do – hey, I do not think for one moment that Paxton and Maxi were in any financial mess or anything – but I guess that Jenni is right. I think that Paxton could have found a way to live a different life but Max would have struggled".

Greg and Ken were having very similar thoughts – one, were the Starrs in some kind of financial situation – more importantly was Mr. Starr in financial trouble? The entire value of Maxi Starr's estate was left to her husband – some $41 million dollars. Was this indeed a motive for murder? The DA would have a field day with this if indeed Mr. Starr was in debt.

Much of what was discussed in the next thirty minutes or so was already known to Greg and Ken but they took notes and would compare the information with what was already known. Then Greg turned the subject to the confrontation between Paxton and Maxi Starr.

"Would you mind walking us through to the room where you saw the incident unfold outside of the house?"

Just as the four were in the process of getting up the telephone rang. Jenni excused herself and walked through to the next room to take the call. The three men sat down again. A minute later Jenni walked back into the room and said to Wil "It is Paxton on the line – he told me about the plans for Maxi's funeral – he would like to talk with you".

This would be the first time that the Wright's had spoken with Paxton since he was arrested for the murder of his wife. On several occasions Wil had thought of trying to contact Paxton but he did not know what to say. On the day that Paxton came home with Greg and Ken he had thought of going over but still he could not. What if Paxton – his best friend - had murdered his wife – it was unthinkable – but what if it were true? He watched from the front window as Paxton drove by the afternoon that he had left his home.

Jenni, Greg and Ken sat in silence while Wil Wright spoke on the telephone with Paxton. It seemed like an eternity but in effect it was no more than maybe a minute or two. Only the odd word could be heard from the other room. The three people sitting alone almost tried not to tune in to what was being said. But they could imagine that it was difficult for both men – what would they say to one another.

They did hear Wil say goodbye to his friend but instead of returning to the room where the others were waiting they heard the door close of the washroom in the main lobby of the house. They could hear Wil Wright blow his nose and the running of water. He was trying to wipe away the tears and clear his head. Another uncomfortable minute passed by before Wil made his appearance.

"Sorry about keeping you waiting." he said. "Paxton will provide us with more details about the funeral service for Maxi." That was all that he said.

"Should we go through to the front room?" and he turned and walked out of the living room. It was not so much of a question as a statement. The other three stood up and followed him without saying a word.

The front room was spectacular. It was indeed large. It faced through glass and sliding doors over the patio, pool, changing room and the ocean. The room had high ceilings with thick dark wooden beams supporting the roof. In the centre of the room were sets of circular shaped sofas in a step-down area that faced onto a 360 degree fire place. In the far side of the room there was a pool table and other games items. There was no TV in the room but Ken thought that there must be a comfy room somewhere nearby where a large screen would grip the viewers in wonderful 3-D. He was correct – leading off from beyond the pool table was the entrance to a TV room – he knew that because as they walked through to the living room Jenni had pointed out some of the features of the house – including storm proof windows and ultra-secure locks on the sliding doors. It was evident that if two people were talking outside on a windy night that no one inside of the house would hear what they were saying.

Jenni Wright took up the lead role as Wil did not seem up to talking at the moment.

"We were mingling in this room – some just sitting around and others standing near the windows – here near the bar counter" as Jenni pointed around the room.

"Maxi was a little loud and she seemed to be mumbling more than speaking properly – slurring I suppose – Pax then took her by the arm and we heard him say that they should step outside."

"You did not think it strange that he asked his wife to step outside to talk with her – as you said it was a little windy – instead of maybe walking into another room in the house." , asked Greg.

"I suppose that inside of the house might have made more sense – but Maxi was standing near the bar and Pax had walked over from near the pool table – he stood for a while next to her and maybe it just seemed the most logical thing just to step outside instead of making more of a scene in the house – but honestly I do not know."

Jenni Wright then described the events that were observed from inside of their home – the slap to Paxton's face – the gathering around Maxi and Paxton when they returned inside of the house – and Wil driving the Starrs home a short while later.

"And neither of you have any idea what might have made Mrs. Starr drink more heavily later in the evening – or what could have led to the confrontation?"

Wil spoke for the first time since his brief one-line report on Paxton's telephone call, "We've gone over the events of that evening over and over again – we just cannot think of anything that got things started. The evening was pretty standard up until then – a bunch of people that really liked one another getting together and sharing great company. We cannot think of anything that sparked off things. We're sorry, but we just do not know".

Shortly thereafter Greg and Ken thanked the Wright's for their time and left their home. As they drove off Ken asked, "What is about Maxi Starrs shawl that is bothering you?"

"I just can't put my finger on it – maybe there is nothing at all but something just seems odd – can you think of anything?"

"No, I cannot. Maybe I've just missed something completely but there is nothing that is bugging me about it."

Greg then added, "One thing we do have to check out is the financial situation of both Paxton and Maxi Starr – Mrs. Starr seemed to like spending money so maybe they were getting into serious debt – and with the downturn in the economy the property development market could have pulled the plug on Paxton's fortune – we need to check that out – and the exact terms on Mrs. Starr's last Will and Testament".

CHAPTER 28

The following morning Elizabeth was in the office even earlier than what was her norm. Today was the report back on all of the interviews contacted by the various members of Greg's team. The "D" part of Greg's DAIIPAS methodology was complete. Not that the approach is ever linear as there are always revisits to witnesses or even new witnesses added to the list – but it certainly was a milestone when all of the initial interviews were complete and a first-cut big picture can be drawn for the team.

Elizabeth had ensured that all professional staff had their notes ready. Greg could be rather unforgiving if there were major holes in the information that had been gathered.

The war room had been set up and refreshment placed at the back of the room – coffee, tea and morning snacks of healthy foods. A short "nature break" would take place about mid-morning but they would work through lunch. Elizabeth would slip in and out of the war room with the light (but again healthy) lunch without so much as anyone looking back at what she was doing. Sometimes Greg would call her into the meetings and sometimes not. This was no reflection of his lack of faith in her confidentiality but over the years there had been cases of personal assistants of leading lawyers being abducted and key information had been lost under threat of violent crimes against them. Greg kept Elizabeth out of some of the discussions to protect her.

Sometimes the meetings would be fairly brief – but still last several hours – other times the discussions went on until late in the afternoon. No matter the duration of the meeting Elizabeth managed the organization of everything required with amazing efficiency. There was no such thing as slipping out to check on emails or anything else – the Sergeant Major would make sure that it did not happen. In truth though the lawyers on Greg's team were all highly professional and they knew the standards of the law firm

183

practice. It was a privilege for them to work for the Greg Winters Law Firm.

The Agenda for the meeting was based on the DAIIPAS interview and data gathering exercises. "D" was for Discovery.

D 4 - Interviews with the group of friends
D3   - Interview with the Wright's
D8   - Interview with Abby Carmichael – added to the list
D2   - Maxi Starr
D1   - Paxton Starr

References would be made throughout the meeting to the police report (D5) and the coroner's report (D6) and other information (D7). Besides the lawyers and associates allocated to the case the Independent Safe Guard was also invited to attend the meeting.

The meeting started right on schedule – Elizabeth made sure of that.

The report back from the team on the interviews with the other neighbors on Ocean Drive tied in very closely to that obtained by Greg and Ken from Wil and Jenni Wright and that obtained by the police reports. There were no glaring contradictions at all.

It became very evident that the group on Ocean Drive were genuinely close as friends and treated each other more like family. The mutual affection was clear. The affection towards Maxi Starr and the assessment of her personality – loving, kind, genuine, full of fun, liked shopping.

Greg and Ken then reported on their interview with Abby Carmichael. Yet again the theme seemed to be one of a very much in love couple who were well liked by their inner circle and also by those that had business dealings with them. Abby's remark that Maxi Starr loved her life style and could struggle if anything happened to her and her husband's wealth was noted. Maxi Starr certainly left the impression with many people that she feared being even middle class.

Greg then raised a theme that seemed to be arising.

"Several people have said that Maxi Starr lived the good life – she could not survive as a regular person – was she or her husband in any financial difficulty?"

The associates that had dug through Mr. and Mrs. Starr's financial record took the floor.

"Mrs. Starr was founder and President of her own interior decorating business. The business has developed substantially over the last ten years in particular. The company won major bids for office parks, building developments that her husband was involved with and even for the decorating of exclusive homes across the country. Where she bid for projects that her husband was involved with Mr. Starr always excluded himself from the review process and left clear instructions that the best bid should be considered. From what we understand Mrs. Starr's business reputation and professionalism led to her winning these projects – but of course we'll never know to what extent there was nepotism involved.

Mrs. Starr had amassed many millions of dollars from her business. We know from the police reports that she left 100% of the proceeds of her Will to her husband – an estimated $41 million – a very tidy sum indeed. Her salary was $100 000 a month but she made her big money out of yearend bonus payments.

The business revenue was down approximately 30% last year as a result of the economic downturn but Mrs. Starr did not let one person go on her staff. From what we've assessed she was extremely well liked by her staff and business associates. Described as a tough-kind person – she got her projects done on time and on budget but always with a smile on her face.

185

Her finances and business ethics appear to be in order. The only beneficiary of her death is her husband."

Greg commented, "So nothing really new on the financial front although leaving your husband $41 million is a tidy sum indeed – anything about her past?"

"No criminal record – two driving offences for speeding – the first in 1997 and the second in 2006 – both times doing about 60 miles per hour in a 40 zone – no violations since 2006.

Taxes are paid on time and no infractions with the IRS. Her accountant is one of the best in her area as is her financial planner. As far as her investments are concerned there is nothing in speculation stocks – no tech stocks – investments were primarily in blue chips like IBM, Proctor and Gamble and the like. She gave generously to charities in the area where she lived.

There were a few incidents while at university but certainly nothing that any normal student would not do. Although she graduated almost thirty years ago some people still remembered her – and great memories too – very beautiful, full of fun etc – they seemed to think that she would be very successful – and she was."

"No DUI violations along the road?' asked Ken.

"No, nothing at all – only the speeding violations – she appeared clean".

Greg called the bio break that everyone was eagerly waiting for. Elizabeth was waiting to bring fresh supplies into the war room. She would have beeped Greg if he overran too late – no one else would have dared to do this but her. Before she had to beep him he announced the break.

Greg called Ken aside as the break started.

"I feel that we are getting nowhere with this – maybe that is a good thing and that the whole event was indeed a tragic drowning of an intoxicated woman. There does not appear to be much on the table right now."

"It appears to be heading that way but Paxton Starr still had the opportunity – most definitely as he was the only other person at home with his wife, as to the motive, well we still have not found a cause I suppose – and we have not as yet found a motivation."

After the bio break Greg and Ken went into the details of their extended interview with Paxton Starr – including his losing his temper with Greg when questioned repeatedly about his wife and whether she drank heavily or not. When they spoke about the story that they were told in the master bedroom of the Starr home there was utter silence in the war room. If the staff in the war room thought that the recount of the bedroom interview was sensitive then they were all taken a little aback by the genuine scene of grief that Greg and Ken had witnessed when Abby Carmichael arrived at the Starr residence.

Many questions were asked if the two lawyers had found any weaknesses in Paxton Starr's recount of the night that his wife had died. There were no doubt some rough edges to the story that they as a defense team would have to iron out with their client but in essence his story could be completely accurate. Greg mentioned that he still found it difficult to believe that one as particular as Maxi Starr would first smartly fold her shawl and put it away and then merely throw her expensive clothes on the floor – have the mental alertness to remove most of her make-up but then be sleepy enough to drown in a hot bath.

Greg was about to lead off directly from the previous point into the concerns raised by the coroner about Maxi Starr's body as found in the bath tub when Ken made a rather unusual suggestion. Greg first thought that Ken was joking but the group seemed to like the idea so Greg went along with it. Ken left the room and walked down the corridor of the suite of offices. Brittany Conrad

187

was a fairly new associate in Greg's firm. She had previously majored in Drama and Acting and spent some time on a TV series before deciding that she wanted to become a lawyer. She had accumulated a fairly large sum of money from her several seasons on the TV show and that paid for her law school studies. Brittany could act and put on accents that would amaze one – as she had done at the previous office Christmas party.

Ken knocked on Brittany's office door and walked in. They sat and spoke for about 15 minutes before Ken came out smiling. During his time away from the war room Greg had called a break in proceedings – much to the shock and agitation of Elizabeth. She had not been prepared and did not have fresh coffee or the lunch ready. Greg had to almost console with her about it. Ken returned to the war room and shared the news with the group. They sat in anticipation – having moved the chairs away from the front of the room.

They did not have to wait long.

The door opened and an apparently somewhat drunk Brittany walked into the war room with a makeshift shawl over her shoulder. She kicked the door closed with one foot – but it did not close completely just as Maxi Starr might have done on the night that she went upstairs after telling her husband that she was going to take a bath and go to bed. Brittany did not overact the part but she was amazing. The group was completely riveted by her performance.

Brittany walked into her bedroom (the war room) and stopped to steady herself up against the end of the bed (the boardroom table). She gathered herself and then walked into her dressing room. She stopped at the closet door and removed her shawl from her shoulders. When she tried to fold it fell onto the floor. She bent down and almost lost her balance in doing so. She stood up and checked her balance against the imaginary closet door. Next she walked to the end of the dressing room and proceeded to remove her dress and underwear. Brittany did an unbelievable job in

188

doing so and male eye brows were certainly raised as she stood and wiggled out of her panties. Several members of staff took very large gulps and swallowed hard. Brittany flicked her clothes away with her foot that she had just removed. She stood naked in her dressing room for a minute and wiggled her shoulders as if to wake herself up. Next she opened up another closet and seemed to be putting on a bathrobe – much to the disappointment of the male members of staff in the room. Brittany then sat down and tried to remove the make-up from her face – several times she screwed up her eyes as if she could not properly focus. She dropped the waste materials used on her face into the waste basket – some of the cotton buds missed the basket. She then stood up and walked to an imaginary door that would have led her to the bathroom. She supported herself with one hand as she opened up the faucets and ran the bath water. The male members of staff knew that she had to remove her bathrobe. They edged forward on their seats in the war room!

Brittany removed her bathrobe and carefully lowered herself into the hot water. She looked as if she relaxed (Brittany was lying on the floor in front of the war room) and she closed her eyes. She died in front of them.

Brittany sat up and smiled and then stood and took a bow. The war room then exploded with laughter and cat calls and whistling.

It took a while before any form of order could be brought to the room.

Brittany had been given the high points by Ken and she had filled in the rest. It was so life like – it could well have been just how things had happened the night that Maxi Starr had died. Greg knew that were still things that bothered him. He made a note to carefully check the photos from the bathroom – he could not recall seeing pajamas in the bathroom.

The lunch break was called and Elizabeth had recovered her composure enough to have the lunch brought in. Normally the

189

group would work through their lunch but today was different. The vivid imagines of Brittany removing her clothes and then later taking off her bathrobe would take a while to subside.

The exercise had proved to be invaluable. Ken's idea had been a stroke of genius.

Once the lunch had been brought in and fresh coffee provided the group did settle down but it still took a while to regroup.

Elizabeth could not understand what had just taken place in the war room.

"OK, with that excitement over let's try to move on" suggested Greg.

Sometimes broad smiles can take a long time to disappear.

"What were the coroner's concerns about Maxi Starr's body?"

"The coroner had several concerns.....one, that Maxi Starr had been found with her face just above the water line – to be exact just over her nose. He maintains that she would have most likely sputtered and woken up if she had slowly slipped under the water to this level...."

Greg interrupted, "But did not Paxton Starr say that he had found his wife submerged and had lifted her body out of the water when he had tried to revive her?"

"Yes, that is true but the coroner says that she died in a more upright position as there was little water in her ears... to him a sign that she could have submerged for a long time... just long enough to drown, that she was then lifted out of the water shortly after she had succumbed and then later re-submerged."

"Can he prove this conjecture?"

190

"It is a debatable point as the sequence of events might have been fairly quick. I am still reading reports on other drowning incidents and seeing what other experts have to say on the subject" said the lawyer dealing with this aspect of the case.

Greg thought for a while and then said, "Make contact with Professor McMillan in New York City. I worked with him years ago on another case but I know that he has previously been used as an expert witness in drowning cases. This could well be the crux of our case so let Ken work with you on this". It was not an offer by Greg but a statement. He had to be sure of their defense on this topic. Paxton Starr's life could depend on it.

Greg then corrected himself, "Sorry son, I cut you off in your report back - you said that the coroner had several points of concern...what were the others?"

"He was also concerned with regards to the actual position of Mrs. Starr's body. The bath in the main bedroom is 6 feet 6 inches long – most likely to accommodate Mr. Starr – the coroner believes that because the bath was non slip that Mrs. Starr would not have slipped down in the water – the weight of her body would have gripped on the surface of the bath and prevented her from sliding down too far. The coroner does not believe that she would have slipped completely under the water line with her entire body."

Greg thought that this was a very real problem for their defense. How could a small person just slide down in a non-slip bath and drown?

"Please find out the name of the manufacturer of the bath tub that is installed in the Starr's home – we need to become experts in bath technologies in a very short order of time. Do you have any other bad news from the coroner's report?"

"Well, in fact there might be – he found dried water marks under the small chair that is situated next to the bath tub. The water was not completely evaporated meaning that it had been there a short while – for instance not days but hours – he does not know how the water got there if Mrs. Starr drowned in the bath tub".

"What is he suggesting?" asked Ken with a puzzled look on his face.

Before he got an answer Greg stood up and almost ran out of the war room. He burst into Elizabeth's office and without waiting for a greeting he blurted out, "Get hold of Abby Carmichael – although the police restricted area in the main bathroom of the Starr home has been lifted please tell her not to clean the bathroom as there may be some evidence that still requires investigation". On the way out of her office Greg turned and said, "Thanks" and he was gone heading back towards the war room.

When Greg walked back into the war room he was confronted with some blank stares from his staff. "Sorry about that." he said "but it just struck me that if Abby Carmichael cleans the floor in the bathroom then we might lose some evidence – or put another way we could not counter the coroner's evidence if it had been removed. We need to try to get to those water stains if they are still there."

Greg did not know if this item from the coroner's report would be significant or not but he was rather peeved that his associate had not brought it to his attention prior to the visit to the Starr home. Not that he would have gained any conclusive opinion on the evidence but that he could have pictured the scene when he was looking into the bathroom. Now he might have to try to picture it in his head – and look much more intently at the photographs taken by the coroner's team at the scene of Maxi Starr's death. Greg would talk with the associate after the meeting had concluded.

All he said was, "Is there anything else that you'd like to tell me?"

Greg did not wait for an answer.

He was about to open up another line of report back when one of the other associates said, "Greg, we have not as yet discussed Mr. Starr's financial situation.

"Oh, right." said Greg. "Please go ahead."

There was not much to report except that Paxton Starr was the major shareholder in his group of companies and that based on the stock that he owned plus his known investments his personal worth was estimated at being around $ 125 million dollars. Greg had expected a large number but not this big. The associate confirmed that since the economic downturn that Mr. Starr's stock value had decreased by some 35% - which meant that all-in-all at one stage his asset base had been about $200 million.

So Paxton Starr had been knocked hard by the downturn but from all accounts he was still very liquid and financially very stable. Would he have murdered his wife for her estimated $ 41 million just to top up his personal reduction in wealth? It was highly unlikely. Highly, highly unlikely thought Greg to himself – but not totally out of the question. If indeed Paxton Starr had murdered his wife then there must be another reason. But it was not his job to suppose that his client might have committed the crime but rather to find him not guilty of the charges brought against him.

Greg thought aloud, "The DA believes that there was opportunity – and we cannot deny that point – was there cause – Mrs. Starr had left her husband an estimated $41 million – but that does not seem to make any sense as he was super wealthy himself – and thirdly that he had the motivation – well, I cannot see right now that he had any cause or motivation to murder his wife. No doubt there are some areas of his account of what happened that evening that do not appear to run smoothly but we can work through those with him.

Oh, by the way did we ever receive feedback from the coroner's office re the coffee mug that we found at the Starr residence?"

193

"Ah, yes, we did." answered Ken. "It was clean – only had black coffee in it just as Mr. Starr had said – and also had his and Mrs. Starr's finger prints. There was nothing suspicious at all."

"Just as we thought I suppose – still strange that no one saw the mug on the kitchen counter."

The ISG had not said a word during the entire meeting – excluding some exclamations while Brittany had performed her bath room routine. He made a bunch of notes.

Greg asked him," Do you have any observations to make thus far?"

Although his role was more procedural and looking for potential holes in their assessments and arguments he had followed the proceedings without missing a word spoken by anyone. In order for him to assess any potential trap that the team could walk into he had to be completely on top of what was going on – but not become involved in the case itself. A retired and respected lawyer like Charles Denham filled this role with tremendous professionalism. There was no doubt that he would come up with a string of items for the group to either further investigate or to ensure that they did not cross the line and impact their case building program.

The meeting lasted for about another hour or so and was brought to an end by midafternoon. A great deal of ground had been covered and progress was being made on the DAIIPAS methodology.

When Greg returned to his office Elizabeth gave him a few minutes and then she tapped on the door. Greg raised his hand for her to come in without even looking up from reading his notes. He knew that it was Elizabeth because of her little tap on his door but also by the smell of the fresh coffee – in his Giants mug.

Elizabeth placed the coffee on Greg's desk and he said thank you. He looked up and smiled at her – more like a big grin. He asked,

194

"You'd really like to know what happened in the war room earlier but you just cannot bring yourself to ask me – well, all that happened was that young Brittany came in and took her clothes off and took a bath."

Elizabeth just looked at him with an absolute dead pan face. Greg rolled back in his chair and burst out laughing. Elizabeth picked up Greg's fresh coffee and turned and walked out of his office. His laughter could be heard throughout the offices of Greg Winters law practice. It took Greg a good few minutes before he recovered – he knew that more chocolates would be required but it was worth it. He had not laughed so loud in a very long time.

Finally Elizabeth made another entrance with fresh coffee in hand. She placed the mug down, sat herself in a chair across from Greg desk, opened her note pad and started to speak. Greg had a difficult time trying to keep control. He knew that another break-out in laughter would cause him to lose his coffee rights for at least a week.

"You had several telephone calls while you were in conference. The first call was from Paxton Starr, he thought that you might like to know the final arrangements for the burial of his wife. The service is next week Thursday. I have all of the details for you – he asked if Ken would also like to attend and I will convey the message to him.

Then Dr. Mills called – you are overdue for your annual medical exam. He said that you have been putting off coming in to see him. The problem is solved – I checked your schedule and found a time slot for you to go in to see him – next Friday afternoon."

This was not a proposal put to Greg. Elizabeth had made the arrangements – an instruction – "you will see your doctor next Friday!" no questions, just a factual statement. Greg knew better than to question it – Elizabeth was paying him back for the earlier laughing incident in his office.

There were a few more items on Elizabeth's list and then she rose to leave. "Will you be having dinner this evening in the office?" She still cared for him he thought!

"No thanks, I'll be heading home at about 6 – thanks for asking."

CHAPTER 29

Paxton Starr's cell phone rang. These days he looked who was calling first before he answered the phone. The caller was Wil Wright – Paxton hesitated for a second and then decided to answer the phone.

"Hi Wil, how are you?"

"Good Pax – real good – and how are you buddy?"

It had taken some prodding by Jenni Wright to get her husband to give his best friend a call. They had only chatted briefly the day that Paxton had informed them of the arrangements for Maxi's funeral. Wil did not know what to say to his friend – it was so awkward – what does one say at times like this. Wil and Jenni had obviously been very shocked when Paxton called them in almost total hysteria after he had found his wife's body on the day that she had died. They had stood by their dear friend – and Jenni's best friend that she had ever had – but when the news broke that Paxton had been indicted for the death of his wife then they did not know how to react. They simply could not – and still did not believe that Paxton could have murdered his wife. That was simply beyond the realm of possibility. They too had read the Press and watched the TV coverage of the developing case against Paxton Starr and they could not believe that there was a possibility that he had murdered his Maxi. The whole thing just seemed to be unreal.

Jenni had finally convinced Wil that he should call Paxton – before the funeral service as she thought that they needed to bond ahead of that sad day. Wil had contended that Paxton had not called him – so maybe he just wanted to be alone. In the end Wil bent under the barrage from Jenni.

"Oh, not too bad considering that my life has been turned upside down and that my face is all over the media of America." There

197

was dryness in Paxton's voice – not dry humor but more like a dry tired sound. There was no doubt that he was taking tremendous strain.

"I cannot imagine what you must be going through." Wil did not know what to say next – what does one say?

"Listen, we know that the funeral is just a few days away but we thought that you might like to come over and have dinner with the two of us – Stacey is away with friends for a few days – so it will just be the three of us – we thought that getting together before the funeral would be great." He just left the invitation in the air and did not know what to add. With their daughter Stacey away, Paxton might feel more comfortable with just the adults around.

There was a long pause on the line. Wil could almost hear his friend thinking about the invitation.

"Gee Wil, I don't know – I am kinda down right now and I am not sure if I want to socialize."

Wil did not reply – he thought that Paxton should come to his own decision.

There was another uncomfortable silence on the line for another ten or twenty seconds and the Paxton spoke, "You know maybe it would be a good thing – thank you I'd like to come over – when did you have in mind?"

Wil was a little taken aback as he honestly did not think that his friend would accept the invitation.

"We were thinking of Monday before Stacey gets back."

"Sure – what time?"

"Should we say 7 and we'll just have a small barbeque?"

198

"Good, that will be fine – see you then."

Wil turned and looked at Jenni she was standing just behind him – she started to sob. Wil walked over and put his arms around her. All Jenni could say was, "the poor poor man." They held each other for a long time.

Paxton Starr sat and thought about the decision that he had just made. Was it the right one? He did not know. Maybe he needed to bond with his friends and receive their love and support.

He was still in deep thought when his cell phone rang again. It was Elizabeth.

"Mr. Starr this is Elizabeth McKenzie from Greg Winter's office – Mr. Winters and Ken Parker will unfortunately not be attending the funeral service for your late wife."

Paxton Starr was neither disappointed nor relieved.

"I understand." he replied. "Is Mr. Winter's available? There is something that I'd like to bring to his attention."

Elizabeth knew that Greg would take the call so she rang his number and said that Mr. Starr was on the line.

"Hello Mr. Winters – I just wanted to inform you that because of the pressures on me and with the media thing being so big that I have decided to take a Leave of Absence from my business. I need some time alone and not having to worry about things that seem unimportant right now."

"I understand Mr. Starr – we'll be in touch soon as there are several things that we need to prepare for." answered Greg.

"Sure, Mr. Winters you know where to reach me."

Greg Winters would have preferred if his client had discussed this sudden move with him first but it was too late now. He just hoped that Paxton Starr was not thinking of disappearing.

Greg had also forgotten to thank his client for allowing members of his team to visit his home and inspect the reported water stains found under the chair in the main bathroom.

CHAPTER 30

The dinner with Wil and Jenni Wright had gone reasonably well. It was awkward at times – in particular when sitting down at a table set for three. Paxton Starr could not talk about the case and the Wright's did not ask. There was more concern as to how Paxton was managing in his personal life. Even on this topic there was not a great deal of discussion. The Wright's knew that Paxton had moved out of his home but they did not press him as to when he thought that he might return.

What the evening did prove – no matter how stiff it was on occasions was that the underlying bond of friendship still existed between Paxton and Wil and Jenni. If anything the short time together was a reaffirmation of their long term relationship.

Paxton had arrived by just after 7 o'clock and bid his friends a good night by just after 9 P.M. The length of the time together seemed to suit them all – the objective had not been to spend a long evening together.

From the other homes on Ocean Drive they could see Paxton's car parked in the drive way of the Wright's home. No one thought of just popping over to say hello. They would chat with Wil and Jenni about the evening soon enough – and Paxton also knew that the telephone lines would light up just after he bade the Wright's goodnight. He was only half right as no one telephoned that night – it was as if no one wanted to intrude in what had transpired. It was only the next morning that Jenni gave the other neighbors a call and updated them.

On the Thursday all of the neighbors of Ocean Drive and their children – now mostly in their late teens or early twenty's – attended the funeral of Maxi Starr.

It was a very sad day and tears flowed as if an angel had passed away. In some respects one had. The media were kept away from the Service and the private burial but a helicopter hovered around like a bee near a honey pot. They seemed to have no respect or comprehension of what was really happening – the final saying goodbye to someone so loved.

Greg and Ken and some other members of the staff watched part of the TV coverage but most walked away as they felt as if they too were participating for the wrong reason. Greg noted from the coverage that all of the neighbors of Ocean Drive could be seen at the service.

The church service was well attended. Family members, friends and business associates and clients of Maxi Helen Starr filled the chapel. At the end of the service just as the attendees were about to leave the silence in the chapel was broken by a single voice. A beautiful voice spread across the chapel and everyone just stopped and sat down again. The voice was so pure, so compassionate and so very soulful. Abby Carmichael had stood up and started to sing – it had not been planned – she just decided to do it. It was the voice of an angel saying her goodbye to another angel. When Abby had finished her song and sat down again there was not a dry eye to be seen.

At the private burial Paxton Starr stood next to Abby Carmichael.

CHAPTER 31

The date for the grand jury had been set.

Greg and Ken felt that they had an outside chance of the two charges brought against their client to be thrown out – the likelihood was however that the grand jury would recommend that the case go to trial.

Greg's team had met several times with Paxton Starr and had prepared him for the proceedings that lay ahead of them. After one of these meetings Greg had planned to head out to his cabin for the weekend but first he had to meet with his client. Unfortunately the meeting had been set for a Friday morning and this had annoyed Greg because Paxton Starr had already postponed the meeting twice because of ill health. In truth Greg should not have been annoyed as it seemed that half of San Francisco had been struck down by some kind of stomach virus. Paxton Starr was one of those that had been laid low. Greg knew that the Friday meeting reduced his time away but work had to come first.

At the meeting Paxton seemed to get the feeling that Greg was more rushed than normal.

"You seem distracted Mr. Winters! Any big plans for the weekend?"

"My apologies – I had planned to go up to my cabin this weekend – needed some downtime."

"Where is your place?" asked Paxton.

"I have a cabin out near Alpine Meadows in Nevada."

"Oh, I know the area – not too well but we did a property development near there some years ago – whereabouts is your cabin?"

"A few miles before town there is a railroad crossing – about two miles passed that there is a sign "Private Road" that turns off and leads up to my cabin. It is a paved road for the first ¼ mile and then a dirt road straight up to the cabin."

"Been up there long?"

Greg was sure that his client was asking questions just to drag out the time. Could he not tell that I am in a hurry to get away Greg thought – but I can't be rude to my client!

"I built the cabin with my late wife – that is where she is buried – on the property of the cabin. That is where I will retire one day."

Finally Greg concluded his meeting with Paxton Starr and he raced back to his SUV. Removed his suit jacket and his tie – tossed them on the back seat and off he went.

His little oasis awaited him.

He just had two nights to relax so he had no time to get together with the town sheriff for a coffee.

CHAPTER 32

The grand jury hearing was almost a non-event right from the beginning. It was very evident that the "forces" were against them and that the recommendation would be that they would go to trial. Greg had argued relentlessly for his client but the decision was clear cut. Paxton Starr would be indicted to stand trial for Second Degree murder and for Criminal Negligence for the death of his wife. There came a point in the hearing that Greg Winters decided to change tactics and allow the proceedings to move against him Pushing too hard now when the odds were against you could only lead to further troubles down the road.

The media were particularly pleased with the decision of the grand jury. There was a distinct air about that the tide was against Paxton Starr. The TV stations and the printed Press had a field day when the grand jury decision came down. Greg felt particularly bad for his client. Somehow he got the feeling that Paxton Starr had expected to be a free man after the grand jury – this in spite of Greg's warning to the contrary. Mr. Starr seemed to take the decision very badly.

Paxton Starr had been away from his position at his company for about two months now – and he had to make a decision of if and when he would return to his office. He had also not returned to life in his home and that was another decision that he had to consider – to return or not. The home was safe and Abby was keeping it clean – but a home needed to be lived in – even more so such a beautiful home. Maybe now it was only a house and not a home. How could he live there alone – and be so lonely?

He had attended two small dinners with Wil and Jenni Wright but as yet he had not returned to the monthly neighbor gatherings. He had been invited – although he knew that he did not require an invitation – but he could not bring himself to mingle even with his close friends. What did they really think about him? Was he indeed a wife-killer? Did they think that he was innocent and that it had all been a tragic string of events that lead to Maxi Starr drowning that night? There was too much sensitivity for him to consider attending the social events. The evenings with Wil and Jenni had been pleasant but both were short and stiff. He knew that they had great affection for him so he accepted their invitations but in reality he had not wanted to attend.

Abby Carmichael still worked at the house three days a week. She enjoyed being in the home but was very sad at not having Maxi around. The days were very long but she tried to keep herself busy – but it is difficult to clean and tidy a room that is still clean and tidy from the last time you were there. She had thought of quitting her job but each time that she thought of contacting Paxton Starr she thought that he might need her when he returned. There was no doubt in her mind that Mr. Starr would be found NOT GUILTY of the charges brought against him. Anyone who had seen Maxi and Paxton Starr together would have felt the love that they had for one another. Abby made up her mind that she would stay in Paxton Starr's employ until after the trial.

After the grand jury decision Greg made time available in his schedule and took an entire week off. He headed out to the cabin and did the normal things. He stopped in at the store just before the turnoff to his cabin and chatted with the owner. He also found the time to say hello to "Chubby" – the middle-aged man who pumped the gas. Chubby had some mental challenges but he loved his job at pumping gas – he had not missed a day of work since he walked into the store one day and said that he wanted to do the job. The sign outside had said "Apply Within" and there he was. Chubby knew every make of car that stopped for gas and who drove them – he mostly likely also knew the license plate of every car too! Greg had always allowed Chubby to fill up his SUV and clean the windshield. Chubby had no idea what Greg did for a living – he just wanted to help and be friendly.

Greg spent the nights at the cabin but on this trip he did some day adventures into some of the small nearby towns. Some he had visited before but others were new to him.

He could feel Mary on his arm as he walked through the beautiful streets and looked on the quaint shop fronts. He treated himself to pancakes and ice cream and hamburgers for lunch – and Elizabeth would never know! Knowing his luck he would walk into his office and Elizabeth would say that he had gained weight and say, "Eating junk food again?" He would feel uncomfortable for days from the variety of foods that he had but he knew that after several days in the office with the health foods put in front of him he would soon recover.

Greg also gave some thought to his future. He so wanted to be with his Mary.

He had to think through his responsibilities to his staff before he made any rash decisions.

In the legal world one must be ready for surprises – and Greg had his share over the years – but not like the ones that he was to have within the next few weeks.

CHAPTER 33

It would soon be an election year. The next year there were certain to be changes in the District Attorney's Office or even with some of the judges. It was likely that the Governor would lose the election due to the impact of scandals within the administration and the appalling state of the economy. But no matter how bad things were an election could still be won based on some good news – particularly news that sat well with the public opinion. All it took sometimes was a small kick to increase the poll numbers to the extent that the election would again be too close to call. Winning a major case in the court of public opinion was one such way of turning the tide. The DA was encouraged to bring forward the Paxton Starr murder trial in order to help build up momentum at the polls.

It was normal that a high profile murder trial could take up to a year or more to reach the courts. Sometimes there was just too much of a time lapse to keep interest in the developing scenario going and as a result the media circus would move onto other "catch of the day" stories. It had also happened before that when the trial did come before a judge and jury other news items stole away the interest completely. The media fed on news and not on old or previously hashed out story-lines. The new Media Relations Consultant for the "powers that be" convinced those responsible to push up the trial of Paxton Starr – to keep it in the public eye and to win over potential female voters. The trial would be an important legal event but more importantly it would be a public relations triumph.

During this time Paxton Starr had decided to return as President of his business and had even decided to move back into his home on Ocean Drive. He still maintained a 24-hour security detail of the property but he had decided that it was time to move back home. He did however not take up residence in the master bedroom but rather in the large bedroom on the other side of the upstairs of the house. If – as expected the trial would be some time in the New

209

Year then he had eight or twelve months until the proceedings commenced. He may as well live at home and in comfort than in a furnished apartment.

He would still not see much of Abby – except that she cooked for him on a Monday evening and left the warm food for him. Once or twice he would arrive home before she left in the early evening. Their greetings were always warm and friendly but Paxton never knew how Abby felt about him. He sensed that the love that they had built up for each other over the years was still there but somehow it seemed to be different. How could it be the same without Maxi being around the house or with he being the accused in her murder?

He had tried to become very realistic about his relationships with those that he worked with and even with his clients. It was very difficult for everyone around him. The invitation to cocktail parties – that Maxi enjoyed so much – had dried up. There were no invitations from business associates to attend baseball games. He was in a new reality and it was uncomfortable. He often thought of what life would be like after the trial – he was sure that Greg Winters was the best in the business and that he would do everything to have his client found not guilty of the murder of his wife. But what would it be like if he was indeed found not guilty – would the invitations to functions come back? Would he simply return to the monthly gathering with his neighbors? What would life be like after the trial and how would he be permanently viewed by some as a wife killer?

He also had not seen much of his friends – but at least he was home now and there were many months ahead before the heat of the trial could further strain relationships again.

He did have one very narrow escape. A senseless decision could well have cost him greatly in the eyes of the law. The terms of his bond were that he could not leave the state of California without the preapproved consent of the district attorney. Up until the time of the near incident he had no reason to leave the state. His

210

development company had a project in Reno and there were problems with the local authorities with the building permits. This was a common practice when delaying tactics required "sweeteners" for the officials to push ahead with the project. Paxton suggested that he and members of his team should drive to Reno for a meeting with the local officials. On the day in question a group of four from his office set off for a day in Reno. The drive was very pleasant and the company in the car was relaxed and Paxton felt completely at ease with his colleagues. Just as they were about to cross into the state of Nevada there was a very large billboard welcoming visitors, "Nevada border 1 mile". There was laughter in the car as the men became excited about visiting the town of Reno. Suddenly Paxton yelled out, "Stop the car! Stop the car now!" The driver pulled over to the side of the road in a full dust cloud and the car came to a screaming halt. It stopped about 50 yards from the Nevada border. If Paxton had left the state of California without the written approval of the DA he could have been arrested and who know what charges could have been leveled against him! It was a very narrow call – just 50 yards and a hell-storm could have broken around his head.

They drove back to the nearest town and Paxton hired a car and drove back to San Francisco alone with his heart still thumping in his chest.

It was early in the following week that Greg received a telephone call from the DA's Office asking him to attend a meeting the next morning. He honestly thought that there would be some discussion about the upcoming trial set to possibly take place in the New Year. He was kept waiting by the DA for almost an hour which annoyed him intensely. Finally when he went in he was politely greeted and asked to take a seat.

The DA went straight to the point.

"Mr. Winters the trial date for the Paxton Starr case has been set. The trial will commence on November 4th and will last for five

211

weeks. The trial Judge will be Rita Marx and the Prosecutor Juanita Lange."

Greg sat in a state of complete shock.

"Mr. Winters?"

Greg had to regroup very quickly.

"But that is less than two months away – we cannot prepare our case by then – it is not enough time."

"Well enough time or not that is when proceedings will commence. That is the decision Mr. Winters."

Greg tried to protest again but the DA just lifted his hand and shook his head. He absolutely enjoyed seeing Greg in a state of shock.

"You have worked with Judge Rita Marx before and you know that she runs a tight no-nonsense court – so you had better bear that in mind in preparing you case. The prosecutor might be new to you – Juanita Lange – do not underestimate her." The DA was still smiling!

Greg had no choice but to work within the system but as he left the DA's Office he felt that the chips were definitely staking up against him. Once he reached his car he telephoned Ken and broke the news to him. An unrepeatable exclamation boomed back down the line! They had less than two months to build their strategy and prepare their client.

Later that day Greg telephoned Paxton Starr and broke the news to him. The same non repeatable word boomed down the telephone line.

CHAPTER 34

The announcement of the date of the trial was the first piece of unexpected news that Greg would receive. The second piece of information was still to come.

To say that Greg's team went into overdrive would be an understatement.

The DAIIPAS methodology was reviewed and any missing pieces of information plugged in. Besides preparing the strategy for the trial the team had to prepare their client. Paxton Starr had only recently reassumed the position of President and Chief Executive Officer of his company when the news broke about the trial date. He had wanted to stay on running the business but finally Greg had convinced him to relinquish the positions again. Greg's argument was "Your entire future is on the line – you need to choose between being a free man and on the other hand possibly spending the rest of your life behind bars – your choice!" The argument was simple and Paxton had agreed.

Mr. Starr had only just returned to his home on Ocean Drive and the question arose if he should stay on at his home or move to a place that was more secluded. This decision was even more difficult than that of relinquishing his position at his company. He had started to feel more comfortable in his own environment and he felt that he could not move into a furnished apartment and be bound-in by glass windows. Greg and Paxton met with the security company that was guarding the home and it was decided to significantly increase the guarding at the home. A more drastic step involved Paxton, Greg and Ken meeting with all of the neighbors of Ocean Drive and requesting their permission to have guards blocking the entrance of the Drive and so keeping the TV stations from entering their secluded road. Greg had to meet with the local town authorities to approve this proposal and it was accepted. In reality though the hungry media circus found their way through the forest beyond Paxton Starr's home and set up a

213

site between the home and the forest. The security company assigned another ten guards to protect the home. The media circus was gaining momentum and the DA's Office was overjoyed.

All vacation time at Greg's law firm was cancelled and he even found this to be a burden. He had planned to spend some time at his cabin and prepare it for the winter but that would have to wait. He thought that he might try to slip away from the city on a Saturday morning and return by the Sunday evening but he would have to see how things worked out. He was also sensitive to the fact that if he slipped away then what was the signal that he sent to his staff? He purged the thought of going away from his mind.

The second piece of information was about to surprise Greg.

Greg was working in his office with the door shut when Elizabeth tapped and walked in. Greg knew that it must be something important as he had asked to be left alone in his thoughts on the case. He looked up over his bi-focal glasses.

"Sorry to worry you but Ken and Charles would like to see you rather urgently".

Greg just nodded his head. By the time he had taken off his glasses the two men had walked into his office. Elizabeth closed the door as she walked out.

"So, what's up that you have to spoil my afternoon nap?" asked Greg.

"Sorry Greg, but Charles has just brought something to my attention that seems to be important."

Greg stood up from his desk and walked over to the conference table. He motioned for the two men to take a seat. He said, "So what is so important?"

Ken looked at Charles and prompted him to speak.

214

"Greg, I was checking the files on the case and making sure that we have everything at hand – well, the strangest thing is that when the police took statements from the people who were at the home of the Wright's on the night that Mrs. Starr died they took 14 statements – that is what is on file – 14 statements – but on the night of the party there were actually 16 people there."

"Charles, what do you mean? 16 people were at the party but only 14 statements taken – surely there must be a mistake – are some statements missing?"

"No, I have checked - according to the witness information there were 16 people at the home for the party – two from house 1, two from house 2, four from house 3, two from house 4 and four from house 5 and two from house 6 – which was the Starr home – but of course with Mrs. Starr having died the night before only Mr. Starr provided a statement. The difference in the numbers is from the Wright home – according to Wil and Jenni Wright it was the two of them plus their 18 year-old daughter Stacey and her boyfriend – a boy from the next road up – but from what the police took down there was no statements taken from either Stacey Wright or the boyfriend Chad Beyers."

"Are you absolutely sure of this?"

"No doubt these kids were never asked for statements".

"Now there is an interesting piece of information." exclaimed Greg.

"Do you have any ideas why they were overlooked for statements?"

"Well" said Ken "we discussed some possibilities before we came through to you – one reason could be that although they were there at the beginning of the party that sometime during the evening they left the party – and maybe out-of-sight-out-of-mind

215

and everyone just forgot that they were indeed there – a second option is that they might have chosen not to give statements by maybe saying that they were not at the house later in the evening."

"And why would they try to avoid having to give statements?"

"Maybe they heard or saw something and thought better just to say that they were not at the house".

"That is a long shot – a long shot indeed but it could be possible I suppose."

At that moment Greg and Ken locked eyes. The identical thought had just passed through both of their minds. Greg blurted out, "They might have heard something – they could have been outside when Paxton and Maxi Starr were having their private discussion – the discussion that no one in the house could hear but there were two people outside of the house – holy crap – do you know what this could mean if this assumption is correct? We could have witnesses to what really happened outside that evening. This could reshape our entire argument for the case. Holy crap!"

Greg walked – actually almost ran – with Ken and Charles back to the office where the discovery had been made. Greg checked all of the records and statements taken down by the police and indeed there where two people unaccounted for – Stacey and Chad. Greg repeated his unholy utterance over and over again. This could turn the entire case on its head.

"OK, this needs to be held in total – in absolute confidence – at this point is it just the three of us that know about this?" The other two men nodded. "Right, then that is the way that it is going to stay until we get to interview young Stacey Wright and her boyfriend. Is she away at school or at home?" asked Greg.

"I will make some discreet enquires and then we can plan our next steps." said Ken.

216

Greg wondered if the Wright's were purposely withholding information that their daughter might have. Why had they not mentioned that Stacey had been at the party with her boyfriend? Was there anything at all behind Stacey and Chad not coming forward with some item of information? Maybe it was all just an omission and there was nothing sinister – but it certainly was unusual – and for the police to have missed it.

Greg wanted to keep his enquiry very discreet so not to alert the prosecutor. There was no need to unleash some potential damaging piece of evidence for the prosecutor to jump all over. Greg decided not to approach Wil or Jenni Wright directly about contacting Stacey. If there was a cover up then they could alert her and any potential evidence could be compromised. He certainly hoped that it had just been an oversight by the police.

"The Solar Murder"

CHAPTER 35

Stacey Wright had graduated high school just a few weeks before the death of Maxi Starr. She had grown up with "Uncle Pax" and "Aunt Max" around her. As far back as she could remember they had been neighbors – best friends to her parents and like her second parents. Paxton and Maxi treated her and Ryan just like their own children. They had spent the most wonderful of times with the neighborhood family on Ocean Drive and it was like their own private happy and safe part of the world. They had spectacular homes, great people living in them and the ocean right on their doorstep. What could be better in life?

Their monthly gatherings were more like a family get together. The atmosphere was inclusive and as young kids there were always games to play – adults to tease them and run around and chase after them – and a variety of bedrooms to fall asleep in. The New Year's Eve party was extra special with fireworks being sent up into the air from the beach – and singing next to the large campfire.

As the young kids grew older they sometimes missed the monthly gathering but they knew that they were always welcome. It was also a great place to bring a friend – male or female – as they were welcomed and made to feel at home.

Things were so much fun when Ryan had still been with them. He was a great big brother and all of Stacey's friends were in love with him. No wonder as he was so tall and powerfully built for his age. Then Ryan ran away and had never contacted his parents once since he just took off. He had changed in the months leading up to his running away – but Stacey could never bring herself to accept that he would not contact her one day. He never even said goodbye to her.

Stacey could almost select which university she would attend after graduating high school but instead she decided to take a year off and do some travelling. She had been to Europe several times with her parents but she was desperate to explore Greece and the Middle East by herself before she settled into university life. She wanted to take Ancient History as her major and could picture herself exploring ancient historical sites after she had graduated. Maybe playing in the sand on the beach in the front of her home had made an impression on her!

She had found a part-time job at a coffee shop fairly near where she lived. Three days during the week from 9 A.M. to 4 P.M. and from 8 to 3 on Saturdays was about as much as what she could handle. The money was not the issue it was more to have something to do during the day. Besides, Chad's Mom owned the chain of coffee shops – so the young man in her life was around most of the time!

Greg had made some discreet enquires as where to find Stacey and he thought that approaching her as she left the coffee shop and having a private conversation with her – and hopefully with Chad would be the best approach. Greg had used an old friend and a very confidential Private Detective to trace Stacey and where she could best be contacted. To Greg's delight he was informed that young Chad would drive Stacey to work in the mornings and fetch her in the afternoons. Hopefully if this practice was used on the day that Greg planned to catch up with the teenagers that he could interview them together. There would be no opportunity for the one to tip off the other before a second meeting could be arranged. On the day that he and Ken had decided to try to catch up with her Ken called in sick so Greg had to investigate the matter himself. In a way he preferred to do this one himself.

Greg did not wish to bring unnecessary attention to the planned meeting with Stacey but at the same time he did not wish for it to be taking place in a clandestine manner. He did not know if any new information would be forthcoming but he had to be careful. Upsetting his strategy now in the case could cost his firm countless hours of rework. And time was not their friend on this case.

220

Greg parked his SUV near the entrance of the coffee shop just on 4 P.M. and waited for Stacey to come out. Just before 4 P.M. a young man pulled up in a car and walked into the coffee shop. Greg hoped that it was Chad. A few minutes later Greg stepped out of his SUV to position himself near Chad's car – he had hardly taken up his position when Stacey and Chad walked out of the coffee shop.

Greg had to act fast while not appearing to be too assertive of intrusive.

"Hello, Stacey." he said. Stacey Wright was surprised to be greeted by a stranger.

"Hello", she said and started to walk by Greg.

"Stacey, sorry to intrude but my name is Greg Winters I am the lawyer in the Maxi Starr trial – would you mind if I ask you a few questions?"

Stacey was taken aback and seemed unsure what to say. Chad replied, "Should you not be talking with Stacey's parents?"

Greg could not afford to lose the chance of speaking with the young people who seemed to sense some danger or reluctance to speak with Greg.

"I would really appreciate a few minutes. This is not a police interview or a statement – just a few facts for the case that I would like to check out – it will only take a few minutes." Greg hoped that he would get a positive response but he was not sure. He held his breath waiting for Stacey's reply.

"Do you have any ID – how do I know who you are?"

"Sure do." said Greg only too keen to keep the conversation going. He opened up his wallet and handed his Driver's License and a Business Card to Stacey. The two teens looked at Greg's

221

identification and handed it back to him. Greg sensed that Chad would have preferred if Stacey decided not to be interviewed by Greg.

"Are you Chad?" asked Greg and put out his hand to greet the young man.

"Yes." answered the teen. "How do you know my name?"

"Well, I am a lawyer and I do know that you are Stacey's boyfriend so I assumed that you were Chad" answered Greg. He added, "Chad, I would appreciate it if you could join us for a few minutes while we chat – I just need to verify some details of what took place at Stacey's parents' house on the night that Maxi Starr passed away – I know that you were both at the party that night but there is no police statements from you – so I need to go over some details – it would really help my case a great deal if you would chat with me."

To his surprise Stacey answered, "Sure, Mr. Winters where would you like to talk?"

"I see that there is a park just across the street how about we sit under a tree on a bench and chat there?"

The three of them crossed the street and found a half-clean bench to sit on.

"What would you like to know Mr. Winters?" asked Stacey.

"Could you just take your time and tell me what events took place that evening – I'll interrupt you if I need to but I'll try not to appear rude in doing so." Greg smiled. He did not mention any potential consequences of not being interviewed by the police. He would leave that as an oversight by those concerned for the time being.

"OK, I'll try." said Stacey

"As you might know the neighbors on Ocean Drive get together once a month on a Saturday for dinner and to have some fun. This "Gathering" as it is called has been taking place since before I was born. Each neighbor takes a turn in hosting the evening. On that night it was our turn to host the evening. If I recall everyone that could be there was in attendance that evening. Chad was with me as we were allowed to bring friends."

Greg nodded that he understood and he waited for Stacey to continue.

"Normally everyone arrives by about 7 P.M.– most people walk to the home where the party is - depending on the weather – I think that everyone did walk that night –" Greg did interrupt, "And nothing seemed out of place or unusual?"

"No, everything was pretty much the same as usual. People would have a drink or some refreshments and just mingle for a while – there was no tension or anything."

"And Mrs. Starr, did she seem in good sprites?" (Greg thought that it was a poor chose of words but he could not correct himself – that would have been like coming straight out and asking if Maxi Starr was becoming intoxicated.)

"Oh, Aunty Max was always full of fun – she had the widest smile and loudest laugh of anyone at our party's – she was the best person to be around. And no, she seemed absolutely fine – mixing with the ladies and being her normal super friendly self.

A little later my Dad started the barbeque outside – the men usually chat together in a group – just as the ladies do too I suppose. The evening just seemed like any other – some of the Dad's played pool inside while the dinner was being prepared – yeah, nothing weird at all." Chad nodded in agreement.

"Chad, I take it that you've been to these gatherings before?"

223

"Yes Sir, I've attended many of these party's before – maybe twenty or so – since I've known Stacey – they are great – good people, real good people."

"In the different homes then?" asked Greg.

"Yes Sir, in all of the different homes."

Greg asked Stacey to continue her description of what happened the night that Maxi Starr slapped her husband.

"Well, dinner was then served – the food was all put out in the front living room and everyone helped themselves and took a seat where ever they wanted. If the weather was good then sometimes we'd sit outside at the homes – everything was just so relaxed. On the night of our party it was windy out so everyone sat inside."

Greg interrupted again (an occupational habit!)

"How windy was it that night?"

"Not real bad – no storm or anything like that just enough to be unpleasant that's all."

Greg again nodded for Stacey to continue.

"After dinner we sat around chatting and some of the wives and husbands played pool – some played darts too if I recall – then Chad and I left the house."

"You left the party?" Greg asked with some surprise.

"Yes Sir, Chad and I left the house – we went down to the beach."

"Did anyone see you leave the house – did you go through the sliding doors?"

There was a slight hesitation before Stacey answered Greg's question.

"No, we left through the front door – I told my parents that we were walking up to Chad's house for a while."

"So as far as your parents were concerned you had left the party."

"Yes"

So that is why Wil and Jenni Wright did not think of mentioning to the police that Stacey and Chad were at the party when the incident between Paxton and Maxi Starr took place. The police must have asked who was at the house at the time of the incident and of course the two teens had already left the home by then.

"About what time did you leave the house?"

The two teens looked at other and then agreed that it had been about 10 30 P.M. – well before the incident occurred.

Greg could have left the subject there but what Stacey then said almost made him fall off of the bench that he was sitting on.

"Mr. Winters we did not go to Chad's house – we walked around my house to the beach in front of our home".

Being an adult Greg now expected what had taken place but he was further surprised with what Stacey said – and he was surprised that she even mentioned it.

"We lay on the beach for a while and looked up at the stars. We loved doing that together. Then we walked up from the beach towards the house – we slipped into the Changing room next to the swimming pool."

Stacey paused.

"It was then that we heard voices – we peeked out of the window of the changing room and Uncle Pax and Aunty Max were standing on the patio."

Greg's hand started shaking with excitement – there had been witnesses to the private discussion held between Paxton and Maxi Starr – Paxton had walked his wife outside so that they could not be over heard by their friends – but he would never have thought that Stacey and Chad were outside in the Changing room. He was not sure if he had just hit the Jackpot or would it prove to be the big breaker of his case for Paxton Starr.

"Why did you not come out of the Changing room?" he asked.

Another long pause before Stacey answered his question.

"Sir, we were naked."

"Oh, right – that would not have been a good idea." said Greg with a mixture of embarrassment for having asked the question in the first place and inward joy at young love.

"Besides." said Stacey, "they were already talking or arguing so we just sat still so that we could not be heard."

"I would have done the same." commented Greg with a smile. For the first time the three of them smiled together.

After a short time Greg then pressed Stacey, "Did you perhaps over hear what Mr. and Mrs. Starr were discussing?"

"We caught every other word because it was windy outside – the wind had really come up stronger just then – but Uncle Pax seemed to say "Max what's up, Max what's up?" Aunty Max looked pale and – and kinda limp – he was holding her by the upper arms – she said something but it seemed as if he could not hear her – he asked again, "What's up – why have you been drinking so much?"

226

"Are you sure about this – that is what he said?"

"Yes, Sir – we could hear him fairly clearly but Aunty Max –well she seemed to be pretty out of it – you could see that she had to be held up."

"How far away from them were you in the Changing room - and how come you could hear with the door shut – I assume that the door was shut!" Greg smiled.

Chad answered that question. "We were maybe 15-18 feet from them. Yes, the door was shut but the change room window was open and we had crept up to just under the window – and we could see out from where we were."

"So you were close enough to hear the conversation – or part of the conversation – but you could not be seen at all – right?"

"Yes Sir." answered Stacey

"Uncle Pax was fairly clear but Aunty Max – well, she seemed to slur more than talk."

Maybe Paxton Starr had been telling the truth all along and that he had taken his wife outside to have a private conversation and to ask her why she had been drinking heavily that evening – maybe she had been very emotional and had slapped him out of frustration and not through anger – Greg's mind was racing all over the place.

"Please go on." he asked Stacey.

"Uncle Pax asked her several times what was the matter – he seemed calm and trying to help her – she then started to say something – and Uncle Pax said "What? I can't understand you – speak slowly" - she tried again but the words seemed to sound funny."

"What did it sound like?" asked Greg.

The two teens looked at each other and prompted each other what the words sounded like that Maxi Starr was trying to say.

"Sir, it sounded real strange – it did not seem to make any sense to Uncle Pax – and less so to us – but it sounded as if she was saying "Kind I Denver, Please, Please - kind I Denver Please! Please!"

Greg repeated it, "Kind I Denver please please" – do you know what she was trying to say?"

"No sir, we thought about it later on but we have no idea what it was supposed to have meant."

Greg took out his note pad for the first time – he had not wanted to scare off the two teens by taking notes of what they were saying.

"Could you please write down what it sounded like to you?"

Stacey took the pad and wrote down in big letters "KIND I DENVER PLEASE PLEASE - KIND I DENVER PLEASE PLEASE." She handed the note pad back to Greg.

"What happened next?" Greg asked.

"Auntie Max repeated what she was trying to say and then Uncle Pax said "No, no Max, no" she raised her voice and repeated what she was trying to say and he said "no, no" again – and then boom she slapped him. We saw it and it sounded like a massive crack – she laid one on him that must have hurt them both."

"You do not know why he said "No, No, Max no" – any ideas?"

"No Sir – none at all."

"And then what happened?"

228

"Uncle Pax held her in his arms and put his arms around her – he held her so gently – I started to cry and was afraid that he would hear me – Chad held me tight so that I would not shake – we were still naked and I was now so cold." Even now Stacey started to cry again and Chad put his arm around her shoulders.

"Uncle Pax then led her towards the sliding doors – we could see that most of the people inside of the house had gathered at the door – they went inside and slid the door closed. I completely broke down and cried. We then got dressed and checked that no one was watching and we slid out of the change room. We walked up to Chad's house and we just sat together in the Den of his home – I could not believe what we had witnessed – they loved each other so much and she hit him – she slapped him so hard! About 2 o'clock in the morning Chad walked me home and I went to bed."

"Your parents were asleep when you got home?"

"Yes – I went straight to bed."

"And what happened the next morning? Did you tell your parents what you had seen?"

"No, we discussed it the night before and decided not to say anything – my parents do not know that I am sleeping with Chad and they would have wanted to know what we were doing outside in the change room".

"Even after you heard what had happened to Mrs. Starr you still said nothing?"

"No sir – the next morning I was still sleeping when my Mom ran into my bedroom and told me that Aunty Max was dead – I did not think of the night before at first as it was such a shock that she had died – I telephoned Chad and we thought that she must have drowned because she had too much to drink – but we decided not to say anything – Mr. Winters are we in trouble?"

"I am not sure – I am unsure if this information is important or not – I will have to think about it – my job is to defend Mr. Starr and I will have to assess if this information is material or not – but I will try my best to protect you – you did trust me in sharing the information and I will do my best to keep you out of the trial." Greg knew that he was lying – this information was material – but he did not know which way.

Greg thanked Stacey and Chad for their time and they walked back across the street together. Greg's SUV was parked just across the street and he was just about to say goodbye to them when Stacey said, "Aunty Max was such a beautiful and kind person – she genuinely loved me and my brother Ryan – they both treated us like their own children – I sat next to Aunty Max when we had dinner the night that she died – just as we were finishing dinner I mentioned to her that today – the night of the party at our house - Ryan would have turned 21."

Greg stopped dead in his tracks.

"Oh, and what did Mrs. Starr say when you told her this piece of news?" asked Greg.

"Nothing – she did not reply."

CHAPTER 36

Greg's mind was in turmoil. He knew that some potential "unknowns" on the case could well be crystallizing into facts – but as yet he could not link the emerging dots. He knew that the information gleaned from Stacey Wright and Chad could have a substantial impact on the case – and even completely undermine the strategy that was being worked on by his team. He had always thought that something must have happened at the party on the night that Maxi Starr died – and although he now thought that he had a link – he did not know what it meant.

When he drove away from the meeting with the two teens all he wanted to do was to sit and think and he could not think while driving – although he had done that too - all too often before. He telephoned Elizabeth and told her that he would be heading directly home. She enquired if he was feeling unwell and he said that he was fine – he just needed to think. Elizabeth informed him that Ken would not be in the following day as he was still ill. Greg made the decision not to go into the office either the next day. Elizabeth was surprised by his decision – something must be up she thought. Her final words to him on the telephone call were "Call me if you need anything."

Greg drove directly home and for the next thirty six hours he lived in a world of his own. Dressed in sweat pants and a pull-over and wearing his favorite slippers he buried himself into the story that was evolving in his mind. Unfortunately he did not have his favorite Giants coffee mug at home with him – or for that matter Elizabeth to bring him fresh coffee or to remind him to eat. Thank goodness for "order in" dinners!

His mind went back to the beginning of the evening that Maxi Starr died. The Starr's had not had an argument or disagreement before they left for the party. Their behavior at the party was completely normal – so even if they had indeed had some falling out beforehand (which was doubtful) there was no evidence of it at the party. Their drinking habits appeared to be normal – her more than him but nothing unusual – before dinner anyway. Then her behavior changed. No one knew why – but they all noticed it. Stacey had mentioned that her brother Ryan would have turned 21 that night. Had that set her off? Why? There was no doubt that the Starr's loved both Ryan and Stacey Wright – like their own children. Was it the news of this milestone birthday that upset Maxi Starr and possibly made her feel morbid? If it was such a big event then why did Jenni or Wil Wright not mention it openly to their guests? Maybe they did not want to unsettle the party? Only they would know why they had not mentioned it to their guests – who were like family to them!

Whatever the trigger was – and assuming that it could have been the news about Ryan's birthday - then why did Maxi Starr not tell her husband the news? Or did he know anyway and decided not to upset his wife by reminding her.   Why would she get so emotional about the news and not tell Paxton Starr?

What was really said outside on the patio? What did "Kind I Denver Please Please" mean? What was Maxi Starr trying to say? According to Stacey and Chad Maxi Starr was slurring – so no doubt – but unproved (except for the coroner's report that she was well over the legal alcohol limit) that she had been drinking heavily after dinner.

Why had Paxton Starr not mentioned this to Greg and Ken when they interviewed him? Was it an oversight or was it intentional? Did Paxton believe that no one heard the private conversation with his wife and therefore there would be no disproving his version of what was said? What would his client do to Stacey if her evidence should perhaps lead to a guilty verdict at the trial? Would he seek revenge from behind bars? Would he do anything if he found out that Stacey provided evidence and he was then found not guilty – would he still possibly seek her out for revenge for trying to pin something on him?

Greg tried to convince himself that Paxton Starr loved Stacey Wright as if she were his own daughter and that he would never harm her just as he had loved Ryan and would not have harmed him. Greg could only imagine the love that Paxton and Maxi Starr had for Ryan and Stacey – he had never been in that position in his life – after Mary died he had not found the love of children as the Starr's had. They never knew how lucky they were to have such a close group of friends and young adults in their lives. He had never known that feeling.

Then there was the issue if what – if anything – he was going to tell Ken. Of all of the lawyers that Greg worked with over the years Ken was one of the very best. Not only that he was a colleague in a firm of defense council lawyers – how could he withhold any information from Ken. But what if the information became public knowledge and Stacey and Chad were then placed in the spot light of the trial. Greg was determined that this would not happen.

Greg did not sleep at all the first night at home. He joked with himself that his brain was too full and that he was in an overload situation. He kept telling himself that he was a defense lawyer and that he should not do anything that could incriminate his client or lead to a guilty verdict in the court. He finally fell asleep at about 5 o'clock in the morning. When he awoke at just after 9 his brain was still full. Not even a long hot shower and an enormous breakfast could loosen the jammed thoughts in his mind. The one thing that he had decided upon was that he had to tell Ken everything.

CHAPTER 37

When Ken returned to the office two days later he had still not recovered from the stomach flu that he had so bravely endured for 48 hours. The dreaded bug had taken his whole family down and it had not been easy caring for the kids and his wife while he felt so ill. Nevertheless he made it into the office as time was so short to prepare for the trial.

To his dismay Greg looked equally as grey faced as what he was. In Greg's case it was from a lack of sleep. Both men would have welcomed a hot drink and to be snug in bed. Elizabeth had scolded Greg when he came in. She had asked – or rather rebuked him by saying, "How are you to function as a top class lawyer if you do not sleep?" He replied that he was a top class lawyer because he did not sleep. That had not been a wise reply. Elizabeth did not bring him his first coffee until he had been in the office for over an hour. And then she brought it in a regular coffee mug and not in his Giants mug. He decided not to pass a comment as he wanted to avoid World War Three.

Ken sat mostly in silence as Greg filled him in with the meeting with Stacey and Chad. So, there was someone outside that overheard most of the conversation between Mr. and Mrs. Starr. Greg had Ken his note pad with the words "KIND I DENVER PLEASE PLEASE". Ken said, "And they had no idea what Maxi Starr was trying to say?"

"No, none at all – but a few things do bother me – this mumbled set of words of course – and I have no idea what she was trying to say – but also Mr. Starr's reaction, "no, no, Max, NO" What was he trying to discourage her from saying? – or doing for that matter – and why he did not mention this to us the day that we interviewed him?"

"Yeah, that seems really strange – KIND I DENVER PLEASE PLEASE – was she trying to say something – was she begging for

235

something – and he was maybe trying to prevent her from saying – or doing it – really odd".

"The question for you and I to answer is – what do we do with the information – confront Mr. Starr with it and who knows what reaction we might get? Would we be exposing Stacey and Chad and then maybe alert the prosecutor that there is a thread worth latching onto – and who knows where that could lead to." Greg looked at Ken as if imploring him for the perfect answer to his question. And of course there was not a perfect answer – there never is.

"How about if I contact Mr. Starr for a follow up – saying that we need to do some more prep work for the trial – he has no choice really to attend – but he might feel less threatened with you not being there – I could then come around to the fact that someone inside of the house might on reflection have heard part of their discussion outside on the patio – it might be a long shot but we'll be protecting Stacey and Chad."

"I think that it might work – he would never know if we've spoken to any of his other neighbors and it is not really a question that he would come right out and ask them – yes, I think that we should follow that line."

Ken went to his office to telephone Paxton Starr as he did not want Elizabeth to put through the call – he needed the request for the appointment to come directly from him. Five minutes later Ken returned to Greg's office and gave him a thumbs up – he also returned with a mug of coffee for Greg which drew a silent stare from Elizabeth as he walked through to Greg's office. That was unheard of in her book – either Greg got his own coffee or she took a mug in for him when he was deeply engrossed in his work. The two men had a low giggle as Ken put the coffee down on Greg's desk and not on his conference table. They acted like two kids being mischievous. They laughed – but not too loud for Elizabeth to hear them. That would have been a foolish act on their behalf. Unbeknown to them Elizabeth had a grin on her face too.

236

The two men met with their fellow lawyers who were working on the case but did not mention Greg's interview with the two teens or what information had been forthcoming from them. Ken mentioned that he was having another meeting with their client but he too remained silent on the topic of the overheard discussion outside on the patio the night that Maxi Starr had died.

They were however not the only two who were aware of the meeting with Stacey and Chad. On the day of the meeting with Greg it was by chance that Chad's Mom had been in that particular store that day – as the owner of the coffee shop chain she did visit the various outlets and she had selected that day to visit the store near where they lived. She was meeting with the Shop Manager when Stacey had come off of shift and left the store with Chad. She saw a man walk up to them outside of the store and then watched with curiosity as the man and the two teens crossed the street and sat on a park bench. For a while she could not place the man who had approached Stacey outside of the coffee shop. Then she remembered – he was the lawyer that was defending that bastard wife killer. How could anyone take on such a role as to defend someone like that?

She sat for a moment and then decided to telephone Jenni Wright. She told Jenni what was happening. Jenni thanked Chad's mother - who she knew to be a real busy-body and interfering type – but nonetheless she was intrigued that Greg Winters had approached Stacey privately and not telephoned the house to see her. Later that evening when Wil returned home she told him of the telephone call. The Wright's decided not to approach Stacey about the meeting with Greg Winters as they wanted to see if she would say anything to them. When Stacey returned home she did not mention her meeting with Greg Winters.

The Wrights' were unsure how to use the tipoff that they had received.

CHAPTER 38

On the day that Ken was to meet with Paxton Starr there was a sudden change of arrangements. Ken was to have met his client at his home on Ocean Drive – a visit that Ken was definitely looking forward to. He had fallen in love with the setting and Paxton's Starr's home and another visit would have been an absolute pleasure. Unfortunately it was not to be. Ken was to have met with Mr. Starr at 2 o'clock at his home but around 12.30 P.M. Ken received a telephone call from his client asking if he could switch the venue to Greg's offices as he had an appointment in the midafternoon in the vicinity of Greg's law firm. Ken completely understood Paxton Starr's reasoning and switched the venue. The only problem was that Greg was in the office and the plan had been for Ken to meet with his client. To have Greg sitting in his office working while Ken interviewed the client alone might have seemed a little strange.

Ken interrupted Greg's deep thoughts and explained the change of plan – and the worst was that the time of the meeting had been brought forward and that Paxton Starr was on his way over to the office park. As they did not know how close their client had been when he telephoned Ken – and they wondered if the switch was well planned and that their Client was already parked nearby the offices – Greg decided that it was too risky to leave immediately just in case he was "caught in the act of skipping out of the office". He pinged for Elizabeth to come through to his office.

He announced, "If you check my Day Planner for today you will see that I have a 2 o'clock appointment with my Doctor." Elizabeth looked at him in disbelief – she knew of all of his appointments and there was no such item in his day planner. She was about to say something when Greg put his hand up and said, "Look carefully and you will see yourself writing it in as we speak." Again Elizabeth looked perplexed as she looked down at Greg's Day Planner in her hand. Greg eased her pain and said, "Elizabeth, I did not want to see Mr. Starr today – Ken is interviewing him and not

239

me. It is unfortunate that I could not be here this afternoon as it clashed with an important prearranged appointment."

A recomposed Elizabeth said with a complete straight face, "Greg, please remember that you have a 2 o'clock appointment." She then turned around and walked out of his office. The two men shared that smile that they had done so often before.

Not ten minutes later Paxton Starr arrived at the law offices of Greg Winters. Greg met him in the main lobby, exchanged greetings and apologized for his prior appointment that he could not miss. The two men shook hands and Greg departed for his long-time planned appointment with his doctor.

Ken Parker met his client in one of the Conference rooms – named *Vertitas* – Truth.

Ken took two bottles of water out of the small fridge in the room and handed one to Paxton Starr.

"There are a few things that I'd like your assistance with – we require the information to help build our case."

"Of course." replied Mr. Starr, "What information do you require?"

Ken asked some questions about the construction of Paxton Starr's home – in particular the name of the builder and the supplier of the bathroom amenities. When Paxton Starr enquired why the information was required Ken explained the potential importance.

Paxton Starr answered the questions freely and where he did not have the information at hand he made notes to investigate and to provide Ken with the answers.

All of the information that Ken required was made available within 24 hours after the meeting. Ken was rather satisfied with the information that he received.

240

Ken had to be careful as to how he raised that subject of the overheard conversation on the night that Maxi Starr died. He was unsure of the response that he would receive from his client. Towards the end of the meeting Ken brought up the topic – "Oh, by the way, we've had some further input by one of the attendees at the party on the night that your wife passed away – they mentioned that although it was windy outside they thought that they heard your wife say something about "Denver" and "please" – do you perhaps recall your wife saying anything outside that night about Denver – or words like that?"

Ken was on the lookout for any change in Paxton Starr's complexion – a reddening of his fair cheeks or a tightening of his lips or narrowing of his eyes. If there was any change at all it was hardly noticeable to Ken.

"Let me think." answered Paxton Starr. "I thought that I had remembered everything that was said outside that night – maybe I missed something – let me think."

Paxton Starr put his hand over his face as if he was in deep thought – possibly it was to control his emotions – Ken could not see through human hands.

"Let me go through from the top – that way I might recall if I missed anything."

Paxton spent the next few minutes recounting his story of what had taken place that evening. He also knew however that if he denied any knowledge of the words that his wife might have said that he could be setting himself up as having left out some item of importance. "My wife was slurring her words and she might have said something about Denver but I cannot put my finger on it." If he acknowledged the truth of the new information and it did not really exist then he could also be setting himself up. Why was Greg not doing the interview? Was this a trap? Are they not my defense lawyers?

241

"To be honest I am not sure of everything that my wife was trying to say – the only thing that I can think of that relates to "Denver" is that we have a chalet near Aspen that we used to go to several times a year – the Wrights and other members of our Ocean Drive group used to join us from time-to-time. If Maxi indeed said something like "Denver please" then maybe she was trying to tell me that she wanted to go away to our chalet. I was more interested in finding out why she had been drinking so heavily that evening – and maybe I missed that she was talking about wanting to go away. The more I tried to ask her about her behavior the more frustrated she became. So to answer your question, the only reference could be to our chalet – but I cannot honestly remember her mentioning it – maybe my friends were mistaken as to what they thought that they heard Maxi say."

Ken decided to kill the topic off quickly and move on to one or two other things that he wanted to discuss with his client.

"Yeah, that sounds reasonable to me – we must remember that your wife was intoxicated at the time." he said. And he then moved onto the next topic.

Greg decided to take a drive and stay away from the office until Ken telephoned him. He drove aimlessly for about twenty minutes and then he realized that in fact he was fairly near to his doctor. He stopped in and made an appointment – this time it would appear in his Day Planner in Elizabeth's own hand. He did so enjoy teasing her but he knew that he could not do without her.

Just on an hour later Ken telephoned him. Greg headed back to his office.

By late that afternoon Ken received confirmation through his sources that Paxton and Maxi Starr indeed did own a chalet near Aspen and that they took week long vacations there twice a year. They usually had one visit in the winter and one in the summer. In this calendar year they had been to the chalet in the winter but had not as yet gone up for a summer visit at the time of Maxi Starr's death.

Had they been clever with their client or had he been clever with them?

After the interview Paxton Starr proceeded on to his appointment.

"The Solar Murder"

CHAPTER 39

The next few weeks just flew by as Greg's team prepared for the commencement of the trial. The media frenzy had subsided for a while but was now being stoked again as the start date of the trial approached. Information and evidence was checked and rechecked, questions were asked from different perspectives and the team put themselves through the hoops and turning any argument that the prosecutor might raise.

The team knew that Judge Rita Marx was a no nonsense type of judge. She would allow arguments to be developed but there had to be a point – if you could not make your point – then she would tell you to move on. Sometimes her telling you to "move on" was not always that polite. But you knew where you stood with her – be clear and concise or face censure. But what was sure is that she disliked wife killers.

The team was more concerned about Juanita Lange, the appointed prosecutor.

She was largely an unknown quantity – she had very sound record and great academic qualifications and had proven herself in the lower courts with some stunning work. She took risks and sometimes they paid off but other times she had seemed to lose her way with too much evidence and too little convincing of the jury. Nevertheless she came into the case gunning for a Second Degree murder conviction – she wanted Paxton Starr and nothing was going to stop her. Oh, to be young and ambitious!

Elizabeth had worked very long hours as indeed had everyone else in Greg's office. She would always find something to do, someone to help – or even just be out of the way while at the same time keeping "her" team fed, watered and warm. If they needed anything Elizabeth took care of it – even driving down to the store to buy a birthday card for a family member of someone on the team – at least when they went home that evening there would be

245

a card for a loved one. In a way she was the silent orchestra conductor or maybe a good sheppard would be a better description. Personally she liked it when she was referred to as the "Sergeant Major" by the team. Whatever the team bestowed on her as a nickname was not important – she was simply brilliant at what she did.

If Ken thought that he was becoming better at what he did as a defense lawyer then he marveled at the work ethic, stamina and perception of Greg Winters. Greg seemed grey and tired on occasions but he could still out work, out think and "out-everything" anyone on his team. He had lost weight over the last few weeks but the team joked that he was like a heavyweight boxer becoming leaner and meaner as the Title Fight came nearer. He was in a world that he loved – but one that had cost him the love of his life. His involvement in the case that he was working on at the time had blinded him to the state of Mary's declining health. He looked up to heaven now and saw her smiling down at him – she said, "You are the best there is – go out and knock them out!"

CHAPTER 40

The Bailiff brought the court to order with an "All Rise" as Judge Rita Marx entered. This was her courtroom and she was going to stamp her control on the proceedings of the case from the very first morning of the trial. The courtroom was packed to capacity. The TV stations had an armada of trucks and equipment outside in the parking lot – a special area which had been cordoned off for them. Judge Marx did not mind the media frenzy as long as they did not interfere with the proceedings of the trial.

If Juanita Lange was nervous she did not show it all – she looked calm and professional – in reality her heart was beating well over the recommended limit and the inside of her shoes felt sweaty. It would only take a day or two and she would be relaxed and at her best.

Greg and Ken had sat in the very chairs before. That however did not make them feel either more relaxed that Juanita Lange or less apprehensive. The sense of apprehension was the same – they fought demons in their stomachs and shakes and twitches all over their bodies. Why on earth would anyone want to become a trial lawyer?

The judge advised the jury of their responsibilities and obligations and left them in no doubt as the importance of their assessment of the evidence that would be presented during the trial. She reminded them to at all times remember that the charges brought against Paxton Starr – the defendant - were Second Degree murder and Criminal Negligence. After her address the judge asked the prosecutor if she understood the message that she had delivered - "I do your Honor" was the simple reply. Judge Marx then turned to Greg Winters and asked him the same question. "I do your Honor".

There was no point in saying anything else at this point in time – and besides which the judge did not want anything else but that four word response.

The judge added some further "housekeeping" issues pertaining to the trial and after only about thirty minutes she adjourned proceedings until the following morning when the prosecutor would begin to call their witnesses.

"All rise" and Judge Rita Marx walked out of her court.

As Greg and Ken were gathering up their papers to leave they looked up and Juanita Lange gave them a very intimidating smile. It was a signal that the battle was about to begin and that she intended to bring down Greg Winters – he was almost more important to her than finding Paxton Starr guilty.

Both men returned the silent communication by nodding their heads.

CHAPTER 41

Juanita Lange made her opening statement the following morning.

"Ladies and gentlemen of the jury we are faced with a clear cut case of a man having murdered his wife – yes, I said "clear cut" not a maybe or could have but a clear cut case. Mr. Starr had the opportunity to murder his wife as he was the only person at home with her the night that she died. Mr. Starr had the cause to murder his wife – they had a public argument that night – and Mr. Starr had the motivation to murder his wife – the prosecution will prove that Mr. Starr stood to benefit by an estimated $41 million dollars from the death of his wife. We have a trifecta in place – opportunity, cause and motivation. Mr. Starr murdered his wife – we will set out to prove beyond reasonable doubt that he committed the crime under which he has been charged – the Second Degree murder of his loving and devoted wife. We are not dealing here with some petty crime but the murder of a woman who could not defend herself against a man much bigger and stronger than herself – a man who stood to gain a great deal by the death of his wife.

There can be no doubt in your minds that Paxton Starr committed the crime under which he is charged. There will be no doubt in your minds that he committed the crime – no doubt at all – and at the end of the trial when you are asked to objectively come to a verdict we will all know that your conclusions will be based on fact and evidence – that Mr. Paxton Starr is guilty – and will be found guilty by you and will pay the price for his crime. Mr. Starr is a wife killer – remember that!"

Greg Winters addressed the jury.

"Ladies and gentlemen of the jury. You are in no ordinary building – this is a special building – outside you will see a statue of a woman holding up the scales of justice – a remarkable symbol – not only a symbol of balance but a symbol of our society – a society

249

where we have the ability to try criminals for their crimes in an open court – in a fair and just manner. We should never lose sight of the fact that we are privileged to uphold a legal system that has stood the test of time – one where fellow man hears evidence and objectively decides the fate of the accused. This tradition goes back many hundreds of years – it has stood the test of test because it is a just and honest way of reaching a verdict. Please remember that fact as you ponder the evidence put before you during this trial.

This is no ordinary room that you are in – you are in a court of the law of the land:

a special place where the traditions of the land – as I mentioned a moment ago – are held sacred – we do not meet under a tree or in a cave or behind closed doors – we meet in a courtroom and hear the evidence in an orderly manner.

During this trial you will be presented with a large amount of evidence – some might appear to be trivial – but believe me that no evidence at a murder trial is ever trivial – rather let me correct myself – all evidence should be heard but the prosecutor will attempt to provide evidence that is not really material to the decision-making process of the case. Some of the evidence will be more substantial and will make you think long and hard about what is before you. Do not be apprehensive about the evidence – both the trivial and the material – they will test your ability to distill the truth.

The prosecutor has said that we have a "trifecta" of events before you. She maintains that Mr. Starr – my client – had opportunity to murder his wife – the woman who was the centre of his universe – his true love – that because he was alone with his wife the night on which she tragically drowned – that he must have drowned her. We cannot disprove the fact that Mr. Starr was alone with his wife – but we will provide sufficient information to question the claim that he drowned his wife – sufficient information to bring you – the members of the jury and upholders of our system of law that I

250

eluded to a moment ago – to bring you to the point of having reasonable doubt that Mr. Starr murdered his wife.

The second pillar of the prosecutors "trifecta" was that my client had cause to murder his wife – after all they had an argument – if indeed it was an argument at all and we simply do not know if it was an argument or not – but my client had this incident with his wife and that was just cause for him to murder her – and to murder her that very night – and of course that would not have raised any suspicion with his neighbors who witnessed the said incident. We will therefore bring into question the second leg of the trifecta – the just cause.

What was the third leg of the wobbly stool of irrefutable evidence set before you? Ah, yes, I remember, it was the motivation. My client who is a wealthy man and whose financial stability is sound – he murdered his wife because he stood to gain an estimated $41 million from the Estate of his wife. He was the sole beneficiary of the estimated $41 million so he obviously decided to add to his wealth by taking away the one person that he valued more than any pile of dollars that he could stack up. Did he think that he could substitute his wife – his soulmate – with a money model made up of $100 bills? I doubt it. I doubt it very much.

The defense team will not only refute the evidence brought before you – the members of the jury – but we will allow you to come to the only logical conclusion in this case – that Mr. Paxton Starr – the defendant is not guilty of the charges of Second degree murder and of Criminal Negligence."

The courtroom had remained completely silent during Greg's opening statement.

Ken saw a man performing at his very best – in control – working the jury – belittling the prosecutor – upholding the traditions of the law – and setting the tone for his defense of Paxton Starr. Ken looked over at Juanita Lange and she sat almost motionless – she did not appear to be at all concerned about the magnificent

251

performance that Greg had just delivered. This observation bothered Ken – had Juanita Lange set Greg up for a big beginning but a poor finish.

Once the court had settled in the following the opening statements Juanita Lange called her first witness.

The first few witnesses were called in fairly short order. The various neighbors on Ocean Drive were called to testify. They were questioned by the prosecutor and then cross examined by Greg. There was nothing startling about the evidence presented or the cross-examination. Each witness in turn told almost the exact same story of the events that had transpired on the evening leading up to the death of Maxi Starr. The prosecutor stayed away from asking questions about Mr. and Mrs. Starr having a caring and loving relationship so each time under cross-examination Greg made a point of asking questions about the evident love between Paxton and Maxi.

The prosecutor had tried to prize information out of the witnesses about the argument between Mr. and Mrs. Starr and that he had handled her roughly outside on the patio of the Wrights' home. She tried to suggest that Mr. Starr had threatened his wife and that his actions of harming her were only delayed until they returned home that night. Juanita Lange was merely fishing and did not really expect to catch anything. Her probing did however serve to possibly raise some doubts in the mind of the jury - for they were her main audience. The more she could raise doubts in their minds as to Mr. Starr's innocence then the greater her chance of having the defendant found guilty.

Her approach also served to keep Greg Winters fairly silent in his seat. There was not too much for him to "Object" to or to counter-punch with. If Juanita Lange could contain Greg Winters then he would lose his force on the case. Ms. Lange was starting slow but already showing a keenness of mind of trial-management. It was management of the witnesses, the jury and of Greg Winters.

The first two days of the trial were therefore pretty insipid – but no doubt the platform was being laid.

After the weekend break the prosecutor "Called" Jenny Wright to the stand.

Although testimony was not of much greater value than that of the other neighbors of Ocean Drive she was closer to Maxi Starr as a friend. The questions posed to her by Juanita Lange were more of a type to highlight the loving nature of Maxi Starr. No mention was made of Maxi's fun times at the party's and her record of sometimes becoming intoxicated. There had been no mention of Stacey or Chad in Jenni's testimony and Greg was very relieved.

Under cross-examination Juanita Lange objected several times to Greg's line of questioning about Maxi Starr. Greg's reply was that he was not attempting to demonize the late Mrs. Starr but to present a balanced view – a view of someone who was not only loving and kind but also of a person who had a complete zest for life – her having a few drinks at these gatherings were not a sin or weakness but a declaration of her embracing life. He set out to paint a picture of Maxi Starr that night – for whatever reason – of having a few too many drinks and then having a tiff with a caring husband – a tiff unfortunately witnessed visually by their close friends – and then tragically falling asleep and drowning in her bath tub that same night. Greg was interrupted countless times by the prosecutor claiming that the so-called tiff was far more substantial than what met the eye and that later that night Paxton Starr murdered his wife.

Greg Winters had an opening that he was looking for. While Jenni Wright sat silently in the witness stand Greg took a few minutes – not too long to gain the wrath of the judge – but long enough to make a telling point – the lack of evidence of the incident between the Starr's as being anything more than a husband caring for his wife so much that he took her outside to try to establish if she was well – or what had been bothering her that evening. He pressed for evidence – and turned to the jury and said, "There is no

253

evidence that something occurred that made a loving husband become a killer! Let me repeat there is no evidence that whatever was discussed between Mr. and Mrs. Starr outside on their neighbors patio that fateful evening led to my client drowning his wife – Mrs. Starr died as a result of falling asleep in her bath tub – a severe tragedy but nothing more – you as the jury cannot read anything more into the situation – your job is to assess the evidence as there is no such evidence before you to the incident seen by the neighbors that evening that it was anything more than a loving husband caring for the wellbeing of his wife."

Jenni Wright was followed immediately to the stand by her husband. The additional dimension that Wil Wright brought by way of evidence was his taking the Starr's back to their home after the incident in his home. He had very little to add besides that he had offered to assist Paxton Starr to take his wife into her home but that the offer had been refused.

Under cross-examination Greg again brought up the loving nature of the relationship between Mr. and Mrs. Starr. Wil Wright confirmed that the relationship between Paxton and Maxi Starr was a loving one – they had never had a public falling out ever before – and that he had been shocked when his neighbor had been arrested for the murder of his wife.

"Mr. Wright, could you please tell the court if Mrs. Starr was able to get into your vehicle unassisted when you took her and her husband home that evening."

"No, my wife and one or of the other wives helped Maxi into my car. Paxton, Mr. Starr went around the other side of the car and put his arm around his wife once she was in my vehicle."

"Mr. Wright could you also tell the court if Mrs. Starr was able to get out of your car unassisted and walk to the front door of their home when you dropped them off."

"When I pulled up outside their front door I assisted Mr. Starr in helping his wife to their front door – Paxton, Mr. Starr came around from his side of the car and assisted his wife out. He said good night to me and apologized for the incident that had taken place – he then put his arm around his wife and led her to his front door."

"Did you drive off or wait once the Starr's had said good night?"

"I waited until they were inside their home and the hall light came on – then I drove through the main gates and I saw them close behind me."

"Mr. Wright, please think clearly now – did Mr. Starr merely have his arm around his wife – or was it something more?"

"OBJECTION your Honor," yelled out the prosecutor. "Leading the witness!"

"Overruled – Mr. Winters make your point please." said the judge.

"Mr. Wright, your answer please." asked Greg

"Mr. Starr had to support his wife as she seemed to still have trouble standing up alone."

"Not to put words into your mouth, Mr. Wright but why was that?"

"As I said earlier – Mrs. Starr consumed a good deal of alcohol at our home that evening."

"Was Mrs. Starr seen to consume alcohol that evening?"

"Yes."

"Would you say – in your opinion of course – and not based on medical knowledge – that Mrs. Starr therefore still appeared to be

– shall we say – still under the weather – when you took her home that evening?"

"Yes."

"No further questions. Thank you your honor."

CHAPTER 42

Juanita Lange called Martin Rees to the Stand.

"Please state your name and occupation."

"Martin Rees, I am the owner of "Bathroom Splendor Inc." – the company manufactures high-end bathroom fixtures."

Juanita Lange asked, "What type of fixtures?" – As if she did not know.

"We manufacture a range of basins, toilets, cupboards and bath tubs."

"Bath tubs – you say – any particular type of bath tubs, Mr. Rees?"

"We specialize in non-slip bath tubs."

"Mr. Rees, for the benefit of the court please explain in layman's terms what a non-slip bath tub is." Greg saw where this line of questioning was going and he was not a happy man.

"We have a Patent on a particular resin that goes into the actual mould of the bath tub itself – this makes the tub itself non slip."

"Mr. Rees – and why is this any different from any other type of non-slip bath tubs?"

"Most other tubs apply the resin after manufacture – a coating in effect - with our tubs it is part of the manufacture process."

"Mr. Rees – I asked you to explain the difference – please do so – clearly in order that the court can understand your explanation."

"In simple terms our tubs retain the characteristics of being non slip whereas with other types the resin wears off of the surface of the tub and over time the non-slip properties deteriorate."

Greg decided to hold back on any OBJECTION as although he knew where the line of questioning was going he wanted to wait for an opportunity and not spoil his chances of the judge jumping down at him.

Juanita Lange looked sharper and stronger now – she was growing in confidence and stature. Everyone in the courtroom could feel the tension rising as they too knew where this line of questioning was going – including a very attentive jury.

"Mr. Rees did your company supply and fit the bath accessories in the home of Mr. Paxton Starr?"

"Yes, we did – we fitted all of the washrooms and bathrooms for Mr. Starr when the house was built."

"You remember this installation? Why would you remember that particular installation from the several hundred that you might do per year?"

"I remember it because it was our first major contract for a home installation – we had previously done up-market hotels and resorts but the contract with Mr. Starr was our first home project."

"Please tell the court how you came to win the contract."

"Objection, your Honor, what is the relevance of the question?" asked Greg.

"Overruled – councilor – please make your point – and now!" stated Judge Rita Marx.

"Mr. Rees, is it correct to say that your company had supplied bathroom fixtures to a property development project managed by Mr. Starr?"

"Objection! What is the relevance?"

"Overruled! – Ms. Lange – now if you please!"

"Mr. Rees – your company was asked to bid for the work at Mr. Starr's home, is that correct?"

"No, we were asked if we would do the job – I advised Mr. Starr that our work was big volume and high–end fixtures...." Juanita Lange interrupted, "And, what was Mr. Starr's reply?" "He stated that price was not an issue – he wanted the best in the home that he was building."

Juanita Lange repeated, "He wanted the very best for the home that he was building - so in order to meet his requirement – and I of course assume that you decided to undertake the project where price is not an issue – you installed the bathroom fixtures in the Starr home."

"Yes."

"Including the main bathroom?"

"Yes".

Greg interrupted the proceedings, "Your honor we have established the fact that the witness installed the bath room fixtures in the Starr home – what is the point here?"

The judge turned to Juanita Lange and said, "Make your point or I will strike the evidence – do you understand Ms. Lange?"

"Yes your honor." Juanita chalked up a point for the prosecution as they were beginning to annoy Greg Winters.

259

"Mr. Rees, what type of bath did you install in the main bedroom of Mr. Starr's home?"

"It was a model NS004 – a non-slip version 4."

"The tub had a warranty as being non slip?"

"Yes" answered the witness.

Greg Winters made a note and place a star next to it. Ken glanced down at the note and understood the message. Greg expected the prosecutor to follow-up with another related question but there was not one forthcoming – he made another note.

"Mr. Rees, what exactly does non slip mean?" asked Ms. Lange – again as if she did not know already.

"The composition of the materials binds the compounds together that produces an outer layer that grips – say hands and feet and prevents the water from acting as a lubricant which could cause the hand or foot for example to slide – which could lead to a fall."

"So a pretty advanced product?"

"Yes."

Juanita Lange had the courtroom sitting on edge – it was clear what she was implying without having had to make her point – could it have been possible for Maxi Starr to have slid under the water in a non-slip bath tub and drowned? Ms. Lange paced up and down in front of the witness for a minute – just long enough to draw out the tension – but not too long to annoy the judge.

"Mr. Rees, this non slip bath tub that you manufacture - would it be non-slip enough to prevent someone say sliding down further into the water once they were in the bath? You said that it would prevent hands and feet from slipping but would it restrain a person once in the tub?"

One could have heard a pin drop in the courtroom.

"Mr. Rees your answer please!" pushed the prosecutor.

"The outer layer of the tub is the same throughout the surface and not just where the arms or feet might touch – once someone is in the tub then they would have to use their arms or maybe their feet to get into the position that they wanted."

"Mr. Rees, answer my question please – could someone slide down in the tub once they were in a position."

"Yes, they could but it would take some effort to do so."

"What do you mean by some effort?"

"They would have to slide down using their arms or legs."

Juanita Lange did not suggest to the witness that someone of Maxi Starr's light frame would require some effort to make herself slide down into the tub – to slide down far enough to drown. Ms. Lange could not lead her witness to make such a statement – that would have brought Greg Winters to his feet and the judge to warn her. Ms. Lange did not have to say it – everyone in the courtroom almost heard the unspoken question – and in their minds they heard what they wanted to hear – that Mrs. Maxi Starr could not have slid down in the bath and drowned. She would have had to push herself further down into the length of the tub to do so. The likelihood of a drowning while asleep was very remote.

This was a major point for the prosecution.

Ms. Lange walked right up near Greg's table and looked at Paxton Starr and said, "No further questions - your witness."

261

Greg Winters rose and addressed the judge, "Your Honor I would like to ask for a brief recess."

The judge looked at her watch and said, "The court is adjourned until 2:30 P.M. this afternoon." As she rose and the Bailiff said "All Rise" the judge walked out of the court.

The afternoon papers would be full of the ace scored by the prosecution in the Second Degree murder trial of Paxton Starr.

CHAPTER 43

As Greg and Ken retired to the room that they used in the courthouse Ken asked,
"How come you did not try to bring down the prosecutor while we were in session?"

The answer was simple and one that Ken would not forget for the remainder of his career.

"The bigger they are the harder they fall – if I had knocked her off right then I might have scored a small point and it could have gone un-noticed – no, we needed to pump some air into this – build up the prosecutor – have the media think that she is on top – then when she falls she falls harder. The next time she tries to make a stunning statement or discovery the jury will not pay as much attention to her. I needed to give her coverage and feel giddy with power. The jury will then begin to see us as the more stable, more logical and more believable. Soon her fire will go out."

Ken thought that Greg's position was high risk – what if it should backfire – if they could not stop the prosecutor – if she gained energy from winning points against Greg Winters.

During the recess their team ate while they worked. Cell phones were buzzing away and notes being taken. Greg would check on the information and request more – he would make notes – walk around the room and drink coffee. He missed his Giants mug – it helped him think.

Suddenly he announced that he was going for a walk and that the team should also get some fresh air. He gathered up his notes and walked out of the courthouse and into the sun shine. It was November but it was still wonderful to be outdoors. As he walked across the street he thought that maybe trials should be held in open parks where everyone could walk by and stop and listen for a while and then walk on. Why must the law be practiced in

263

courthouses – hold them outside so that the world could appreciate the law – and not be fearful of it.

He sat on a bench and pictured a trial being held in front of him. He listened in as the evidence was presented and the lawyers jiggled with the truth, manipulated thoughts and discredited witnesses. It was like watching a circus with each performer trying to outdo the other one – "No, look at me, I am best", or "Watch me, watch me I'll twist the information better than what he can!" Was a trial a circus? He hoped not – Greg had spent his life as a defense lawyer and there was no doubt that he had enjoyed his career. But that could still have made it a circus.

Greg's mindless wonder was sharply interrupted as he was recognized by a TV reporter and who with her camera man in toe came running towards him.

Greg escaped the charging rush of the reporter and made it back inside the safety of the courthouse. He was not sure if the circus inside the court was better or worse than the one outside. Whatever the answer he had other things to think about now.

CHAPTER 44

Martin Rees was reminded that he was still under oath.

"Mr. Rees, prior to the recess you told the court that the bath tub that you installed in the main bedroom of the home that my client was non slip. Is that correct?"

"Yes sir."

"You also told the court that the manufacture of the bath tub incorporates the non-slip resin into the material – it is not an add-on afterwards."

"Yes sir, that is correct."

"Mr. Rees, you expressed the opinion that this bath tub – Model NS 004 -if I recall would most likely prevent a person from slipping further down into the water – unless some effort was expended in doing so – is that general opinion still valid?"

"Yes sir, it is."

"You also stated that your product has a warranty of being non slip – is that what you said under oath?"

"Yes, the non-slip bath tub has a warranty."

"Mr. Reed, unfortunately you are not providing the court with full disclosure – may I remind you of the consequences of misleading a court of law while under oath."

"Objection, Mr. Reed answered my question under oath, your honor" blurted out the prosecutor.

"Overruled, please continue councilor" answered the judge.

"Mr. Reed – allow me to provide some general information – maybe that will prod your memory – do most warranty policies carry a time and condition clause?"

"Objection, The defense is prompting the witness your honor."

"Overruled – councilor I have now said twice that the defense can pursue his argument – do not let me say it a third time."

Greg continued without the threat of being interrupted in the foreseeable future.

"Mr. Reed, your answer to my question."

"All warranties have a time and condition stipulation in the contract."

"Such conditions exist in your warranty terms and conditions?"

"Yes sir, they do"

"Right then let us first deal with the "time" aspect – what is the warranty period of the NS004 – as manufactured in the year that the bath tub was installed in my clients home?"

"At that time the warranty was 10 years – although it is 20 years for the newer models".

"Mr. Reed the new warranty period is of no interest to the court – my client purchased his bath tub – and all other bathroom items from your business over 21 years ago – please repeat for the court – what was the warranty on the bath tub in Mr. Starr's home at that point in time."

There was a substantial stir in the courtroom as the witness answered the question.

"The bath tub had a 10 year warranty."

"Thank you for clarifying that for the court – to make it clear to the court the said bath tub was therefore out of its warranty period." Greg spoke very slowly as he made this telling affirmation of the facts.

"Your Honor", chipped in the prosecutor, "Most products stand good for longer than what is stated – the product should still have remained non slip."

"Councilor that might be so but your argument was based on the warranty and the importance of the product being non slip – now there appears to be doubt to that fact – your interruption is therefore out of order." Judge Marx knew that the prosecutor had lost ground under the cross-examination of her witness.

"Mr. Winters, do you have any further questions for the witness?" asked the judge.

"Yes, your Honor, as a matter of fact I do – may I continue?"

The judge waved her hand indicating that Greg should continue.

"Mr. Reed, we still need to address the aspect of the conditions of the warranty of your NS004 bath tub. Allow me to digress for just a moment – a warranty is an agreement between a seller and a purchaser that in good faith a sound and functioning product is provided in exchange for a predetermined amount of money. The seller is on the hook to repair, replace or provide some form of compensation to the buyer if the product is defunct or does not operate as described that it would by the seller. The buyer on the other hand is responsible for maintaining the product in a certain manner during the warranty period. Do you agree with this pen picture of a warranty?"

"Yes sir, that is fairly accurate."

"Now allow me to come to my point – the warranty for your product is not what is in question – rather it is the maintenance of the bath tub – in truth not the maintenance but rather the usage."

Greg walked back to his table and picked up a piece of paper. "Your Honor I would like to submit as evidence a laboratory report by "Science Inc." of Los Angeles, California Greg distributed the report to the judge and to the prosecution team.

Greg continued. "The coroner's report found traces of a soapy fluid in the lungs of the late Mrs. Starr. We obtained a sample of the fluid and had it analyzed by two separate labs in LA – neither of which knew the source of the fluid – the results, one from "Science Inc." and the other from "Brown Research" identified the fluid as bath oil. A lavender scented bath oil. The same make and scent as the bath oil that was found in Maxi Starr's bath room. So we know that Maxi Starr not only added bath oils to her bath the evening that she died but – and even more importantly for this case – that from samples taken of the surface of the bath tub that these oils had been used many times. In the reports that I have just submitted as evidence to the court it clearly states that the bath was in fact covered in this oil".

 Greg paused for a second then continued, "Mr. Reed, the resin that your company puts into its products makes the surface become non slip is that correct?"

"Yes sir."

"In your opinion what impact would there potentially be if the continuous use of bath oils have on the properties of your non slip bath."

"Objection, your Honor, the witness cannot speculate on the impact of the bath oils on his product – he has no scientific evident in front of him to make a far comment."

"The witness will only provide an opinion Mr. Winters, no more" commented the judge.

"Your opinion if you please, Mr. Reed."

"Bath oils could have the effect of reducing the ability of the resin to provide a non-slip surface – it could reduce it significantly"

The judge called for silence in the court several times before order was restored.

"So let me recap for the court." said Greg, "We have identified an issue with the term of the warranty – a 10 year warranty but the bath tub in fact was installed over 21 years ago – so there is nothing to suggest that the non-slip qualities of the bath tub still had efficacy – there might have still been non slip qualities but there is a doubt.

Next, the constant use of bath oils by Mrs. Starr could have resulted in the surface of the bath tub to be more slippery than normal – and in fact negate the benefits of having a non-slip bath installed in the first place."

Greg turned towards the jury and said, "Beyond reasonable doubt – beyond reasonable doubt – these are the key words. It has just been illustrated that reasonable doubt exists in the charge of Second Degree murder – that is all it takes is having reasonable doubt."

Greg turned back to the witness and said. "I have no further questions."

"Does the prosecution have any further questions?" asked Judge Marx.

"No, your honor I have no further questions."

269

The judge adjourned the case for resumption two days hence. Maybe she realized that the prosecutor had some major healing to do.

CHAPTER 45

The following day when Greg arrived at his office there was a pile of mail waiting for him on his desk. Elizabeth brought him his coffee and they discussed a few things that required his attention. She did not want to get in his way as she realized that he would want has much time with his team as possible. She did however point out that there was an invitation from Todd Hornsby – a very notable lawyer who Greg had known almost all of his professional life.

"Mr. Hornsby's assistant called to say that there was an invitation being delivered to you – it is Mr. Hornsby's retirement dinner for two Mondays time at 7 o'clock. She mentioned that her boss was hopeful that you could attend although he knew that you were so tied up with the trial. She did ask that I bring the invitation to your attention".

Greg opened the letter and read the invitation. Where had the years gone? He must have known Todd for over thirty years. What a delightful man in every way – a very good lawyer, a part-time lecturer at a local university, a published author and best of all a devoted husband and father.

Greg thought about his own retirement. Would that day ever come? He was in his late 50's but he knew that he did not have five or six more years of practicing law in him. He had thought that the previous trial was his last one and then this one came along. Would he be tempted into others after the conclusion of the Paxton Starr case?

He felt that every day away from Mary was a day that he could not make up – a lost day of being near her.

He had found new energy in this case and felt that he performed well thus far – or was it his team that was just getting better as each case added to their experience? Maybe it was both. On this

271

case every member of his team not only came with their A game but much more. Was it a final tribute to him? Was it a way of saying goodbye? He did not know. How could he ever live without them – with Ken and without Elizabeth.

Greg looked up and Elizabeth was still sitting across the desk from him. She would have waited all day if necessary.

"Please reply that I would not miss the dinner for a million dollars – but if he had 1.5 million I would rather take the money!"

Later that morning Elizabeth telephoned Mr. Hornsby's assistant and told her that Greg Winters would be at the dinner. She did not mention anything about the money – she thought that it would have been in bad taste - besides the fact that Elizabeth could not comprehend that amount of money.

CHAPTER 46

The next witness called by the prosecutor was Myles Smith.

"Mr. Smith could you please tell the court your occupation." asked Juanita Lange.

"I am a Certified Financial and Estate Planner."

"Mr. Smith, how long have you been in this profession?"

"For almost thirty years."

"Please tell the court, was Mrs. Maxi Starr one of your clients?"

"Yes, Mrs. Starr was one of my clients."

"When did Mrs. Starr become one of your clients?"

"Mrs. Starr became a client of mine about twenty years ago – I have done all of her financial planning since then."

"Is Mr. Starr one of your clients too?"

"No, Mr. Starr has never been a client – I only worked for Mrs. Starr and not her husband."

"To confirm, Mr. Smith, you did Mrs. Starr's financial and estate planning, is that correct."

"Yes."

"Mr. Smith – over the years did Mrs. Starr's ability to investment and her investments increase?"

Juanita Lange was expecting Greg Winters to interrupt the examination of the witness but he did not.

"Yes, as her personal wealthy increased through the development of her business she invested more money and her portfolio of investments also increased in worth."

"Mr. Smith what was the estimated worth of Mrs. Starr at the time of her death?"

"Approximately $41 million – in stocks and a $25 million life policy - but since then with the down turn in stock values the worth today is about close to $32 million – including the life policy you understand that the value of the investment portion of her portfolio goes up and down as the market fluctuate."

"That is a great deal of money is it not?"

"Yes it is."

"And who was the sole beneficiary of Mrs. Starr's estate?"

"It was her husband, Mr. Paxton Starr."

Although this item of news was well known by those that had been following the case there was still a stir of exclamation throughout the courtroom.

"Order, there will be order in my court!" Judge Marx would have no audience participation in her courtroom.

Juanita Lange continued, "Mr. Smith am I correct in saying that the proceeds of Mrs. Starr's estate is being held in trust until after this trial is concluded but if Mr. Starr is found not guilty that the full proceeds will be paid to him?"

Still Greg Winters did not interrupt the examination of Myles Smith.

"Yes, that is correct."

274

"I have no further questions your honor."

"Your witness councilor." said Judge Marx addressing Greg.

To everyone's surprise Greg said, "No questions at this time your honor."

The prosecutor then called the coroner to the stand.

After some basic questions Juanita Lange asked the coroner to provide an account of his call to the Starr residence the morning that Maxi was found dead.

"When you arrived at the residence was Mr. Starr in a state of shock?"

"Objection! Your honor, the witness is a coroner and not a physiatrist. He is not qualified to assess the mental state of my client." interrupted Greg.

"Sustained! Councilor, do not attempt to lead the witness."

"Yes your honor."

"Please detail for the court your findings when you entered the bathroom of the Starr residence."

"I entered the bathroom at 9:46 A.M. - Mrs. Starr was in the bath tub – submerged to about just above her nose line – I tried to find a pulse but she was dead."

"What was the approximate time of death?"

"My initial estimate was that she had been dead for about 9 -10 hours - this placing her time of death at about midnight to 1 A.M. that morning. My comprehensive examination of the body in the mortuary confirmed my original estimate"

"Doctor, if this estimate is accurate – and we have no reason to doubt it – then Mrs. Starr died say within one hour of her returning home from the neighborhood party."

"Objection your honor, the Doctor cannot prove what time Mrs. Starr came home from the party." interrupted Greg.

"Overruled, the court has established that Mr. and Mrs. Starr arrived home at approximately 11:45 P.M. After she consumed coffee she retired up stairs and her drowning could have occurred any time after midnight." Judge Marx had a very good memory.

Juanita Lange continued.

"Doctor, Mrs. Starr was found in the bath tub with the water level just above her nose line – please describe for the court if this position – with the water line – is consistent with a drowning accident."

"The drowning line – if that is what you are describing – is not so much the issue as we believe that Mr. Starr moved his wife's body."

"Then Doctor, what is the issue!" The prosecutor was leading him along nicely and Greg knew it. But he decided to wait.

"What is important is the rate at which the water entered her body."

"Explain."

"If one were asleep or in a potential state of drowsiness – as might have been the case with Mrs. Starr then the water would have entered the mouth slowly. In most cases the person would wake up and they would begin to choke or splutter as the body alerts them to take action. If the person did not wake up then the water entering the mouth would still be slow and it would take some time for the person to drown."

"Approximately how long could this process take? And, Doctor, in the case of Mrs. Starr what was different from the description that you have just provided?"

"In the case of Mrs. Starr the evidence of the water in her lungs and the stress of her body was that the water entered her body at a faster rate than what I would have expected – the drowning could have occurred within a minute or two."

Again Greg just sat and waited.

Was he waiting to catch a fly or would he be caught?

"So, Doctor in your professional opinion the drowning of Mrs. Maxi Starr did not fall into the norms of a tragic drowning accident – is that correct?"

"Yes, that is correct".

"You therefore suspected fowl play and alerted the SFPD of your suspicions."

"That is correct."

"Doctor, please state your understanding of who else was in the Starr residence at the time of Mrs. Starr's death."

"Objection, your Honor – the doctor has no way of knowing if perchance there was someone else in the home – it might be a remote possibility but the doctor cannot be expected to comment – even by implication if Mr. Starr was the only other person in the home that night."

"Sustained – please rephrase your question to the witness."

"Doctor, to confirm then, in your professional opinion Mrs. Starr death by drowning was not a tragic accident?"

"In my opinion it was not."

Juanita Lange pressed home her advantage.

"You put forward your evidence to the police department and the District Attorney's Office?"

"Yes, that is correct – the evidence was verified my members of my team and we presented our findings as you described."

"And based on these findings an Arrest Warrant was issued?"

"Yes."

"Doctor, is the person who was arrested in the death of Maxi Starr in the court today?"

"Yes. It is the accused, Mr. Starr."

A ripple went through the gathered audience in the courtroom. Everyone of course knew that the accused in the trial was Paxton Starr but bringing him clearly into focus as a potential wife killer brought a strong response.

Juanita Lange paused for a moment to allow the impact of the audience to settle in. she savored every moment. The atmosphere excited her. After another half minute she continued her examination.

"Doctor, your team inspected the entire bath room, is that correct?"

"Yes, that is correct."

"Was there any other evidence that surprised or intrigued you?"

278

"Objection your honor, leading the witness." interjected Greg.

"Sustained – councilor move on please."

"Doctor, tell me about the evidence that you obtained from the floor of the bath room."

"My team found almost dried water stains on the floor – away from the bath tub and almost under the chair on which the deceased bath robe were found."

"And what is the significance of these almost dried water marks?"

"The water samples matched those from the bath tub – the water was fairly fresh and had the traces of the bath oils used by the deceased – we believe that the water stains were left some time after the bath tub was filled – indicating that possibly someone with wet hands might have sat in the chair after Mrs. Starr had commenced her bath."

"And so indicating what exactly doctor?"

"That there is a strong likelihood that someone else was in the bath room after Mrs. Starr climbed into the bath."

"Doctor, I do not see the significance – could the water marks not have been made in the morning when Mr. Starr said that he found his wife dead in the bath tub?"

"No I do not believe so – as by then the water marks would have more liquid – spots of water versus dried watermarks – no, the water drops were from about the time that the deceased died."

"Are you absolutely sure about this Doctor?"

"Yes."

"Thank you, your honor – I have no further questions."

"Your witness, councilor!" the judge addressed Greg.

Greg sat for a moment before rising to speak. There appeared to be a swell of anti-feeling towards his client at that point in time. He could feel – he had felt it many times before over the years – maybe it was beginning to stick to his skin. Do not become angry – do not come out punching – do not further upset or annoy the jury – be logical, slow and precise – be professional and do what you are skilled at doing.

Greg paced up and down the front of the court for a few moments and sensing that the judge was about to bring him in line he asked, "Doctor, in your testimony you seemed to avoid using medical terms to describe the drowning of Mrs. Starr – why was that?"

"I suppose that I wanted to keep things simple."

"For whom did you make things simple, Doctor? – To perhaps dumb things down so that the jury could keep things simple to understand – or maybe you think that they are un-intelligent and that medical words might confuse them – is that what your intention was Doctor?"

"No."

"No, is that your simple answer? Doctor, you are a highly trained man, a chief coroner – one of the best in the city – you know how to speak in medical terms better than anyone – I've even had the pleasure of hearing you confuse an audience on a number of topics – but today you never used one medical term."

"Objection, your honor what is the significance?" yelled out Juanita Lange.

"Overruled – continue councilor but make your point."

"Thank you your honor. My point – and allow me to be simple – is that the learned Doctor avoided using medical terms in order to engage the jury – if he confused them then he might not have assisted the prosecution's case."

"Objection your honor – is the councilor saying that I tampered with the witness."

"Overruled – your last chance before I strike the questions from the record."

"Again, thank you your honor." Greg knew that he could not push his line of questioning too far with gaining the wrath of Judge Marx.

"Doctor, when you inspected the bath tub in which Mrs. Starr had drowned did you notice the water level in the bath tub?"

"Yes, we photographed the bath tub with Mrs. Starr still in the tub – the water level was high."

"How high, Doctor? Say 70%, 80%, 90% of the capacity of the bath?"

"If I recall the water level was about 80-90% of the capacity."

Greg walked over to his table and produced a photograph that he submitted as evidence. "You will notice that the water level in the bath tub was upwards of 90% plus – indeed it was very close to the top of the bath". Greg walked over to his table again and produced another photograph taken by the coroner's team.

"You will also notice that there are puddle marks on the floor next to the bathtub – most likely caused when Mr. Starr pulled his wife out of the water and tried to revive her."

"Objection, your honor how is this relevant?'

"Overruled – please continue councilor – come to your point please!"

"The significance of the water level is this – the high water mark suggests that Mrs. Starr took a full bath that night – with her body weight the water level rose to the levels as shown in the photographs that I have distributed. We know from all accounts given that Mrs. Starr had consumed a great deal of alcohol the night that she died – that she was still intoxicated when she returned home – the blood alcohol level showed almost double the legal limit in her body. Her state coupled with the effects of a hot bath – with bath oils – made the deceased fall asleep in the bath tub. The significance of the high water level mark is that she did not have to slide down very far into the water to drown.
Drowning could indeed have occurred fairly quickly as the water level was so high – opposed to the position say if the water level was low and Mrs. Starr would have had to slide down much further in to shallower water."

"Objection, your honor the water level could not have played a part in the death of Mrs. Starr."

The judge turned to the coroner and said, "Doctor please provide an answer to this theory."

Greg stood and waited.

"It is highly unlikely that the water level could have affected the drowning."

Greg sprang into action.

"Doctor, did you say that it was unlikely?"

"Yes."

"Pray tolerate my knowledge of the English language but if something is unlikely does that mean that there is some possibility of it being "likely?"

"I suppose." answered the coroner.

Greg walked away from his position near the witness and spoke – his words were directed at the jury – "Beyond reasonable doubt, beyond reasonable doubt – that is the essence of a legal trial – if there is in other words reasonable doubt then a jury in any case cannot find an accused guilty of a crime. Doctor, thank you for providing the court with a plain and simplistic testimony – something that we could all understand – and being just as simple you provided – under oath I might add – that the drowning of Mrs. Maxi Starr could have occurred within a short period of time due to the high water level in the bath tub."

Greg held the pause in the courtroom longer than what Juanita Lange had done. It was almost as if he was counting to a number higher than the seconds that she had kept the court waiting.

"Doctor, you also mentioned something about water drops – or water marks – or almost dried water marks under the chair where Mrs. Starr had placed her bath robe. Is that correct?"

"Yes, that is what I stated."

"And, Doctor, you maintain that these water stains – water marks – were there from about the same time as when the deceased drowned. Is that correct doctor?"

"Yes, that is correct."

"So, therefore in your professional opinion it is beyond the realms of possibility that perhaps, just perhaps of course, that Mrs. Starr started running her bath water, felt the temperature of the water with her one hand and then sat on the chair waiting for the bath tub to fill up – and remembering of course per your own scientific

283

evidence that Mrs. Starr had almost double the legal limit of alcohol in her blood stream – and that she might have selected to sit down on the chair because she could not stand up by herself!"

"Yes, I suppose that it could have happened like that."

"In other words Doctor there is no clear evidence here to implicate my client – merely conjecture, speculation and unsubstantiated poppy cock – Doctor, this is a court of law – a court of law doctor!" Greg turned and faced the jury. "A court of law – where beyond a reasonable doubt means something – this is not a playground to entice a jury – it is a court of law."

Greg turned back to Doctor – he walked right up and stood directly in front of him and said, "Thank you Doctor. I have no more questions your honor." There was confusion in the court as the judge called for silence. Several requests had to be made before silence returned.

The judge asked the prosecutor if she had any more questions and she replied that she did not. Had Greg Winters succeeded in casting doubt on the Second Degree murder charge against his client? It appeared as if there were doubts about the conclusions drawn by the coroner. The apparent importance of the time taken to drown and the water stains under the chair in the bathroom now appear to be in doubt. All it took was to have "beyond reasonable doubt" in the minds of the jury.

CHAPTER 47

The prosecutor advised the judge that she had no more witnesses to call at that time.

A one day recess was called by the judge – much to the dismay of Greg. Thanksgiving was soon approaching and he knew that a one week break from the trial would then take place. He did not want to lose the advantage that he believed that he now had. He did not want any surprises to come from left field. This was the time to strike home the advantage. This was not the time for a one day break in proceedings. He wondered what the motive of the judge was in calling a timeout.

When the trial was reconvened it was the defense team that was now front and centre. Greg called his first witness – Abby Carmichael.

"Please state your name for the court."

"Abigail Carmichael – everyone calls me Abby."

There was a mild ripple of laughter through the court. Abby's charm and forthrightness was already evident.

"Abby what was your relationship with Mr. and Mrs. Starr?"'

"I was employed by them at their home."

"Were you their housekeeper?"

"No – I had no title – did not want one."

A further ripple of laughter ran through the court.

"Why not?" asked Greg with a smile.

"There was no need – I cleaned, I cooked once a week – I managed the gardener – sometimes I shopped – whatever needed doing – what title would that be? No, I needed no title – no Sir, if God wanted me to have title he would have given me one!"

The courtroom was called to order. Judge Marx however seemed to enjoy the touch of life in the court and the candor of Ms. Abby Carmichael.

Greg then explored several questions relating to how Abby became employed with the Starr's and how long she had been in their employ.

"How would you describe the relationship between Mr. and Mrs. Starr?"

"Oh, they were in love – they were so much in love with one another."

"Was this love visible to you or just from what you heard from others?"

"There love for each other was plain for all to see – it glowed like God's sun."

"You are in no doubt about their evident love for one another?"

"No sir – they were in love and more – they even liked each other…"

The laughter in the court was spontaneous and it took several calls for order before Greg could continue – having had to wipe away a tear of laughter from his eye.

"They liked each other!"

"Yes sir, they were in love but more importantly they liked being in each other's company – they did things together – they laughed a great deal – they were best friends and soulmates – yes sir, they were in love and they liked each other too."

"You never saw them argue?"

"Objection, your honor, the defense is leading the witness."

"Overruled." said the judge.

"Ms. Carmichael, your answer if you please."

"No sir, I never saw them argue – I never heard the one say a bad thing about the other one either."

"Thank you, No further questions."

"Your witness." said Greg.

Juanita Lange had not found Abby's engaging personality to be charming at all – in fact she had found it to be insulting – she was going to take it out on the witness.

"Ms. Carmichael, you seem to have been well inclined towards Mr. and Mrs. Starr – that is correct is it not?"

"Yes – they treated me like family."

"Like family – that is interesting – like family – is that why they paid for the education of your children?"

Abby Carmichael hesitated for a moment – the Starr's had insisted that no one ever know that he paid for Abby's children to have a good education – both secondary and for their college. No one – not even her children knew about the kindness of Paxton and Maxi Starr. How did the prosecutor find out about this?

"Objection, your honor what is the relevance?"

"Overruled – you have one chance to make your point!" warned Judge Marx.

"Ms. Carmichael, may I have your answer please!"

"Yes, Mr. and Mrs. Starr paid for my children's education – they were being kind."

"Councilor what is your point?"

"Ms. Carmichael was highly indebted to the accused and his late wife – she was well paid, invited to family functions, included in Mr. Starr's company year-end parties – she owed her life to them in a way – she would therefore stop at nothing to protect them – she was inside the Starr home and witnessed the relationship between the couple – if she saw or heard anything she would not tell the court – I propose your honor, that Abby Carmichael is not a reliable or honest witness".

"Objection, your honor this is ludicrous. Ms. Carmichael is under oath – why should she lie under oath – there is no point to this line of questioning or supposition."

"Ms. Lange I do not see the point of your line of questioning – other witnesses have vouched for the love between the accused and his late wife – move on or I will strike your cross examination from the record – do you understand?"

"I understand your honor." Although reprimanded Juanita Lange believed that she had planted a seed in the minds of the jury.

"Ms. Carmichael, during your time in the employ of the accused and Mrs. Starr did you ever see them distraught or unhappy – or were they always as happy as what you have indicated?"

"They were a normal couple – a couple in love – but they had their sadness."

288

"Can you describe one of these events in order for the court to understand that the Starr's were not heavenly-beings always happy and never sad." The comment was full of sarcasm Greg Winters erupted immediately and rose from his chair, "Objection, your honor – what is the meaning of mocking either the witness of Mr. and Mrs. Starr?"

"Sustained, councilor, this is your last warning!" Judge Marx was growing very weary of Juanita Lange.

Juanita Lange nodded but seemed hell-bent on sustaining her verbal line of attack.

"Ms. Carmichael, please tell the court if you ever witnessed any sadness in the Starr household."

"Yes, I did."

"Could you please share that with the court?"

"It was several years ago. I came to work on a Monday morning and the devil must have visited". Before Abby could finish her sentence there was another round of mild laughter through the court. The judge did not call for silence as the touch of Abby's humor was much needed fresh air in the courtroom.

Abby continued.

"I parked my car and walked into the house. I heard Ms. Maxi crying and I rushed through to the Living room. She was huddled in Mr. P's arms. Mr. P came over as I walked into the room and told me that Ms. Maxi's parents had been killed in a car crash in the early hours on the Sunday morning. I sat next to her on the couch and cried with her and prayed for the souls of her parents. She was like them – both wonderful people."

The court sat in silence as Abby Carmichael told of the sad scene that she had been part of. She told the story with such heartfelt

289

sadness that many a tear in the courtroom was shed. Then she continued, "That was not the only tragedy that weekend – young Mr. Ryan from next door to Mr. and Mrs. Starr had gone missing and the police had been alerted and were trying to find him. Mr. and Mrs. Wright had telephoned the police on the Sunday after Ryan had not come home the night before."

Greg's mind was working overtime trying to recall the incident of the death of Maxi Starr's parents and the disappearance of young Ryan Wright. Either he could not remember that co-incidence or he had dismissed it. He looked at Ken for assistance but Ken seemed equally as forgetful. Greg's mind was still spinning when he was brought back to the present as the prosecutor was talking.

"These two events took place the same weekend – no doubt this was not a happy time."

"No, it was not. I stayed all day with Ms. Maxi – the men and the police were out trying to find Mr. Ryan – and they were also visiting all of the young man's friends – but they came back in the afternoon – Mr. Ryan was not found. They looked for a long time but he must have run away – and he never came home."

"That was on a Monday you say, was there anything different about the house or that you will not find on a regular Monday?"

Greg was about to object but decided to hold fire.

"Yes, it was not a regular Monday."

The court seemed to hang on Abby's statement – what could have been different?

"Please tell the court what was different?"

"The neighbors hold a party once a month at the different homes on Ocean Drive – and on the previous Saturday the party had been at Ms. Maxi and Mr. P's home – these adults make a mess so it was

290

no regular Monday – the house was messy and who had to clean it me, of course who else!"

The court again experienced a ripple of laughter. Ms. Abby Carmichael was charming and so endearing.

Even the prosecutor had a smile on her face which was rare.

"It must have been a very tough day indeed." Juanita Lange added.

"Yes, it was – trying to comfort Ms. Maxi – trying to tidy the house – and then sitting with her some more – it was a day sent from the devil."

Greg's mind was trying to link dots – and not knowing if the dots were supposed to be linked or not in the first place. - a party at the Starr residence – Ryan going missing – a party at the Wright residence and Maxi Starr getting upset. That was too much to consider and there was definitely no suggestion of any linkage. "No, Greg" he said to himself, stick to the facts and the evidence.

The prosecutor moved on to another topic.

"Ms. Carmichael I believe that you were out of the country at the time of the death of Mrs. Starr."

"Yes, I was in China."

"Was your trip planned well in advance?"

"I have been thinking of going to China since I was a child."

"That was not my question. I did not ask you for how long you had being thinking of going to China – I clearly asked you how long in advance did you plan your trip – a week, two weeks or maybe four weeks perhaps."

Juanita Lange was dead set on bullying Abby Carmichael again.

"If I recall I booked to go on the trip about two weeks before I departed."

"Was the timing of your trip your decision?"

"Objection, your honor – what is the relevance of the question?"

"Overruled." said the judge. "The witness will answer the question."

"I had been thinking about going to China for a long time – Ms. Maxi had been prodding me to go for a long time too – she knew that it was a childhood dream of mine to go to China – but I had been putting it off for years."

"And what made you change your mind and decide to go at that particular point in time?"

"Mr. P had also been prodding me and the one day when I came to work he was home with Ms. Maxi waiting for me to arrive. He told me that they had a gift for me."

"What kind of gift?"

"Mr. P told me that they knew that I had wanted to go to China but that I could not make up my mind to go – so he had made a deposit with a Travel Agent up in the village and that the money could be used for my trip – and not only that he had booked a departure date for me."

"So the accused, Mr. Paxton Starr made a deposit with a travel agent for you to go away on a particular date is that correct?"

"Yes."

"How much was this deposit for?"

292

"He told me that it was for $5000."

"That is a great deal of money – sufficient to tempt you to go away!" The courtroom was again buzzing with speculation about the motive of the accused to insist that Abby go away on a particular date – and that he had laid out such a large sum of money to convince her to go.

"And what was the date of departure Ms. Carmichael?"

"It was the Friday - a week before Ms. Maxi died."

There was a loud murmur across the courtroom and Greg and Ken exchange worried looks.

"Ms. Carmichael, let us be clear here – after years of prodding by the deceased – and with no result in having you make-up your mind to go to China – Mr. Starr – the accused prods you to go – and then lays down money and even books a date for you to depart – does that not seem rather odd to you?"

Abby Carmichael say silent for a moment – as another ripple of anticipation ran through the courtroom.

"Ms. Carmichael?" The prosecutor was pushing home the advantage – the advantage of raising suspicion over the timing of the trip and of Mr. Starr's payment for Abby to go away while he planned to murder his wife?

"Yes it might appear to be odd – but I understood why Mr. P wanted me to go away at that particular point in time – there is an annual Flower Show in Beijing and that is one of the events that I always wanted to attend."

"So, then the accused planned the murder of his wife while he sent you off on an adventure that you could not say "no" to, is that it, Ms. Carmichael? Was he playing you?"

293

"Objection, your honor – this is speculation, pure speculation."

"Sustained".

"Ms. Carmichael you said that Mr. Starr paid for your trip to China."

"No, I did not say that." replied Abby.

"But Ms. Carmichael under oath you stated that the accused made a deposit of $5000."

"I know that I am under oath – so may the Lord strike me down and kill me if I lie under oath."

Once again Abby Carmichael brought the tense courtroom to a state of laughter.

After some composure had been returned the judge turned to Abby and said, "Ms. Carmichael – please answer the question and we know that you are under oath – this is a court of law" Judge Marx was smiling which was rather unusual.

"Mr. P said that he made a deposit with the travel agent. I went to book my trip but I did not use the money – I paid for the trip myself."

There was yet again another ripple throughout the courtroom.

"You did what?" said the prosecutor.

"I paid for the trip myself – I did not want Mr. P's money towards my trip – it had been a lifelong dream of mine to go to China and I was going to pay for it – which I did. I think that the money from Mr. P must still be with the travel agent."

The prosecutor was not a happy camper – part of her argument of Paxton Starr paying for Abby to be away had just fallen apart.

294

"Judge – I would need time to confirm this piece of evidence – could I suggest a short recess in order that we are able to report back to the court."

The trial was adjourned for an hour. Upon reconvening the prosecutor produced a FAX from the travel agent showing a $5000 credit on Abby Carmichael's account. She had indeed paid for the entire trip herself. She had also proved that she did not lie under oath as so accused by the prosecutor.

The prosecutor said that she had no further questions and Abby Carmichael stood down from the stand. The woman had a certain aura about her – something that attracted people to her – an honesty – a pure simple heart – and no wonder why the Starr's had loved her so much. No wonder why the court of Judge Marx had also fallen in love with her.

The judge asked Greg Winters to call his next witness and to the surprise of the judge, the prosecutor and the court he said that he had no further witnesses. His strategy had been to beat down the witnesses of the prosecution but then not allow the prosecutor to beat down any of his witnesses. The less the opportunity he gave to the prosecutor the less likely was the chances of some "out of left field" piece of evidence that might come up – and confuse the jury. In the planning sessions with his team he had kept saying "let's keep it simple – no chance for slip ups!" There had almost been one or two already but Greg did not wish to press his luck. Some information that he and Ken had was not of the concern of the court – so it would remain outside of the trial.

The judge allowed three days for the defense and prosecution teams to prepare their final statements. The trial had moved along faster than what had been expected.

On the following day however the judge's assistant requested an urgent telephone conference call with Juanita Lange and with Greg Winters. The judge had a death in the family the previous night. The judge had decided that because the delay would take the trial into the following week – which was Thanksgiving – the trial would only resume on the Tuesday after the holidays – a break of almost ten days. There was nothing that either Greg or Juanita could do but to agree.

CHAPTER 48

Greg was not at all happy with the delay in the trial as he did not want the members of the jury to have time to think too much – he would have preferred the closing statements, deliberation and the verdict in fairly quick order.

On the Friday before Thanksgiving week Elizabeth reminded him that on the following Monday was the retirement dinner for Todd Hornsby. In all honesty Greg had completely forgotten about the dinner and in all likelihood he would have missed attending the function. Then he thought "no" Elizabeth would have reminded him on Monday again and almost forced him to attend. Never underestimate an organized woman and her Day Planner!

On the Monday evening Greg left the office and drove to the venue of the dinner. He was warmly welcomed by armloads of lawyers whom he had met and worked with over the years. It certainly did not take too long for Greg to relax a little – and avoid all discussion of his case – and begin to enjoy the evening. He lost count of how many lawyers had stood up to say a few words about Todd Hornsby. Some speeches were very heartfelt goodbyes while others were unbelievably funny and bordering on libel. Todd was an amazing good natured man and of course he took all of the comments in his stride.

As the evening wore on some of the lawyers – who had very smartly taken cabs to the venue and would take cabs home - became rather intoxicated.

Greg was sitting at a table chatting to some old friends when one of the intoxicated lawyers walked up and started talking with them. Try as could, he could not make himself understood – one of the lawyers at the table stood up and said, "Mike, you've had way too much to drink – how about we get you a cab home." Mike mumbled something in reply and everyone burst out laughing – the poor man was incoherent. The lawyer who had spoken with

Mike took him by the arm and led him away – and hopefully into a cab and on his way home. Greg was enjoying the good laugh when all of a sudden a flash exploded across his brain. He sat in disbelief for a moment. "Greg, are you OK buddy?" said one of his old pals. "Oh yeah, sure – excuse me I need to take a leak." Greg stood up and as he walked towards the wash room he stopped at the bar and picked up a number of paper napkins. He then walked into the wash room and sat in one of the stalls. He took out his pen and wrote out in big bold letters "KIND I DENVER PLEASE PLEASE". He held the napkin up and read out what he had written". Then he read it again but tried to slur this time. Again and again and again he read out the words on the napkin. Once he felt that he had the right level of intoxication he read the words again and again.

He sat silent for many minutes after he had read out the words. Then he folded the napkin and put it in his pocket. He thought he knew what Maxi Starr was trying to tell her husband the night of their incident on the patio at Wil and Jenni Wrights home. But why was she trying to say it?

Greg washed his face and dried it very slowly on the paper toweling. When he walked out of the wash room he walked around the dining room until he found his old friend Todd Hornsby and bade him goodnight and wished him a happy retirement. Todd pleaded with Greg to stay but to no avail. Finally Todd took Greg in his arms and gave him a big man-hug "Well old buddy you look after yourself and do not wait too long until you retire too – I'll need a tennis partner!"

Greg did not feel comfortable to drive home so he found a coffee shop near the restaurant. He sat sipping several cups of coffee until he felt sufficiently sober to drive home. Before he realized it he had been sitting there for over two hours with the staff edging to go home. As he walked to his SUV he thought that even these days the two drinks that he had at the party was getting too much for him. He had all of the Scotch up at his cabin and it would most likely last him a good few years.

It took Greg 40 minutes to drive home and after another round of a few mugs of coffee he took a long hot shower. All the time his mind was working overtime – KIND I DENVER PLEASE PLEASE.

He had a restless sleep that night but was in the office early the following morning.

He dare not tell Elizabeth about how many cups of coffee he had consumed since the previous night. When she walked into his office with the large Giants coffee mug he accepted it gladly – anything else would have raised her suspicions.

Greg also decided not to tell Ken of the thoughts that had bounced through his mind the evening before – his experience of sitting with his pants on in a washroom stall looking at a napkin and trying to sound like an intoxicated person would remain his secret.

Although Greg had several invitations to visit with friends for Thanksgiving he decided to drive to his cabin for a few days. He still had a number of magazines that he wanted to read on renewable energy – plus a few other less stimulating topics – anything to switch his mind off for a few days. He did however sit and draft his closing statement for the trial. After he had read it through he tore it up and rewrote it.

He was walking through the local town when a voice behind him said, "Hey, stranger, new to these pasts?" There was no mistaking the burly voice of Sheriff Norm Wilson. The two men shook hands. Sheriff Norm asked why Greg had not contacted him if he was in town – he chuckled as he asked Greg if he had finally given up drinking coffee. When Norm Wilson heard that Greg would be spending Thanksgiving alone at the cabin he would not hear of it. After much pestering Greg finally accepted Sheriff Norm's invitation for dinner. On Thanksgiving Day Greg enjoyed himself more than what he had in many years. Sheriff Norman and his sister were splendid company.

299

CHAPTER 49

When the trial recommenced on the Tuesday after Thanksgiving all that remained was the closing arguments, the instructions from the judge and the deliberation of the jury. Not trivial matters by any means. In all too many cases the swing of opinion of the jury had only been achieved right at the end of the trial. Greg and Ken still believed that even though the prosecutor had stumbled several times in the trial that the jury had not as yet made up their minds on the upcoming verdict. It certainly was not cut and dried – it never was.

The media circus had taken a break over the Thanksgiving week but were now back in full swing. One could not avoid it – every newspaper, the online media, social networks and every TV station was covering the story. Talk-Show hosts would interview experts on topics related to the trial and even on topics completed unrelated. News feeds the media and increases viewership – viewership increases advertising rates and the stockholders become very happy. There is little moral fiber in much of the reporting and in the case of an accused wife-killer there is little sympathy. A leading female State Congresswomen had all but called for the accused to be drawn-and-quartered. Those that made the laws at federal level seemed to lose all sense of responsibility when it came to speculating on the guilty verdict of the court. If a man is accused of murdering his wife then he is guilty in the court of public opinion.

Paxton Starr had been sheltered from the media as far as was possible during the trial but there was no doubt that he had taken a great deal of strain. He had lost over twenty pounds in weight and he looked very drawn and pale. His bush of blonde hair had suggestions of grey flicks in it now. As the trial progressed he had retreated more and more into his shell. Sitting in the court day after day had served to almost drug him into a state of semi-consciousness – in all likelihood he could not remember much about the proceedings that had taken place. He was the subject of the trial and yet he almost seemed self-detached – as if he was watching an old black and white movie in slow motion without a sound track. Maybe his mind had shut down and it was a way of it trying to preserve itself – and how would it react when the verdict was read out?

Would he experience the high-of-highs or the low-of-lows? Would he care? Either way he would still be without his Maxi. A verdict would not change that. Nothing could bring her back. Nothing would ever be the same again.

How could he sit in his SUMMER or WINTER rooms and experience the joys of life without Maxi being with him. He had hardly walked into those rooms in his home since she died and he could not see himself ever wanting to relax there again – if he was found not guilty of course. He had not slept in the main bedroom or used the bathroom since Maxi had died. The one guest suite upstairs had become his new home. If he was home and Abby was at work then she would encourage him to move back into the bedroom but he could not bring himself to do it. Life would be different now – life already was different and it could become a great deal worse.

Paxton Starr had witnessed Ken and particularly Greg in action. He was so pleased that he had thought of approaching Greg Winters to defend him when he sat in the Holding Cell at the police station all of those months ago. His life had changed since that summer day. Paxton had watched Greg in action but his mind had drifted in and out of the reality of the situation throughout the trial. Greg Winters was the best in the business and had one of the keenness minds that he had ever come across. He was sure that Greg had not missed much that had been said or implied since they first met. He knew that Greg was selective in what evidence he wanted to present or not to present – Greg's task was to find his client not guilty of the murder of his wife. That is all that Greg was focused on.

Paxton Starr's attention was drawn to the proceedings in the court. The prosecutor had commenced delivering her closing statement.

"Ladies and gentlemen of the jury – at the outset of this trial – this trial of a potential wife-killer – we set before you three main principles – three main determining factors that led to the charges being brought against the accused, Mr. Paxton Starr. Allow me to remind you of these three points. Firstly, opportunity: Mr. Starr was alone with his wife the night that she mysteriously drowned in her own bath tub. Secondly, there is cause: Mr. and Mrs. Starr had a public argument, albeit one that was witnessed, but it was not heard because it had taken place outside on the patio of the residence of Wil and Jenni Wright. They had argued over something important – was it over the consumption of alcohol consumed by Mrs. Starr? We will never know, but almost within an hour of the argument Mrs. Maxi Starr was dead. A coincidence, I think not! Add to this the fact that Mr. Starr had begged, if not pleaded, with Abby Carmichael to go away on vacation at that same time – it begs the question if the entire set of events was preplanned by the accused. Was indeed the said argument even staged - the accused would have needed an excuse to bring attention to his wife's condition that night so that when she drowned in her bath tub, it would appear a tragic accident. Finally, there is motive: we heard from Mrs. Starr's financial planner that Mr. Starr was indeed the sole beneficiary of his wife's estate, a sum that varies as the market goes up and down, but is estimated to be over $40 million dollars. A sum that is likely to rise in value when the stock market recovers!

We are faced with three key pointers that I have laid out before you. The defense has tried to argue against these points but they have failed – repeat they have failed – in disproving any of the points raised. Mrs. Starr was murdered on that fateful night. The statement by the accused of his actions that night when the couple returned home from the party is a fabrication. Mr. Starr might even have suggested to his wife that she take a bath to relax – and then later walked up the stairs of his home and like a coward

303

drowned his wife. Let me repeat that statement – Mr. Starr drowned his wife. We might never know what his true motives were – the money or whatever other reason but that night he became a wife-killer.

Ladies and gentlemen of the jury the charges brought against the accused, Mr. Paxton Starr are Second Degree Murder and Criminal Negligence – you have no option based on the evidence presented at this trial to have him found guilty as charged. Thank you your Honor."

There was not a sound in the courtroom – a far cry from the day that Abby Carmichael had testified. It is so strange that one room – a courtroom – can witness days of more light testimony and days when verdicts are handed down. Greg had often wondered if he had been in the room used at the Nuremberg Trial and heard all of the testimony delivered by both witnesses and by the Nazi members how he would have felt. Then what would the feeling be if he had returned well after the trial and sat in the same run-down room if the atmosphere would have completely vanished? Maybe the walls would have absorbed the horror and stained the room forever – but maybe the room was just a room and there would be no trace left of the trial. What if both the world and the room had forgotten? Greg thought of the day that he had walked across the street from the courthouse and sat on the park bench. That day he had thought that trials should be heard outdoors and that anyone could listen to the proceedings. Then they could walk on. Maybe that way more people would remember trials. Courtrooms are such sad places.

"Mr. Winters, your closing statement." said Judge Marx. Maybe her thoughts were the same as Greg's about courtrooms being such sad places. He made a mental note to add that to his closing statement.

Greg Winters rose very slowly from his chair. He walked towards the jury and then he stopped for a moment. He looked at them and said.

304

"Ladies and gentlemen of the jury – a courtroom is such a sad place – we hear witnesses support or condemn an accused – we hear very personal and sometimes graphic details of private lives – we hear of the love of a man for his wife – we hear of how she died – and some might imply how he was involved in her death. We argue about points of order and procedures – we use strategy, tactics and terms of phrase to move the jury one way or another. Sometimes it smacks of theatrics.

The walls of this courtroom have memories of everything that has ever been said here. These memories will last long after this and other trials are over.

It is our duty under the law to bring the accused in a case to trial - to hear the evidence and for you – the jury to come to a decision. We pride ourselves of our legal process – that it is open and fair. In my opening address to you I mentioned the statue of a lady that stands outside of this building – she holds scales – scales of justice – signifying balance. We need balance to have a fair legal system.

The essence of any legal case is the presentation of evidence. We've heard the prosecutor repeat herself that my client had the opportunity, the cause and the motivation to murder his wife – the woman that he loved. While we agree that Mr. Starr was alone with his wife on the night that she tragically died – no evidence – absolutely no evidence has been presented that even remotely points to my client being involved in the death of his wife. The evidence brought by the coroner was put into question – there was doubt in his mind – and confusion in his professional evidence as to how Mrs. Starr died. If the coroner cannot be sure then who can? We heard from the expert who installed the bath tub in which Mrs. Starr drowned – and what was his conclusion at the end? That a non-slip bath tub over 10 years in age and with the regular usage of bath oils loses its non-slip properties. Where, I beg you, is the evidence that links Mr. Starr to the murder of his wife? We heard about drops of water on the floor – and where did that line of evidence go? Nowhere – it went nowhere.

305

We acknowledge the fact that my client stands to benefit by a large sum of money as the result of his wife's death – some $40 plus million. But we also discovered that the terms of Mrs. Starr's last will and testament was signed many years ago – it was not a recent change that could have occurred as a result of pressure from her husband. And need I remind you that my client is already worth four times the amount of what his wife left him.

Is there cause? Is there motive? Absolutely not! The flimsy evidence produced was smoke in the sky to distract you from the basic and underlining truth that my client did not murder his wife. The prosecution failed in every way to produce anything that merits the time of this court – the memories left behind on these four walls will be one of a reckless case against my client – a case that has proven absolutely nothing. I mentioned that the courtroom is a sad place – it indeed has been a sad place these last few weeks – dragging an innocent man through the mud for no reason whatsoever. Is that not sad?

So, ladies and gentlemen of the jury I put to you that there has been no evidence linking my client to the murder of his wife. The law requires you to make your decision based on facts – and in this case none of the so-called facts stood up to cross-examination. The law also requires that guilt is proved beyond reasonable doubt – the only doubt that has been proven in this case is that of the evidence presented.

In closing I therefore ask you to consider the requirements of the law – to apply just reason and to come to the only conclusion that there is in this case – a verdict of not guilty. Thank you, your honor."

There was not a murmur in the court after Greg Winters had concluded his closing statement. He had been dramatic, direct, to the point of the law and had gripped the court with his delivery and imagery of what justice was supposed to be.

Judge Rita Marx broke the silence.

She instructed the jury as to the decision that they were required
to make and the conduct that was required of them. After she had
completed her instructions she turned the proceedings over to the
jury and adjourned the case until they had reached their verdict.
It had been a very interesting Tuesday in Judge Rita Marx's court.
Now the dreaded period of waiting began.

CHAPTER 50

The media circus seemed to be on steroids. The city was filled with speculation on the case. How long would the jury sit? Why would they take that long? Did the evidence stack up against the accused? Each News Anchor and TV station had their expert panel – every detail – real or fictional was examined. Had Greg Winters been too overbearing? Would this influence the jury? Had the prosecutor dropped the ball – would the jury still side with her? If Paxton Starr was found guilty what would the sentence be?

Greg had ensured that Paxton Starr would be under secure guard and completely out of sight during the period that the jury deliberated the case. Greg had arranged a secluded and well secured home for Paxton Starr to move into for the duration of the deliberation.

In truth Greg had not organized this – Elizabeth was given the instruction and through their network they obtained the location of safety and seclusion for their client. They had used this residence before and after shaking off the Press brigade that was following them and changing vehicles Paxton Starr disappeared from the public eye.

This is a difficult time for a legal team. Matters were now out of their hands.

Still it was very nerve racking – everyone was on edge. Greg and Ken and the other members of the team that had represented Paxton Starr drank more coffee that what was normal for a set of human beings to consume. Elizabeth was not happy with this but it was a battle that she was not going to win – and a battle that she had lost before while the firm of Greg Winters and Associates waited for the verdict.

The jury received their instructions on the Tuesday – how long would the wait be?

On the Friday morning Greg's office was notified that the jury had reached their verdict. The court would sit at 1 o'clock.

Greg's mind had been split on two different topics over the last few days. The number one priority was of course on the trial and what the verdict would be. He had spoken on the telephone several times to his client and assured him how confident he was of the outcome. Inwardly he was not that sure – one can never be too sure of these things.

The other topic on his mind was that of his own future. Had this been his last case?

He had promised himself that after the previous case that he would retire but then this one just seemed to slip in. He had many things to consider but those thoughts would have to wait for his full attention – not now there were other more important things at hand.

Greg and Ken arrived at the courthouse at about 11 o'clock. Any time after that could have been sheer madness to try to get near the court. The vehicle and security that brought Paxton Starr to court arrived just on noon. Greg briefed his client on what will take place once they were called to the court. Paxton Starr had aged a great deal in the last few months and he looked even worse that day.

The one o'clock time came and went and it was closer to 2 P.M. in the afternoon when they entered the court and waited for the judge and jury to enter.

Once everyone was settled the judge asked the Jury Foreman to rise.

"Have you reached a verdict?" asked the judge.

The judge asked the Bailiff to bring the sheet with the jury's verdict written on it. The judge read the note.

"Will the defendant please rise."

Greg Winters and Paxton Starr stood up.

"In the case of Second Degree murder in the death of Maxi Starr how do you find?" asked Judge Marx.

The Foreman answered.

"We find the defendant NOT GUILTY."

There was an explosion of noise in the courtroom and the judge had to call for order several times before silence was returned. Greg had cast an eye at Paxton Starr and he saw the color rush out of his face and then return. His cheeks were red and he was holding back the tears. Greg glanced at Ken and just nodded his head.

"So say yea one so - so say yea all?" asked the judge.

"We do your honor."

The judge then asked, "In the case of Criminal Negligence how do you find?"

"We find the accused GUILTY."

"So say yea one so – so say yea all?"

"We do your honor."

Again there was an outburst of emotion inside the courtroom and the judge had to call for order several times before there was a semblance of silence. Already the news of the verdicts was known to the outside world through all of the social networking devices that were being used inside of the courtroom. Greg could only imagine the frenzy when he had to address the media. That was how this story began with Greg having to face the media after the not guilty verdict of his previous client. Not an activity that he enjoyed doing.

Judge Marx spoke, "The accused will remain in custody until I deliver the sentence – today is Tuesday – I will deliver sentence by next week Tuesday at 10 o'clock."

Greg asked, "Your Honor, in view of the high bond already in place with my client could I suggest that he be allowed to remain on bail while you consider the sentencing?"

"The motion is denied. Bailiff, please escort the accused and take him downstairs for holding until next Tuesday. I would like to thank the members of the jury for their deliberation on the case. Your duties are now dissolved and you are dismissed. Please assure that you abide by the rules and regulations that apply to you as being members of this jury."

"The court is adjourned until sentencing." Judge Marx rose and left the courtroom.

Greg told his client that he would see him shortly in the holding cells – and a very confused and distraught Paxton Starr was led out of the courtroom.

Ken shook Greg's hand and congratulated him on the not guilty verdict. As they stood speaking Juanita Lange walked right by without even acknowledging Greg's out stretched hand. He thought, "She still has a lot to learn about decorum – she reminds me of me when I was young and cocky!"

When Greg addressed the media he thanked the judge and the jury for their deliberation and handling of the case – he believed that logic and common sense had prevailed and that the prosecutor had failed in providing any evidence that implicated his client in

312

the death of his wife. A reporter then asked, "Does that mean that he did do it and the prosecutor just failed to prove it – or is he really not guilty?" At first Greg was loath to respond to the question and then he replied, "The answer to that question does not matter and has no relevance at all – but what is important is that in the eyes of the law – the law that we respect as a community – that he was found not guilty by a jury of the people and for the people. We respect and trust the legal system."

It took Greg almost two hours before he could get to see his client. There was no doubt that Paxton Starr was very disappointed by the verdict pertaining to Criminal Negligence. Greg and Ken tried to comfort him by saying that although the next week would be very difficult they would prepare an Appeal once the sentence had been handed down by the judge.

There was not much activity in the week that followed. Greg did not really approve of celebrating a not guilty verdict in his offices after a trial but he did accept the congratulations of his staff and a firm hand shake from Elizabeth. He did not know however, if congratulations were in order. His feelings were not based on the fact that he had maintained a 100% record on defending clients on murder charges but rather on the ringing in his ears from a conversation that he had overheard in Joe's Diner all of those months ago. "The lawyers who get not guilty verdicts for wife-killers are just as guilty as the guys that commit the crimes." He could not remember the exact words used that day but the ringing in his ears would not stop.

Over the next few days he spent a great deal of time with Ken in preparing for a potential Appeal to the Paxton Starr sentencing that would come down on the following Tuesday. There were many things for them to discuss. The discussion even spread out to a private dinner that Greg invited Ken and his wife to. After the sentencing of Paxton Starr Greg would also arrange a private function for his staff – or rather Elizabeth would arrange it.

313

"The Solar Murder"

314

CHAPTER 51

The following Tuesday came around quickly and Greg and Ken were at the courthouse early to avoid the media circus that had already gathered. The not guilty verdict of Paxton Starr had not gone down well with the public although the legal opinion was that it was the correct decision.

Paxton Starr was brought into the courtroom and was seated next to Greg and Ken.

Once the court was brought to order Judge Marx addressed the court.

"The jury in this case found the defendant guilty of Criminal Negligence. Why was that? The jury came to the conclusion that although the deceased, Mrs. Starr, had consumed a substantial amount of alcohol on the night that she died and by all accounts was not in a sound state of mind when she returned home with her husband – and was therefore not of a sound functioning mind – and should not have considered taking a bath in the condition that she was in – the defendant had a responsibility for his wife's wellbeing. Granted his emotions were wrought as a result of the events of the evening – but he did not consume much alcohol himself – and therefore was of reasonably sound mind and therefore he should have either prevented his wife from taking a bath or even have assisted her. Even if he had consumed more alcohol than what was reported that in itself is no excuse – he should have known better and acted in a responsible manner.

The law must look at this situation from a legal perspective – in other words what is required under the law and not be driven by any outside events – such as the events of that dreadful evening when Mrs. Starr died.

However, outside of the law one must take into account the love that very evidently existed between the defendant and his late

315

wife. This court has heard from all witnesses that were close to the couple that they were genuinely in love with one another. Although being in love is not excuse for Criminal Negligence one must consider that in the defendant's state of mind that night he must have had great feelings and high emotions for his wife – she was in distress for some reason and in trying to comfort her she had hit him. No, I do not believe that he acted in revenge – I merely believe that he did not think at all about the consequences of his wife taking a bath in her condition.

I have therefore come to the following conclusion. The verdict of this court was that the defendant was guilty of Criminal Negligence – and I concur with the verdict. The sentencing of the defendant is as followings – will the defendant please rise – Paxton Starr you are therefore sentenced to serve 21 days in prison plus one hour. Your time served in detention up to and including today is 21 days – this will count as time served.
You will be detained and taken to a cell in this building where you will be held in solitude for one hour – at the end of that time you will be free to go.

"May you have long and fond memories of your wife."

This court is now dismissed."

There was not much time to congratulate each other before Paxton Starr was taken away to serve his one hour in a cell in the basement of the courthouse building.

Once Paxton Starr had left the courtroom Greg just sat down in complete exhaustion. He could not feel his body at all. Ken was shaking his hand and patting him on the back but he felt nothing at all. It was over – it is all over. He had nothing left inside. A court official thought it a good gesture to bring Greg and glass of water and he thought that it was the nicest thing that had ever happened to him in a court of law.

The prosecutor now had the grace to shake hands with Greg and Ken. Greg knew that Juanita Lange would become a major force as a prosecutor and he was glad that he would not have to face her in the future.

Greg addressed the media again – and his dislike of having to do so was only tempered by the fact that the interview was very short. He went and waited for his client in a reception room in the cell area.

When Paxton Starr emerged at the end of his one hour confinement – which had seemed like ten years to him – he embraced Greg and Ken and held them so tight that they gasped for breathe as they each took turns with their client. They sat for a few minutes and spoke and then Ken called for their vehicle to be brought up. The media circus was waiting for them but they whisked Paxton Starr away – away to the beginning of a life as a free man – but one forever without his wife.

CHAPTER 52

It was now early December. The previous six months had flown by – as time always does when there is a case on file. Greg and his team had paid so much attention to the Paxton Starr case that they had lost track of the days, weeks and months. On reflection the delay in the conclusion of the case until after the Thanksgiving holidays had been a blessing. Greg's staff had always been home for Thanksgiving – there was no way that anyone would miss it – but some years the strain had been unbearable. This trial had been tough and also drawn to an end over the holidays but this time it felt a little different. Greg had given most of the staff an extra day off in order that could have a longer time at home. Some had done some work late at night when the family was in bed but generally the holiday time had been a truly wonderful experience. The pressure was also more on Greg to prepare for the end of the case so in reality there was not much work for the lawyers to do.

The final invoice was prepared for their client. The deposit amount of $1 million that Paxton Starr had made had been exceeded. The invoice for the remaining amount was signed off by Greg and payment was received within 48 hours. The case was closed and all administration was soon wound up.

There were other potential cases stacking up and already a smaller case had been taken on. The firm is a living entity and can only survive on a continuous inflow of fee income.

Elizabeth had planned the annual staff year end dinner. Several years before she had found a small inn just outside of the city that had a retired 5-Star hotel chef. He now only cooked for select groups on Friday or Saturday nights. The menu was spectacular and after the first year the staff lobbied to go back there again. Elizabeth now booked the dinner one year in advance. Spouses or companions joined the staff and by having an intimate gathering in a private dining room was very special. Many of the staff selected to stay over after the dinner – Greg's offer was either a limo to and from the venue or the night accommodation.

The dinner was the second Friday of December. On that day Greg closed the office at 2 o'clock and allowed his staff to go home and get ready for the dinner or arrange for babysitters.

Pre-dinner drinks were at 7 o'clock and the dinner commenced at 8. A quartet played softly in the background and all was set for a wonderful evening.

There were no formal speeches to be made that night as it was not Greg's style. He did make a point however of thanking all of the spouses and partners for their understanding and support during the year. All he could promise was the same pressure the next year.

The evening was a sheer delight and Elizabeth had outshone herself with the organization. By about mid evening two stand-up comics came in for a short skit. It was uncanny how the one looked just like Greg and the other one like Ken. Elizabeth was getting her vengeance back at them for teasing her the entire year! In the middle of their skit a third comic entered the room – this one was unbeknown to Elizabeth as she had only arranged for the first two. The third one was dressed just like Elizabeth in full office wardrobe – the gathering roared with laughter. Greg and Ken had overheard Elizabeth planning the skit about the two of them and they then telephoned the comic company afterwards and arranged for a third member to be added. The three-person skit session had the audience crying with laughter. At the end of the set Greg and Ken presented Elizabeth with a boutique of flowers and each one gave her a kiss on the cheek. Everyone stood up and clapped their applause for their Sergeant Major.

At about 11 o'clock Greg called for their attention.

"Sorry to bust up your fun but I would like to say a few words. For those of you that are sober could you please take notes and share it with the others over breakfast!" He paused while the group became silent.

"We have just come to the end of another trial and another outstanding effort by every member of the team. From backroom to frontroom everyone in the firm pulls together and helps to make us successful. And make no mistake we have been successful over the years. But a time does come when some of us need to take stock and consider our future – our next challenges in life. I now have reached such a point. I have decided to retire from the practice – this news might not be a surprise to some of you – it might not even be a shock – and it could even be a relief to others!" Greg smiled but no one was laughing.

"I will be leaving the firm officially at the end of December but in practical terms I will be saying goodbye next Friday – so only one more week of having me around." There was still no laughter in the room. "I have great pleasure in announcing the Ken will be the Senior Partner in the firm – he is a man who I have admired for many years – an exceptional lawyer and a fine man. I know that he will lead the new firm with great success. He will have me around for a while as I will act as a consultant to the firm for about a year – so you will see me from time to time.

I will be selling my apartment and moving full time to my cabin near Alpine Meadows. I feel that that is where I want to be – in the country and near to my beloved Mary. I need to find the peace of being with the woman that I still love so much."

Greg wiped away a tear – as did so many others in the room.

"So, I therefore propose a toast – to old friendships and may they never die – and to the new firm – may it prosper and grow!"

Everyone stood up and shared the toast with Greg. There was not a dry eye in the room. Ken was the first to walk over and hug Greg – then the lineup of others behind him. Elizabeth stayed back and was last. She hugged Greg and he kissed her on the cheek – he

321

whispered in her ear that he would be taking his Giants coffee mug with him. Elizabeth buried her head on Greg's shoulder. Everyone in the room knew that they had tremendous respect for one another.

The party did not want to breakup that night and it was well after 3 o'clock in the morning before the final whiskey glasses were put down and people trooped off to their bedrooms. Those that had decided to have a limo service that night had kept their drivers waiting a long time before they went home.

It was the end of an era.

CHAPTER 53

Greg sold his apartment within a few weeks and agreed to an early close date. Within the month he was packed and moved out. He gave away most items of furniture as the cabin was reasonably well fitted out. Plus the theme of the décor in the cabin was not city-style so there was not that much that would blend in. He was amazed at the amount of books and legal publications that he had piled up in the apartment. He had little time to sort through many of them but he did dump those that were well dated. Why he had kept them he never knew – most likely because he never had time to look at them in the first place! The majority of the books would be transported to the cabin where he would sort and dispose – well that was the theory anyway.

Greg had never before accepted an invitation to spend Christmas Day with Ken but this year it felt different and he accepted and enjoyed a wonderful evening with the Parker family. After Christmas he moved permanently into his cabin.

New Year's Eve was spent alone but that did not perturb Greg at all. He had never really managed to stay up until midnight just for the sake of saying "Happy New Year" and then going to bed. He had a quick coffee with Sheriff Norm on New Year's Day. His friend was on duty that day so they sipped a coffee or two before duty called.

By the end of the first week of January Greg had properly moved into the cabin. Many years too late - but better late than never as the saying goes! He had too much stuff and the next week or two were spent throwing out things and getting rid of boxes and bags. On garbage collection day he would drive the maximum allowable load to the main road and drop it off.

Greg had brought with him a number of magazines on renewable energy and on electronic equipment. He wanted to research some topics that interested him. He spent hours reading up on alternative sources of energy and searching online for further information. He was determined to make a few changes to the cabin as soon as possible. His target date was the early spring. There were also a number of changes that he wanted to make on the inside of the cabin.

He drove into San Francisco and spent a considerable amount of time in an electronic gadgets store. Several hours later – and several thousands of dollars lighter – he walked out with what he wanted. He purchased all of what he needed in the city including some lumber that he could have purchased in Alpine Meadows.

He had hardly ever used his workshop and in the winter it was not an easy task to first tidy it up and then to get to work on some things that he wanted to make. His knowledge of woodwork was scant but he still managed to make one or two things that he required. The other things he had made in the city.

Soon he moved his renovations – if that is what you could call them – inside the cabin. Besides anything else it was warmer inside.

He had decided what he wanted done with the renewable energy. He had decided against replacing the roof as it would detract from the rustic look of the cabin. Instead he decided to erect solid thick wooden pylons around the side of the house – where the forest would hide them – or rather where the pylons would blend in. On top of the pylons the construction company would build platforms for the photovoltaic panels. The electricity generated by the sun would be directed down the pylons to battery packs that would be housed on the ground. These batteries would provide some of the electricity required for the cabin.

Greg signed the contract with the construction company and the renewable energy company and by the end of February during a mild period of weather the foundations were laid and the pylons of heavy beamed wood were erected. Once the foundations had settled in early March the renewable energy panels were installed and the alternative power source was all ready and operational by midmonth.

Greg had also completed the internal changes that he was making. Everything was finally all done and he was ready. He tested all of his new toys and everything worked perfectly. One of the safety features was a trip wire that he positioned on the road just at the turnoff to his property. As a vehicle drove over the wire it would trigger a buzzer in the cabin. He would then know if someone was driving towards the cabin – first on the short tarred strip of road and then on the dust road. All-in-all he would have about a five minute warning if a visitor was on his or her way.

On a visit to the town to see Norm he was quizzed by his friend as to why he had used contractors from the city and not local businesses that could have done with the business. His only answer was that he wanted the cabin to remain private and that although he dearly liked the local folk he did not want them talking about how much he had spent on his renovations. Sheriff Norm did not accept the reasoning but it was not his business.

"Once the days are warmer and the sun is bright then you should come out and visit the cabin and I'll show you what I've done." Sheriff Norm accepted the invitation. He had only been to the cabin once before – when Mary Winters had been laid to rest.

The road to the cabin was turning from snow to mud and soon the warming weather would turn them to a hard dry dust. The seasons change too soon sometimes.

Ken had spoken with Greg once or twice a week on different matters and had been impressed how energetic his former boss sounded. Physical work and thinking about new things had certainly turned Greg's life around – he was in the place where he wanted to be. Greg had also telephoned Elizabeth every so often. She denied emphatically that she missed him but deep down she knew that she did – he was a one-in-a-million man to work for. In truth the entire office did not seem the same.

Greg was in town one day picking up some groceries when he was stopped by one of the locals. "I see that that guy whose butt you saved last year is back from completing a big project somewhere in the Middle East – why should he go and help them build anything?" It was neither a question nor a statement – merely an idle comment.

Greg purchased a newspaper and read an article detailing Paxton Starr's recent return from the grand opening of a large apartment block complex. His company had built it in the United Arab Emirates and it was the largest apartment complex built in the Middle East. Greg thought, "That must put a few dollars in Paxton's personal coffers!"

Greg thought it time that he visited his old colleagues and so he arranged a date for a lunch in the office. Ken wanted to run a few things by him on a case that they were working on so Greg decided to make a day of it. He spent a few hours with Ken - in Greg's old office – and then enjoyed a lunch ordered in by Elizabeth. Around midafternoon he drove down to Joe's Diner and purchased himself an entire cheesecake to take back to the cabin with him. The four hour drive back to his cabin was filled with expectations of going home again.

During the next few weeks he threw out even more of his old law journals and other items that at this stage of his life that he classified as junk. Twenty years ago he would have found every logical reason to keep them –just in case he needed to refer to something in the future. Now the papers were worthless as the laws and opinions had changed so often. He carried out more bags of papers to his SUV and dropped them off at the garbage pickup point. Greg thought that the truck driver must have thought that the guy who lived up in the cabin had tons of junk to throw away – in truth the truck driver never even thought about it – he just picked up what was there and drove on.

When the dirt road to his cabin was becoming drier as the season changed he thought that it was time to telephone an old contact. "Sweaky" Jones or whatever his real name was. "Sweaky" had provided Greg with some valuable information over the years. Even good lawyers have their own resource pool! "Sweaky" could find out anything on anyone. Just give him the assignment and make sure that you paid his fee in cash and he would deliver. The transactions were always cash – one cannot trace old used bank notes.

Greg dialed "Sweaky's" private number. "Hello, what you want?" "Hello you old rat bag." said Greg. "Mr. W How are you? Where you been lately?"

"Oh, I retired a while back now I am out near Alpine Meadows."

"Yeah, I heard that you had retired – no good lawyers are left in the city now."

"So how are you Sweaky?"

"Business is slow – very slow."

"Sweaky" Jones knew that if Mr. W called that there was something that he wanted – it would have been poor business practice to say that things were good – that would be like driving the price down.

"Sorry to hear that – maybe I could help." Greg provided "Sweaky" with directions of how to drive to the service stop and grocery store that was about 15 minutes before the turnoff to Greg's cabin. Greg would have an envelope with instructions and a bundle of cash – made up of a few fifties but mostly a stack of twenty and ten dollar bills – nothing that would raise suspicion. It was a big envelop.

The following afternoon Greg walked into the grocery store and bought a few items – including a large coffee. He put the groceries in his SUV and then went and sat on a bench on the side of the store. In the summer one could buy burgers and hot dogs and eat them under the umbrellas on the side of the store. A few minutes later a car pulled up. A man got out and also bought a large coffee – what better place to drink it than outside on a bench in the spring sunshine. The man picked up the bundle that was next to Greg and sipped his coffee and then got up and drove away in his car – in the direction that he had come from. Greg finished his coffee and was about to walk to his SUV when a voice said, "I always thought that you were a spy!"

Greg looked up at Chubby the service pump attendant who was standing in front of him.

"I saw that man pick up the secret information that you left for him – I seen it in the movies – I saw what you did – you're a spy!"

Greg was not sure how to answer Chubby and he did not want him speaking all over town about what he had seen.

"Oh, hello Chubby – how are you today?" But Chubby just looked at him.

"Well, Chubby, you caught me – but it was a test to see how good you are – we need your help and we wanted to check you out first." Chubby said," I don't believe you – you're a spy!"

"Actually I am not a spy – but I'll tell you about that in a moment – but we really do need you help – will your let me explain our plan?" Again Chubby just looked at Greg.

"OK, Tell me but you had better be telling the truth."

"I understand – well, as I said I am not a spy – actually I am working under cover for NASA – you know our Space Agency – well we've been tracking a Russian satellite that has been sending beams down to earth that interrupts our communication with the Space Station. In my cabin we've built a tower with special lenses

328

and it takes photographs of the satellite every time that it passes over us. The man who took the photos from me takes them back in complete secrecy to our research offices in San Francisco – and there they analyze the photographs. Chubby this is really very top secret."

"You sure? This is no lie?"

"No, Chubby it is the truth – but it must remain top secret – do you understand?"

"You sure? Is this the real truth?"

"Yes, it is the truth. And let me tell you how you can help. There are some bad guys hanging around here – or some guys that might be coming to visit me – nasty Russian spies. They would do anything to stop NASA. Your job is to telephone me at my cabin as soon as you see one of these guys or see the fancy car that they might be driving. Could you do that – could you do that for your country – and never tell anyone about it?'

"You want me to help NASA on a top secret assignment? Why me? What can I do?"

"The test that we did earlier showed us that you do not miss a thing that happens here. You see everyone that stops here and you see everyone that passes by – no one passes here without you seeing them. Right!?"

"I suppose. What must I do?"

Greg got up walked back to his SUV. He had an old newspaper on the back seat. He tore off the page with the photo of a man. Greg jotted down his telephone number at the cabin and also the type of car that the man drove. He walked back to Chubby and said, "This is the Russian spy that might come to visit me – if you see him you call me immediately – can you do that? We are counting on you?"

329

"Will my name be in the papers if we catch him?"

"No, unfortunately not – this must remain a NASA secret."

"I have always wanted to serve my country. I'll call you if I see him. You have my word." Chubby stepped back from Greg Winters and gave him a salute which Greg returned. Chubby stuffed the page from the newspaper into his overalls and walked away.

Greg was not sure if he felt terrible about lying or pleased with himself about his spontaneous performance. He thought "You should have been a lawyer!"

In any event he now also had an unexpected ally.

CHAPTER 54

True to his word it did not take "Sweaky" Jones too long to come back with some information. His network had confirmed that on Friday week a construction conference was being held near Reno and that the person in question from San Francisco would be attending. The Friday in question therefore looked like a possible date. Greg agreed. "Sweaky" had never failed him before.

Greg spent the next week or so tiding up the cabin, visiting with Mary and walking around the forest near his little place of heaven. He completed the paper work that required his attention.

The following week he drove into town and visited his bank and the local town offices. It was unfortunate that Sheriff Norm was out of town for a day on a police conference.

On the Friday in question Greg rose early as there was much to do. He took his breakfast outside and then walked over to Mary and stood next to her while he drank his coffee. He then took a walk down his drive way and sat on his favorite tree stump – with another mug of coffee in his hand. After lunch he checked that all of the batteries of his renewable energy system were working. Then he settled in to read some old case files that he had kept. Finally he took a long shower and dressed.

In the late afternoon he telephoned his friend Sheriff Norm Wilson. To his surprise Norm answered the telephone. "Sheriff Wilson." Greg greeted his friend and then said, "Sheriff I've completed all of the renovations up at the cabin now and I know that I owe you a guided tour – I was wondering if you could make it tomorrow morning." Norm Wilson checked his Day Planner and replied, "Sure, what time?" They confirmed 11 o'clock as the time that Sheriff Norm Wilson would visit Greg. Just before Greg hung up the telephone he said, "Sheriff, I've also redone Mary's resting place I must take you over to take a look".

His dinner was steak, eggs and greasy bacon. Elizabeth would have scolded him if she were there.

It was about 10 o'clock when the telephone rang. It was "Sweaky." All Greg said was "Thank you" and hung up.

Around 10:30 P.M. the telephone rang again. The voice said, "Hello, this is Chubby, I saw the Russian spy. He stopped his car just away from the gas pumps and called me over – he asked how far it was to the railway lines as he was lost – he did not sound like a Russian. Did I do good by calling you?"

"Yes, thank you Chubby you did very good. NASA will be very proud of you – but remember this is top secret – no one must ever know."

"I understand sir." Chubby put down the telephone in the call box and saluted.

Greg walked out of his cabin and over to where Mary lay. He kissed her headstone. Then he bent over and placed an envelope at the base of the stone and secured it with a small rock. He turned and walked back inside the cabin. The front door was closed but unlocked.

Greg walked over to his liquor cabinet and looked inside. There were so many unopened bottles of whiskey. He had stockpiled them for the winter – in fact he had been stockpiling for years already – but he hardly ever had a drink. There is not much fun in drinking alone. He took out an open bottle and poured himself a shot – he enjoyed the aroma – and then thought "what the heck" and just drank it. He followed with a second and a third until his chest burned like crazy. Could he force another drink down – he poured another slug but only drank half of it.

Ten minutes later the buzzer went off in Greg's cabin. He turned it off and turned off some of the lights in the cabin. Greg went into his office and pressed a button.

Everything was silent.

Some minutes later the power went out. The electricity outside had been cut at the switch box.

Greg moved around the darkened cabin. Then he heard the creak of the dried wood on his front steps. The front door was very slowly opened. There was another creek.

Greg half-stepped out of the shadows and said, "Is anyone there?"

It took a second or two and then a single shot rang out.

Greg Winters fell to the floor.

He groaned in pain from the bullet wound. He had taken the shot in his right upper chest. He lay on the floor with an ever bigger blood stain covering his dark shirt. A figure walked towards him in the half-dark. He leaned over Greg

"Hello Mr. Starr." said Greg.

Paxton Starr turned down his hooded top and said, "How did you know that it was me Mr. Winters?"

Greg was in great pain but thanked himself for drinking the several big shots of whiskey. He did not know if it was helping deaden the pain but knew that it would most likely have been worse if he had not forced the liquor down his throat. He coughed and the pain wracked his body.

"I knew that you would come to visit me – I was just not sure when."

"And why would you think that I would come to visit you?"

"Because I am the only living person who knows that you murdered your wife."

Paxton Starr did not answer Greg at first. He looked at Greg's wound and the amount of blood that was seeping through onto Greg's shirt. He then said, "I was never a good shot – but you most likely remembered me telling you that once – I can hardly hit anything at more than 15 feet – I shot too soon." He paused then said, "Not to worry I think that you will bleed to death – I'll wait until it happens just to make sure."

Paxton Starr then walked around the cabin switching on lights to make sure that the power was indeed off. He knocked over lamps looking for hidden bugs that the sly Greg Winters might have planted. He could not find any.

He walked back to where Greg lay on the floor. He pulled up a chair and sat in front of Greg. He placed his hand gun on a table and looked down on the man that had saved him in court.

Greg looked up at him and said, "Why don't you humor a dying man and tell him what happened that night?"

Another minute or more passed before Paxton Starr spoke.

"I suppose that you deserve to know – and yes, I had to kill you because if you ever spoke then I would be ruined."

"Why don't you tell me what happened at Wil and Jenni Wright's house – that is where the real tragedy started to unfold – I am I right?"

"Yes, you are right that is where it started – but before I tell you my story I have a few questions."

Greg was not sure if he would live long enough to answer the questions and then to hear why Paxton Starr murdered his wife.

"You can tell me when you first suspected that I killed my wife."

Greg answered, "On the day that I took on your case you said, "Please do anything you can to make me a free man – that sounded odd to me – you wanted to be a free man – and there was no thought of your crime – you just wanted to be a free man."

"Yes, I remember that mistake – I cursed myself when you left me that day – it was an error."

"What else? What else bothered you about my story?'

"I was confused if you recall about your wife's shawl."

"Ah yes, I could not see where you were going with that one – and then you just dropped it."

"Your wife was very particular with her things – everyone said that and we could see it too. But that night she was intoxicated – she walked into her dressing room and most likely the shawl fell from her shoulders as she tried to take it off – I believe that she left it lying on the floor – just as she did with her clothes. But the shawl was in her closet neatly folded. It was folded because you picked it up and put it away. This proved to me that you did not merely walk into your bedroom that night and lie down on your bed and go to sleep – you walked around the room – and even more likely had been into the bathroom. When you picked up the shawl and folded it was after you had murdered her – like a sign of regret – you found it and put it away as she would have liked it done. But you did not see her dress lying on the floor at the back of the dressing room."

Greg coughed up blood and was struggling to speak.

"When you folded the shawl and put it away you did not notice that all of the other shawls had the fringe endings facing outwards on the shelf – all neat and tidy as your wife had placed them there. The shawl that you folded and put away had the fringe edges facing inwards towards the back of the closet. If your wife had put it away the shawls would all have been facing the same way. I knew that you had put it away."

Paxton Starr again sat in silence for a minute or more and then he spoke in a very soft voice. "You are absolutely right – that is exactly what happened – I put the shawl away – I found it after I had been into the bathroom."

Greg sputtered, "One more thing – you suffer from an enlarged prostate – I checked your medical records – but when we spoke to all of the witnesses that night no one saw you go to the washroom. After you had a number of drinks in your home later that night you just had to go and pee – you walked into your bedroom put down your coffee and then walked into the bathroom to relieve yourself."

"My, you are a very observant and astute man, Mr. Winters!"

"Tell me what happened that night - tell me how it was affected by Ryan Wright's disappearance."

"Alright – I'll tell you. Ryan was like a son to us – we loved him and Stacey like our own children. You know that. He was a real good kid – but like all kids he was going through a bad patch. His parents knew that he was drinking and most likely taking drugs.
It was a terrible time for Wil and Jenni. Ryan was 16 and a big strong kid."

"Was he drunk at your home the night that he disappeared?"

"Yes – he was right out of it – eventually Wil took him to the door of our home and told him to go home and go to bed."

"He came back didn't he – after everyone had left?"

"Max went upstairs to get ready for bed and I decided to have a quick swim – I remember that it was a brilliant full moon. I came

336

out of the pool and was walking towards the sliding doors to the kitchen when I heard Max speaking loudly."

"It was Ryan?"

"Yes. He must have snuck back into the house when I was swimming. Max had come downstairs and had been standing in the kitchen when all of a sudden the light was switched off – she turned around and he was there – he said that he was going to rape her – I heard her saying "No, No, stay away from me!" – I did not know who it was but I saw him from behind – the big figure – he was wearing a hooded sweater – as I came into the kitchen he must have heard me and he turned around – all I saw was the knife – a big gleaming knife in the half light – he came towards me."

"Did you kill Ryan Wright?"

Paxton Starr continued as if he had not heard Greg's question.

"He came towards me with the knife – I – I panicked - old Paxton Starr panicked – I tried to back away and I slipped on the wet kitchen floor – I fell to the ground and as I turned over he was astride me – on my chest – both hands were on the knife and he was about to plunge it into my chest. I thought that I was about to die but I could not fight back – I was too terrified to do anything. The next thing I heard was a heavy dull thud and he fell limp on top of me. There was another thud and then another. I lay still on the floor with the intruder on top of me. Finally I managed to push him off of me and all I saw was Maxi standing over me holding the skillet – she had hit him over the head – she had saved my life – my tiny wife had saved me – big old soft Paxton – she had saved my life."

"I turned the intruder over and to my horror I saw that it was Ryan – I felt his pulse – he was dead – no, Mr. Winters, I did not kill Ryan – my wife did."

Greg could hardly talk now he was in such pain.

337

Paxton Starr continued.

"Before I could tell my wife that Ryan was dead I heard the skillet fall from her hand as she fainted. I crawled over to her – she was out cold. I picked her up and carried her upstairs. I put her to bed and thought that I'd tell her what had happened when she woke up. I went downstairs again and checked Ryan again – I don't know maybe I was hoping that he was alive – but he was dead. I sat on the kitchen floor next to him and cried like a baby – like the baby that I was that night. I had to protect Max – whatever happened I had to protect Max – if I called the police she would go to jail – my little Max could never survive behind bars. She loved life too much – her clothes – her lifestyle – she would not survive in jail.

So I went to the garage and put on my overalls and boots – I found an old blanket in a closet. I rolled Ryan in the blanket and put him on over my shoulder. He was heavy – so heavy – with a shovel in my one hand and carrying Ryan I started to walk towards the forest. I walked and walked and walked – how I found the strength I do not know. Once I was inside the tree-line then I put him down and rested. I looked at the full moon – and I remember throwing up as if my inside wanted to come out.

I knew of a rocky crop in the forest as it turns back towards the cliffs. I picked up Ryan and walked on until I reached the spot. Max and I used to walk there some Sunday afternoons and sit on the rocks and look out over the ocean. I never went back there after that night. I forced Ryan's body deep in between the cracks – as far as it would go. Then I gathered rocks, stones – anything that I could find and covered his body. The public never go there and I was sure that no one would ever find him. I had made him a deep tomb. I decided not to use the shovel as I thought that the noise might carry so late at night. I walked back to the house and was surprised that it was after 5 o'clock in the morning already.

338

I washed the overall down stairs – and burnt the blanket. I went into the kitchen and scrubbed the floor and then washed and rewashed the skillet – I remember the next week buying a new skillet and telling Max that I did not like the old one anymore – so we threw it out. She never suspected anything. The shock of the death of her parents must have prevented her from recalling Ryan's death.

I went upstairs and Max was sound asleep.

I showered in the guest bedroom – the longest shower that I had ever taken in my entire life. It was 6 o'clock by the time I fell into bed next to Max.

I would tell Max in the morning when she woke up.

The telephone rang after 9 o'clock and for a second I could not remember what had happened the night before – then Max said, "Are you going to get that!" – I answered the phone and it was the police department telling me that Max's parents had been killed in a car accident. I was speechless – they told me that police officers were on their way to our home to provide further details. I gave the news to Max and she broke down and sobbed – she was so heartbroken. Then I remembered about Ryan – how could I break the news to her then? Should I tell the police when they came by? Should I go and see Wil and Jenni – I did not know what to do. A short while later the police arrived. Max had not remembered a thing from the night before. I thought that once the shock of hearing about her parents had sunk in that she would remember – but she never did."

Greg said in a very weak voice, "Not until the night of the party." Greg was not going to mention that Stacey had mentioned to Maxi Starr that on it would have been Ryan's 21st birthday. He was going to protect Stacey and Chad.

"Yes, not until the night of the party - when we noticed that Max was drinking so much. I asked her to walk outside with me. I asked her what was wrong, and why she was drinking. At first I could not understand her then I understood what she was saying."

Greg whispered, "KIND I DENVER PLEASE PLEASE."

"Yes, "KIND I DENVER PLEASE PLEASE."

Greg pronounced the words that Maxi Starr was trying to tell her husband.

"KIND I DENVER PLEASE PLEASE – your wife was saying
RYAN I REMEMBER – POLICE POLICE."

"Something must have triggered Max's memory – for the first time since the night that Ryan had died. She remembered what had happened over four years before. She was trying to tell me that she wanted to tell the police but I said "no" we will not do that."

Greg remembered that Stacey and Chad had heard Paxton Starr saying, "No, no, NO!" to his wife outside on the patio. The young people had correctly heard what Mr. Starr had said – and they had been so close to interpreting what Maxi Starr was trying to say.

Paxton Starr continued.

"When we arrived home I did make Max coffee and we sat in silence in the kitchen. Then she said that she wanted to take a bath. I walked with her to the bottom of the staircase – she walked up a step or two so that she was at my height – she bent forward and kissed me and said, "tomorrow I'll call the police" – then she turned and walked up the steps. I returned to the kitchen and poured myself a drink – and then a second. I did not know what to do – I knew that Max would not survive in prison – she would die. I honestly did not think about murdering my wife – you might not believe me but I did not think of taking her life – she was the centre of my life – my soulmate and my love.

340

I poured my coffee and then walked up to the bedroom. I said, "Hon" when I came into the room but she did not reply. The bathroom door was closed so I did not expect that anything was wrong. I put down my coffee and as you guessed I had to go pee. When I was done I walked through to the bath room section and said "Hon" again – then I saw her – she must have been asleep in the bath tub. I spoke to her but she did not answer me – she was out cold – asleep like an angel.

I sat on the chair and looked at her – naked and so beautiful – so fragile – so small.

I could not let her go to jail – I thought that if I took her life while she was sleeping that it would be painless – and although I would have to live with the pain for the rest of my life at least she would not have the pain. It all seemed logical at the time. I stood up and walked to the bottom of the bath tub and took her by the ankles and gently pulled her body down into the water. Her face then went under the water and she slowly began to take it in through her mouth. I held her like that until I was sure that she was dead. I then sat on the chair again and looked at her – she still looked like an angel. Now she was one.

I felt exhausted and walked through to the bedroom and lay down and fell asleep.

The next morning I awoke and put my arm out to cuddle Max but she was not there. I called out for her thinking that she had already gotten up. Then I remembered. I ran through to the bathroom and saw my baby still in the water. I grabbed her and cried and cried. What in heaven's name had I done! You know the rest – I telephoned the police – I was a wife killer. While waiting for the police I found Max's shawl and I folded it and put it away".

Paxton Starr sat in silence for what seemed like an eternity. Then he spoke, "So, there you have it Mr. Winters – my wife killed Ryan and I killed my wife – Ryan's body was never recovered and I am

341

sure that his remains are still wedged in the rocks where I left him."

There was no response.

Gregory Winters was dead.

Paxton Starr checked that Greg was dead – once confirmed he then set about ransacking the cabin to make it look like a youth gang attack. He broke open the liquor cabinet and spilled whiskey on the floor and threw broken bottles around. He then carefully walked out of the cabin and disappeared into the dark night.

The only living person who knew that Paxton Starr had murdered his wife was now dead.

CHAPTER 55

The Saturday morning broke bright and sunny. Over breakfast Jenni Wright said to Wil just how excited she was that the group that lived on Ocean Drive was finally meeting at Paxton's home again that night. It was the first time that Paxton had agreed not only to attend a monthly party but also to host one.

Paxton Starr only returned home after 3 A.M. that morning but he awoke feeling as if a giant anchor had been cut away from his side. The events of the previous evening made him feel free and independent again – he truly now felt a free man. He was looking forward to meeting with his friends that evening. It had been almost nine months now since he had attended a gathering of his of friends.

Abby Carmichael did not normally work on a Saturday but Mr. P had asked her if she would come in that afternoon and evening to help set up for the party. She had readily agreed.

Sheriff Norm was at work early that morning as per his usual routine. He had every intention of leaving the office at about 10 40 A.M. to drive to Greg's cabin. He was looking forward to his visit and to inspect the changes that Greg made. Unfortunately Sheriff Norm was called away to a serious traffic accident and was tied up until almost 1 o'clock. He had tried to telephone Greg to tell him that he was running late – but Greg's telephone just rang. On the third attempt Norm Wilson left a message that he would be late.

Just after one o'clock Sheriff Wilson turned his vehicle off of the main road and onto the dirt road that led up to Greg's cabin. As he approached the cabin he marveled at the breath-taking view across the small lake with the cabin situated on the other side. From the police SUV he could not see any obvious sign of renovations but then again it had been many years since he was last up with Greg – attending Mary's burial.

As he parked the vehicle he called out for Greg but there was no response. As he was about to walk up the steps onto the front deck he noticed that the door of the cabin was broken and standing open. "Greg, Greg – are you okay –it's Sheriff Norm – Greg?"

There was no answer from inside the cabin. Sheriff Wilson became very nervous and he slowly drew out his firearm. He walked up the steps and pushed the door open with his one boot. "Greg, Greg." There was no answer. The sheriff walked very slowly into the cabin – he immediately saw that the place was in a mess – those bloody kids he thought to himself – then he edged in through the small lobby and into the living room – it was then that he saw legs lying behind a couch. Norm Wilson rushed over and as he turned the corner of the couch he looked down and saw the dead body of Greg Winters.

"Oh no, oh no, Christ Almighty, oh no, Greg!" The big man knelt down on one knee and tried to find a pulse. Greg's body was cold – he had been dead for many hours.

Sheriff Wilson moved very swiftly for a big man – he ran back to his SUV and called in Emergency Services. He walked back inside the cabin and had a quick look around for any obvious evidence. He tried the lights and realized that the power had been cut off – he stepped over broken liquor bottles and knocked over tables and chairs. The desk draws in Greg's office were broken open. All first impressions pointed towards one of those forced entry attacks that were becoming common across the State. He had just been briefed on this type of attack at the conference that he had attended the previous week – the same attacks that Paxton Starr had read about in the newspapers.

Within a few minutes the sound of sirens could be heard coming down the main road. A dust cloud arose as the speeding police vehicles came screaming to a halt outside of the cabin. Sheriff Wilson walked inside the cabin with the doctor and members of his team. They had hardly started their assessment of the situation when the sheriff of Carson City walked in – he was always called in when murders were reported in the smaller towns.

Every police officer that was at the scene of the murder knew Greg Winters – most of them personally – but all through his many cases. They were all equally as shocked at the shooting death of Gregory Winters.

The initial estimate of the time of death was between 9 P.M. to 11 P.M. the night before – some fourteen hours earlier. While the investigatory team took photographs and marked out the crime scene Sheriff Wilson walked outside for fresh air. He was a long-time serving police officer – a professional – but professionals cry too.

By now the team was spreading out looking for unusual tire prints on the dirt road – but of course they would not find any. Paxton Starr had parked his car on the paving just off of the main road – around a corner from the road so that no passing car could see it. There would also not be any sand from the dirt road on the tires of his car. Sheriff Wilson was walking around outside of the cabin when he remembered that Greg had been insistent that he should look at the clean headstone on Mary's grave. Norm Wilson walked the short distance to where Mary Winters was at rest. The grave stone was indeed clean and neatly kept – Greg was obviously very proud of the way that he kept it.

Sheriff Wilson was reading the wording on the stone when he looked down and saw a brown envelop at the base of the headstone. A single small rock had kept it from blowing away. The big man bent down and picked up the envelope – to his utter surprise it had the words "Sheriff Norman Wilson" written on the front. He was confused to say the least. It felt as if there was a note and a key inside. He hurried back to the cabin and called some of his officers together.

Norm Wilson carefully opened the envelope. There was a key inside and a handwritten note from Greg.

345

"Dear Sheriff Wilson,

My dear friend - this key fits a panel behind the picture frame in my office in the cabin. The information will be self-explanatory.

Thank you so much for your friendship over the years.

Fondest regards, Greg".

All of a sudden they were no longer dealing with a random murder but did Greg know who was going to attack him?

The police officers walked into Greg's small office. One of the officers removed the picture frame on the wall behind Greg's chair. There was a panel and a small key hole. The officer inserted the key and the panel came away in his hands. Many pairs of eyes looked in at an array of electronic recording devices. The officer removed the disk from the one tray and looked at it – he then placed it back into one of the other machines and pressed PLAY. Greg's computer switched on. Then the recording on the disk began to play.

For the next thirty minutes the police officers stood in total disbelief as they watched the entire set of recordings of what had taken place the night before in Greg's cabin. The recording started with a darken room and then Greg's saying "is anyone there", then the sound of a shot. A figure then came into picture and the policemen could not believe what they then witnessed. They heard the cabin being broken apart. They then saw the figure walk out of shot again and what sounded like the front door being kicked in. Then there was just an empty picture with no sound.

They had just witness the planned killing of Greg Winters and they knew who had committed the crime. Greg had laid a trap and Paxton Starr had walked into it.

"Wait a minute." said Sheriff Wilson "the power was cut to the cabin so how was the recording made?"

The officers traced the cables from the back of the panel of Greg's office through to the back of the house and then outside to a covered box. Inside the box was a set of batteries and they were connected to cables that ran up the large wooden pylons that peaked out over the top of the side of the cabin. On top of the pylons were solar energy cells - capturing sun rays and turning them into electricity – the electricity was saved in the batteries and which powered the electronic devices in Greg's office. The officers traced the wiring from the control panel along the floor line to a number of wooden beams that held up the interior of the cabin. Small cuts had been made into the beams and the wiring placed inside. Attached to each wiring set were small cameras – some six in total in tiny pin holes that could not be seen with the naked eye. Greg's living room had become the filming set of his own murder. In the panel of electronic gadgetry were six recording devices – each connected to a different camera strategically imbedded into a wooded post in the living room. In a way Greg had all of the angles covered. He must have planned this for months – and indeed he had from the moment that he moved into the cabin. He knew that Paxton Starr would come and kill him once the season changed and when there would be no tire marks in the snow or mud.

The officers were discussing calling in the local district attorney when they received word that the story was beginning to break of an incident that had occurred at a local cabin. Pretty soon the media would arrive and all hell would break loose. A barricade was erected at the turnoff on the dirt road to Greg's cabin and reinforcements were called up from neighboring communities to secure the access to the cabin via the forest. A make-shift command station was set up outside of the cabin and frantic activity was taking place.

The DA was contacted and based on the electronic evidence viewed at the cabin he contacted his counter-part in San

347

Francisco. All parties were patched into a conference call. Sheriff Wilson briefed everyone on his discovery of Greg's body, the envelope that he had found and the playback of the scene that had unfolded in the cabin the night before. There was stunned disbelief – and utterances of very foul language over the call – besides the fact that Greg was dead they could not believe that he had rigged up his living room, knew that he would be murdered and had even invited Sheriff Wilson over to his cabin – knowing that when he arrived he would find Greg's dead body. The story was also too incredible to believe. And why would Greg sacrifice his life to catch Paxton Starr?

The evidence found at the crime scene would have to remain in the State of Nevada. Paxton Starr would have to be tracked down and arrested and then brought to Nevada to be charged with the murder of Greg Winters. It was key however that the information about the murderer not be leaked to the Press as Paxton Starr could then run – if he had not run already. It was agreed that the SFPD would establish Mr. Starr's whereabouts and then keep him under surveillance until the paper work could be done to secure an arrest warrant. In the meantime Sheriff Wilson would make a statement to the Press but no mention would be made of the vital evidence that had been found at the murder scene.

The first media vehicles had already gathered at the turnoff to Greg's cabin – and just in time the reinforcements arrived to secure the entrance to Greg's property through the forest. The overhead helicopter could not be stopped from flying over the property.

The media were advised that a statement would be made shortly – in reality though it took almost another 60 minutes. The timing coincided with the confirmation that in the late afternoon Paxton Starr was at his home on Ocean Drive.

CHAPTER 56

Saturday afternoons were leisurely shopping time for Elizabeth McKenzie. She had her favorite produce market that she used to visit – making a stop for a glass of freshly squeezed orange juice at the small "Nature Shop on the corner". Her shopping baskets were full of jars of homemade soups from "Maria's Soup and salad" and with packets of milk. After she had finished her fresh juice she was going to walk back to her car and drive home. She had personal things planned for the evening including a stroll through the streets where she lived. A safe part of town and walk in the spring just before sun set was an injection into the soul.

Elizabeth saw a crowd gathering outside of a TV store and she was frustrated as it meant that she would have to step onto the road with her heavy parcels to get around them. As she was passing the crowd she heard the TV reporter say "So, to confirm our breaking news story – From Alpine Meadows – the well-known and recently retired San Francisco lawyer Greg Winters was apparently found shot dead in his cabin this morning – information is still coming in but it appears as if Mr. Winters was shot sometime last night. His body was found by Sheriff Norman Wilson who had a prior appointment with Mr. Winters."

Elizabeth stopped dead in her tracks. It felt as if her body had kept moving but her mind had heard something that it could not comprehend. She turned very slowly and looked up at the TV in the store window. The headline scrolling across the screen was, "BREAKING NEWS leading lawyer believed to be shot dead." Then the reality hit her and her confused mind gave way to what she was reading on the screen and what she thought that she had heard as she had walked past the store. Elizabeth screamed and dropped her parcels. The bottles of soup broke as they hit the paving. She fell to her knees and screamed and screamed and screamed. Those standing in front of her at the window turned in shock at the screams from behind them and saw Elizabeth lying on the paving. She was like a rag doll laying on her side now and

349

whimpering and shaking. As the crowd gathered around her someone called 911 for an ambulance.

Ken Parker was at home with his family on the Saturday afternoon. He enjoyed watching a Saturday matinee baseball game on TV – and dosing off from time to time – as most men do while watching sport alone. His head was nodding from side to side when during a break between innings the TV station highlighted a BREAKING NEWS story. Ken was asleep but his wife was in the kitchen and she thought that she heard something about Greg Winters. "Hon, was that something about Greg that I heard on the TV?" Ken was asleep on the couch. His wife walked through to the TV room and said, "Hon, there was something about Greg on the news." Ken woke up and took a few seconds to pull out of his deep afternoon slumber. Ken's wife turned up the volume on the TV. "We have breaking news from Alpine Meadows, it is believed that there was a shooting incident at the home of the famous lawyer, Greg Winters – it is unconfirmed but we believe that police found Mr. Winters dead in his home earlier this afternoon. The reports are so far unconfirmed but a Press statement is expected within the next few minutes. We will cross to our reporters on the scene shortly."

It took a full few seconds before either Ken or his wife reacted. Mrs. Parker burst into tears and Ken said, "Oh my God, no, Oh my God no – say that it is not true." He leapt to his feet. His home and cell phone began to ring at almost the same time. In an electronic age bad news travels very fast.

The next few minutes were spent on the phone talking with colleagues and trying to reach the SFPD. He had to try to find out as much as possible about what had happened. Finally he reached someone that he knew but there was no more information available.

Ken's wife called him back to the TV room as the Press statement was about to begin. The time was 4:30 P.M. – over three and a half hours had elapsed since Greg's body had been found by his dear friend.

Sheriff Norman Wilson was introduced by a police department Press Officer.

"Ladies and gentlemen – I am Sheriff Norman Wilson of the Alpine Meadows police department. I wish to confirm that an apparent break-in and a shooting incident occurred at the home of Mr. Gregory Winters sometime last night – this morning I had a prior appointment at the home of Mr. Winters – I arrived at his home at approximately 1 P.M. and found Mr. Winters on the floor in his living room. I called for backup which arrived about 15 minutes later. Mr. Winters was pronounced dead at the scene. At this time we do not have a time of death – that will only be determined once a post mortem on the deceased has been conducted – we estimate however, that he was shot late last night. The home of Mr. Winters had been ransacked – we are investigating if the incident was robbery. At this time we have no further information that we have available. We will keep you informed as more information becomes know. Thank you."

Police statements are never satisfactory in the eyes of the media and barrages of questions were fired off by the different reporters. Sheriff Wilson had walked away from the microphone and his Press liaison officer made a closing statement.

"We have no suspect or suspects in mind at this point of time – the investigation is under way and will continue for some time." And in response to one question he said, "Mr. Winters was shot once in the upper body and it proved fatal."

The TV stations were all relaying coverage of the Press statement and aerial photos of Greg's cabin with the police vehicles parked outside. The news channels were already covering stories on Greg's life as a well-known lawyer – and his recent defense success in the Second Degree murder trial of Paxton Starr.

351

Paxton Starr was at home with Abby preparing for the neighborhood party that was to take place there later that evening. No TV or radio was on in the home as Abby had her iPod plugged in as she was cleaning and dusting the down stairs rooms.

To say that Paxton Starr was assisting in getting the house ready for the party was not totally accurate – in fact not accurate at all. He was in his office deep in thought with his office work. Even when the front gate bell was rung with the delivery of the food and drink for the evening it was Abby who let the delivery van in and signed for the order. She packed the common room fridge with beer, wine and pop. The meat for the barbeque was placed in Tupperware containers and put into the fridge. In all likelihood Mr. Starr had never even heard the delivery van arriving or leaving.

Wil and Jenni Wright were pleased to have Stacey home for the weekend and they were all excited about visiting with Paxton Starr that evening. Chad had also been invited and he enjoyed playing pool with the men – and then maybe later he and Stacey would walk down to the beach and find a secluded spot.

It was just as they were getting ready to leave to walk over to the home of Paxton Starr that Stacey received a text message from a friend. The message read, "Just read that Greg Winters – Mr. Starr's lawyer was found murdered!!!!"

Stacey came running into her parent's bedroom screaming, "Mom read this read this – oh my God – can you believe it?"

Jenni Wright looked at Stacey's iPhone and her eyes almost fell out of her head. Wil took the phone from his wife and said, "Oh no, oh no – he had retired after Pax's trial – how terrible!"

They spoke about Greg Winter and how brilliantly he had defended Paxton Starr – what a terrible thing to happen just as one retires. They turned on CNN and watched a brief story that was being covered on Gregory Winters.

352

It was time to walk over to Paxton Starr's home and they were sure that he had heard the news – and that it would be discussed at the party that evening.

In fact Paxton Starr had not heard the news – from his office he had gone to the spare room – that was still his bedroom – and he had taken a shower and proceeded to get ready for the party. Abby had used one of the down stairs bedrooms to change into something more presentable when the guests arrived. She would settle everyone in and then say good night and drive home.

It was just after 6 P.M. when the first of Paxton Starr's guests arrived. Wil and Jen and Stacey and Chad were the first to arrive. Wil could not wait to discuss the tragic death of Greg Winters with Paxton. "Terrible news about your defense lawyer." said Wil. "What news is that?" answered Paxton. "Have you not heard what happened?" asked Jenni is surprise. "No, I have not heard what happened to Greg Winters?"

"Uncle Pax, he is dead – he was murdered in his cabin last night – someone shot him!" said Stacey. "Did you not hear the news – it is all over the TV stations?"

"Oh my God, No – are you serious – no, I had not heard – oh, my God, that is terrible." Paxton Starr seemed so surprised to hear the sad news.

"Abby, Abby – did you hear the bad news – the lawyer who defended my case – Mr. Greg Winters was murdered last night – this is terrible news!"

Abby Carmichael had not heard the news either and she started to cry. "Praise his soul oh God, praise his soul!" she said and walked off crying into the kitchen.

As the other guests arrived over the next thirty minutes or so they all spoke about the terrible murder of Greg Winters. The death of such a good man seemed so out of place on the patio of a beautiful home overlooking the ocean – with the guests holding drinks in their hands.

All this time the police surveillance of Paxton Starr's home was still taking place.

There had been a delay in obtaining the Arrest Warrant and then the required paper work to transfer the suspect to the State of Nevada to be charged with the murder of Gregory Winters. The police were eager to move in and execute the warrant but they had to be sure that all legal considerations were well in place – they did not want some smart lawyer proving that there had been an error or a loophole in the proceedings.

The time was now well after 8 P.M. and still the order had not been given. A SWAT team was on standby within 5 minutes of the Starr residence and when the order was given they would storm over the grounds of the property and prevent the suspect from escaping.

It would be another hour before the support vehicles that were waiting to drive up Ocean Drive were ready. These vehicles would whisk Paxton Starr up to the Nevada border where he would be transferred to the local authorities and taken in and booked.
There was much to plan and many armed police personnel were anxious to break up the happy environment in which Mr. Paxton Starr found himself – his life style was soon to change.

CHAPTER 57

The gathering of the neighbors on Ocean Drive – or at least a gathering that included Paxton Starr – had been a long time in coming. Having the event in his home was also rather special. There was no doubt that everyone missed not having Maxi with them. In many ways it was awkward having an event in her home – in the home in which she had died – and not having her there. No one expected that it would be easy but they felt that it had to be done - for their sake and for that of Paxton. They all needed to bond together again – like the extended family that they were.

There had been some discussion about the death of Greg Winters and in a way that distracted the conversation away from that of missing Maxi Starr. The group was all stunned with the murder of the lawyer who had defended Paxton.

As the evening wore on and Abby had tried to take her leave but no one would hear of it. Her plan was to be gone by around 8 P.M. but that time had come and gone. She was a character in her own right and the ladies in particular asked her to stay longer. She was very hesitant to do so because she was well out of her station in life but she did feel that the offer to stay was very genuine so she agreed to stay until 10 P.M. – after that time she did not feel safe in driving home alone. Jenni Wright teased her by saying that they would organize a cab home for her if she wanted to stay later than her own defined time to leave.

Paxton Starr was in a fine mood and appeared to be very relaxed. His group of friends was very pleased for him. As the evening progressed Paxton consumed his first beer, then later a second and was now into his third – not like him at all. He then felt the urgent need to relieve himself. His urgent need could not have come at a worse time. There were three wash rooms on the ground floor of his home and all were occupied. He bounded up the steps to his spare bedroom – his new residence as he had not moved back into the main bedroom that he had shared so many memories with his wife. The bathroom in the spare bedroom was also occupied. He thought, "Gee, all of a sudden everyone has to pee at exactly the same time!"

Reluctantly he walked into the main bedroom and through to the bathroom. There he stood and relieved his very full bladder. He had closed the bedroom door and then the bathroom door. He could not hear the disturbance that was about to break out downstairs.

The final pieces of planning were in place for the arrest of Paxton Starr. The legal matters were all in-hand – it was time to execute the arrest warrant. The "go" signal was given. Without sirens or lights on the SWAT vehicles approached the Starr residence. The officers who had come through the forest approached the side of the house in complete silence. They held station not 50 yards from the home. None of the men who were standing talking on the patio even heard them approach. At 50 yards they stopped until they received their next order.

The team that approached the front of the house stopped at the main door and then burst in and twenty men filled the lobby within a second. The ladies who were sitting in the common room screamed in fright – was it a home invasion? The SWAT team filtered through the house as the men came running in from the patio. As they did so the SWAT team outside stormed the patio and secured all exits to the home.

"Where is Paxton Star?" asked the lead member of the team. The men who had come running in from the patio were immediately ordered to be silent. When members of the SWAT team are heavily armed and tell you to remain silent you do exactly as you are told. The women were too terrified to even scream again.

"Paxton Starr?" One of the ladies pointed upstairs with her finger.

The officer in charge signaled with his hand and five men were speeding up the staircase. They did not make a sound. The lead
356

office stopped outside the door of the main bedroom and listened. He nodded. One of the men stepped away to guard the corridor which lead down to the other bedrooms – he would soon be stopping one of the men who had been using the bathroom in the other bedroom.

The bedroom door was slowly opened and a face carefully peeked around the door. Again one man stayed back at the door while three other approached the bathroom door. Again they stopped and listened. They heard the sound of a man relieving himself. The officer thought, "Buddy soon you'll be pissing your pants."

The three members of the SWAT team burst into the bathroom with raised firearms.
"Paxton Starr?" If they had been ten seconds earlier Paxton Starr would certainly have peed all over himself. He had just zipped up his pants and was about to wash his hands when the door flew open. He almost jumped clean off of his feet.

"Paxton Starr – are you Paxton Starr?"

"What is the meaning of this – who the hell are you?"

The lead officer stepped forward – he felt like smashing his assault rifle into Paxton's abdomen but he thought better of it. All he said was, "I'll ask the questions – are you Paxton Starr? I am not going to ask you again!" Paxton shook his head affirming that he was. The officer spoke into his radio "We have him – he is up stairs."

Paxton tried to speak but nothing would come out – his throat was completely dry.
The officer put his finger to his lips signaling to Paxton to remain silent.

A minute later a senior police officer walked into the bathroom. It was the SFPD Chief of Police. He introduced himself. "Mr. Starr, I am Chief of Police Martinez of the SFPD – I have a warrant for your arrest. You are being charged with the murder of Gregory

357

Winters." Chief Martinez read out Paxton's rights. Finally Paxton Starr found his voice and said, "Are you crazy? I did not kill anyone – killing Greg Winters, that is madness."

All Chief Martinez said, was, "Tell that to the judge."

"Read him his rights. Cuff him!"

Paxton Starr was led down the steps. All of his friends were standing on one side as he was walked out through the door. Abby had opened the gates for the police vehicles to come up to the front door. Paxton Starr did not look at his friends as he walked passed them – then he was placed into a vehicle and it sped away with several support vehicles and sirens wailing.

Wil Wright stepped out from where the group had been herded together. He asked, "What is happening?" A member of the SWAT team answered him. "He is being charged with murder". "Murder, murder – he was found not guilty in the death of his wife – he can't be charged with that again!"

"No sir, he can't – he is being charged with the murder of Gregory Winters."

The lobby of Paxton's Starr was silent. A totally stunned silence! A jaw dropping silence!

"We believe that he shot Greg Winters in his home in Alpine Meadows last night."

All they remember the police offer saying was, "Okay folks the party is over."

Paxton Starr had been arrested for murder in the bathroom in which he had murdered his wife – but of course at the time his friends did not know that fact.

CHAPTER 58

On the Sunday the police department in Nevada made a Press statement that a person of interest had been detained in the murder case of Greg Winters. It did not take too long for the news to come out that Paxton Starr was the person of interest. The public could not understand why a client who had been found not guilty would then take the life of his lawyer. Speculation abounded as speculation would. What did appear to be obvious was that Gregory Winters must have known that his client had committed the crime for which he had been charged – the drowning of Maxi Starr – but had still so successfully defended him – how could any respectable person do that? The public failed to ask the question about what the true role of a defense lawyer is – to defend their client.

Ken Parker was particularly worried about what had happened and why Greg had not entrusted him with some key evidence – let alone entrust him as a friend. There were so many unanswered questions – just speculation at this point in time

Paxton Starr had requested a lawyer when he had arrived in the holding cells of the Carson City police department. When a lawyer appeared on the scene the preliminary charges were read out – and the police made reference to some revealing evidence that had led them so quickly to seek out and arrest Mr. Starr. When the lawyer and members of the District Attorney's Office and other key persons were present the police department played the disks that had been recorded in Greg's cabin the night that he had died. Although the images were sometimes dark because of the fact that the power had been cut inside the cabin one could still clearly make out the scene that had been played out in Greg's self-made studio that night. There were clear images of Paxton Starr with the hood down and his blonde hair showing. His face was clear and crisp on some of the images. Besides the noise of the shot that hit Greg Winters – and even the flash of the hand gun that Paxton Starr had used – there was his vivid description of what had happened the night that Ryan Wright disappeared and where he had hid the body. There was the account in Paxton Starr's own words of how he had found his wife asleep in the bathtub and how he had held her by her feet and pulled her under the water line. Throughout the screening of the different disks of evidence Paxton Starr sat completely motionless in his chair.

At the end of the presentation of the evidence that lawyer met privately with his client. Would any self-respecting lawyer take on the case to defend Paxton Starr? The lawyer in question had no qualms at all about taking on the case – he was a defense lawyer and besides the potential fee income would be substantial.

The legal wrangle over the evidence and the charges against Paxton Starr would take some time to sort out. The question remained as to why Greg Winters would put his own life on the line to bait and catch his former client.

When the lawyer appeared at the end of the meeting he had a one page drawing that he handed to the police as evidence. Paxton Starr had insisted on drawing a detailed map as where he had hidden Ryan Wright's body – now almost five years before. The document was recorded as evidence.

The news being made available to the public was still very sketchy and this only served to fuel the media. Every news channel across the country was covering the story.

Stacey Wright was so upset on the Monday following the arrest of Uncle P – if she could ever call him that again was another question – that she decided to stay at home all day. Wil and Jenni also decided to stay home on the Monday. Their front door bell rang late on the Monday afternoon. If only they had known what news awaited them they might not have answered the door.

Stacey opened the door and saw two senior police officers standing there. They asked if Mr. and Mrs. Wright were home. Wil Wright came to the door and the one officer asked if they could come in – they had some information that had come to light regarding the disappearance of their son. Stacey said, "Oh my God" – and ran screaming for her mother. Jenni Wright came through as her husband was offering the policemen a seat in the front room.

"Stacey, do you want to stay?" asked her father. He did not receive a reply as Stacey was already seated next to her Mom.

The one police officer then said. "We have received some new evidence regarding Ryan." Before he could continue Jenni Wright broke down crying. "He is dead – oh God – I can tell by the look on your face that my son is dead!" She buried her face in her hands and Wil put his arm around his wife.

"Our evidence has led us to believe that a body buried nearby in the forest up the road could be your son. We will be sending out a team tomorrow morning to try to locate the site and to verify if it is your son – at this stage we do not know – but we wanted you to be aware of our investigation."

"Do you know if it was an accident? How did you come across the information?" asked Wil.

"I am sorry but I cannot disclose that information at this point in time – we will try to locate the site in the morning and will, of course, keep you posted as to our findings – more than that I cannot tell you right now. I am sorry."

None of the Wright's slept that night. They had waited so long to hear some news about Ryan – hoping and praying that he was still alive and that he would return home one day. Jenni Wright had never stopped believing that Ryan was alive – she could not allow herself to think otherwise. Wil had often wondered what had happened to his son and how he might have failed him – was there more that he could have done for Ryan while he was going through a terrible teen phase. Fathers always blame themselves - they have to – it is their duty in life to protect and provide for their families – for their children – and when something goes wrong it is always their fault. Wil would live with that thought for the rest of his life. Stacey had looked up to her big brother. She absolutely idolized Ryan. He was her hero – and even as her own brother he was her knight in shining armor. In her book – at the age of about thirteen at the time she could only see the good in her hero.

The next morning the stream of police vehicles drove down Ocean Drive just after first light. Wil Wright had telephoned his neighbors the evening before and told them of the new developments. Several of the wives came over after breakfast to be with Wil, Jenni and Stacey.

It did not take long before the media picked up on a story that the police were investigating a lead on an old case of a teen that had disappeared. At that point in time there was no linkage to the teen being Ryan Wright or that the lead on the case had come from the arrest of Paxton Starr – not then at least.

It did not take the search team long to locate the spot where Paxton Starr had indicated that Ryan would be found. Police security recovery tents were erected and a no fly over zone was put into effect. A police road block was established at the entrance to Ocean Drive and entrance to the forest was blocked on all sides.

The search for Ryan on the days that he had gone missing did not cover that area of the forest. The grid maps used at the time of the search indicated that no search had covered that area. They had come close but not close enough. Not that it could have saved Ryan but maybe if his body had been discovered all of those years ago then justice – no matter how difficult that it would have been – would have come down on Paxton and Maxi Starr. The early discovery of Ryan's body would also have ended the living hell that the Wright's had gone through for almost five years.

Many police hands were used to carry away the rocks that hid the crack into which Paxton Starr had jammed Ryan's lifeless body. He must have had the strength of a man possessed that night to have

362

carried the amount of rocks that were covering the entrance to Ryan's tomb. Wearing his workshop gloves had saved his hands from cuts and bruises which would surely have been queried by Maxi and others the day after Ryan had been killed.

After about thirty minutes of removing the rocks the police made their discovery.

The remains of a human body were recovered and moved into one of the tents that had been erected. No sooner had the remains been removed when the story started to break over the TV stations that the police had found what they had been looking for. The media have "long eyes" and can see from nearby hill tops.

Ryan Wright was soon identified from a description of the clothes that he was wearing on the night that he had disappeared and from the remnants of his Driver's License. It was important that this news be relayed to the Wright family before the media blasted something across their stations. The investigation of the scene would still take several hours but there was no point in keeping the Wrights on edge.

When the police car pulled up in front of their home everyone knew that the news was bad – how could it ever be good!

The police would not make a statement in front of the group of friends from the other homes on Ocean Drive – the friends walked outside knowing that the hammer was about to drop.

"We can confirm that the remains that we found in the forest were that of your son – we are very sorry." The reaction was – to say the least – was heartbreaking. Being a police officer is not a career for the faint of heart.

"Did our son slip and fall in between the rocks?" asked Wil.

The police officer hesitated before answering the straight forward question.

This would be the most difficult news to deliver.

"I am afraid not – your son was murdered – the information that we received indicated foul play but it was only when we discovered Ryan's body that we could confirm the injury that we had been informed of – and please understand that the coroner will have to conduct his autopsy – but we did want to share the information with you before the media broke the news."

At first the word "murdered" did not seem to register with either Wil, his wife or with Stacey. Then the impact of the message sunk in – like the aftershock of an earthquake.

"MURDERED! Ryan was murdered!" Wil could not contain himself. "Ryan was murdered – oh my God!"

Jenni and Stacey Wright fell into each other's arms again – who would want to murder Ryan? Was it the punk kids who were providing him with drugs at school – those bloody little bastards!

Wil Wright tried to gather himself as he held back his tears and tried to control his urge to puke on the floor.

"What information led you to locate our son?"

"Mr. and Mrs. Wright – Stacey – this is very difficult – and please this information cannot leave this home until the police department makes a statement." Before he went any further he remembered that the Wright's had some of their neighbors with them. That would be a problem – as they would have to be locked down until the Press statement was made.

"I am afraid that your visitors will have to be placed in shut-down until the police make the statement – which will be made once I give them the go-ahead."

"Our friends should hear the news with us." said Wil – "they are our closest friends and like family to us".

The police officer did not think that it was wise but the Wright's insisted. Against his better judgment the wives were ushered into the room. They were informed that the information that they were about to hear was still confidential – but that the Wright's had made the decision to have them present. The visitors were told that they would be in a shut-down for a while after he had shared the news with them – he asked that all cell phones be handed to his colleagues until it was time for the Press release.

Once everyone had taken their seats again and all devices had been gathered up then the lead officer spoke.

"I have just informed Mr. and Mrs. Wright that the remains that we found this morning were that of their son. Ryan had been murdered – he had received a blow to the back of the head – the coroner will conduct his autopsy but it appears as if there had several blows – and that was the cause of death. Ryan was not murdered at that site – he died somewhere else and was then carried there and entombed between the cracks in the rocks."

He paused but there was just stunned silence in the room – except for the noise of the tears running down the cheeks of everyone in the room.

"Mr. Wright asked me what information had led us to the discovery of the scene were Ryan was found – well, - we arrested a suspect in another murder over the weekend and he provided us with the information that led us to Ryan."

No one in the room had linked the discovery of Ryan's remains with the other sensational murder news – and the arrest of the murderer that they had witness just a few days before.

The officer knew that the news that he was about to break to them would be stunning. He took in a deep breathe.

"The source of the information came after the arrest of Mr. Paxton Starr for the murder of Greg Winters."

"What! What does Paxton's arrest have to do with Ryan's murder?" sputtered out Wil.

"All the information that I am able to provide to you at this point in time is that visual and audio evidence was obtained from the scene of Mr. Winter's shooting – from that evidence we have established beyond reasonable doubt that Mr. Starr was involved with your son's disappearance."

The news could not get any worse for those gathered together in Wil and Jenni's home. Their dear friend had not only murdered his wife but had also murdered their son – it just could not be true. Wil Wright uttered a string of foul language words – words that Stacey had never heard him use before. If Paxton Starr was present in the room Wil Wright would have attacked and killed him with his bare hands.

"That F---ing bastard murdered my son!" Wil repeated.

"Actually no, Mr. Wright he did not – by all accounts he did not murder your son – he – well – he disposed of your sons' body – your son was killed by Mrs. Maxi Starr."

The police officer had never seen so many pairs of eyes get so big and intense in his entire law enforcement career – they were like glazed balls of jelly – big and shiny but without any sign of life – and then the emotion came through. Intense screams of anguish and an outburst of tears and sobbing. It turned the police officers stomach to have to sit there and break this news to people who were so very close to one another.

Jenni Wright was the first to muster up the ability to speak. "It must be a mistake – Maxi, Maxi, would not have hurt Ryan – she loved him – they both loved him – I do not understand!"

Now was the time that he had to tell them what had happened the night that Ryan had died.

"I am very sorry to have to tell you this – but Mr. Starr has confirmed the evidence that we found – he confirmed it to us in his own words in front of his lawyer and the DA in Carson City. Please allow me to explain what happened the night that Ryan died. You know that he was apparently intoxicated that night – we know that at the Starr residence that Wil told Ryan to go home – he did not – after the party was over he returned to their home and entered through the opened sliding door into the kitchen – Mr. Starr was swimming and he left the door open – when he returned to the house he heard his wife fighting off an intruder that was wielding a knife and who had said that he was going to rape her. When Mr. Starr entered the kitchen the intruder heard him and turned with knife in hand onto Paxton Starr – Mr. Starr said that he slipped on the wet floor from where he had been standing – the intruder jumped on top of his chest and raised the knife with both hands and was about to plunge it into his chest – then there was a thud – Mrs. Starr hit the intruder over the back of the head with a skillet. She had saved her husband's life by attacking the intruder. Mr. Starr then saw that the intruder was Ryan – he was dead. He was about to tell his wife that she had hit Ryan when Mrs. Starr fainted.

Mr. Starr carried his wife up the stairs and put her to bed – he had every intention – or so he says – of telling her what had happened when she woke up. He felt a coward by falling over when an intruder approached him with the knife. His wife had saved his life.

Mr. Starr said that he could not visualize his wife in prison for what she had done and that he could not find it in him to telephone you to say what had happened. He decided to bury Ryan in the forest – he carried him into the forest and then cut back to the rocky outcrop where he covered Ryan with rocks. His wife was still out cold when he returned from the forest – he decided that he would tell her what he had done in the morning when she woke up. It was the next morning that Maxi Starr received the news that her parents had been killed in an auto accident – and it seems as if the shock of that news blocked out the memory of the incident of the previous evening. She never remembered it at all – so Mr. Starr decided to never mention it – it remained his secret that he bore for almost five years."

The officer felt like a story teller who had gripped the attention of his audience. He had cast a spell over them and when he had completed his tale – to that point anyway – they all sat in silence. The officer then continued.

"It remained a secret until the night of your party – the night that Mrs. Starr died – something that happened that night brought back her memory – and she wanted to tell the police what had happened the night when Ryan attacked her."

"What would have brought back her memory?" asked Jenni Wright – it was a robotic question as the full shock had not yet settled in.

Before anyone could respond Stacey answered the question.

"It was something that I said." Everyone in the room turned and looked at Stacey.

"What could you have said that brought back her memory?" asked her Dad.

"After dinner I mentioned to her that Ryan would have turned 21 that day – maybe it was the thought of Ryan's 21st birthday that brought everything back."

CHAPTER 59

The following week two church services took place. The one was the funeral of Gregory Winters. The service was held in a chapel near Alpine Meadows. It was hopelessly too small for the number of people that came to say their last good bye to a good man and an outstanding lawyer. Chairs were placed outside of the chapel and the service was broadcast to those that could not squeeze inside. Prosecutors and defense lawyers, district attorneys and police officers, coroners and colleagues joined together in a simple celebration of a man's life. Elizabeth sat with Ken and his wife. Next to them was Abby Carmichael. Everyone from Ocean Drive attended the service – including Stacey and Chad – Greg had not betrayed them. In a corner under the tree outside sat Chubby from the gas station – he was so sad that his friend from NASA had died – but so pleased that the Russian spy had been caught – and he would never tell as Greg had sworn him to secrecy. Chubby felt that he had served his country – but he would have liked a badge or something.

Greg was laid to rest next to Mary. He had left clear instructions of what he wanted – a matching stone – the color had long since been ordered from the cutting yard. Only a few people attended the burial at the cabin.

A day after Greg's funeral Chief Martinez received a telephone call – the caller asked if he could come by the police station. Later that day Greg Winters doctor arrived at police headquarters. Chief Martinez had no idea why the doctor wanted to see him.

"I was Mr. Winter's doctor for many years. I knew him very well. About a year ago – last summer in fact – Mr. Winters came to me for an annual physical examination. During the examination he told me that he was experiencing headaches – we conducted tests and discovered that he had a brain tumor. At that point it was present but inactive – the diagnosis however was that it would grow and that it would become terminal. Greg asked me to keep the news confidential – which of course I would anyway. We monitored the situation – and frankly I think that his last case accelerated the growth of the tumor. We saw that it was beginning to grow in size. Greg refused any treatment. By December last year we knew that his time was limited – he asked me how long he had to live and I stated that it is always impossible to tell – personally I thought that he had less than a year – most likely far less than that. Greg knew that his life would begin to change dramatically within the next few months. Personally I think that by cornering that Paxton Starr fellow for the authorities it was his way of not only bringing justice down on a murderer but by ending his own life quickly before the pain and suffering set in."

Chief Martinez could share this information and it was his duty to do so. His first call was to Ken Parker. Ken then shared the news with his staff. To them Greg was their ultimate hero.

The other service that took place was that for Ryan Wright. His remains were returned to his parents about a week after his body had been uncovered. For the people on Ocean Drive it was a terrible week.

CHAPTER 60

Ken Parker thought of how Greg was to have become a consultant to the law firm. He now understood the Greg would always be that consultant. One chair in the war room was always left empty.

Elizabeth McKenzie received a letter at the office requesting her to attend the reading of the Last Will and Testament of Gregory Winters. She had never thought that Greg would remember her in his Will. On the day of the reading of the Will she arrived at the law firm and took her seat.

Once the lawyer had gone through some preliminary points he commenced the reading.

"And to Elizabeth McKenzie" The lawyer handed Elizabeth an envelope. She opened the card inside. She smiled. All it said was, "Elizabeth thank you for being my friend, Yours Truly, Greg."

Elizabeth would have been content with her card as she knew that Greg had called her his friend – not merely an employee with whom he got on with and trusted.

The lawyer then continued, "To Elizabeth McKenzie I leave the sum of two million dollars. I also leave my cabin in Alpine Meadows – fully paid and without debt – including a credit with the local town authorities that would cover taxes, utilities and other costs for the duration of her life."

Greg's visit to the bank and town authorities just before he died had been for a good reason.

Elizabeth could have been blown over by a feather.

Greg had left her two million dollars and his cabin!

Two months later she resigned from the law firm of Ken Parker and moved to Alpine Meadows. She had all of the electronic equipment that Greg had installed removed. Elizabeth moved into the second bedroom even though it was much smaller than the main room.

She gave away most of the furniture and bought new ones at the stores in Alpine Meadows. Everyone in town knew of the intense love that Greg had for Mary and felt good about the fact that Greg had left the cabin to a dear friend – and if per chance there was any gossip then the local sheriff would put a stop to it. Sometimes Elizabeth would drive into town and meet the sheriff for a cup of coffee. If the sheriff ordered a greasy burger and fries Elizabeth would order a salad and herbal tea.

Paxton's lawyer had tried to put forward the case that his client was not mentally fit to stand trial. The motion failed. The trial for First Degree Murder and for Damage to Property proceeded quickly. In due course Paxton Starr was found guilty on all charges and sentenced to twenty five years in jail without parole. He paid the Deceased Estate of Greg Winters $25 000 for damages to the cabin.

The state of California also laid charges against Paxton Starr – being an accessory to manslaughter and discarding human remains – as well as withholding evidence from the police. Paxton Starr was never brought to trial in California. He died two years later of prostate cancer before his trial commenced. In his Will Paxton Starr left the value of Maxi's estate – now worth well over $41 million again, to Abby Carmichael. Abby visited China often. She also sponsored a youth program in her neighborhood and named it in honor of her late husband.

Elizabeth took painting lessons but after a year or so grew weary of her new hobby. She then turned to writing. Her first novel was entitled, THE SOLAR MURDER – about the life of a well-known defense lawyer. Her book became a number One Bestseller.

Other books by Stan

"From my hilltop – a living history of South Africa" (ebook)
This book takes a unique look at the changes in South Africa, as narrated by an old marula tree (Professor Marula). It is a must-read for all South Africans!

"Reflections of heaven" (ebook)
A collection of 26 faith-based poems.

Both books are available from:
The Endless Bookcase
www.theendlessbookcase.com/epub/e-books
Amazon (all sites)
www.amazon.com
www.amazon.ca
Kobo
https://store.kobobooks.com/
Nook (Barnes and Noble)
http://www.barnesandnoble.com/u/NOOK-Book-eBook-store/379003094

The Solar Murder (ebook)
If you would like this book in electronic format, it can be purchased from any of the above websites.

The Solar Murder (printed)
If you would like a soft copy version of this book you can purchase it from The Endless Bookcase website.

In Canada, The Solar Murder (printed) is also available from the author Stan Daneman. To purchase directly from Stan please send him an email at: **sdemail@rogers.com**.

Stan's website
www.booksbystandaneman.com

Other e-books by The Endless Bookcase

All of our books can be found at:
www.theendlessbookcase.com/epub/e-books

We have a variety of e-books available including;

Novels
'Sarina' by Bob Hambleton

Crime novels
'Dead on Arrival' by Katie Gray

History
'A Perspective on Pendley: A history of Pendley Manor' by Bob Little

Music
'How to get off the Sofa and Sing like a Professional (Opera) Singer' by Robert Little

Learning and Education
'Perspectives on Learning Technologies' by Bob Little

Exercise and Health
'How to Get Off the Sofa and Start Running' by Annie Page
'Increase Your Heart Health Easily' by Adam Shaw

Short Stories
'The Hovering Tales Series' by Bob Hambleton

Thank you for reading!